TONGUE TIED

BRANDI SPENCER

Authors 4 Authors Publishing
Marysville, WA, USA

Published by Authors 4 Authors Publishing
1214 6th St
Marysville, WA 98270
www.authors4authorspublishing.com

Library of Congress Control Number: 2023940709

E-book ISBN: 978-1-64477-175-4
Paperback ISBN: 978-1-64477-176-1
Audiobook ISBN: 978-1-64477-177-8

Edited by Lisa Borne Graves

Cover art ©2023
Images and Cover Art Illustration by Period Images, Pi Creative Lab and Mary Chronis. Cover Text, Background, Logo, and Branding by Practically Perfect Covers. All rights reserved.
Interior Design by Brandi Spencer

Author photo courtesy of 3rd Gen Photography.

Authors 4 Authors Content Rating and copyright are set in Poppins. Headings and titles are set in Athena. Kennard's handwriting is set in Almendra. Calosandros's handwriting is set in Sundisk. Conora's handwriting is set in Viner. Boinee's handwriting is set in Brackle. All other text is set in Garamond.

Tongue Tied

Brandi Spencer

Authors 4 Authors Content Rating

This title has been rated XS, Extra Strong, appropriate for adults, and contains:

- frequent graphic sex
- extreme language
- moderate violence
- moderate alcohol use

Please, keep the following in mind when using our rating system:

1. A content rating is not a measure of quality.

Great stories can be found for every audience. One book with many content warnings and another with none at all may be of equal depth and sophistication. Our ratings can work both ways: to avoid content or to find it.

2. Ratings are merely a tool.

For our young adult (YA) and children's titles, age ratings are generalized suggestions. For parents, our descriptive ratings can help you make informed decisions, but at the end of the day, only you know what kinds of content are appropriate for your individual child. This is why we provide details in addition to the general age rating.

For more information on our rating system, please, visit our Content Guide at: www.authors4authorspublishing.com/books/ratings

DEDICATION

To anyone else with "the wildness" inside,
may you embrace your uniqueness
and find love and acceptance along the way.

WORKS BY BRANDI SPENCER

Healers' Kiss:

Kiss of Treason
Kiss of Destiny
Kiss of Legacy (2024)

Tied Tongues

Gifted Hearts:
Short Love Stories of Carum Sound

"Her Dearest Treasure"
"I Loved You Tomorrow"
"Seeing Through Him"
"The Veiled Queen"

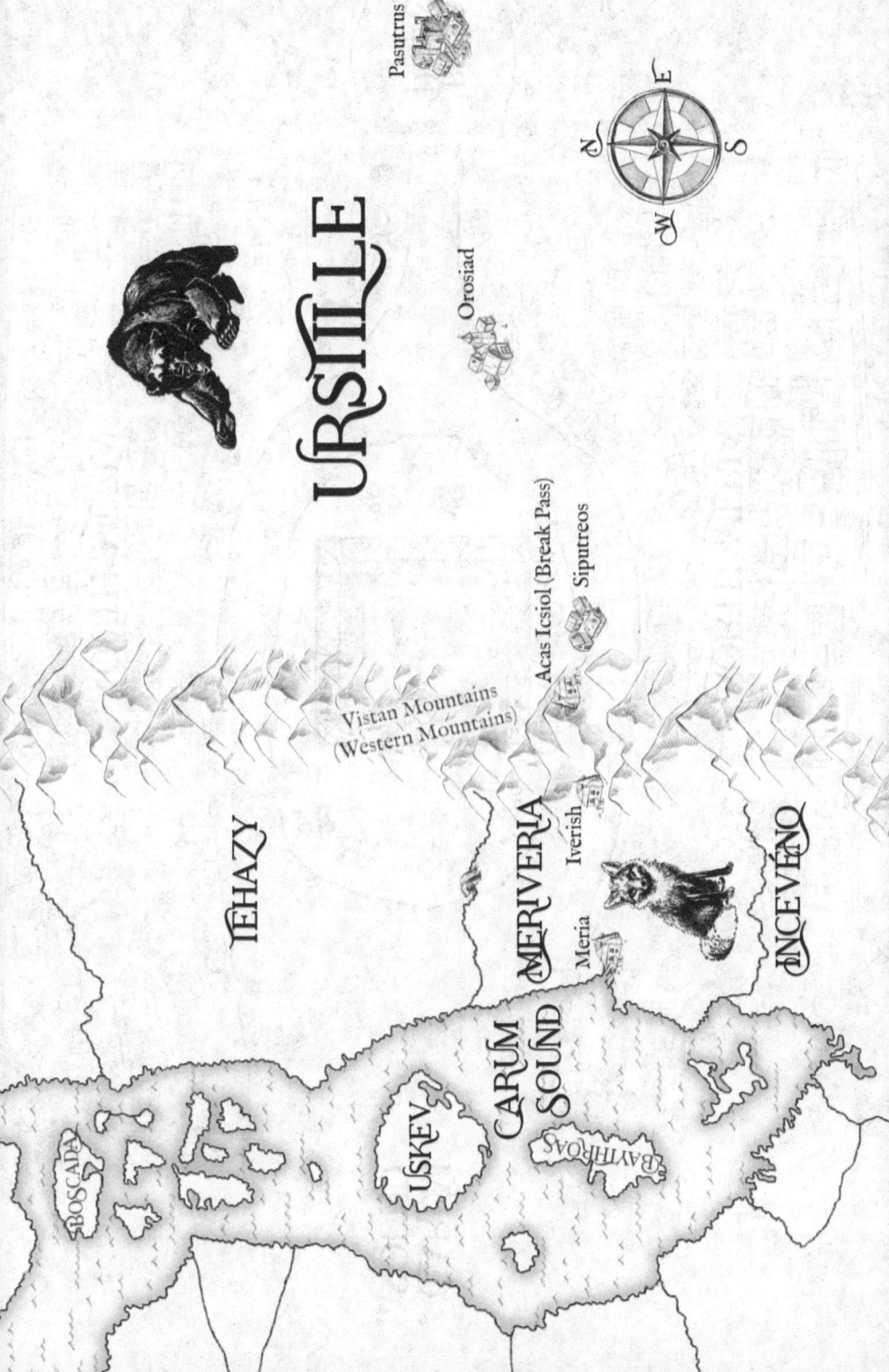

Pasutrus

URSILLE

Orosiad

Vistan Mountains
(Western Mountains)

Acas Icsiol (Break Pass)

Siputreos

TEHAZY

MERIVERIA

Iverish

INCEVENO

Meria

CARÚM SOUND

USKEV

BRAVITHRÓAS

BOSCADA

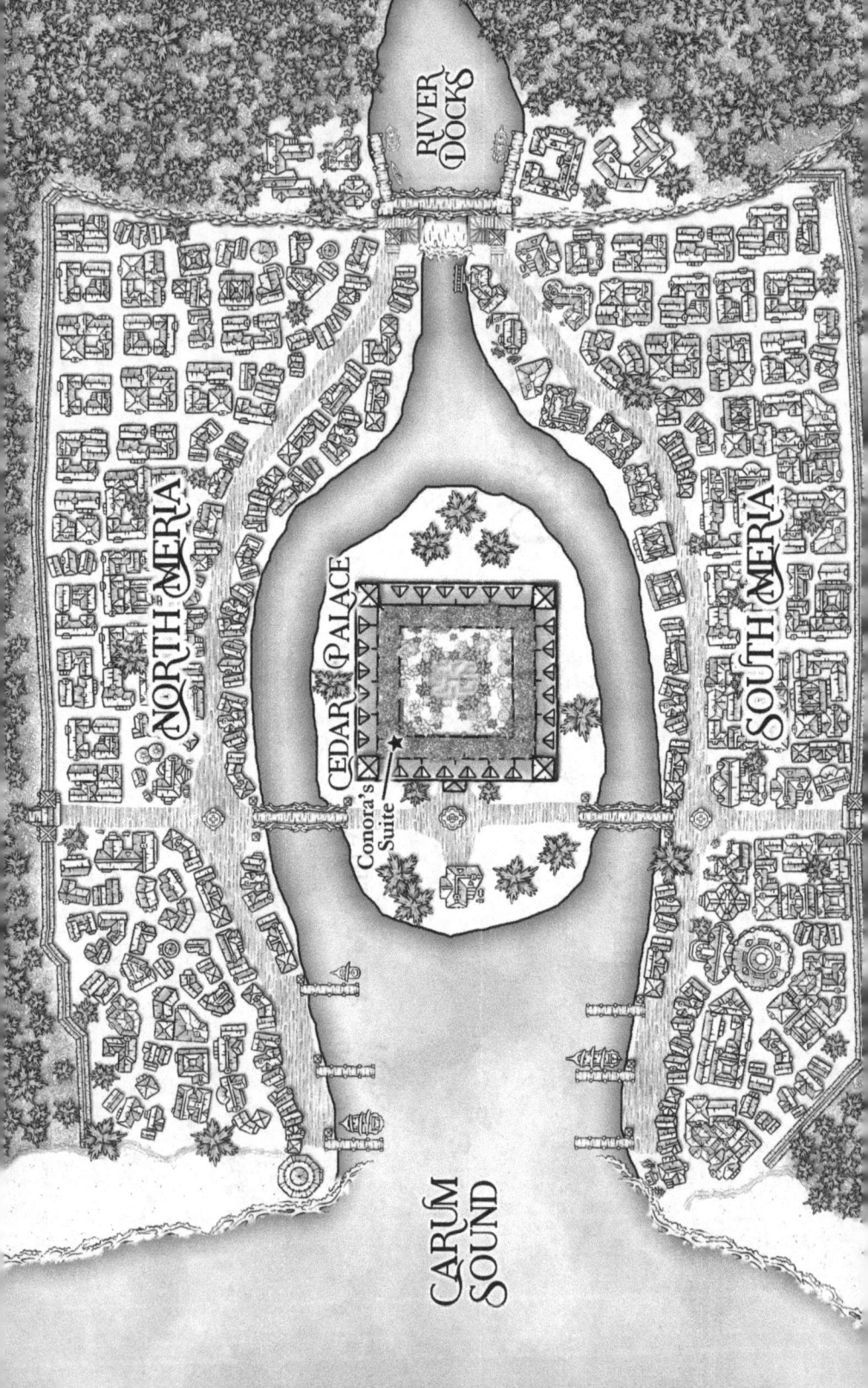

RIVER DOCKS

NORTH MERIA

SOUTH MERIA

CEDAR PALACE

Conora's Suite

CARUM SOUND

PASUTRUS

IMPERIAL PALACE

Nobles

Empress

Emperor

Calosandros

Nursery

Nobles

Celudos
Ucusioya

Kitchen

Servant Tunnel

Celudos
Iarosa

Nobles

Celudos
Ucuisa

Public
Bath

Library

Throne
Room

Imperial
Office

Treasury

Nobles

PRONUNCIATION GUIDE

For a more complete list, including IPA phonetics, visit
BrandiSpencer.com/pronunciation

Names

Abhenric – ə-BEN-rik

Agilee – ə-GEE-lee

Anabusos – AN-ə-BOO-sohss

Barbenia – bar-BAYN-yə

Baythroas – BAYTHE-rohss

Boinee – BOY-nee

Boscada – Bohss-CAH-də

Calosandros – CAL-ohss-AN-drohss

Doivrie – DOY-vree

Doneron – DAHN-er-ahn

Elgatha – el-GAHTH-ə

geoduck – GOO-EE-duck

Iverish – IV-ə-RISH

Jibiam – jib-ee-əm

Kennard – KEN-ərd

Melaine – mə-LAYN

Meria – MAIR-ee-ə

Meriveria – MAIR-ə-VAIR-ee-ə

Nemonee – NEM-oh-nee

nuil yos – nweel-yohss

Odelia – oh-DEE-lee-ə

Orosiad – OR-oh-see-ahd

Oulley – oo-LAY

Pasutrus – PAH-soo-TROOS

Rhonwin – RAHN-win

Quintos/Cuintos – KWEEN-tohss

Siputreos – SEE-poo-TROHSS

Tehazy – tə-HAYZ-ee

Urstille – er-STEEL

Urstillian – er-STIL-ee-ən

Uskev – OOS-kev

Valerzan – VAL-er-ZAN

Urstillian Sounds

A – w<u>a</u>nt

B – <u>b</u>oy

C – <u>c</u>at

CH – lo<u>ch</u>

D – <u>d</u>og

E – h<u>e</u>lp

G – <u>g</u>oat

I/EE – k<u>iwi</u>

L – coo<u>l</u>

M – <u>mom</u>

N – <u>n</u>ope

O – p<u>o</u>l<u>o</u>

P – hoo<u>p</u>

PH – <u>ph</u>one

R – bu<u>rr</u>o (rolled)

S – <u>s</u>ee

T – <u>t</u>oo

TH – <u>th</u>em

U – d<u>u</u>de

Y – <u>y</u>es

TABLE OF CONTENTS

1

ALL OF CARUM SOUND

Oingioros pan Camaos Carum

Princess Conora was taking a much-needed break from talking to humans. Unfortunately, the more upheaval Meriveria faced, the more necessary the overwhelming royal hospitality became. But animals were simple. So, when a servant had complained about a dog barking incessantly, Conora took the opportunity to use her Animal Speech.

She crossed her arms and stared down the one-year-old sled dog. *No.*

Please, the dog yipped back.

Conora refused to flinch. She needed to show the adolescent pup who was in charge. *Too young. No out for your first heat*, she haw-ruffed.

The dog growled.

And no howling or digging.

She gave a doggy pout and whimpered.

Conora rolled her eyes. "Nope. Won't work." She gestured at her mouth. *No yapping, or you get the muzzle.* It was a warning, not a threat. Conora could never bring herself to order it, but someone else undoubtedly would do it.

The dog sat, though her front paws never stopped moving. *I good! I good! I—* She sniffed at the air. *Males.*

Ugh. Conora spun on her heels in time to see a dog cart pass outside the pen, then turned back and sighed. *Ignore that.* With her brother and sister-in-law's coronation in two days, there would be no shortage of traffic to and from the palace.

And Conora really had no time for this. Kennard and Odelia had called a meeting in the Advisory Den for the four grandilords and trusted royal family members. This included Odelia's mother, Hortensia, but Conora was the only worthy kin from Kennard's side.

Tehazy, Meriveria's neighbor to the north, had been raiding their border with increasing frequency until they were forced to declare war. Father had failed so spectacularly as a leader that Kennard and Odelia had

1

enacted and completed a bloodless coup within days; if Father hadn't lost his throne to Kennard, the Tehazians would have soon marched in and taken it.

In the few months they'd been in power, Odelia had been sorting out neglected domestic affairs in between bouts of morning sickness, while Kennard was restructuring what was left of their military. But no amount of restructuring could produce soldiers, and they were running out of subjects to enlist.

The dog tapped her front paws faster. *Scratches?*

Conora laughed. *Last ones!* She crouched and buried her fingers deep in the fluffy white fur behind both ears. It was almost soft enough to make yarn if the rest of her weren't gray and brown, but the wool dogs for shearing weren't kept on the royal islet with the working dog kennels for fear of accidentally breeding mutts. Funnily enough, her ancestors had had the same fear regarding the human subjects of their kingdom, but fortunately, they were much less successful there...

A soft breeze and the fluttering of feathers barely preceded the voice of a winged Flight messenger. "Your Highness?"

Without looking up, Conora nodded and waved behind her head. "I know. I'm coming." She touched the tip of the dog's nose with one finger. *Remember, be good.*

By the time she turned around to leave the pen, the messenger was gone. She shook the stray dog hair from the skirt of her sky-blue ramie gown. At least she didn't have any sleeves to worry about, thanks to the summer heat. She made her way inside the Cedar Palace, adjusting her plain gold circlet and straightening her delicate necklace of tiny citrines. As much as she loved her more glittering attire, ever since Kennard and Odelia deposed Father, Conora had chosen subtler, simpler styles. It was partly due to a need to not overstep the new, more understated king and queen. But she also couldn't deny the part of her that longed to distance herself from Mother's outrageous vanity and clawing ambition.

The woman was gorgeous and decadent, the pinnacle of Elgathan beauty—and a cruel bitch to anyone she deemed beneath her. Of course, most people never noticed because her Allure made her, well, alluring to anyone without blood ties to her; they would find her charming, even as she insulted them.

Conora smiled as she approached the ultimate target of Mother's ire—Queen Odelia. Her short stature and pastel coloring marked her as a

Vistan, which had annoyed Mother enough when Kennard and Conora made friends with Odelia and her brother as children. To Conora, the four had practically been siblings together—though the older two *clearly* didn't share that sentiment.

The Advisory Den was in the midst of a much-needed remodel: a rich blue and green cloth covered some of the large square table in the center, and yellow and white banners hung across the walls, both hiding a pervasive inlay of fierce fox faces—the emblem of Elgatha. How long before Kennard commissioned a new table and walls? Mother would *love* that. She'd already been fuming about Odelia being too sensitive and covering the symbol of their people.

But they weren't Elgathan anymore—not officially anyway. The marriage of Kennard and Odelia had united them all as Meriverians. And Conora couldn't begrudge Odelia such changes when most of the Vistan dynasty had been massacred by Elgatha. If not for Conora's family, Odelia's wouldn't have had to spend generations in hiding.

Kennard was uncharacteristically somber. His wild brown curls, which normally added a bit of boyish charm, gave him an air of manic distress as they half covered his crown. He cleared his throat and feigned a bright smile. "So...any chance someone has news for us before we begin?"

There was a long, awkward silence.

Grandilord Patricius crossed his arms and raised a red eyebrow. "Did the meeting with Uskev not go well?"

"They did offer funds."

"But not the men we need?"

Kennard sighed. "Unfortunately, they have none to spare."

The grandilords groaned and started muttering.

Odelia fidgeted uncomfortably until Kennard kissed her temple. She instantly calmed, then kissed his cheek.

Conora looked away. She was happy for them—really, she was—but aside from the familial discomfort, it was a constant reminder of what she had never experienced...and likely never would.

"Is it any wonder our kingdom has failed to make allies?" Grandilord Straton scowled. "You can't draw up treaties if you're too busy making doe eyes at each other."

Odd. Straton had been one of the Vistan nobles who witnessed their wedding.

"Would you rather the queen and I didn't get along?" Kennard asked.

"We would rather see you practice some decorum, Your Majesties," Grandilord Doneron said.

Conora rolled her eyes. Of course, Doneron would care about formalities above everything else, though it was refreshing to see him show some spine.

"It's not for us to admonish our sovereigns," said Grandilord Rhonwin, who owed his position to his loyalty to Kennard and Odelia. "Besides, we cannot blame this situation on their affections. Gonfrid destroyed our army and foreign relations before they took the throne, and Uskev is the only nation that's given them a chance to try diplomacy in person."

"And that diplomacy matters little if Uskev has nothing for us," the other Vistan, Grandilord Patricius, finally said.

Odelia sighed. "Which is why we need a plan. We need troops, and it's clear that Meriveria is on its own. There must be a way to find more soldiers here."

Patricius shook his head. "How? Vist has already given more than its share of men."

Rhonwin ran a hand over his face. "Nothing like a draft to endear me to my new grandrion."

"But even doing that, Elgatha doesn't have enough men to make up the deficit," Doneron said.

Conora held back a sigh. Well, they might as well all learn to speak Tehazian—assuming the Tehazians let them live.

Odelia crossed her arms and cocked her head. "You keep saying 'men.' What if we allow women to join the ranks?"

Conora perked up. That was certainly a new idea.

Doneron gasped. "You cannot be serious."

"Why not? I was stationed at Fort Solace. Did you need to see another demonstration of my ability to handle a weapon?"

"But you are exceptional, Your Majesty," Straton said.

Odelia scoffed. "The scores of women we've pardoned for wielding weapons have proven that I'm not."

Rhonwin frowned. "You would force other women to endure what you did in Solace?"

"No, volunteers. There are brave women who would be eager to protect their home."

"Vistan women, perhaps, but Elgathan women are not so foolish," Doneron said. "That was why the old law only applied to them."

4

Wow. Conora didn't have training in any kind of weapon, but she wished she had so she could knock him on his pompous ass. "If a woman has combat skills, what is so foolish about helping?"

"Even Her Majesty left the battlefield to bear children. How helpful will others be?" Doneron didn't hide the contempt on his face.

"And who will be protecting all those women from their fellow soldiers?" Rhonwin asked.

Conora laughed to release some of her anger. "Is that all women are to you? We all must be protected to marry and produce babies, or we have no value?" She crossed her arms and pushed back from the table.

Breathe in, breathe out. She had to control her feelings before they welled up into tears. Crying—even angry crying—would not convince these men that women were worthy to serve their kingdom. She should've been used to the idea anyway. As a princess and second-born, she had one role: providing backup heirs.

Not that she'd ever fill that role.

Kennard was well on his way to providing more than enough for himself, and Conora knew she'd never marry. It wasn't even a matter of want; it was her fate. She'd been foolish enough to pester a Seer for answers, and the words would haunt her forever: *There is no lover for you in all of Carum Sound.* Odelia had tried to console Conora by telling her that Carum Sound wasn't the whole world, but it might as well have been. She'd never seen anyone from beyond the region.

Odelia's mother, Hortensia, picked the conversation back up, but Conora hardly heard her. She turned toward the wall to better collect herself and looked up at the map of Carum Sound hanging there. So many kingdoms...

Conora walked over for a closer look. The sound itself and its islands took up much of the middle of the map. The western peninsula never paid much heed to other Carum Sound nations, more concerned with the open ocean to their west. Baythroas, Uskev, and Boscada were the largest of the nine island-bound nations. Meriveria sat between Tehazy and Incevéno, all of them flanked by the sound to their west and the Vistan mountains to the east. And past the Vistan mountains...

Kennard raised his voice. "Then Giver help us because there are no options outside ourselves. We've reached out to every nation in Carum Sound."

Every nation *in* Carum Sound.

"Carum Sound isn't the whole world."

"Conora…" Odelia said, her voice etched with concern.

"Look." Conora pointed to the far eastern side of the map. "On the other side of the Vistan mountains, we share a border with Urstille. They're huge and share a border with Tehazy as well. Surely, if anyone could benefit from allying with us, it would be them."

They all stared at her in shock.

"What?" Conora put her hands on her hips and smiled. "Are you all embarrassed that you failed to notice something so obvious?"

Odelia covered her mouth, and Kennard shook his head, looking disappointed.

"What? Why are you shaking your head at me?" The solution was right there!

"Conora, we absolutely cannot ally with Urstille," Kennard said.

"Of course we can."

"Did you daydream through all of your history studies?"

"Not all of them, but it's difficult to pay attention to details about a kingdom we have no dealings with." Conora face burned. They knew her attention could wander. Did her brother have to humiliate her about it?

Kennard sighed. "We don't have dealings with them for a reason."

"And we desperately need an ally, so refresh my memory on what reason would be good enough to reject them."

Odelia put a hand on Kennard's arm. "The border has been closed since the original Treaty of Meriveria. Before that, Urstille used to attack Vist. They regularly raided our towns, slaughtering men, pillaging, and kidnapping women to take back to Urstille. It was the driving incentive for Vist to create the treaty, as it gave Vist the added power of Elgatha to seal the pass on the eastern border."

Conora raised an eyebrow. "And?"

Patricius pinched the bridge of his nose. "You're telling us that you want to save us from a nation who broke faith and raided us by trusting one who used to conduct worse raids?"

"Two hundred years ago!" Conora tried to pull back her frustration. Were they all really this dense? "They could've changed by now, but"—she waved her hands wildly for emphasis—"nobody knows because the border is sealed."

"And unsealing it could double our peril," Straton said.

"Or it might save us," Conora said. Great Giver, how could they not get this? "Two hundred years is a long time. A hundred years ago—half the time, mind you—our ancestors massacred Odelia's, and now she and

Kennard are joyously in love and building a family together. The best things that have happened to Meriveria have come from rejecting the pain of our past."

"You mean asking the Vistans to reject the pain of their past," Kennard said. "Odelia trusts me despite our ancestors, but we cannot ask the rest of Vist to trust an entire nation with such a past when it affected Elgatha so little."

Oh, forget it. If they were just going to be stubborn... Conora slumped into her chair. "By all means, share a better idea." She turned to Odelia, willing her to remember the same conversation Conora had. "But perhaps the Giver is pointing us there."

Odelia looked at Rhonwin, who nodded, obviously reading some thought she'd directed at him—Listening was such an off-putting Gift—and considering that his wife had been the Seer in question, Conora didn't need Listening herself to know what Odelia was thinking.

Odelia closed her eyes, inhaled, and said, "We're out of other choices to protect Meriveria, and I am not bearing triplets for nothing. I want to send a request to Urstille."

Patricius looked at her, horrified. "They might destroy us."

Odelia stared him down. "'Might' is better than 'will,' and Tehazy is sure to. I choose risk over assured destruction."

"I don't like it. What do the rest of you think?" Kennard asked.

Straton shook his head. "We teach our children that Urstille is the evil that will visit them if they misbehave. No."

"I believe it's worth trying," Doneron said.

"So, the Elgathans, Conora, and Odelia for it and the Vistans and I against," Kennard said, then turned to Odelia's parents. "What about you, Hortensia and Abhenric? You've been quiet."

"Abhenric said Meriveria would fall without allies," Hortensia said. "I wouldn't reject the only one you might have without seeing what they have to offer. It can't be worse than not acting."

"As much as I distrust Urstille, you don't want to know what I've Seen will happen without allies," Abhenric said.

"Between Moira and Abhenric, you have two Seers steering you this way," Rhonwin said.

"Who are we to fight destiny?" Odelia crossed her arms and gave her husband a pointed look.

Kennard sank into his chair. "How do we want to word our request?"

2

A FORGOTTEN ENEMY

Thia Nudos Icporul

Calosandros wanted to run. He couldn't change his past decisions, but the sight of Agilee made him wish he could. A vain, selfish, greedy woman like her—he'd known better than to let her into his bed. It had been six months since his five-week mistake, and yet here she was in the private audience that Emperor Quintos and Mother had called.

Calosandros eyed Agilee suspiciously as he bowed to the emperor. Whatever the matter was, it wasn't a child—thank the Giver. Not only had he been more than careful, but she was as slim now as she'd ever been.

Mother folded her hands together and sat back as far as her tucked brown wings would allow. "Lady Agilee has shared with us her concern that you've grown distant..."

Calosandros raised an eyebrow. "Distant? That certainly isn't how I would describe it."

"Do not interrupt," the emperor snapped.

Calosandros swallowed and nodded. "Yes, Father."

The emperor motioned to Agilee. "Tell the prince the proposal you shared with us."

She gave Calosandros a pitying smile. "I understand how close you are with Captain Anabusos, and I'm willing to participate or even step aside if we produce an heir."

Calosandros blinked and shook his head. Anabusos and he had been friends for a long time, but that suggestion was not going to happen. "What makes you think any of that would appeal to me?"

"Everyone knows how Anabusos feels about you," Agilee said.

Calosandros shrugged. "And his feelings will, unfortunately, remain unrequited. My sexual orientation is not compatible with his, which we both have been well aware of for years."

"Ladies talk," Mother said. "We know you haven't been with a woman in some time."

8

"That doesn't mean I've been with men. I have two functioning hands."

The air was sucked out of the room. A loud silence hung for a few beats.

The emperor's eyes grew wide. "Son, you could have anyone you want in the empire. Why would you do that to yourself?"

Calosandros looked at the floor as heat filled his face. Had he really just admitted his sexual drought? "That is my choice and my concern. Regardless, Lady Agilee is as deeply mistaken about the current state of things between us as she is about the nature of my friendship with Anabusos."

"I see..." the emperor said. "Lady Agilee, leave us for now."

"Yes, Your Imperial Majesty." Despite her angry pout, she bowed and left.

As the door opened for her, a servant with huge black feathered wings entered, then tucked the extra appendages over his back and bowed. "Your Imperial Majesty, I know it is not the time for messages, but I come bearing one from beyond the Western Mountains." He offered him a sealed letter.

"From Carum Sound?" The emperor put on the thick golden spectacles that hung from his neck, took the missive, and frowned. "How can you be sure? This writing looks like nonsense."

The Flight messenger put a hand on his heart. "I received it myself. The border gate to Vist opened, and a man with wings as blue as the sky flew through with his hands over his head. I couldn't understand a word he said when he gave me that, but before I could ask him anything, he flew away again, and the gate slammed closed again behind him. If it weren't for that paper, I'd swear I hallucinated the whole thing!"

"If this is a hoax, you will pay dearly." The emperor whipped off his glasses and pointed the letter at the messenger, whose feathers began to tremble.

The brief flash of words on parchment sent a thrill up Calosandros's spine. Despite the claim of foreign text, he had read the word "Urstille" on its surface. The spread of Urstillian throughout their empire had rendered his Gift of Speech less useful every day.

"Calosandros?" The emperor held the letter toward him without looking away from the messenger.

Calosandros bounded to him and eagerly snatched it up. The first contact in two centuries, and he'd be the first to read it. The paper smelled strangely fresh: pine and cedar and something he couldn't quite pin down. A silver fox wearing a flower garland pressed in wax sealed the crisp cream-colored paper, and on the opposite side was a simple address in neat writing.

"What does it say?" the emperor asked impatiently.

"It's addressed to the current ruler of the Kingdom of Urstille."

"*Kingdom?*" the emperor sneered.

Mother put a hand on his arm. "It has been two hundred years, darling husband. We've heard nothing of them. Perhaps they don't know we have an empire now?"

He scoffed. "Don't be soft, Nemonee. Their ignorance is of their own making."

She smiled as if she hadn't heard him. "Well, at the very least, if our son can read the writing, it must be a real language. Might we let this fine messenger go back to his post before Calosandros opens it?"

The emperor waved him off. "Yes, you're dismissed."

"Thank you, Your Imperial Majesties." The messenger bowed, then didn't waste a moment to retreat.

Calosandros broke the seal and unfolded it.

> Your Majesty, Ruler of Urstille,
>
> Greetings, friend. You are no doubt surprised to see our border unsealed. Carum Sound has changed since the gate was locked. You know the kingdom this message originated from as Vist. However, the union of Vist with Elgatha has become permanent, creating the new kingdom of Meriveria. Currently, Meriveria is at war with one of our common neighbors, Tehazy.
>
> While Urstille and Vist have been enemies in the past, we cannot deny that Urstille has been a strong and worthy adversary. In the current fight, Meriveria could use a portion of that strength. An alliance with us could reopen trade between our nations, and the union between Vist and Elgatha would mean that trade access would reach the coast.
>
> We hope to meet with you or one of your ambassadors in Meria as soon as possible to discuss terms in more detail. May the Giver smile on a new era of peace and alliance between our kingdoms.

Sincerely,
Her Majesty, Queen Odelia of Meriveria
and
His Majesty, King Kennard of Meriveria

It was a long message to translate directly. With Speech, he would have to work back and forth one sentence at a time, waiting for someone to speak Urstillian to reset his language, then repeating the message. That would take far longer than anyone in the room had patience for.

"Was the letter real?" the emperor asked.

Finally, Calosandros could speak his native tongue again. "Vist and Elgatha combined to make the kingdom of Meriveria. They're at war with Tehazy and want an alliance with us, troops for trade. It's signed by Queen Odelia and King Kennard. If you want to read the whole thing, it would be easiest for me to translate on paper."

The emperor shook his head. "Don't waste your time. Why would we care about trade with their little kingdom?"

Calosandros shrugged. "They say Meriveria reaches to the coast. I imagine that means they also have port trade with all the seaside nations."

The emperor's eyes lit up as he grinned. "All the way to the coast? It has been some time since we expanded the empire... With a foothold there, we'd be unstoppable..."

"Should I draft a reply?" Calosandros asked.

"Yes, and prepare some troops to set out at once. If we're doing this, I'll need to send you as my representative. They're desperate enough to open the gate, which means they'll agree to anything. You know the procedure. We're going to get our first portion of Carum Sound."

Calosandros knew the procedure well, so practiced that he could assemble the needed forces and supplies in two days. He would be sent to a foreign kingdom and use their desperation to get them to sign more debt than they could ever hope to pay. When the kingdom inevitably fell delinquent, Urstille would oh-so-generously offer to take care of the kingdom's subjects itself—by absorbing them. Many places did fare better as part of the Urstillian Empire as they raised their standards of education and culture and gave them access to the empire's vast resources. Calosandros didn't want to admit the exceptions to that improvement.

He nodded. "I'll get to work at once."

"Just a moment," the emperor said. "I want to know the state of my right hand. Going over the mountains means you'll be gone for some time.

11

You're already twenty-five, and I still have no assurance that you won't be the end of my line. Now, is the obstacle a matter of body or desire? There are remedies you can try for either."

Calosandros's stomach turned sour. This wasn't a conversation he wanted to have with anyone, let alone his parents. "Neither. I just..." How could he say what he really wanted? That he couldn't fathom a lifetime with anyone he'd been with? That being with Agilee had felt empty? The concept of love was anathema to most of Urstille, especially the emperor; to love someone was to let them own you. Calosandros wasn't foolish enough to want that, but to feel just some kind of connection, to wake up next to a woman who stirred more than his loins, what would it be like?

The emperor sighed. "I knew you were too soft when you were Gifted with Speech, but this is an opportunity to correct that. These Vistans...Meriverians—whatever they're called now—they've always been too sensitive. It's the reason they had to seal that border. Their men were weak, and their women were easily swayed by the sight of Urstillian prowess. I'm sure this current war is the result of such weakness again."

He leaned back and propped his feet up. "So, go to this Meriveria. Let yourself experience their feelings for a while and see how they fail. And when you return with their crown, you will settle down with Lady Agilee."

Calosandros grimaced. "Does it have to be her?"

The emperor raised an eyebrow. "Did you have someone else in mind?"

"Literally any other eligible lady?"

"I'll take it under consideration."

Twelve days later, just after dawn, Urstillian troops approached the border at Break Pass, nestled at the lowest point of the Western Mountains, two thirds of a mile above the rest of Urstille. An abundance of timber and mining kept the remote town bustling, though not quite enough to call it a city. It had potential—without the wall at the rear center of the town, it would make a formidable trade hub. Of course, a fair number of buildings would have to go first. Having no through-traffic, many denizens had established homes and businesses right on the old road, blocking portions of it in random clusters. Calosandros had to order his soldiers to break formation and weave their way between and around structures to reach the border wall.

The gate itself looked almost haunted, covered in moss and abandoned in the shadows of the newer parts of Break Pass. The guards stationed to watch the Urstillian side had dubbed it "Shit Pass" because so many of them had gone nearly mad from sheer boredom. Calosandros half expected the ancient gates to remain shut, but before he could even ponder signaling, they creaked open, revealing a darkly shaded passageway through the thick stone wall.

Though, from the bright daylight, it seemed to lead to nowhere, Calosandros had his soldiers reset their column quadruple file as they funneled in. Only twenty feet in, they reached the other side, where they found a dense forest and a road so choked with vegetation that the Urstillians were forced to switch to single file again. At least the forest sheltered them from the summer sun, but this path would be a problem for transporting supplies. However, since the plan was to leave the bulk of his troops here at the border to await the outcome of negotiations with the Meriverians, Calosandros ordered those left behind to widen and clear the road from the wall to wherever it became viable again.

This proved to be half a day's march down the mountain, where a handful of little log homes nestled partway into the rocks surrounding a clearing. Even at the edge of the trees, the air was still refreshing, noticeably cooler than home. As Calosandros stepped out from the woods, he heard a sharp gasp. To his right, a petite copper-haired woman ran for one of the houses and slammed the door closed. He didn't blame her—it was a sensible move for someone who lived in the middle of nowhere.

However, Calosandros didn't need to remind his troops that harassing the locals was forbidden until the kingdom was theirs. A clean image was always an integral part of the emperor's plans when first conquering a kingdom.

And one did not upset the emperor's plans.

Calosandros took a moment to pull out a map and check his surroundings better. A ledge at the clearing's edge promised a decent view. And how it delivered! Coniferous trees stretched at his feet for miles and miles, a thick rolling blanket of verdant spikes, stretching north and south as far as the eye could see, that abruptly ended at sparkling dark turquoise water near the western horizon. He'd never before seen a body of water so large that its far side couldn't be seen clearly nor uninterrupted flora beyond the size of a city. Well, not entirely uninterrupted—here and there, small holes appeared in the forest with flickers of blue lakes inside. His

13

fingers itched to capture it all, and he reached into his pocket for his sketchbook.

A whistle broke the mesmerizing effect of the vista. "Do you think there's actually a kingdom under there?" Anabusos laughed and clapped a thankfully gloved hand to Calosandros's shoulder. Normally, the summer heat would make his friend's Ice a welcome Gift, but it wasn't so necessary on this side of the mountains.

Calosandros nodded. "It does look wild, doesn't it?"

"With all these woods, I fear this morning's slow pace will continue."

He crossed his arms in thought. "A kingdom can't run on roads like that. They must have better transportation as we get away from the border." He scanned lower in the forest, closer to their feet and directly ahead of them. "There!" He pointed out a break snaking through the trees, then a river on the map. "That must be the Ablure River. Our destination is at the mouth...somewhere...under all the trees."

Anabusos failed to hold back a smirk.

Calosandros rolled his eyes. "And my map shows the capital of Vist at the other end of the river, which shouldn't be far." With his finger, he followed the river backward until it turned into a good-sized lake that looked to be only a mile from the bottom of their cliff. "See? You can just make out buildings on the edge of that lake. I'll bet that's Iverish."

Anabusos's smirk turned into a smile. "Shall I relay orders to move on?"

The city of Iverish snuck up on the Urstillians. One minute they were walking through the forest—which, if anything, had grown thicker—and the next, they stepped between trees and onto a boardwalk around a lake. From this vantage point, Calosandros could finally see the ring of buildings bunched together around it and tucked into the forest. Several small boats sailed around the lake, and the city hummed with activity.

Calosandros had no trouble seeing over crowds here. Most of the adults only reached as high as his shoulder. And they made for an interesting view, seeing the tops of gold and copper heads. Though Urstille had blonds and redheads too, they were a rarity, usually the result of Vistan lineage cropping up. Even their "Vistan-towns" had, at most, maybe a third of their population with light features. But in Iverish, it looked to be almost the whole city.

And most of the city seemed to be filled with women and children—the few men were notable for their fitted pants amid all the skirts. How could they stand having their balls squashed like that all the time? No wonder their ancestors had trouble keeping women in the kingdom.

A shortage of men. The kingdom would likely pay almost anything to replenish their troops. The Meriverian letter had said as much, but the confirmation would make negotiations easier for Urstille.

It was a pity, really. The city was beautiful and didn't appear to lack resources. What would they gain from this alliance with Urstille after the war was over? They'd be stripped of what was here, and in return, the order of Urstillian rule would barely touch this place. Calosandros had managed the journey today, but what about when the pass filled with snow or a rockslide? It would only be a matter of time until this place descended into anarchy. He'd have to set the current rulers up as puppets to make it work here.

Calosandros had never wanted it less. He'd never enjoyed taking over territory, but this felt even more wrong than usual.

A young blonde squealed with delight and ran past him, a letter in one hand and a red ribbon streaming from the other. She threw her arms around another blonde who looked like she could be her sister. "He sent it! Even from Solace!" Both women dissolved into fits of laughter and tears.

As Calosandros walked on, he noticed more and more young women with red ribbons—not all of them by any means, but enough that they had to mean something—in their hair, around their necks, around their wrists. It was a striking display for the otherwise conservatively-dressed Vistans, who scarcely bared their arms and shoulders and were clothed all the way down to their knee-high boots. Calosandros nudged Anabusos.

"Yes, Your Imperial Highness?"

"What do you think the ribbons are for?"

Anabusos shrugged. "The latest fashion?" He flashed a charming smile at a redhead, who giggled and ran to her friends.

Calosandros sighed. "Forget I asked. And eyes ahead. You know these people are off-limits—especially to you."

Anabusos feigned shock, hand over his heart. "Who, me? I have no idea what you mean." He lowered his voice and teased, "Wanting to keep me for yourself?"

Calosandros laughed and shook his head, then pretended to scratch his nose with his middle finger. He sobered as they climbed the stairs of an inn.

"But truly, Anabusos, I doubt you'll find enough to satisfy you with the locals anyway."

Anabusos frowned. "Yes, I noticed. It'd be more trouble than it's worth."

Inside, a pale blonde woman blinked and looked at them askance for a moment before giving them a concerned smile. "Do you need help?"

"How many rooms do you have for tonight?" Calosandros asked.

"Oh. I thought maybe you'd been—" She looked them up and down, then shook her head. "Never mind. We have more than enough for you two to each have your own."

"We have fifty soldiers to house tonight," Calosandros said. "We are here at the invitation of your king." He reached into his bag and produced the letter, holding it up for the innkeeper.

"Oh!" The woman put a hand to her mouth, trailing a crimson ribbon from her wrist. "I have twenty rooms, but only eleven are open."

"We'll take all of them, thank you." Calosandros turned to Anabusos and waited for him to reset his Speech.

"Yes, Your Imperial Highness?"

"We have eleven rooms. Save one for me and two for the female soldiers. You and the other male soldiers can sort out the last eight."

"Of course." Anabusos gave a quick bow, then left to retrieve the small contingent of soldiers on the outskirts of the city.

Calosandros turned back to the innkeeper and waited an awkwardly long time for her to speak first. Finally, she blushed bright red. "How silly of me! You're a Speaker, aren't you? I should've known better, but I got a bit distracted by your...um...clothing, and—"

He began gathering coins from his bag. "What do I need to settle for the rooms?"

She put her hands over his and shook her head. "Nothing. If you're here to help our men come home, it's the least I can offer."

He stared at her, dumbfounded. She couldn't be serious. What kind of innkeeper turned down payment?

She handed him a pile of keys. "Make sure your men come down for dinner too. If there's any other way I can help, please let me know."

"I did have one question."

She smiled and nodded.

"I've seen those ribbons around. Are they for a festival or something?"

"You really are from far away, aren't you?" Her smile turned sad as she ran a finger over the ribbon on her wrist. "They're called ribbons of intent.

Men offer them to women they want to woo, and if we accept them, well..."
She held up her wrist. "Every woman you see wearing one has a
sweetheart...somewhere."

Calosandros nodded. "I hope we bring your sweetheart home safely."
Why had he said that? He didn't know her or her sweetheart. He couldn't
even guarantee that Urstille would join the fight. He needed to focus. "How
much farther to Meria from here?"

"That depends. I'd say a week if you're marching, but with only fifty
men, you could take a couple riverboats and be there in half a day."

Forget having his soldiers sleep on the floor. They could reach the
palace that night. He handed the keys back to the innkeeper. "Thank you so
much for your help, but we won't need the rooms—not tonight at least. We
will dine here, though." He handed her a few gold emperor coins as well.
"For your trouble. Which direction are the docks?"

After dinner, true to the innkeeper's word, Calosandros found several
boats available to the west of the inn. After introducing himself and his
purpose in the capital, he hired three to take him and the soldiers down the
river. Though the current carried them well, groups of rowers Gifted with
Strength propelled them even more swiftly, and they reached the docks in
Meria not long after sunset.

As they disembarked, a soft continuous roar and a salty breeze wafted
over them. Even the pervasive scent of pine couldn't overpower it. But the
dark was frustrating. What kind of city only had lights on the river docks?

One of the riverboat captains pointed straight ahead down the pier,
then to the left, farther downriver along docks. "You just keep following
the riverbank, Your Imperial Highness."

Calosandros crossed his arms. "I see nothing ahead. How do I know
you haven't dropped us in the middle of the forest?"

The captain put his hands up. "I promise you can't miss the Cedar
Palace."

Still uneasy about the dark city as they stepped off the pier,
Calosandros sent Anabusos to scout ahead of them downriver. Within
minutes, Anabusos was back, grinning. "I think you'll like this."

Several paces downriver, a thick railing came into view, cutting across
their path. The railing continued past the docks over an arched bridge,
under which the river seemed to disappear as the roaring grew louder.

Calosandros followed Anabusos to it, where a whole city opened up thirty feet below them with flickering lanterns illuminating its streets. From the base of a waterfall, the river cut right through the center of the city until it reached the sea, and at its mouth, a tiny island held what had to be the Cedar Palace. It was bigger and more brightly lit than anything else, and a pair of grand bridges linked it to both riverbanks.

The Urstillians took a staircase that zigzagged down the hill on the north side of the river for what felt like forever. Thankfully, there was a pulley system to lower their gear to the bottom. By the time they approached one of the bridges to the palace, Calosandros was ready to fall asleep in any kind of lodging, even a bedroll in a tent, though he hoped the Meriverians would not keep their gates shut at this late hour.

The guards did indeed let them in, but without a royal welcome as the king and queen had long since retired for the evening. Calosandros didn't mind; it would give him more time to prepare himself for the meeting and negotiations. He ordered his soldiers to remain quiet as they entered and avoid disturbing the palace residents. As tired as they looked, it wasn't all that necessary, but Calosandros wouldn't take a chance on that.

Once inside the Cedar Palace, the name became obvious. The palace looked to be made entirely of yellow- and red-cedar, lending a warm glow to everything. Intricate inlays and carvings covered the walls and floor, interrupted by rich blue curtains along large windows that faced the sea.

Servants soon arrived to greet the Urstillians. Though dressed like the Vistans, these people otherwise looked more like Urstillians: taller, with bronze skin and dark hair and eyes—Elgathans. A man with graying hair explained that the male soldiers could be housed in the servants' quarters and guard barracks, with the female soldiers in some place called the DiOrto apartment. Calosandros relayed the information, then translated back and forth as more specific arrangements were assigned.

As soldiers dispersed, Calosandros heard a *yip, yip* behind him. He'd lost his war dog, Dunos, years ago, but the sound of barking still reminded him of his four-legged comrade. Curious about the kind of dog to make such a tiny bark, Calosandros turned and was instantly rendered speechless.

A woman knelt next to a fluffy brown dog, putting them eye-to-eye. Her deep maple hair fell around her in soft curls and waves down to her waist, reflecting dark gold and copper in the candlelight and framing a flawless tawny complexion. The midnight blue dress that floated over her slender form was far too fine to belong to a servant or even a lower noble—a

18

grandilady perhaps?—and while the skirt pooled on the floor below her, the shimmering neckline framed her like a gilded portrait.

But it was her face that had stolen his tongue. The strong structure, full lips, and long lashes would have been enough to make her the ideal Urstillian beauty, but she had the warmest brown eyes he'd ever seen. As she gingerly lifted one of the dog's front paws, her expression of raw compassion and concern somehow filled him with peace and fervor until he felt his chest would burst with feeling. When she opened her lovely mouth, she didn't speak words—not human ones at least—but canine barks and huffs and whimpers.

Animal Speech! Calosandros had rarely encountered Animal Speakers. The few so Gifted typically lived out in the wilderness, but here she was in the middle of a palace. Like his own Gift of Speech, the natural state of Animal Speech was empathetic and sympathetic. This was a woman who might actually understand him, might *connect*.

He hadn't noticed a red ribbon on her, though it was hard to believe a beauty like her wasn't spoken for. He glanced at her fingers. No marriage band either.

Giver's hands, but if he'd imagined the ideal woman for himself, she'd never have compared to the exquisite jewel before him. Calosandros considered introducing himself—he was *the* imperial crown prince, wasn't he?—but a quick sniff of his body disabused him of that notion. The beautiful lady was likely to attend tomorrow morning's royal meeting anyway.

"I believe that all of your party has been accounted for, Your Imperial Highness," a servant said behind him.

Calosandros suppressed a jolt at the sudden intrusion and turned back around. He couldn't help but ask, "Who is the lady over there, the one with Animal Speech?"

"That is the king's sister, Her Royal Highness, Princess Conora."

Princess? No wonder she was single. Few men could be worthy of speaking to her, let alone woo her—thank the Giver Calosandros was one of them!—though it was intriguing that she'd managed to avoid being married off in royal negotiations...

Calosandros tried to clear his head as he followed the servant to the guest suite, but a plan was already forming. If it worked, it could be the solution to more than one of his problems.

19

3

A WELCOME SHOCK

Icpoiba Siad

Conora could've kicked herself. How had she missed the Urstillians last night? She wouldn't let it happen again. After all, the alliance had been her idea. They'd sent a letter the week before to announce their arrival, and while some were alarmed to hear that Urstille had become an empire, Conora saw an opportunity for an even more powerful ally against Tehazy.

Too excited to sleep, she'd woken early anyway and wasted no time getting ready. Fussing with her curls would take too long, and she didn't want to wait for Raina, her new lady's maid, to help her—Conora had managed without one anyway before Odelia took charge. At least her hair was behaving enough this morning to leave it down. She picked one of her favorite summer gowns, a camas-blue chiffon that complemented her warm features and seemed to float when she walked—the flattering deep neckline wouldn't hurt her chances of guiding destiny her way either. A matching gold and amethyst tiara was the perfect finishing touch to add a little sparkle without making her shine too much.

Satisfied with her choices, Conora went straight to the throne room—which turned out to be empty, save for a few servants. She'd arrived much earlier than necessary, but she didn't trust herself to return in time if she left, so she took her seat on the dais to wait.

Kennard and Odelia showed up after what felt like ages, dressed in their matching crowns and coronation clothes. He shot Conora an annoyed glare.

What had she done now? She wasn't late this time.

He whispered something to Odelia, who scoffed. They each looked toward Conora before whispering back and forth.

Conora was getting just about fed up when Odelia glared at Kennard and raised her voice. "It's the height of summer. What else is she supposed to wear?"

Conora checked her dress. It wasn't new, and this wasn't the first time she'd foregone a few of her undergarments this summer. Nobody had ever mentioned anything to her before.

A servant approached them. "The Urstillians are ready. Shall I send them in or wait?"

Kennard sighed. "Send them in." As the couple cuddled together on the double throne they'd unveiled at their coronation, he turned to Conora. "Remember what they're known for, and be prudent."

Conora shrugged. "I haven't forgotten." Remembering wasn't the issue. She simply didn't need such patronizing fuss.

"Please, be careful with your words," Odelia said to him.

"Of course. Why wouldn't I be?"

"I'm 'very visibly claimed'?"

"We're both claimed." He gave her a mercifully brief kiss.

Odelia scoffed. "You're lucky that I know you well enough to know what you really meant. Just remember that the Urstillians don't."

Conora couldn't help but smirk at the reminder that, for all her brother's scolding, he had his own impulsive smart-ass streak.

The outer hall doors opened with the usual triple drumbeat while the brown-winged steward flew to the ceiling. "Presenting His Imperial Highness, Crown Prince Calosandros of the Empire of Urstille."

Conora's heart raced at the announcement. Finally!

But her excitement had in no way prepared her for the Prince of Urstille. He was sexuality itself chiseled into the form of a man. Bronze flesh rippled over thick, hard muscles as he strutted toward her, most of his body visible under his singular scant tunic-like garment. The rich crimson piece tied at one shoulder, with a fine leather and gold belt slung at his waist. The skirt portion only reached halfway down the prince's thighs, piquing Conora's curiosity at what he could possibly be wearing underneath—not much, or it would show... Even his footwear oozed sensuality. Instead of boots, leather sandals snaked up his sturdy calves.

If it weren't for the attire, Prince Calosandros might almost look Elgathan. Almost. Though carefully groomed, his mid-length wavy black hair and beard lent to his intensely virile bearing.

As the prince passed the ladies of the court, he smiled back politely to their staring. But when he looked up and saw Conora, his eyes—green as new cedar and stark against his dark lashes—lit up with a sort of passion that she couldn't quite place. It read as desire, but that couldn't be right; she had to be confusing her own emotions for his.

His gaze didn't waver from hers, the fervor of it nearly unbearable. But she couldn't look away either, not as long as he focused such passion on her. Just before he reached her, he gave a smirk that said, *I have a secret for you.*

Then he turned to Odelia and Kennard, leaving Conora to catch her breath.

She rose with them as the steward began introductions: "Their Majesties, Queen Odelia and King Kennard."

Instead of bowing as expected, Prince Calosandros exchanged nods with Kennard, *then* Odelia, ignoring the order of their introduction. Conora prayed it was an oversight.

"Her Highness, Crown Princess Conora," the steward said.

Conora tried to temper her excitement at his renewed attention as she curtsied. Calosandros held out his hand, and she didn't hesitate to offer hers back.

His voice was husky as he murmured, "I especially look forward to knowing you," then brushed his lips across her knuckles.

Heat filled her body, and her face felt aflame, but she did her best to limit her reaction to a demure smile. Surely, it was an error in translation that her lust-filled mind had twisted. He must have meant he looked forward to *getting to* know her. A simple error from a non-native speaker—not that she'd detected an accent. And yet, the most primal part of her hoped he'd meant what he said.

Conora had always been deeply uncomfortable with being leered at before, so what made this so different? She saw it when his eyes met hers once more: he didn't eye her like prey; in spite of all his cocky swagger, his face was full of earnest hope and awe.

As Calosandros stepped back, Conora sat again, still holding his gaze until Kennard cleared his throat. The prince snapped his attention to the king.

Kennard forced a smile. "Welcome to Meriveria, Your Highness."

What was his problem? He knew the prince should've been addressed as "Imperial Highness," and they needed to impress him!

Calosandros narrowed his eyes at Kennard but nodded. "Thank you for the invitation. I wish it were under better circumstances." Still no foreign accent, he spoke Meriverian perfectly.

There wasn't a chance he'd learned it that well naturally. He had to be a Speaker. That would make negotiations more convenient. It also explained why she read his expressions so easily. Most Speakers and Animal Speakers were like that— Frog nuggets. He was probably doing the same to her.

"How was your journey?" Odelia asked.

"Fine, thank you." Calosandros tilted his head and smiled curiously. "You remind me of an old poem that the Vistan immigrants brought with them before the border closed. It's an honor to see 'the Maiden of Vist' in the flesh."

Odelia chuckled and placed a hand on her growing bump. "As you can clearly see, my maidenhood has gone the way of my homeland."

"Well, His Majesty is still a fortunate man," Calosandros said.

Kennard, ever enamored with informalities, said, "Calosandros, that's quite a long name. May I call you Cal?"

"No." He wrinkled his nose, then grinned knowingly at Conora. "But Her Highness is welcome to."

It was obvious he intended some kind of innuendo with his retort to Kennard's request. She failed to hold back a laugh at her brother's expense.

Calosandros turned back to Kennard. "Given that you've unsealed the border, I assume that your situation must be dire, and time is of the essence, so I won't waste any more time getting to the terms we have for you."

How refreshing to see such directness from a human. Most people needed to make inane amounts of small talk before considering any real discussion. Conora usually had to count on animal conversation for that.

Calosandros unfolded a paper from one of his guards. "In return for our military support against Tehazy, Urstille will expect Meriveria to provide food and shelter for our troops as well as the following over the next five years: two hundred full mature logs each of spruce, pine, red-cedar, fir, maple, and yew; one thousand pounds each of crab, salmon, clams, oysters, and mussels; two barrels of mint oil; fifty pearls; one thousand yards of silk fabric; and three thousand skeins of worsted dog wool."

It felt like someone had thrown ice water on her. Urstille was asking too much. Even if they saved Meriveria from Tehazy, they could never afford to pay all that without ruining their kingdom.

Kennard inhaled slowly. "Is that Urstille's only offer?"

Something in Calosandros's smile reignited Conora's hope. "There is one alternative, which I prefer myself, to be honest."

"What is it?" Kennard asked, his voice filled with desperation.

"One hundred logs of each wood, five hundred pounds of each seafood, five hundred yards of silk, fifteen hundred skeins of dog wool,

23

and…" Such a massive concession had to have a catch, but Calosandros barely hid his own desperation as he lowered the list and looked straight at Kennard and finished with the most obvious object of his desire: "Your sister."

Conora froze. How could something feel both inevitable and unfathomable?

"*What*!" Kennard pressed up from the throne, only held back by Odelia. "How dare you! My sister is a princess of Meriveria. She is not a commodity to trade."

Odelia whispered to him until he settled down, then said, "I apologize for the outburst, Your Imperial Highness. My husband is fiercely protective of those he cares about, both our subjects and family. What he was trying to say is that we have no right to give you Conora's hand. Such a decision is hers alone. We cannot force her to marry anyone, not even a crown prince, and would, therefore, have no way to honor such an agreement."

Calosandros nodded. "I understand. I learned a little about your customs on the way here." He pulled something out of an unseen pocket, then approached Conora, his trembling only perceptible when he leaned in close and took her hand. He held what looked like a piece of his garment, one of the ties from his shoulder—on its own, the red silken strap would work nicely as a ribbon of intent.

Conora put a hand over her racing heart and gasped. "Is that…?"

He smiled and nodded, then leaned just a little closer to speak for her ears alone. "I do not seek a reluctant bride. From your reactions, I believe you feel the same desire, the same connection that I do, that there is potential for great passion between us."

Overwhelmed, Conora could hardly parse her thoughts. "I… I…" She settled for a slight nod.

Still holding the ribbon, he clasped her hand to his chest with both hands and moved his head to make his gaze meet her averted one. "Your queen is correct to say this is your decision, and I understand it is much to ask of you. If this proposal offends you, I will not mention it again. But I've traveled to many kingdoms, and I can say without exaggeration, you are the most exquisite woman I have ever seen. It would be the greatest honor to one day have you by my side as my empress."

What could she say? All of Meriveria was at stake. And had she not longed for a moment like this? She'd always imagined spending some time as sweethearts to become familiar before a man proposed marriage, but did that matter if he was the right one to ask?

24

There is no lover for you in all of Carum Sound.

This was her chance.

Before she could second-guess her choice, Conora whispered, "You have to tie it on me."

Calosandros gave a tentative half smile. "Is that a yes, then?"

She nodded. "Yes, I agree to my part."

He exhaled, then beamed as he gently wrapped the ribbon around her wrist and finished it with a tidy bow. "Thank you, Princess. Your courage only raises your esteem." He stepped back and turned his smile to Kennard. "Her Highness has agreed to uphold her part if you agree to the terms of our second offer."

Her brother's face screamed, *No!*

But it was Odelia who politely addressed the prince. "You have given us much to think about. May we have some time to discuss the options? You are welcome to tour our palace and enjoy yourself while we deliberate."

"Of course, Your Majesty. It is your kingdom that's running out of time, so take as much as you think you can afford."

4

AN INCOMPLETE CONFESSION

Icloidoidois Icangalar

Calosandros held his posture as he left the throne room. Unsure where else to go, he headed in the general direction of his guest suite. When he reached a seemingly empty hallway, he stopped and leaned back against a wall, hands on his knees. He'd never been personally invested in negotiation outcomes before, and his head swam with the rush of emotion.

"What was that?" Anabusos's sudden question startled Calosandros out of his stupor.

He put a hand on his chest. "What?"

"That was the weirdest royal introduction I've ever seen. That king lost his shit. What the hell did you say to him?"

Shit. Calosandros hadn't thought this part through when he planned what to say to the Meriverians. He'd successfully sized up Princess Conora—who was somehow even more breathtaking up close—and by some miracle, she gladly returned his affections. Giver, he'd pulled that off faster than he thought possible, and his encounter with her had been woefully brief. Hopefully, the king wouldn't completely lose it and sequester her away before Calosandros could see her again.

Anabusos put a hand on Calosandros's shoulder. "Are you okay? You seem...out of sorts."

"More than okay." He relaxed into a smile. "Meeting Princess Conora was absolute joy."

"Was she the pretty brunette you tied a piece of your chiton on?"

Calosandros sighed. "I want her so badly, it was all I could do not to pitch a tent in there."

Anabusos laughed. "Fair enough. I doubt I could've resisted those eyes. She looked ready to pounce on you."

"If she had, the king really would've lost his shit. He did not appreciate my attention to her."

"Wait. That's what that was all about? Giver, this kingdom's so repressed. Shame. The princess seems like she'd be quite frisky."

Calosandros smirked. "Oh, she definitely has a wild streak. She's an Animal Speaker."

"Oooh...you are so lucky the rules don't apply to you. Just yesterday you were warning me not to mess with the locals, and now you're flirting with the sexiest one. Hoping to break your dry spell soon?"

"To be honest, I was thinking she might make a good empress."

"Always so ambitious. One thing at a time, my friend. Why don't you work on seducing her a little more before you make grand plans for your future?"

Calosandros's hopes rose. "Are you offering to help me?"

Anabusos wiggled his eyebrows suggestively. "Is that an invitation?"

"You wish."

With an exaggerated shrug, Anabusos snapped his fingers. "Damn. It was worth a shot."

Calosandros snickered. "Is there anyone you've ever closed your bedroom door to?"

"And risk missing the infinitesimal chance someone changes their mind? What fun would that be?"

Calosandros clapped him on the back with a full laugh. "And you call me the ambitious one."

"Did you have something in mind for me to do?"

"Not yet, but I'm sure something will come up. After the king's reaction, I'd be shocked if some kind of sneaking isn't involved to be alone with her."

"Should I shadow you until then, or do you need some reconnaissance for negotiations with the Meriverians right now?"

"That's a good question." Calosandros stroked his beard. Information would be invaluable, but where to even start? Better to assess the situation more before directing Anabusos to spy, lest he waste time searching all the wrong places for who-knows-what. "Why don't we start with the shadow?"

5

SPARKS

Duroidosio

Conora waited until Odelia closed the door to her office, then threw her arms around her shoulders and whispered excitedly, "You were right. There is someone for me."

"We cannot accept these terms." Kennard just had to rain on her happiness.

Conora gasped. "What? We must!"

"She's right," Odelia said. "Like it or not, Urstille is our last hope."

He dug his hands in his hair. "So, we sell ourselves to them instead of falling to Tehazy? There must be something else they want, something we can use to negotiate."

King or not, Conora wasn't about to put up with his nonsense. She planted a hand on her hip. "He told you. He wants *me*."

"That's not an option."

"Ken, she could save our kingdom," Odelia calmly pointed out.

He gaped at them. "Have you lost your mind? I am *not* selling my sister!"

"You wouldn't be," Conora said. "I'm a willing participant. I want to do this." That was an understatement, but it wasn't as if she could tell her brother how hot her ardor was burning. He would always see her as his *little* sister, the one to be protected from his shenanigans.

Kennard sighed. "It's not a freely made choice. It's coercive enough that he asked you publicly, but he's holding our kingdom for ransom."

Conora scoffed. "It doesn't matter whether I marry for love or to save Meriveria. This is my choice, something that gives me a purpose beyond being an unnecessary spare heir at the end of what I expect to be a long line."

Kennard put a hand on her shoulder, his worried brow eerily making him resemble their father more than usual. "You're not thinking about this clearly. You can't trust him. Whatever he told you, this isn't about love."

Apparently, the resemblance didn't stop at his expression. Conora rolled her eyes.

Kennard moved his face in front of hers to force her to meet his gaze, then shook his head in disgust. "You think a man who coerces you will respect you? You think he sees you as anything other than an object to buy?"

She suppressed the urge to shove him away. "So what? I'll be a future empress, for Giver's sake!"

"Conora, you can't possibly know what you're agreeing to. We don't know him or Urstille, and what we do know isn't promising. They're a very carnal people. He's likely to be an unfaithful or—Giver forbid—a violent husband. We can't, in good conscience, condemn you to that."

Conora crossed her arms to hide her clenched fists. "I'm aware of the risks, and I don't care. He's handsome and charming—"

"Handsome and charming? He's a boor!"

She glared at his interruption. "—and even if he turns out to be a terrible husband, it'll still be a small price to pay to protect the thousands of lives in Meriveria."

"That's easy to say now. What about when you're stuck in Urstille, miserable and apart from everyone you know and love?"

"If Odelia can risk her life for the future of this kingdom, why can't I risk the rest of mine?"

"This will end poorly, and I refuse to be part of it. *I will not sign.*"

"Have you looked at the recent maps of Urstille? I will be empress of that one day. *Empress*! If you ruin this for me, Kennard, I swear to the Giver..." They hadn't brawled since they were children, but Conora was dangerously tempted to slap him now.

"You'll what? I'm trying to protect you!"

Odelia threw her hands up. "Enough!"

Kennard gave an annoyingly smug nod. "Thank you."

"I was talking to you," Odelia snapped.

He spun around. "Excuse me?"

"Leave Conora alone. She's a grown woman, and you're not her father."

At least *somebody* acknowledged that, at eighteen, she was not a little girl anymore.

He practically growled as his body clenched. "You would agree to this?"

"It's her choice."

"A hastily made one."

Conora laughed at the hypocrisy. "Because you took so long to deliberate before eloping with Odelia and launching a coup?"

Kennard put up a finger. "That was different. We were in love and already had a long-established friendship. That particular event may have been quick, but on the whole, our courtship took time."

Ha. Maybe if by "courtship," he meant years and years of denial. Conora smirked. "Well, not all of us need more than a decade to work up the courage to get married."

He rolled his eyes. "Oh, of course, you're right. I should've proposed to Lia when we were eight years old."

"No, but you could have four years ago," Conora said.

Odelia sighed. "Please, Conora, I want to help you, but you know the situation was more complicated than that." Her expression said, *Not helpful.*

"How much time would satisfy you?" Conora asked. "The longer you wait to sign, the more soldiers we lose and the closer Tehazy comes to overtaking us. And let's not forget that it'll take Prince Calosandros time to send word back to Urstille and have his troops brought across the pass and through Doivrie to our northern border."

"She's right," Odelia said. Conora enjoyed how much she kept repeating that.

"But why Conora?" Kennard groaned. "He must have a reason for asking for her hand so quickly. He's clearly older than us. He's a future emperor, and if he's so 'handsome and charming' as you both seem to think, why hasn't he married already? What is he hiding? Maybe she wouldn't be his first wife. For all we know, the Urstillians might keep multiple wives. That could be why they used to steal Vistan women. Or maybe he's killed his previous wives. We don't know."

"Ugh. That's it." If Conora had to listen to him talk anymore, the childhood brawls were definitely returning, and she could kiss Odelia's support goodbye if she laid a hand on him. She headed for the door. "If you're just going to spin wild theories and other nonsense, I'm going to do something productive."

"Like what?" Kennard asked as if he'd gotten the better of her.

Literally anything would be better, but she grinned as she thought of what she really wanted to do. She flung the door open and said over her shoulder, "Entertaining our guest."

"Conor—!"

The slamming door cut off whatever tirade he was about to start.

Conora flipped her hair over her shoulders and walked away with her chin up. This was a wonderful day so far, and she wasn't about to let her brother ruin it—and Meriveria's future—with his stupidity.

She was halfway down the hall when she realized two guards, Gerid and Thaum, had fallen into step behind her. Ugh. She'd forgotten about her new hires, a stipulation from Kennard to allow her to participate in negotiations.

"I don't care where you go or what you do as long as you have guards," he'd said.

Conora was determined to test that promise.

She didn't have far to go. As soon as she rounded the first corner, she spotted Calosandros in animated conversation with one of his soldiers.

He lit up when he noticed her, blurting, "Conora Duboinee, tra oin cal so icida?" It was strange to hear her name with all the vowels fully rounded, but way his *r*s rolled off his tongue was pleasantly reminiscent of purring.

"Could you repeat that in Meriverian? I haven't had time to learn any Urstillian yet."

His cheeks bloomed red. "I'm afraid you caught me thinking aloud. I said, 'Princess Conora, how are you so beautiful?'"

"I thought I heard you say 'Cal' in there somewhere. Which word would that have been?"

"Beautiful." His tone implied *like you* underneath.

She felt bad for the stray giggle that escaped and clearly wounded him, so she quickly clarified, "You don't want my brother to call you beautiful?"

"Does he usually ask visitors that?"

"Not exactly. He likes nicknames. It was an effort in friendship."

"Nicknames? I'm not following. What is that?"

"You know, shortened names. Calosandros becomes Cal. Kennard and Odelia become Ken and Lia."

He tilted his head. "He just changes people's names? Lovers use pet names, but why else would you call someone by something that isn't their name or title?"

She laughed. "I'm not sure anyone can explain him."

"Do you at least know why my proposal so deeply offended him?"

"That is much easier to explain. I take it that your understanding of Meriverian courtship is rather cursory?"

31

Calosandros cleared his throat as another blush crept up on him. "Well, we only entered your kingdom yesterday... How badly did I miss the mark?"

Conora put a hand on his arm. "Your proposal itself was lovely. I'm still touched by it." Now it was her turn to blush. "It was the audience that was a bit...inappropriate."

He blinked. "Oh. I wouldn't have guessed that. What is the appropriate audience?"

"None, actually. Ribbons and proposals are given privately here. It lets a woman make her choice without worrying about publicly embarrassing a rejected man."

"Interesting. That's surprisingly progressive."

Conora balked. "What's so surprising? Do we seem so backward to you?" Whether he meant it or not, it was hard not to take offense.

"I wouldn't say backward—you have plumbing and clocks and cities—just a bit restrictive. You don't seem entirely free."

"Is anyone entirely free?"

"Wow. Fair enough." He laughed. "Looks like I can add wit to your growing list of virtues. I think I chose well." He suddenly sobered. "Unless this is your way of telling me you accepted my proposal just to spare me embarrassment?"

"My *yes* was genuine. I'm not so deeply concerned with public opinion that I'd uproot my life for it. And I do not give my word lightly either. I stand by my decisions."

"And yet I see questions on your face," he said softly.

"A few." Curse Kennard for sowing doubt in her mind. She couldn't deny the validity of some of it. "Perhaps I could show you around the palace while we discuss them?"

He took her hand and kissed the back of it. "As you wish, Your Highness." Then he promptly wove his fingers between hers and pressed himself close to her side.

The sudden intrusion into her territory caught her off guard. She involuntarily took a step away before realizing but stopped short of dropping his hand. It was something she'd always instinctually done when people came too near, but without knowing that, Calosandros could misinterpret and take it personally. She tried to play it off as a directional choice. "Why don't we go this way?"

"Of course." If he noticed, he didn't show it.

Behind them, Gerid and Thaum began to follow at a distance.

"What would you like to know first?" Calosandros asked.

"What is your intention for me—I mean, your expectations for a wife?" Lovely. One question in, and she was tripping over herself.

"Have you not been taught royal and marital duties?" he asked cautiously.

"Yes, I understand the basics, but there are multiple roles for a consort, and I want to make sure I know which ones to fulfill. Are you looking for a companion? A bedmate? A trophy? A means to an heir?" She paused before quietly adding, "Perhaps love?"

"Trying to produce an heir is all I can rightly ask of you, isn't it? I cannot make you entertain me, nor can you promise sexual satisfaction. And love, well, that can be outright impossible sometimes. Despite the way your king looked at me, I'm not a monster. I won't place more demands on you when I'm already asking you to leave your home and family behind."

Something in Conora's chest relaxed, a tightness she hadn't noticed growing. Maybe Kennard's paranoia had been for nothing.

"I appreciate that." She exhaled, then discreetly shook out her free hand. "And what is it that you want?"

He tilted his head again. "Didn't you just ask me that?"

"I asked what you expected. Now I'm asking what you *want*. What do you hope for? What do you desire in a wife?" His eyes had told her in the throne room, but she wanted to hear it from his lips.

He frowned, then looked behind them. "We have an entourage."

Gerid and Thaum and the Urstillian soldier Calosandros had been talking to were trailing several paces behind.

She gave a dismissive wave. "An annoyance we'll have to live with for now." She poked his arm with her index finger and teased, "Trying to dodge my question?"

"I don't know. It's...it's not something I've ever been asked before."

"There isn't a wrong answer, you know. It's just however you feel about it." She continued teasing, flirtatiously leaning toward him.

"Ha. Abstract feelings. Urstillians do not talk about that. Hunger, thirst, arousal—visceral feelings you can address directly are what we're concerned with."

Despite the undeniable presence of that last feeling, the tightness in Conora's chest crept up again. "So, the connection between us that you spoke of, is it all lust, then?"

Calosandros stopped and sighed, then grasped her other hand. "I said we don't like to talk about those feelings, not that we don't have them." He lowered his voice. "To be honest, I often find that hard. It's taken me a long time to learn to bury such thoughts."

The brief glimpse inside him called to her. It was the same thing she'd seen in his eyes when he had been on one knee. She longed to unbury that vulnerability, to embrace and protect it.

"So, where are we going on this tour?" he asked.

And just like that, it was gone.

Desperate to see it again, she pulled him toward the stairwell. "I thought you'd enjoy a light snack."

He let go of her hand and wrapped his arm around her waist, seductively whispering, "I've never seen a kitchen upstairs before. Or are you being coy in front of your guards?"

Her pulse raced from the proximity, a tempting double-edged thrill of craving and unease that stimulated her every impulse. Conora involuntarily sped up her pace, forcing Calosandros to let go and chase her up the stairs, all the way to the top. There, she grabbed the door and whipped around to face him as he stopped inches from her. His expression of restrained longing as she stayed just out of reach was thrilling. She couldn't keep from teasing him just a little more.

With a sly smile, she said, "Tell me if you've seen this before."

He reached for her just as she opened it, and he stumbled through the doorway. He turned completely around, then back to her, looking utterly perplexed. "Okay, I'm lost. We went up all those stairs. How did we end up in a bramble patch?"

Seeing an opportunity for some privacy from her glorified chaperones, she quietly locked the door to the roof as he marveled at the spiny plants around them. She walked to a banister behind an archway breaking through the thick brambles, then beckoned with her finger for Calosandros to follow her. When he reached her, she gestured over the railing. "We're on the rooftop garden. Do you like raspberries?" Reaching past him, she plucked a ripe one from the vine and held it in front of him for a moment.

Then he just ate it—right off her fingers!—without warning. Conora let out a startled squeak and tried to back away, but his arm came behind her.

"Careful! Are you okay? You almost ran into that bramble." He gently pulled her forward, then relaxed his arm.

It was too much at once. Her senses weren't just stimulated. They were on fire. She'd underestimated the space under the archway, and his close proximity was dizzying. "I think I'm just a bit warm. All the hot air rises up here, and with everything so close together, the body heat..."

Stop talking. Giver, stop talking!

Conora gripped the railing and looked out over the inner garden below, burning with embarrassment at being so quickly overwhelmed. What she wouldn't give for a bird to fly by and distract her from all of it.

A hand on her back made her jump. Again.

She hung her head.

Calosandros leaned next to her on the railing, careful not to touch her this time, his voice soft. "I'm sorry. I'm not sure what exactly I did, but I feel like I upset you somehow."

Conora shook her head. "No. You're fine."

He sighed. "I know you were asking me questions, but I have one for you."

She kept her eyes on the garden as she said, "Ask it."

"You keep shying away... Are you...afraid of me?"

"No!"

"I understand if you are."

Conora wanted to find a deep dark hole to crawl into. "I don't fear *you*. It's overexcitement, fear of this moment where you see me reacting because everything around me is too much."

"Well, I don't know about you, but I have plenty of time to spare right now. Why don't you slow down and explain it?"

"I thought Urstillians didn't talk about feelings."

He laughed. "You aren't Urstillian yet. And not talking doesn't mean I can't listen."

She looked over at him for just a moment. He was patiently waiting but intently focused on her.

"It's so much easier to talk to animals. They're not adept at deceit, and when they communicate, the message is straightforward. But people? We'll say one thing with our words, another with our tone, and another with our bodies. And we lie all the time, even when we don't intend to. So many conflicting messages. Add all that to what my father calls 'the wildness' in me—nobody likes to talk about that."

"What is 'the wildness'?"

"Do you ever feel too many things together? Where every smell, every touch, every noise, every sensation fights for your attention at once?"

Calosandros nodded. "When too many people are talking over each

35

other, I can tell if they're speaking different languages, because my mind gets..." He wriggled his hands beside his head.

"Swarmed?"

"Exactly!" His eyes lit up. "It makes it difficult to speak back."

"That's how it always is for me around most people. I try to hide it well, but as you can see, it doesn't always work, and the panic when that happens makes it harder to hide, which means more mistakes, and on and on."

He stroked his beard. "You said *most* people, so there are exceptions? Because I very much want to become one."

"You're not offended or worried?"

"Why should I be offended by something you cannot help?" Calosandros offered his left hand palm-up, the way one would approach a skittish dog. "My affections are an invitation, not a demand. Whenever you are comfortable with touch, I will be receptive."

Conora gingerly placed her hand over his, more hovering than touching. When she was sure he wasn't going to close his fingers, she let her hand rest. She hadn't noticed before how surprisingly soft and warm his skin was. Though he had the expected callouses from fighting, he clearly cared for his hands enough to use lotion.

"Better?" he asked gently.

Conora nodded. She traced her fingers down his, pausing at the base where a ring rested. He didn't resist at all when she flipped his hand over to see the top of the ring, which looked to be a signet of a bear.

"That's the imperial crest. I'll have a smaller one made for you in Urstille." Calosandros held up his other hand and flipped it back and forth. "Nothing on this one—yet." He winked.

Conora flourished her left hand, where she kept her own signet on her thumb. "Same for me. My crest was supposed to be updated soon, but I guess there's no point in it now."

"May I see it?"

She brought her hand closer and let him hold it steady for viewing, noticing that he kept his grip open.

"Oh, I see. it's missing the flowers that I saw in the letter to Urstille."

"The fox is Elgathan. Queen Odelia contributes the Vistan flowers to the crest."

He opened his hand more, but now that she didn't feel captured, she didn't want to move away, so she decided to test her own boundaries. She took a step closer to him and slid her hands up his forearms, savoring the thrill of pressing her limits on her terms.

He smirked. "Maybe you could keep the fox as a souvenir. It suits you."

"How so?"

"When I was a boy, there was a fox den near one of our palaces. Nobody else knew where, but they knew it was close, because a little vixen kept showing up all the time. None of the servants could get near her." Calosandros grinned. "But I could. The vixen was clever and knew they were trying to catch her."

"You approached her softly, like you are with me now."

He nodded. "They called her wicked and sneaky, but I respected her and brought her little treats. She was so sweet, she played with me like a puppy, wagging her bushy tail. She even led me to her den sometimes. She eventually disappeared. I like to think she found a mate."

"I'll take that as a compliment. You know, foxes are some of the most faithful animals you can find. They mate for life." Conora found herself with her hands on his brawny chest, his hands lightly resting on her hips. She'd been so engrossed in his story, she hadn't noticed the magnetism slowly drawing their bodies together.

"Is that something else you have in common?"

"I supposed that's why I've never accepted a ribbon before today. What about you?" Her cheeks warmed as she brushed her fingertips over his signet ring. "Bears are anything but monogamous."

He blanched. "I hadn't intended to bring it up so soon, to be honest. But I'm trusting that—after being so open yourself—that you won't laugh at me." He slowly leaned to her ear to whisper in the lowest possible voice, "I've only taken three lovers to my bed."

Only three. He was horribly embarrassed by a number that Conora couldn't even imagine for herself. It was more than the number of ribbons she'd been offered in the two and a half years since she'd come of age.

"Sorry, I should clarify," he abruptly amended. "That's in total—not together—all separate..."

"Oh. That—that hadn't even crossed my mind." Never. That it was a possibility worth mentioning spoke volumes about how different Urstille was. And she had been overwhelmed by a simple touch. It was a wonder he hadn't laughed at how frigid she must seem by comparison.

"That came out all wrong. Yes, things are different in Urstille, but that doesn't mean— Conora..." Calosandros grazed her cheek with the backs of his fingers and gently tipped her chin until they were eye to eye, a whisper apart. "It's true that you won't be my first, but you are my only now, and Giver willing, you will be my last." Every inch of him declared his earnest honesty, his body language swearing an oath to match his words.

He closed the small distance between them, pausing for a heartbeat, his breath on her lips. But the flood of warmth inside Conora was rising, and she held still. Then his lips seized hers, and a heady mix of hunger and excitement drowned out the world. His beard felt like velvet under her hand as she moved her hands upward and settled them behind his neck to steady her weakening knees. When his hand shifted backward and pressed, she gasped at the gripping sensation on her buttock, and his tongue prodded her lips. Already lost to pleasure, she opened her mouth to let him do as he would.

With a quiet, throaty moan, Calosandros plunged in, dancing his tongue against hers, luring her to push back into his mouth. It was the hand on her breast that unchained her, and her hips reflexively moved against his. Too soon, his hands were on her hips once more as he broke the kiss, softly pushing her away as the door finally clicked open behind them.

He touched his index finger to her lips. "Just a taste, my little vixen."

6

HUNGRY

Pundoidia

It took every ounce of restraint Calosandros had to walk away from Conora when she responded so eagerly to his kiss. But he wasn't an impetuous youth anymore, and he couldn't afford to botch what he'd set in motion.

Anabusos clapped his back as they exited the rooftop. "Impressive recovery. I thought you'd blown it completely. What did you say? Because—a kiss that sexy?—she is *ready* to fuck."

"I just had to listen to her. Poor woman has been stifled here. I did tell her one story. Do you remember the vixen I used to play with when we were young?"

Anabusos sputtered. "W-why would you tell her that story?"

Calosandros smiled and shrugged. "I think she liked it. She is an Animal Speaker, after all. And Meriverians aren't so quick to laugh at a bit of softness."

"That much I understand fine, but the way it ends..."

"What? How she wandered off?"

Anabusos opened his mouth, then frowned and shook his head as if thinking better of it. "Never mind. Stick to your fluffy stories if that's what gets the princess's attention." He glanced backward. "Speaking of attention, we have new shadows."

"How long have they been there?"

"I'm positive they weren't there before you met the royal family. I think they started following us from the roof."

Shit. So, the king's need to control things hadn't ended with his outburst. If he was going to spy, Calosandros wouldn't feel guilty about his own tactics. He whispered, "Inventory and squad reports until dinner."

"Yes, Your Imperial Highness." Anabusos bowed, then peeled off in another direction.

They both knew the code well enough. Anabusos would scout out the palace guard and staff numbers and rotations, but first, he would start a chain of orders that would spread through the ranks. Every fifteen minutes or so, a different random soldier would visit Calosandros at his guest quarters, which he would conspicuously occupy. There would always be at least one or two with legitimate business, but most of them would be decoys.

It usually confused local spies regarding whom to follow since they typically had trouble distinguishing Urstillian military ranks unless they'd worked with them before. It also added to the impressive reputation of the bustling empire. In reality, Calosandros would be bored out of his mind until dinner.

This time at least, he had a passionate kiss with a beautiful princess to occupy his daydreams.

While Calosandros had initially hoped that Conora might seek him out at some point, by dinnertime, he was buzzing with anticipation. He ended up trading that nervous energy for awkward silence as he and King Kennard waited at the table for the queen and the princess. The king bore himself more like a sullen youth than a prudent monarch. He'd probably been spoiled rotten; he still needed to experience real disappointment and opposition.

The queen's arrival seemed to stir the man for a moment before his perpetual scowl returned. It was hard not to notice her waddle in and wrangle her swollen form into the chair next to him, but Kennard didn't acknowledge her at all. They'd been so cozy in the throne room. Did the king normally direct his temper at his wife, or had something happened between them? Or maybe the affection itself had been a farce?

Calosandros was dying to break the ice and get closer to finding out, but just as he opened his mouth to speak, he saw the true focus of his desire enter the room. He couldn't stop grinning like a fool as he stood and offered Conora his hand. "Your Highness, how is it that you're even more beautiful than when I last saw you?"

"Perhaps it's just hunger." Her coquettish smile teased him with innuendo.

"Hardly." He kissed her hand and, for less than a breath, let himself savor the perfume of her flesh. Then Calosandros pulled out the seat between him and the queen.

"Before you sit, I need to ask a favor," Conora said carefully, her dark eyes sparkling like rich brown garnets in the candlelight.

Anything for those eyes.

But when he looked down at her hand to see what she offered, his heart sank. It was the ribbon of intent he'd given her. Nobody had told Calosandros about this part of tradition, but it was universally obvious: a return of his gift would be a rejection of his offer.

This was all supposed to be for trade negotiations, so why did it feel like a knife in his gut? Regardless of his feelings, her reaction made sense. He had pushed her too far with that kiss.

Calosandros stuffed his pride down as he took the red ribbon back. "Oh, I understand..."

However, Conora didn't seem regretful in the least as she brushed her hair back and bared the flesh of her neck to him. "I was hoping you could retie it somewhere more advantageous for viewing...since my hands are sometimes in my lap, of course."

Calosandros could hardly breathe. In the blink of an eye, she'd brought him as low as possible, then somehow raised him higher than before. Giver, she was glorious.

He moved behind her and draped the ribbon over her shoulder, letting it trail down her chest. Resisting the urge to follow it down, he picked it up with his other hand and gently slid it around her neck. As he moved closer, she was taking deep, steady breaths—contending with as much temptation as he was. He knotted a tidy bow, carefully avoiding the stray tendrils that tried to curl into the ribbon, then stopped himself short of kissing the tender skin of her nape, settling instead for grazing it with his fingertip as he pulled away.

Conora's smile was infectious as they took their seats. She pushed her hair behind her shoulders and straightened in her chair, chin held high, making a grand show of her new accessory. Foreign as the custom was, seeing her choose to wear it so boldly swelled his chest with pride.

The room fell quiet as the king pushed back his chair and stood. "Our Meriverian subjects, both Elgathan and Vistan, we thank the Giver for the food before us, for the Gifts we've received, for the unity of our people, and for our..." He glanced uncomfortably at Calosandros and cleared his throat. "...for our Urstillian guests, who bring with them the hope of peace."

When the Meriverian nobles began filling their plates, Calosandros took that as the cue to do likewise. Most of the spread looked and smelled like seafood, but it was the freshest he'd ever seen. Other than freshwater fish and the occasional clam found in the lakes and rivers at home, he'd only ever seen it smoked, imported from long trade routes around the mountain range.

Conora slid a spiny red crab leg onto his plate. "You'll want to try this."

What had prompted that? Calosandros blinked and raised an eyebrow at her.

She shrugged. "You seemed a little lost."

"Only completely. Thanks for the rescue." He laughed, then picked up the cup of dark purple liquid in front of him.

At least he recognized the sweet but tart flavor of blackberry wine. This one was delicate and smooth; the Meriverians were putting out their best, though an interesting choice under the circumstances. They must've planned out the menu before today. Not a chance they would have purposely served something so similar to blackberry ink—a key component to a wedding ceremony. It was a Giver-given sign he was doing right. It had to be.

Calosandros took another long swig, imagining himself with Conora and a brush dipped in blackberry ink...

Down the table, Anabusos laughed loudly, then yelled, "Okay, Prince! Whose cocks are being served on the table?"

Calosandros nearly spat, the wine burning his throat a bit as he quickly swallowed. "*What*?"

"They look like cocks!" Anabusos hefted a platter of food that undeniably fit the description as the other Urstillians continued laughing hysterically.

Regardless, Calosandros couldn't let them insult their hosts. "Shut up!" He waved at Anabusos to sit, thanking the Giver that the Meriverians didn't understand Urstillian.

"What was that about?" Conora asked casually.

Calosandros looked nervously at the king, who was smirking. Was this some kind of test? He turned back to Conora and tried to find a diplomatic way of explaining in front of his intended's prudish family. "Well...given my current understanding of your customs and your personal inexperience, I don't think it would be wise of me to teach you such words until after I've wed you, but my people would like to know what's on that plate. To be honest, I'm a bit surprised myself. I didn't think Meriverians would eat such things."

42

"Oh, those are geoducks," Conora said simply as though she were discussing the weather and not a plate full of genitals.

He wrinkled his nose. "Gooey ducks?" That sounded thoroughly unappetizing. Then a more horrifying realization struck him. "If those are—how big are these ducks? And...I'm afraid to ask why they're gooey."

Conora gave him a small, polite smile and patted his hand. "They're not from ducks. Geoducks are a type of clam."

He put a hand on her arm. "Sweetheart, those are the opposite of clams."

"They really are clams. They're dug up from the beach."

She had to be playing some kind of game. Calosandros lowered his voice to show his seriousness. "Do you eat them?"

Conora nodded. "They're a delicacy, although Odelia's never been fond of eating them."

Calosandros couldn't resist turning to the king. "I'm so sorry, Your Majesty."

The king and queen burst into sidesplitting laughter, giggling harder when they looked at each other, until the queen shook her head and tried to push herself up from her chair. "Sorry. If you'll excuse me."

She only wobbled for a moment before the king had his arms wrapped around her. He turned to the table. "I'll be right back. I want to accompany her for a little while." Then he ushered her out of the room.

Calosandros chuckled. "I'm not sure which is stranger, the geoducks or those two."

Conora laughed. "Definitely the latter."

"Any chance you could explain?"

"About my brother? You'll have to be more specific."

Calosandros scooted his chair closer and leaned in. "He seemed sullen and dismissive of her when we sat down, but I swear I saw him kiss her a few times anyway. And then just now...I have no idea what that was about."

Conora shrugged. "They're still newlyweds."

He raised an eyebrow. "I don't understand. There must be more to it than that."

With a long pause, she fidgeted and bit her lip, then exhaled sharply. "I...I'm sorry. The best I can tell you is that the constant physical affection is normal for the two of them. Please don't ask me to explain why."

"Is it that you don't know or can't tell?" he whispered.

She blanched and shook her head to say, *Don't ask.*

This probably wasn't the right place anyway. If she was going to give him information, he needed to get her alone, and for all the effort that was going to take, he had much better ideas of what he wanted to do alone with her.

"Let's talk more about you, then."

She playfully posed a hand under her chin and batted her eyelashes at him. "What did you want to know?"

He draped an arm over the back of her chair and gestured at a large geoduck on her plate. "You never answered my question."

She opened her mouth and leaned toward it in a way that made him envious of the food. Then she stopped a few inches short. With a mischievous giggle, she sliced the tip off, popped it into her mouth and smirked.

Unsure whether he was more aroused or threatened, he said, "Go ahead and swallow first."

A deep blush came over her as she covered her mouth and laughed. So, she *did* know and had simply been toying with him.

After she'd stopped laughing enough to finish chewing, Conora cleared her throat and briefly slid a hand over his knee, whispering, "I'll leave that to your imagination," before returning to her food.

Calosandros took a long drink of wine, trying his best not to let his fantasies run wild. He needed to change the subject and cool off before the king returned. "What has the rest of your day been like?"

"I spent most of it with my mother. She left the palace today."

"Your mother?" he asked, surprised. "I don't remember meeting her this morning."

"Oh, she's no longer welcome in the throne room, not since Kennard and Odelia took over. They barely conceded to letting her live here for a while."

"Why keep her here if she's unwelcome?"

Conora leaned closer to whisper more quietly. "She has Allure. I think they were trying to contain her influence."

Allurists were dangerous. People couldn't help but adore them just for existing, and unscrupulous Allurists could bend almost anyone to their will with a smile.

"Why send her away now?" Calosandros asked.

"Kennard is afraid she'll give me ideas for how to snare myself a future emperor."

Calosandros leaned in close enough to brush his lips across her ear as he whispered, "As if you need any, my little vixen."

Conora giggled and blushed.

As Calosandros glanced over the table, the king returned to his chair, glaring murder at him. Poor timing. Calosandros needed to smooth things quickly. "Your Majesty, we must thank you for your hospitality. Perhaps some of my entourage could favor you with some of our music?"

Conora's eyes lit up. "Please, say yes, Kennard! I want to hear it."

"Only if Your Imperial Highness participates in the first song." The king smiled smugly, clearly not realizing what he was asking for.

Calosandros did his best not to gloat. "It would be my pleasure."

After picking out a few soldiers he knew to be skilled with drums and strings, he directed them to borrow instruments from the Meriverian musicians. He knew exactly what to play.

7

AN INTIMATE DANCE

Icanar Dus

Conora sighed. "I wonder if he'll play a ballad for me."

Kennard rolled his eyes. "The Urstillians probably favor military marches, and even if he did play for you, you'd never understand the words anyway."

"Why must you be so determined to dislike him? He's been nothing but sweet to me."

"Because he's sweet *on* you—though 'sweet' isn't really the right word for it," said the man who couldn't keep his hands and lips off his wife.

"Shouldn't I want my husband to lust after me?"

"He's not your husband."

"Not yet," she singsonged.

"Conora, you don't have to do this," he pleaded. "We can negotiate something else, but I can't do that unless you stop encouraging him."

Such melodramatic worry deserved to be mocked. "So...encourage him more. Got it."

Calosandros played a few notes on a lyre, then nodded to his people, who began a slow but energetic song with languid percussion and a light melody. The way his fingers moved over the strings, quick and soft but precise, awakened a desire to feel them on her skin. He gave Conora a smile that said, *This is for you.*

But it was the rich bass of his voice as he sang to her that warmed her inner thighs. Though the lyrics were all in Urstillian, the meaning was perfectly clear: sensuality, a seduction call from him to her. As he played, he sauntered across the room toward her, his gaze drinking her in, thirsting for her like wine. She wanted, needed to be in his arms again, kissing and exploring one another for more than just a fleeting moment.

Just a taste, my little vixen.

Just a taste would not do. Conora wanted it all.

Calosandros knelt before her as he sang the last verse. He stopped strumming, and the last few words rang in his bewitching voice alone. His eyes promised all she desired. As the final note faded, he kissed her hand.

"That was beautiful." Conora put a hand on his broad chest, bracing to avoid throwing herself in his arms.

Kennard cleared his throat, playing the killjoy once more, but Conora refused to acknowledge him.

"Oh, sorry." Calosandros turned to a musician who'd walked up to him. "You probably want this back. Thank you for letting me borrow it." He took both of her hands as the Urstillians began another, more vigorous song. "Do you dance?"

"Yes...but not with a partner." Not only did that involve close touching, but the open body language of dancing was overwhelming in its own way.

Calosandros nodded. "That's usually the case for me as well, I suspect for the same reason. If that's the case, under the circumstances, wouldn't that be all the more reason we should this time?" He smiled and stood, then held out his hand.

Though a little wary of pressing her boundaries so publicly, she trusted him enough to let him pull her to her feet. After all, her trust that morning had been more than worthwhile.

"I don't know how to do this," Conora confessed as he led her to the middle of the floor.

"You don't have to. With our Gifts, you and I are made for this. Just react to me. You can fight me or meld with me, whatever feels natural. We trust our bodies to speak to each other."

Conora prepared to give him her other hand for the usual couple's dance pose, but Calosandros grasped her hips and pressed their bodies together, starting at their waists and working up their spines, pausing for a second as their lips almost met. She held onto his shoulders as he drove them back and forth and side to side, their bodies melding and undulating as one. Resistance to him didn't exist, not without defying herself. Inertia held them together as he slithered his hands up her sides to take her hands.

Then she was spun around until he pressed against her back, his arms possessively wrapped around her waist. She answered by leaning into the embrace, tipping her head against his chest. He brushed the back of his hand down the side of her face like he had before their kiss, but this time, he continued down her neck between her cleavage, down to her navel, sending shivers of anticipatory pleasure.

47

The *clank* of dishes and loud scuffle of a moving chair broke Conora from her rapture. Kennard was standing with his fists clenched, his face twisted in disgust.

No. He was not going to ruin this for her.

When Calosandros spun Conora back out of their embrace, she paused at the outermost point to meet her brother's gaze. She gestured across the ribbon of intent around her neck, *Back off.*

Then she was face-to-face with Calosandros once more and losing herself in the rhythm with him. It didn't matter what other people said. She'd never felt more real than she did in his embrace. He was her exception, the lover meant for her, and she would follow him home.

Conora whispered, "We need to be alone, but the guards have been ordered to follow you."

"I noticed."

As a spontaneous plan occurred to her, she spoke quickly, lest the song end. "There's a hedge maze in the garden in the center of the palace. Wear a cloak or poncho, and meet me at the entrance at dusk. In the middle of that maze is a gazebo. Pick someone you trust who could pass for you in the dark, and send them to wait in the gazebo as soon as we finish dancing. Oh, and I'd bring a bit of meat if I were you."

Nobody questioned Conora taking her dogs for a late evening walk in the garden. Seemingly satisfied with the safety of the situation, Gerid and Thaum gave her plenty of space. After all, who would bother to assault a princess flanked by a massive pair of exceptionally trained and loyal canines? Certainly not someone with a Gift like Speech. Conora settled on a bench near the maze and rested a hand on each dog. Spruce's silky fur was mostly black, while Cloudy lived up to his name in an overly fluffy silver coat.

Spruce perked up first and nosed Conora's hand. *Your mate coming. I smell.* He sniffed her. *Yes, same smell.*

Not to be outdone, Cloudy wagged his generous gray plume of a tail and trotted off. *I meet him. See if he is safe man.*

Conora crossed her arms. *Yes, he is a safe man! Come and sit, Cloudy.*

You sure? Cloudy huffed but obeyed.

Spruce's nose went wild, along with his tail, his blue eyes wide. *Treeeeaaats!*

Calosandros's smile grew wider as he approached. "I see what the meat is for. Who is this?" He knelt a few feet away from the dogs and held both hands palm-up, offering a bit of dried meat in each.

Conora smiled back. *Go to him on your name.* "Spruce and Cloudy."

As the dogs took their treats, Calosandros gave them scritches behind their ears. "Such good boys. Boys, right?" He peeked below for a second.

"Yes, they're very good boys."

They wagged like mad, panting doggy smiles.

He good. He nice, nice man.

I like him.

Calosandros slowly stood up straight. "Are they protective, or am I allowed to touch you?"

Conora stood to meet him, keeping her voice low. "They should behave." She tiptoed and leaned to whisper, "I told them you're my mate."

He grinned.

"Oh, I should clarify. They're very present creatures. They don't plan relationships out like we do, so it's the closest concept they understand."

Calosandros slipped his hands to her waist and laughed. "That makes sense, though I still like how it sounds."

Conora sighed. "We should get moving before my guards become interested. Follow me. Keep close, keep quiet, and don't stop moving until we reach the center." *Spruce, Cloudy, block guards.*

She spun on her heels and rushed into the hedge maze, following the route she'd had memorized since childhood. She could probably run it with her eyes closed, which was fortunate with the sun slipping away. Calosandros was steady behind her, one of his hands on her back most of the way. Though a bit unnerving for her, it was a sensible strategy for him to not get turned around.

When they reached the wooden gazebo at the center, Calosandros wrapped his arms around her. "Finally."

Conora put a finger on his lips. "Not quite yet."

His frown looked adorably confused.

"We'll only have a few minutes alone in here before my guards catch up, even with my dogs distracting them." She reached into her cleavage and pulled out a key. "Or we can follow the rest of my plan and have as much of the night as we want."

He took the key and turned it over in his hand. "Your room?"

She nodded. "It's in the northwest corner of the garden. I tied a light blue ribbon around the door handle to help you find it."

"But the guards will follow us when we leave."

"That's why I had you send a decoy—you might want to wake him up." Conora pointed out the Urstillian soldier slumped over on one of the benches.

Calosandros poked the man in the shoulder until he began to stir. "Anabusos."

"That's also why I told you to wear that cloak," Conora continued. "If you put that on him, it should be enough to fool someone from a distance in the dark. I'll leave first, then him, and the guards should follow. Then you should be able to sneak out of here a little while later when it's cleared out."

Calosandros removed his cloak and set it on a bench. "I can think of one thing that would make this more convincing. Anabusos?"

"Mios, Duboinos?"

"Loee noee yid caee ichnara."

Anabusos raised an eyebrow and cocked his head, then shook it, and shrugged. "Tee."

Conora was absolutely not prepared for what came next.

Both men grabbed their tunic-like clothes from the bottoms and yanked them up over their heads, leaving them wearing nothing but their sandals. Not a thing—well, other than two things Conora hadn't seen on humans before—animals were not shy about mating. Admittedly, the men's penises did look more accurately like geoducks than she'd expected. They passed their clothes to one another and pulled them on as if it were a perfectly normal thing to do.

Calosandros looked at Conora. "Loee tee icpila?"

"What?"

"Are you okay?"

Conora shook it off. "I'm fine. I just wasn't expecting you to change...whatever your clothes are called."

"It's a chiton. Mine is red and missing a shoulder, and Anabusos's is blue."

"Right... I'm going to go now. Tell Anabusos it was nice to...er, meet him? Have him count to fifty before he leaves."

As she left the gazebo, Conora remembered Mother's advice: "Do whatever you must to whet his desire, but don't sate it." Logical as that had sounded before, it wasn't at all helpful now for handling her own wanton urges.

8

BOUDOIR DIPLOMACY

Camprulos Duosa

Satisfied that both Gerid and Thaum had left her sitting room to take up their posts in the hallway and closed the door behind them, Conora retreated back to her bedroom and locked that door. She drew all her curtains, careful to make sure every seam closed completely, then checked her appearance in the mirror as she waited for Calosandros. The tiara and necklace could go; she didn't need either of them tangling in her hair if things went as expected. By the time she'd tucked the jewels away in their proper boxes, both dogs had perked up and were quietly huffing that her mate was here.

With a click, the door from her bedroom to the garden eased open, bringing a waft of salt and lilies. Calosandros slipped inside, then hastily closed and locked it behind himself. He held out her key and the blue ribbon she'd tied to the handle. "I figure you wouldn't want to leave your door marked, in case the guards become curious."

"Thank you." She took the items and bent down to stash them in the drawer of her bedside table.

Before she fully stood back up, his hands were on her hips. "I've never waited so long for the sun to set."

He pressed in close, as he had for their dance, then brushed her hair over one shoulder, nuzzling and trailing teasingly soft kisses down her neck until she sighed and leaned against him. When he slid his hand forward, just above her pelvis, it sent flutters through her and set her heart racing. His merest touch drowned out the rest of the world—almost.

Cloudy nudged her hand with his cold nose. *Oh no. You hurt? I help you. Wake up!*

Conora groaned and knelt to meet the dog. *No, my friend. I do not want help.*

Cloudy tilted his head and glared at Calosandros. *You whimper. He hurt you.*

No. Sometimes happy humans make bad sounds. You leave me and my mate alone. Unless I call for you or Spruce, do not help.

Fine. Cloudy sulked over to the big doggy bed in the corner of the room.

She stood facing Calosandros, running her fingers up his arms. "Sorry about that."

He laughed. "My dog used to do the same thing. He usually had to wait outside."

"Don't worry about them." She hoped it didn't come to that. Having circumvented the guards, if her instincts about Calosandros were wrong, the ability to call the dogs to her at a moment's notice was her last defense. It was a dangerous game, but inflamed with passion as she was, she still had *some* sense left—for now.

His hand had barely grazed her cheek when his mouth was on hers, and she deepened the kiss with her next breath. But he briefly retreated, moving to the corner of her mouth, her cheek, her jaw, her neck... As he passed her décolletage, her pulse quickened with each kiss. They were creeping toward reputation-cracking territory, and—Giver help her—she wanted nothing more. When he'd almost reached her cleavage, she inhaled sharply, raising her chest to meet him as he buried his face and seized her breasts with both hands.

Did he mistake her moan of pleasure? Because he let go then and raised his head, settling for neck kisses, with his hands resting on her shoulders, his thumbs tucking just under the straps of her dress. "Do you want more?"

"Yes," Conora sighed, without a second thought.

He pulled the shoulders of her dress down her arms, and a cool rush of air caressed her bare breasts, followed swiftly by his warm hands and the moist heat of his mouth over her nipple. She could barely stifle her squeaking moan at the titillation. Her pelvis pressed against him of its own accord, and she clung to his waist to keep from falling. But he pushed back until they fell onto the bed, his firm chest bearing down on her loins in slow rolling waves of carnal joy.

Calosandros panted. "Ah, so hot." Pulling up to kneel on the edge of the bed, he yanked his chiton up and off, baring his full muscular glory once more. Only, this time, the folds of her chiffon skirt obscured him from the waist down. "Much better." He grinned, then stalked toward her on all fours and pinned her down with a vigorous kiss.

Her instincts overcame her again, her body drawn toward him.

He chuckled. "I knew you had a wild streak. Let's indulge it." He kissed her and began pulling her skirt up—the last barrier between them.

The logical part of her mind finally woke up. At least, it woke just enough to protest, though not enough to think of what to say. Conora didn't want to ruin what they had going, just block this one route forward. She tried to raise her arms to push him back, but the shoulder straps of her dress restrained her. Moving the rest of her body would only signal encouragement. Quickly running out of options, she blurted the first thing she could think of: "I'm a virgin!"

Calosandros froze, staring uncomfortably at her for a moment. "What... I'm sorry, but...I don't know what I'm supposed to do with this information..." He tilted his head quizzically. "Are you asking me to stop? To be careful? Telling me you're scared? Do I need to slow down and make sure you're aroused enough?"

Of course. She'd managed to find the stupidest thing to say. She took a deep breath, fighting back the overwhelming emotional whiplash.

"Conora..." He brushed a dark curl away from her face and kissed her cheek. "I don't mean to shame you. I just want to know what you need so I can pleasure you."

"I don't want you to stop. It all feels so good. But I can't do that yet—not under my skirt."

"I didn't cross any boundaries before that?"

She shook her head.

He smiled and rubbed his thumb over her cheek. "I can work with that." He smoothed her skirt back down between them.

Then he kissed her soundly, and as his tongue penetrated her mouth, his groin slowly thrust against hers in a long, smooth rhythm. While she instinctively moved with him, the sensation of his hands on her breasts again made her buck with increasing pressure. Even their breathing took on the rhythm as they panted together. It was almost unbearable, the euphoric fervor building through her flesh, and then it burst in sudden but soothing release.

Calosandros rolled to his side next to her and kissed her shoulder. "I certainly felt that. You are so delightfully reactive."

Conora wanted to revel in what sounded like a compliment, but her skirt had stuck to him a bit, and her nether region had cooled almost instantly as he left her. She raised herself up on her elbows for a better look. With absolute horror, she gasped as she noted a huge viscous spot soaked into her skirt.

Calosandros tried to suppress a laugh. "Are you sure about the not-under-the-skirt rule?"

"I'm sorry. That's so embarrassing!"

"Sorry? For what?" He gently grasped her chin and turned her head to him. "Never apologize for coming—and certainly not with me. I take pride in bringing you to such a beautiful climax."

Her voice squeaked as she whispered, "I've never made a mess like that by myself."

"Well, that 'mess' is going to serve us both very well when you're ready. Is there a particular reason you don't want me under your skirt? I didn't question it at first—I thought it might be a fetish—but it seems a bit new to you."

Confused, Conora furrowed her brow. "Of course, it's new to me. I'd never accepted a ribbon until this morning."

"Well, yes, I understand that much; you just told me you were a virgin. So, what experiences *have* you had?"

"Not counting my own hand?"

He laughed. "I didn't count it for myself."

"None."

He sat up. "Wait. None? At all? Nothing?"

She cringed. "I probably should thank you for my first kiss too."

His jaw dropped; then a look of pure guilt softened him. "I swear I had no idea. I wouldn't have moved so quickly if I'd known."

"That's why I didn't tell you. I didn't want to slow down. I wouldn't have stopped you at all if I didn't have to."

"Why do you have to?" He wrapped an arm around her waist. "We both have passion and desire, and neither of us is spoken for by anyone else. Why can we not fully explore that?"

Conora sighed. "Because, above all else, I'm a princess of Meriveria. I can't raise arms to save my people. My maidenhead is the one thing I have to bargain with to that end."

He shrugged. "Why would the state of your hymen matter? I asked for a wife. I never made it conditional."

"I'm inexperienced, but I'm not naive. I wouldn't be the first woman to give in to fine promises, only to be used and abandoned when a man's had his fill."

"My fill? Of you?" He raised an eyebrow. "My little vixen, nothing less than taking you home will satisfy me. If I had any inclination of turning my back on this deal, I'd ask you to run away with me instead."

She'd already shared so much with him. Could she admit that she had considered it—fleeing the danger here to live as his empress? Stranger though he was, she trusted in the tenderness he'd shown. "Please don't tempt me. I can't be that selfish. Even if I trust you with myself, that doesn't guarantee you won't return to your original offer if you believe you might already have your heir."

His scrutinizing gaze smoldered with silent intensity, making her squirm. When she thought she couldn't take any more, he asked, "Is that the only obstacle? You're saying there's no other reason you would change your mind?"

She nodded. "I am duty-bound to my people."

"Giver, I could love you." He gave her a quick yet forceful kiss. "Do you have wax and writing supplies in here?"

Blinking at the abrupt subject change, she pointed across the bed. "I keep a little in my other night table."

He rolled over and scooched away from her, then began going through the drawer. "Perfect." Snatching up the items, he bounded out of the bed.

Conora shamelessly enjoyed the sight of his robust backside as he strode to her mirrored dressing table and sat. After Calosandros wrote for what felt like ages, Conora's curiosity got the better of her. The waist of her dress seemed to be holding her skirt up decently enough, so she pulled her arms out of her bodice rather than try to put it back on properly to follow him.

As she neared, he looked up and smiled. "Perfect timing. What do you think?" He leaned back and gestured for her to read over his shoulder.

By the great and favorable laws of the glorious
Empire of Urstille, this declaration is made between His
Imperial Highness, Crown Prince Calosandros of Urstille,
and Her Royal Highness, Crown Princess Conora of
Meriveria, of our complete willing consent and full
faculties, to take each other as husband and wife.

In honor of this union, on behalf of the Empire of
Urstille, His Imperial Highness offers the Kingdom of
Meriveria military aid in exchange for 100 full mature
logs each of spruce, pine, red-cedar, fir, maple, and yew;
500 pounds each of crab, salmon, clams, oysters, and
mussels; 500 yards of silk; and 1,500 skeins of worsted

> *dog wool. Urstille shall recognize this offer, without any
> further alterations in its favor, at any time that
> Meriveria wishes to agree to such terms.*

Conora had slowly relaxed into an embrace from behind him, resting her head on his shoulder. "You reversed the order. Instead of waiting on Kennard and Odelia to make an agreement, we elope and force them into that option?"

"Exactly. Either way, you will come home with me, but your people are in no danger of me backing out of Urstillian aid." He tugged on her arm, guiding her to sit on his lap. "To make this legal, I need to write it in Urstillian too. Any chance you remember how to say anything? I only need a word or two."

She chanced the intensity of looking deep into his green eyes as she said in her best Urstillian pronunciation, "*Cal.*" And she was not disappointed.

"Mmm... Nuil yos sioria..." He growled and kissed her fiercely. Then he seemed to remember himself as he pulled away, smiling besottedly and putting a finger on her lips. "Ca icoindara."

Calosandros covered the writing at the top of the page and began writing. After he had a couple lines down, he uncovered the Meriverian text and worked back and forth. Conora pressed herself to his chest, partly to keep from being crushed against the table and partly to listen to the soothing softness of his breath falling into sync with hers. In a matter of moments, he wouldn't be a stranger anymore; they'd be bound together for life. She wouldn't be alone.

"*Conora.*" Her name rolled out like a purr as he put the pen down and picked up a stick of cobalt blue wax.

"Finished?"

"Almost." He removed his signet ring. "Do you have yours ready?"

She held out her thumb and let him take her ring too, then grabbed the pen and signed her name next to his at the bottom. Hot blue wax dripped over the page in a wide oval, and he pressed the rings into it together, leaving impressions of a bear and a fox.

"Now what?" she asked.

"Now we do whatever *my wife* desires."

She grinned. "What I desire?"

He nodded solemnly. "I take pride in my responsibilities, and you are officially dearer than anything to me now."

"The first thing I desire is to know what *nuil yos sioria* means."

He blushed a little as he laughed. "My sexy little vixen."

"It sounds pretty in Urstillian."

"When you've learned the language enough to speak it back to me, I can call you that more often." Kissing her neck, he slipped her signet ring back on her thumb.

Conora puzzled at the casual gesture. It was so reminiscent of a real wedding but didn't seem to signify anything. "Is there really nothing else we're supposed to do? It feels odd not to perform some kind of ritual, especially for a royal wedding."

"And here I worried *I* rushed *you*. We can plan a wedding to pledge our devotion with your family later."

"So, which one is real?"

"Both," he said as though it were the most obvious thing in the world. "A marriage contract is legally binding, of course. It's just not a wedding."

Conora had never heard of the two being separate things before. The distinction didn't make perfect sense—though it was hard to think with him softly caressing her—but she understood the most important part: the contract was legally binding. Though her kingdom was unlikely to recognize the union without a witness or officiant, the surety of his imperial seal was enough for her. So, she kissed Calosandros for the first time as her husband, delighting in the very idea of calling him that.

He pouted, eyes smoldering, as she pulled away. Every muscle flexed with tension to follow, but he merely pivoted in his seat to watch her back up a few paces. He must have noticed her staring, because he smirked and spread his knees apart more. "Wanting a better view?"

A flush of heat flooded her cheeks and between her thighs. "Something like that." She reached behind her back for the ties near her waistline and pulled. With a flutter of fabric, her gown slid down her legs, pooling at her feet.

Calosandros's biceps bulged as he gripped the table, his gaze roving over her flesh so thoroughly, she could feel his lust growing—not to mention *seeing* it growing...and throbbing. His chest heaved as he said under his breath, "Please, don't be teasing me." When his eyes met hers, she could scarcely move under the weight of his pleading passion. "No more obstacles? No more boundaries?"

Conora shook her head, and in the next heartbeat, he hefted over his shoulder, leaving her to watch his back upside down as he ran and tossed her, squealing, onto the middle of the bed.

He put a finger to his lips and tried to shush her as they both giggled. "You're going to get us caught."

She shrugged. "I've made stranger sounds than that before."

"Is that so?" He traced his fingertips down her body. "I wonder...how many I'll hear tonight."

He pressed on her clitoris, smiling when she gasped at the jolting sensation. With just one finger, he slid up and down her lower lips until she squirmed. And then that finger was sliding inside, wriggling and sending pulses through her. He retreated all too soon, only to plunge back in with two fingers. She couldn't help but moan at the strange feeling, immensely pleasurable yet twinged with the discomfort of stretching.

Calosandros slowed. "Do you want to stop?"

"No."

He brushed her hair out of her face with his other hand. "I need to know if something doesn't feel right. I don't want to hurt you."

Conora panted. "I trust you."

He nuzzled her ear. "Enough to fuck to completion?"

She gasped out, "Yes."

He removed his fingers and realigned himself so the thick tip of his shaft gently pressed against the opening. His hand still slick, he slid it over one breast, then the other, failing to make purchase as he grasped, though somehow magnifying his touch. He nipped at her nipple, then flicked it with his tongue. "Relax, dearest." He continued licking between words. "There is only us...only now...only pleasure."

Then he covered her breast with his mouth, sucking hard and squeezing her other one until the sensation overwhelmed her. With a whining moan, she spread her legs farther, removing all resistance for him to slip inside. Despite the strain of novelty, the way he filled her took her breath away with rapture. Once he started moving, she lost all sense of time or place. He was right. There was only them, entwined as one, bringing truth to the motion of their dance together.

At one point, he seemed to pull away, pausing for a moment at the edge of withdrawal and looking as if he were about to speak. Then he shook his head and growled. "We are bound." He thrust in harder and faster than before, and it was all she could do to brace herself from being shoved into the headboard by his pounding force. "Look at me," he begged between panting.

When their eyes locked, he instantly slowed almost to a stop and grunted, his whole body shuddering. Deep inside her, a soft flitting feeling told her what he was doing: the completion he'd asked for. She held his stare, one of total vulnerability and a tenderness for her that she wished could last forever, and she reached up to stroke his silky bearded jawline.

He kissed her slowly, as if to savor the taste of her lips, then broke away and rolled onto his back, sighing and panting. "That was..." He exhaled sharply, then turned his head toward her, his eyes not as vulnerable but still regarding her tenderly. His hand found hers, weaving their fingers together. "How do you feel?"

Conora's words failed her. How could she compress all those feelings into anything that made sense? After a couple false starts, she finally managed to say, "Like your wife."

"Is that good?"

"The best."

Calosandros sighed into a smile and snuggled close to her side to kiss her.

Conora awoke with Calosandros curled around her back, his arm holding her firmly, his hand filled with her breast, and a noticeable erection wedged between her thighs. Parts of her body ached from being used in unfamiliar ways, while others responded with carnal desire. And when Calosandros let out a contented hum and squeezed her, that carnal desire began to win out. She writhed against him.

His voice was husky in her ear. "Does my little vixen have a morning appetite?"

She turned in his arms and pushed him over onto his back.

He laughed. "Oh, you want to take the lead this time?" With a grin, he folded his arms behind his head. "I won't object. Let's see how wild you get."

The desire burned hotter than she'd ever known possible. She found new sympathy for the animals in heat that she'd talked down before. All she wanted was to feel him inside her again, no matter the method. Without hesitation, she straddled him and centered herself. Unlike the night before, she had no reservations or tension about the act. She simply bore down upon him, relishing the thick penetration.

As she rolled her hips, desire built again. "Touch me," she pleaded.

He fondled her all over, his hands constantly moving and grasping, sending her in the throes of ecstasy. She wanted to scream, to cry out her ravishment, but she used what little self-control she still possessed to snatch up a pillow to stifle herself.

That's when Calosandros's hands stopped wandering. He planted them firmly on her ass and moved her hips back and forth in a faster rhythm. Conora buried her face in the pillow and muffled a yelp from the increased intensity. She closed her eyes and arched her back, gasping for air as the rest of her body released in pulsing waves.

It took a moment to realize he'd stopped moving her, his hands relaxed on her thighs as he smiled up at her. He tucked her hair behind her ear. "So beautiful. How did that compare?"

She collapsed next to him, caught in a fit of giggles. "Amazing. I'd do it again if I could move right now."

He grinned and tiredly pumped his fist into the air. "Victory is mine. It seems I've tamed my little vixen."

"Are you sure 'tamed' is the right word?"

"Well, as close to it as you could ever be."

She laughed and rested her head on his chest, only to pull right back up from the slick skin. "Ugh. We're so sweaty." Chancing a sniff of herself, she immediately regretted it. "Oh, great Giver."

He turned his head away from her. "Would you please draw us a bath?"

Utterly lost, she furrowed her brow. "Calosandros, who are you talking to?"

"Your servant." He shrugged and waved across the room, then looked back at Conora. "Sorry, should I have let you give the order?"

Conora's blood froze. "What?" she squeaked, too mortified to look in the direction he'd indicated as water began splashing in the bathtub.

"I don't know her name. She walked in while you were riding me—closed the door behind her very discreetly, I must say."

It had to be Raina; she was one of the few servants with permission to enter her rooms and the only one with a key. Conora had forgotten to account for the maid since she'd never originally intended for Calosandros to sleep in her bed. "And you didn't say anything?"

"What? She's just doing her job. It's not like she's a guard."

Conora struggled to breathe as panic rose up her throat.

"Dearest, why are you upset?" Calosandros sat up and pulled her close, rubbing her back.

"That was a private moment," she whispered. "Everyone in the palace is going to know. *Everyone.*"

"Isn't that the plan?"

"The plan is to push Kennard and Odelia into signing, but I think that will work much better if we come to them on our terms. If rumors come to them that you were found in my bed, they'll be too furious to hear the rest of it. And what if she tells the guards?"

"I think they would have burst in here already if she was going to tell the guards anything."

How could he be so calm about this? Stories shaming Conora would be out of the palace and into the city by the end of the day.

"The bath is ready. It'll make us both feel better, and I'm sure we can just talk to your servant. I have more than enough funds to bribe her if we need to." He hopped out of bed. "I'll be quick." With a playful pat on her bum, he added, "You can join me in the tub after you piss."

She shot him an ornery pout. "I hope you aren't expecting to direct all my bodily functions."

He turned toward the door to the toilet and, as he walked off, called over his shoulder, "Hardly, but I do expect you to continue practicing basic sexual hygiene."

When the door closed behind him, Raina approached the bed and whispered, "Your Highness, is there anything you need? I added some kinnikinnick and mahonia root to the bath for your, uh, womanly health and in case you're, um...*sore*."

Conora self-consciously pulled the blanket up to cover herself. "Thank you, Raina. Do you normally carry that with you, or did you somehow know I'd need it?" What if someone had been spying last night?

Raina bowed her head and shook it. "Oh, no. Sorry to worry you. They're simply useful remedies to have on hand. If I'd had any idea what you were doing, I would've tried harder to avoid interrupting." She put a hand over her heart. "I am honored to serve such a brave princess."

"I don't know what you mean. I feel anything but brave."

"The dogs said the prince is your mate, that you said not to interfere. And I saw the contract on the table."

Conora gasped and clasped the blanket tighter to her chest. "The king cannot know about this. Please. You cannot tell anyone until I can talk to him."

"Of course not. After you heroically sacrificed your virtue to protect the kingdom, I will gladly help you however I can."

It felt wrong to call Conora's eager collaboration a sacrifice, but at least Raina understood what she was trying to do.

61

Calosandros opened the door and casually smiled at Conora as he strutted in and slunk into the tub. "Mmm, that's perfect." Eyes closed, he slipped his head under, his dark wavy hair turning to smooth black as he rose back up.

How was he going to leave her room in the light of day without anyone else seeing him? Well over six feet of gorgeous muscle—it wasn't like she could hide him behind her skirt. She didn't have all day to think about it, though, so she scurried to the toilet to relieve herself, trying not to think about her continued exposure to her maid. There were so many servants moving about in the morning that Raina would definitely prove useful, but the details escaped Conora for the moment.

When she came back out to the bedroom, Raina bent down and picked the chiton up from the floor. "Do you want this washed?"

Calosandros shrugged. "That would be great if I had anything else to wear."

"I can fetch another from your rooms if you wish."

"That might be difficult. I'm afraid none of my people understand Meriverian."

"But you can write in Urstillian," Conora said. "Send her with a note. I can seal the outside so it looks like I'm sending it. It would probably look more suspicious if one of us didn't try to contact the other this morning anyway."

Calosandros offered her a hand as she stepped into the tub with him. He cuddled her back against his chest and kissed the crook of her neck, humming contentedly. "Mmm...my clever little vixen, what other ideas do you have?"

Conora's stomach growled. "Raina, do you think you could bring enough breakfast for the two of us? Would that justify needing a cart?"

"Possibly? But they might question your sudden appetite."

"Oh, that part is fine. The trick is whether you could move it with the prince inside."

Raina nodded. "I'm stronger than I look." Considering the maid was as tall as Conora and much sturdier, that spoke volumes.

"Then, I have a plan. Fetch me some paper."

9

FOOD FOR THOUGHT

Grados ia Ictir

By the time Calosandros could eat breakfast, it was almost time for lunch. While they bathed, Raina had delivered a letter from "Conora" to "Calosandros," making a show of it. He'd written the text himself, a message to Anabusos requesting a fresh chiton. A blank paper with his seal was tucked inside the first letter. When the maid ostensibly returned with Calosandros's "response," she brought the folded garment in her apron pocket. While he and Conora dressed, Raina procured a cart laden with breakfast for two. She unloaded the cart in Conora's sitting room, where Calosandros hurried to cram himself underneath before anyone else entered from the hall. He'd barely concealed himself with the cloth covering when the door opened, followed by heavy footsteps.

Conora said, "Prince Calosandros and one of his officers will be joining me for breakfast. Since you both must watch over us, I've ordered extra food for you as well. Please, help yourselves."

A man said, "Thank you, Your Highness, but shouldn't we wait until you and the prince have eaten?"

"Oh, he won't mind. Urstillian traditions are different. And there's more than enough food. I'm sure it will be much easier to guard me if you aren't hungry or still eating."

Another man said, "That's very gracious. Thank you."

Then Raina pushed the cart out into the hall. The maid moved Calosandros through so many long stretches and turns that he completely lost track of where they might be in the palace at any given moment. When she stopped, there was a long pause before the cloth cover lifted, right in front of a stairwell. Calosandros crawled out and bounded up the stairs, not wanting to linger in case one of the guards watching the entryway decided to approach the maid.

It was a somewhat clever design, the way the guest hall didn't connect to anything else on the second floor, leaving it easy to guard the single stairway that accessed it and preventing guests from wandering into

63

residences without notice. It simply failed to account for trusted palace staff colluding with the guests.

To the left of the stairs, Calosandros found his suite, where Anabusos was waiting for him, looking deeply annoyed.

"Why come all the way here just to turn around and go back?"

"Because, as far as the Meriverians know, I have been in here since last night. If I appear from anywhere else, there will be questions, and this is a bad time for questions."

Anabusos crossed his arms. "I understand that. But why go back after you just had all night with her? Yeah, it feels good to break a drought, but this kind of excess can be dangerous. It's asking to get caught."

Calosandros scoffed. "Thanks for the vote of confidence, Anabusos, but this is part of the plan. The two of us joining her for breakfast was what allowed her maid to get a cart."

"Us? Why am I part of this?"

"One, to get more food. Two, she wanted to thank you for your part last night. Three, you're going to have to meet eventually, and *I* am asking for that time to be now." Calosandros gestured for Anabusos to walk through the doorway.

He acquiesced, sulking. "With all due respect, it still doesn't make sense. Are you planning to spend the whole meal translating between us?"

Calosandros was immune to the bad mood, still basking in the bliss of Conora's bed. He clapped his arm over Anabusos's shoulder and led them to the stairs. "It gives me a chance to use my Gift more. Besides, since when do you turn down an invitation from someone beautiful?"

"Are you referring to yourself or the princess?"

"Like it matters to you."

Anabusos laughed. "Fair point."

As they exited the stairway, two guards fell in step behind them.

"Our shadows are back," Anabusos said.

"Good. I want them to see me leave." Calosandros glanced at the guards, one ridiculously muscled, the other practically twitching while trying to match their relaxed pace. "Looking at their forms, I see Strength and Speed. They won't understand us."

Anabusos exhaled and stretched his neck. "I will admit the one upside is that I stole your bed last night. It's *so much* nicer. What about you?"

"Never slept better." Calosandros purposely didn't elaborate, letting the silence stretch on, knowing exactly what his friend was actually asking. He bit back a smile as the obnoxious tension grew.

Anabusos groaned. "You're killing me. I have to know what it was like with an Animal Speaker. Just a little detail—a tiny one!"

"It confirmed my decision that I don't want anyone else."

"You're joking. We come to this repressed kingdom, and you have the best sex of your life?"

"Not exactly yet, but it will be."

Anabusos raised an eyebrow. "What the hell does that mean?"

"What she lacked in experience, she made up for in passion. With a little practice, she—"

"I'm sorry. Did you say lack of experience?" Anabusos sighed. "Please tell me you did not fuck a virgin."

Calosandros glared. "Don't be cruel. She hasn't had many opportunities for exploration, and I won't hold that against her."

"If she lacked opportunities, then she probably lacked supplies. Where did you get *sitrecayus*? I didn't have any in my pocket last night, and I didn't find any in yours."

"She didn't drink any."

"So, you found a sheath?"

"No."

Anabusos stopped cold, agape. "You, of all people? I don't know anyone more responsible and adamant about *sitrecayus*. You never trust a woman into your bed if you don't watch her drink it yourself. And you, what, got so desperate that you risked only pulling out?"

Calosandros cleared his throat and pressed Anabusos forward. "We need to keep moving."

Anabusos's eyes looked ready to pop out. "Oh shit... You didn't."

"Anabusos."

"You fucked a virgin without any protection whatsoever? Have you lost your mind? That is a recipe for a royal bastard that everyone will instantly blame on you. Not to mention that she's the sister of a king who hates you, so you've probably started a war. Am I missing anything?"

"Plenty, and keep your voice down," Calosandros snapped. "I am perfectly sane and was clear in my decisions last night. As I told you before, I chose her to become my empress, and she will. She and I signed a contract of—"

"You married a woman you've known for less than a day? That's even worse! I didn't think it was possible, but you somehow found a way to make this all crazier. And you've made me an accomplice, which means the emperor will have my head when he finds out what I helped you do." Anabusos put a protective hand around his throat.

"He's the one who told me to settle down, create heirs."

"I doubt he meant choosing the next woman you stumble across."

Calosandros pivoted to get in Anabusos's face, fingertips on his chest. "Now that you know she's my wife, you will not disparage her again. She is a princess by birth and by marriage, and you will respect that. I permit you to speak candidly to *me*, but to attack *her*, you cross the line. Are we clear?"

Eyes wide, Anabusos swallowed and nodded. "Yes, Your Imperial Highness."

Calosandros turned and continued walking. "Ultimately, all of this should work toward our deal with Meriveria. Part of it has already been enacted, so they'd be fools not to take the rest of it. If they decide their kingdom is not worth saving, I still get a wife with royal lineage, and she gets to follow me home to live in safety and luxury." He tapped a finger to his temple. "See, it's much more logical than you give me credit for."

"So, you need to talk to the king again, right? How does this breakfast with your new wife factor into the plan?"

"She's the one who will talk to him again. I'm sure she will be far more effective than I could ever be. Who knows the king better than his sister?"

"And in the meantime, we simply wait?"

"Precisely."

Anabusos tilted his head. "Huh. I can't say we've tried this strategy before."

Calosandros laughed. "Well, by its nature, I'm the only one who can, and I can only try it once."

"That's a hell of a gamble from the most careful man I know."

"I am careful. Perhaps it's not as much of a gamble as you think."

Despite the outburst from Anabusos, he was cordial at breakfast. As for the guards, if they suspected anything about last night, they kept it to themselves. Calosandros tested them a bit by greeting his beautiful bride with a kiss and wrapping his arm around her waist, not dropping his hold, even as they sat to eat. He merely moved his chair closer.

From under the table, Spruce pressed his snout between them and whined, his eyes huge and shining. Calosandros picked up a piece of meat to offer, but Conora growled at the dog until he slunk away.

"Such a faker!" She laughed and rolled her eyes. "He's testing you. He eats well, and he knows better than to beg at the table."

Calosandros sheepishly set the morsel back on his plate.

"Oh, don't feel bad." Conora stroked his arm. "I appreciate the impulse to feed him. If you really want to give him treats, you can set them aside for later. I just don't want him harassing humans when we're at the table."

"Ah." Calosandros nodded and chose some gristly pieces to tuck into a napkin before returning to his meal.

He'd inhaled half a plate of food when Conora set down her fork. "I'm so sorry. I should switch sides with you."

Calosandros raised an eyebrow at the random offer. "Why?"

"So you don't have to eat with your left hand."

"Are you implying that I'm clumsy with a fork?"

"No, sorry..." She frowned and shook her head. "I didn't realize you were left-handed. I could've sworn you used your right hand yesterday, but I obviously misremembered."

"I'm not, and you didn't." He waved the fork in his left hand and winked at Anabusos, who bit back a laugh in understanding. Though not the kindest thing to do, this was a game Calosandros could never resist since he could only play it once with any given person.

She looked at both her hands, then eyed him sideways. "Are you ambidextrous or just desperate to hold me?"

"A man can be both."

A surprised smile lit her face. "Really? You're the first I've met. How does it work—can you use both hands at the same time or just equally well?"

He laughed. "Eating with both hands is a bit much. It's useful for fighting, though. Almost makes up for a non-combative Gift."

"Any other uses?"

"Remind me to show you the next time we have paper and pencils." He grazed her ear with his lips to whisper, "or in bed."

Her blushing grin was adorable. It deserved to be captured.

Calosandros got Anabusos's attention and tasked him with fetching his sketchbook and roll of oil pencils after they finished eating. He normally liked to keep a small one on hand but had been so preoccupied with his plans for the princess that he'd forgotten to grab them.

Most of the afternoon was spent drawing Conora, her dogs, and various flowers she excitedly picked for him. Despite the inferior supplies—his best paints and charcoals didn't travel well—she oohed and ahhed every time he switched sides to rest a hand or layer new colors without smudging as he swiftly worked outward, completing the drawings at a rate that seemed to continually surprise her. None of it felt like false flattery or sarcasm; she genuinely reveled in watching him, and he wanted to draw anything that would keep her smiling.

But he couldn't demand her attention forever, and the all-too-familiar duties of a princess came calling. Calosandros and Anabusos were left in the garden when Conora had a scheduled meeting with Elgathan lords. As much as he would rather her stay, he admired her spirit and ambition to serve her people.

He nudged Anabusos and, after his assent, said, "I told you she'll make an excellent empress."

"Probably. For all our sakes, I hope you're right. I can sympathize with your attraction, but it's disturbing to see you so smitten."

"I'm still in control of myself."

Anabusos crossed his arms. "What are the terms of your contract?"

Calosandros sighed. "I figured you'd ask." He reached into his pocket and retrieved a copy he'd made earlier that morning while waiting for Raina.

After reading it over, Anabusos massaged his temples. "You've undercut the emperor."

"As his son, I am within my rights to use my future inheritance to pay the bride price." The words tasted like dirt. Calosandros did not want to buy and possess her like some royal asset. But explaining the connection he felt with her would only further his friend's theory. He had to stick to the logic of the situation.

"All the more incentive to have negotiated better. But you walked in woefully out of practice against her strongest weapon." Anabusos slung an arm over Calosandros's shoulder. "I'm guessing she wouldn't screw you until you came to her terms."

Technically, Calosandros had written the terms, but being weak with lust would be more easily forgiven than purposely scheming against the emperor's interests. He hung his head as though Anabusos had surmised his shame.

"I can't say I wouldn't have given in, and I don't even have the excuse of temporary celibacy insanity." Anabusos squeezed his shoulder. "All is not lost. With the right leverage, you might still talk the king into better terms."

"That would take a miracle. The man hates me."

"Lucky for you, I see a very sexy miracle right now. Look." He pointed across the garden to a large window. "Isn't that the king?"

Calosandros squinted. Though it was hard to see the man's face well as he was locked in a passionate embrace, with a woman blocking him completely from the front, King Kennard's unruly curls were unmistakable, and the room looked like an important office. His partner was a petite blonde, but unlike the heavily pregnant and precisely adorned queen, this woman was slender, with hair that fell down her back in wild gold waves. With the monarchs in the middle of a spat, the king had obviously found an outlet for his urges, and private offices had a well-established history as havens for powerful men's trysts.

"It looks like the king is not so righteous after all," Calosandros muttered.

"He certainly has a type, doesn't he?" Anabusos said. "Not that I'm complaining. This is the best show I've seen since we got here."

The couple's hands were all over each other, and the king lifted her onto his desk, grabbing at her dress and burying his face in her bosom. She tipped her head back, though not quite enough to reveal her face. He left her for a moment and began closing curtains, confirming that he definitely was the king.

Anabusos scoffed. "What a tease! Just when it was getting good... Ooh! He missed a spot."

"Anabu—"

His friend was already sneaking closer to the window where the king, in his haste, had left a gap in the drapery. Anabusos waved Calosandros to follow. "This could be great intelligence," he hissed.

Calosandros rolled his eyes but knelt next to him in the bushes. "You just want to jerk off."

"Says the man who's been combining business and pleasure for the past two days. We might be able to see who the lady is."

He shifted around to get a better view, but the lady still faced away from them as she straddled the king. "No good. There's plenty for your purposes but none for mine." Calosandros stood and dusted himself off. "I'm going to try from the inside." He'd seen enough to verify their actions, so if he could catch her leaving, he would have enough to use against the king.

Counting the number of windows he passed, Calosandros walked inside and backtracked past an appropriate-looking number of doorways. He ended up right next to the throne room, in the direction he remembered the Meriverian royals leaving via a side door after their meeting. So, this had to be the king's office. Calosandros crept close and put his ear to the door, but the voices on the other side were indistinct. Then he heard a woman laughing close to the door, and he backed up a step. He'd soon see who this lady was.

She yanked the door open much faster than he'd anticipated for a clandestine mistress, and Calosandros nearly jumped in shock.

It was Queen Odelia.

Disheveled, wild-haired, and flushed pink from head to toe, she was nevertheless the queen herself. Holding her round belly, which clearly protruded from this angle, she gasped, eyes wide with as much surprise as he felt. Then she exhaled and smiled. "Was there something you needed, Your Imperial Highness?"

Shit. He hadn't expected to need to explain himself. "Uh...no, I just...I was exploring your lovely palace."

Though her nose crinkled in momentary confusion, she smiled and nodded before urgently waddling away. Whatever the queen thought, she was clearly preoccupied with other matters, and Calosandros accepted it as a minor blessing.

As she walked out of sight, quick footsteps slapped the hardwood behind him, and when he turned, Anabusos called out, "Wait! It's the queen! I saw her face!"

Calosandros slumped and ran a hand over his face. "Thanks, Anabusos. That was useful information two minutes ago."

"You could try to talk to the king right now. We know for sure that he's in a good mood."

True, but that also meant he had sex fresh in his mind, which was the last thing they wanted him thinking about. They needed him to set aside his feelings and look at the deal rationally. Better to trust Conora to choose the moment.

Calosandros shook his head. "Dinner will be soon enough. Let's hope his good mood lasts until then."

10

BROTHERS-IN-LAW

Thematiarosio

To call dinner awkward would be an understatement. Beyond his secret marriage to Conora, Calosandros had to sit with the king and queen, having spied on them screwing less than an hour ago. He couldn't mention a word about any of it, but no matter whom he looked at, those were the only two topics he could think about, so he kept his mouth shut.

Eventually, Queen Odelia mercifully broke the silence. "Prince Calosandros, I'd love to know more about the man interested in my sister-in-law. Do you have any brothers or sisters?"

Calosandros shrugged. "None that I know of—certainly no legitimate ones at any rate." It was unlikely. They'd have to have been from before he was born, because the emperor had been injured not long after that, and if anyone had a claim, they'd had more than enough time to make it by now.

Kennard scoffed. "Why am I not surprised?"

Calosandros pretended not to care. It wouldn't help his case to argue. "What about you, Your Majesties? Other than your sister, of course."

"My brother, Valerzan, is a few months older than Conora," Odelia said.

Odd that Calosandros hadn't met him yet. "And where is he?"

Odelia paused, her smile faltering. "He's in the Land of Blue Skies."

"I'm not sure I'm familiar with that region."

The king flung his fork down and glared at Calosandros. "He's buried with a pinecone in Iverish."

Conora's hand was soft on his shoulder as she whispered, "He was killed in battle protecting my brother."

Calosandros nodded solemnly. "I'm sorry." He felt like such an ass. Having led enough soldiers into battle in foreign lands, he should've guessed that a land he'd never seen on a map might be a reference to the afterlife.

Eyes shining with unshed tears, Odelia shook her head. "I brought up the topic. I should've realized I'd have to answer it myself."

"Was there something else you wanted to know?" Calosandros smiled, desperate to talk about anything other than what was clearly still a fresh wound.

"How many wives have you had?" Kennard leaned back in his chair, eyes narrowed.

"None." Calosandros tried to laugh off the not-so-veiled insult. "What about you? Do Meriverian men go through so many wives that you'd expect me to have had my share?"

Conora snickered. "Hardly, especially my brother. He's been smitten with Odelia for most of his life."

The king put his arm around his queen. "And I will be for the rest of it." He gave her a kiss on the temple before continuing, "I must say, it's surprising that an imperial prince has been unable to find a bride yet at—how old are you?" He snuggled closer to the queen.

"Twenty-five," Calosandros said, "and I assure you, if I'd wanted to marry by now, I would have, but until recently, I had yet to find a woman who possessed the qualities I desire." He looked to Conora and took her hand under the table, hoping to impart how sincerely he meant every word.

"Would youth be one of those qualities?" the king asked, dripping with derision.

Calosandros cocked his head. "What do you mean?"

"My sister is quite *young*."

His stomach soured. If that were true, not only would the marriage contract be invalid, but wittingly or not, he would have committed a monstrous offense last night. He turned to Conora. She appeared to be two, maybe three years younger than him, four at most. "But you look—I mean, I assumed you were at least...of age, if not older." His heart anxiously slammed against his chest as he leaned closer and whispered, "Are you?"

"I am and have been for two years now. My brother is being ridiculous." If Conora could kill with a glare, the king would've been dead.

Calosandros put a finger up. "Just to clarify, what would be the—"

"He's still seven years your senior," Kennard said.

Seven years difference from twenty-five would make her eighteen—younger than he'd assumed but more than old enough to consent. If she'd been of age for two years, then Meriverian laws had to be the same as Urstillian ones in that regard. Calosandros shrugged off the disgust the king had tried to impart. "You're plenty old enough to marry in your land and mine."

Queen Odelia put her hand on the king's chest. "I don't feel well, love. Could you escort me upstairs?"

He kissed her. "And now you're fine."

Ugh. Telling his consort how she should feel? It reminded Calosandros too much of his parents. Perhaps that's why he couldn't hold back anymore. "You have an awfully suspicious mind," Calosandros accused the king. "How much younger than you is your wife?"

"I'm not sure. She might be the older one for all I know." The king laughed. "People have questioned many things regarding Odelia and me, but I can promise that an age gap has never been one."

Conora rolled her eyes. "Compared to you, a week would be an unfathomable difference."

So much for Calosandros's jab. The king might actually be crazy. How could they not know how old they were?

Conora leaned into him. "They were born the same day."

At least it made some sense, but what were the odds of that happening? He blinked and shook his head. "On appearances, I'd guessed that the queen was not as old as you, let alone the king."

"Are you calling my wife immature?" the king asked.

Calosandros smirked. "Immature? Not her, no." The king? Absolutely. "But she is quite small for a grown woman."

"Well, I am Vistan," Odelia said. "We're all short."

"You must not encounter many in Urstille," Conora offered—again proving herself to be a supportive consort.

"Certainly no full Vistans anyway," the king muttered.

Calosandros focused on the cordial conversation with the women at the table. "Vistan ancestry is common there." He smiled at Odelia. "I have some on both sides. That's where I get my eyes, and I know some people with bright hair, but it doesn't seem to affect height much in our people."

"Huh. You sound almost proud of that," the king sneered.

Now Calosandros was certain the king was losing his mind. "Why not? Won't your own child be part-Vistan as well?"

Kennard scoffed. "Oh, I wouldn't dream of comparing myself to your ancestors."

The queen cleared her throat and lifted her water cup. "Well, I, for one, think we *all*"—she shot a look at her husband—"should thank the Giver that we are not our ancestors nor responsible for their choices."

Conora followed suit. "Agreed!"

The king nodded and blushed as though chastened by something, though Calosandros couldn't imagine what.

Conora laid a hand on Calosandros's arm, her touch instantly calming. "Would you like to see the beach after dinner? The sunsets are wonderful this time of year."

It didn't matter where she wanted to go, as long as he could enjoy the peace of being alone with her. He grinned. "I believe I've had my fill. Lead the way."

He put his arm around her waist and stood with her, but the king called out to Conora, who sighed.

"Yes, Brother, there will plenty of guards for both of us." She leaned over the table to hiss, "Stay out of my love life, and attend to your own." Turning back to Calosandros and taking his arm, she flashed the most beautifully confident smile, then led him to the inner garden.

"Do you mind if the dogs walk with us?" she asked as they neared her suite.

"Of course not."

When she opened her bedroom door and began to walk through, a large hand gripped his shoulder.

"His Imperial Highness is not permitted in here," one of the guards said.

Conora groaned. "Fine. I only need to grab a couple things anyway." She turned back to Calosandros. "I'll only be a moment, *Cal.*" Her voice slipped into the cutest accent for the last word in what must have been his language. She kissed his cheek, then slipped away.

Calosandros took two steps back and crossed his arms. Ridiculous as the situation was, the men were merely following orders and had no idea how futile their efforts were. He had and would continue to spend more time in there than in his guest suite, king's orders be damned.

With the dogs running ahead of them, Calosandros followed Conora as she approached what looked like the edge of a small cliff before the sea. But a small path wound sideways down the bluff, leading to a broad stretch of smooth pebbles. Here and there, sun-bleached logs broke the monotony of the gravel that extended seemingly infinitely to the south. To the west, the pebbles gradually grew smaller as they neared the sea.

As striking as the water had been from the mountains, seeing it spread nearly to the horizon in front of him was even more awe-inspiring as the quiet rolling thunder of the waves alternated with the hissing foam on the rocks and sand. The wind picked up, chilling the air and carrying a more pungent version of the scent Calosandros had noticed on the Meriverian letter.

Conora closed her eyes and deeply inhaled the briny air with a contented smile. It was certainly a unique smell. A pang of guilt jabbed at Calosandros as he realized she might be trying to memorize the aroma; they wouldn't encounter it in Urstille.

She dropped the large bag she'd been carrying and pulled out a leather belt. "Ever gone wading?"

"Only in fresh water and not in a body this big."

"Well, then..." She grinned, then hiked up her skirt until the hem reached her knees and started securing it with the belt. "I guess it's my turn to show you a new experience. You'll want to take off your sandals."

"And walk on the rocks with bare feet?"

"They're smooth enough. You don't want to soak your shoes in salt water; trust me." She slipped off her boots and dropped them by the bag.

Calosandros untied his sandals, then placed them with her boots and took her offered hand. "I'm guessing your guards would object to making this a swim?"

Conora laughed. "Of course they would. They're sane."

"Is there something wrong with the water? Should I be worried?"

"Oh, wading is fine. It's just a little cold to get your whole body in there. You'll see." She chased after the receding surf, stopping a few feet past the highest point where the water had touched.

The gravel here was more like coarse sand, soft and wet underfoot, squishing as they stepped. Calosandros wiggled his toes in it and watched the indents they made.

And then the surf rolled up again.

He yelped. "Shit—shit—shit—shit... *Fuck*! That's cold!" The icy water nipped at his heels as he high-stepped back out.

Conora doubled over laughing.

"You call *that* a little cold?" he yelled.

She stopped laughing long enough to wheeze out, "You get used to it after a minute."

"It's like soaking your feet in a glacier!" Married less than a day, and his wife was trying to kill him.

Sighing, she wiped her eyes and trudged up through the water to him. "I swear it's refreshing. Your face..." She stifled a giggle. "I guess we're even for this morning now, Prince Hand-Confusion."

When she tried to finish her taunt by tickling him in the rib, he dodged and pulled her flush to him.

He whispered close to her lips, "I should've guessed my little vixen would be a trickster."

"Not intentionally...this time."

He chuckled. "I'll have to be careful not to cross you." Then he kissed her deeply, her body so soft and warm against his in the crisp breeze.

Conora pulled away, panting and smiling, her eyes shining like dark amber in the setting sunlight. "Since wading was a bust, how about watching the sunset together under a blanket?"

"Sounds like a marked improvement."

"I must warn you, after the dogs wear themselves out running the beach, they'll demand cuddles."

"As long as they don't try to separate us, I won't object to our furry friends."

Soon they were settled on one of the driftwood logs, a huge blanket wrapped around them, with Conora's head on Calosandros's shoulder. The sun on the horizon painted the clouds in soft fire and flickered over the surface of the water. The small sketchbook and pencils he carried were insufficient to capture the vibrant color, but he attempted it anyway.

After filling two pages, he set the book down, realizing he was currently better equipped to cherish the beauty in his arms. He kissed her neck, then took advantage of the blanket's concealment to fondle her breast and enjoy her soft gasp of pleasure. Sliding his hand between her thighs had her arching her back against him. Though sexy, it was not subtle.

One of her guards approached them warily. "Is Your Highness all right?"

She laughed lightly. "Yes, thank you, Gerid. I was just yawning. It's been a long day."

Gerid narrowed his eyes at Calosandros as he continued addressing Conora. "Of course. We'll be here if you need us."

Calosandros glared back at the insolent guard and whispered to Conora, "How much longer must we abide this bullshit?"

She didn't respond for a long while, either oblivious to his question or serving him angry silence—he couldn't see her face to discern which it might be. Finally, she turned so that she was standing between his knees.

Her eyes only met his gaze for a moment before flicking downward. "I'm sorry. I should've talked to Kennard. I fully intended to, but I let myself get distracted by anger. He was being such a..." Her face screwed up in frustration.

"Fucker?"

She jolted, eyes wide, then frowned. "Don't call him that."

"Are you defending his behavior?"

"Not at all. I'll admit he's acting boorish lately, but you shouldn't call him...things like that."

He sighed. "He's your king. I know what it's like. No one is supposed to be allowed to speak ill of the emperor either."

Conora shook her head. "I don't care that he's king, but my brother is a good man. I don't believe he's earned such words."

"Why? He's rude and overbearing. He even tried to control the queen at dinner."

She cocked her head. "What do you mean? When did he try to control her?"

"When she wasn't feeling well, he just dismissed it and told her she was fine."

"Did he kiss her first?"

He thought back for a second. "I think so?"

"Then she was fine."

"What? It's not like he can decide how she feels. And what does a kiss have to do with it?"

She shrugged. "I don't know why it works that way. Ask the Giver why he made Healing so weird."

Calosandros tried to shake the confusion from his head. "Did you just imply that the king is Gifted with *Healing*?" Something must have been translating wrong with his own Gift.

"I didn't imply. It's common knowledge that he and Odelia are Healers."

He laughed. "Very funny. What are their real Gifts?"

"I know the odds of two Healers finding each other are ridiculous, but from what they've told me about their Gift ceremony, it wasn't a coincidence."

"But the twentieth Gift is just a legend. People aren't actually given that one. Other empathetic Gifts are rare enough. The empathy needed for a Healer—how would they even function around other people?"

Conora tilted her head again and giggled. "Empathetic Gifts aren't rare. You can find an Animal Speaker at any kennel or farm. Even my maid is one. Ports are lined with Speakers' offices. Granted, Listeners are a bit harder to find, but I've met a few of them as well."

"Perhaps living in the shelter of the palace brings you close to more special people. I've traveled widely, and I haven't found that to be true."

"And perhaps we aren't like your empire here." She huffed and crossed her arms. "Being a princess doesn't make me ignorant. I've toured the kingdom before, and I've read the census reports."

"This kingdom isn't that large."

She pulled out of his arms. "Don't insult my kingdom or my family when you know nothing about them."

"Am I allowed to comment on what I have seen? Because I can only see what they choose to show me."

Her bottom lip quivered. "If everything you see connected to me is so terrible, why marry me? I'm one of my people."

"I see more to you than that. What we share is greater than where we come from." He stood and reached for her hand. How had his desire to be closer to her unraveled so quickly to drive her away? "And I'm sorry for insulting your people. Most of the subjects here have been kind and welcoming. What I mean is that you deserve better than to be trapped by a selfish and childish king. I want to free you." Not wanting to further insult her intelligence, he stopped short of explaining how much worse the trap would be if the empire were to control Meriveria.

Conora took a deep breath as her eyes welled up. "I'm grateful for that—truly, I am. But you have no idea what we've been through here. Compared to my father's rule, my brother is the better we deserve. He and Odelia are doing their best with the mess they inherited, and they haven't had much time to fix it yet."

Calosandros squeezed her hand. "You're right. I have no way of knowing what your father was like. All I can do is take your word for it and hope that the king eventually warms to me enough to show the goodness you say he has."

She worried her fingers. "What if... Would you..." After a sharp inhale, she blurted, "You could meet my father."

What good would a gravesite visit do? Calosandros squinted at the almost-gone sun. "Maybe we should wait until daylight."

She nodded. "Daylight doesn't make much difference in his prison cell, but getting some sleep first would be a good idea."

"Wait. He's alive? How is your brother king?"

"Kennard and Odelia deposed him after their wedding," Conora said matter-of-factly.

"Really?" Calosandros gaped. Who would let a deposed monarch live?

"It's a long story, and I don't know most of the details of how they pulled it off because I asked not to be involved. Until I learned the full depth of my father's treachery, I didn't want to take sides."

"If you sided against your father, does that mean we can refer to *him* as a fucker if he acts like one, or will you that upset you too?"

"I suppose." Conora blushed. "Do all Urstillians speak like you do?"

"How so?"

"Sometimes you sound like you belong on the docks more than a palace."

"Oh." Calosandros sat back down. Though she hadn't imparted judgment in her tone, it still hurt. "I must have picked up a commoner's accent the first time I heard Meriverian."

"No. I mean your choice of words."

He raised an eyebrow, not sure what she meant.

She scarcely squeaked a whisper, "Like 'fuck.'"

"What?" He snorted as he failed to contain his laughter. "You and I can fuck like rabbits, but the *word* is embarrassing?"

Her face was deep red now. "It's considered crude."

"Is there anything your people don't use a euphemism for? It makes it very difficult to understand what anyone means."

Conora laughed. "Now you get it. Welcome to Meriveria."

"I guess I should try it, then..." He contemplated what to try as he slowly pulled her onto his lap, then whispered, "Have you thought of tasting my geoduck?"

She giggled, wrapped her arms around his neck, and whispered back, "Does that come with an offer to taste my clam?"

"Of course. If you can get me past your guards again, we'll have a feast." Though he felt completely ridiculous speaking this way, he enjoyed how much it seemed to amuse her.

"If? Have a little more faith in me, *Cal*." She pulled back to smile saucily at him, then added, "I hope you're prepared for dessert *and* breakfast."

11

HUMILIATION

Icnaboir

Since Father's arrest, Conora had visited him only once, on the eve of her grandfather's execution. Strict justice should have demanded Father's death too. It was Odelia's mercy alone that had spared Father—not that he ever appreciated it. The fool had done nothing but spew pure vitriol for her, even when she'd brought Conora to him. If it weren't useful to helping Calosandros understand things, Conora wouldn't have been willing to visit Father again, but she supposed she could take the opportunity to say a final goodbye before she moved to Urstille—or, more likely, a good riddance.

So, late the next morning, with Gerid, Thaum, Anabusos, and another Urstillian soldier several steps behind, she and Calosandros followed the guard captain down the damp, mildewy prison corridor. The hair on the back of her neck stood on end. In the creepy prison basement of the palace, being shadowed by a team actually felt necessary.

When she shivered, Calosandros put his arm around her, grounding her with his calm strength. "We can turn back if you're not ready," he whispered.

She shook her head.

"Then breathe, Conora."

A howl pierced the air. *Conora!*

She clenched her fists, partly in anger at herself for flinching. "I hate when he does that."

Before she could change her mind about this visit, the guard captain was well ahead of them, unlocking the door at the end of the hallway. He bowed to Conora, then turned to her guards. "Gerid, for Her Highness's privacy, I shall entrust you to lock the cell and return the keys to me when you are finished."

As the door creaked open, the reek of unwashed filth wafted out with the echoing rattle of chains. Father's dingy clothes hung more like rags off his haggard frame. His long curly hair had matted into greasy strings that fell over his shoulders as he jumped up from his cot and clung to the bars that blocked the open doorway. He smiled at Conora. "You came back to me!"

But his gaze flickered to Calosandros, whose hand still rested on the small of her back. Wide-eyed horror took over, followed swiftly by simmering rage. "What is the meaning of—"

"*Cal.*" Conora tried to breathe through her mouth as the pungent smells of wet dog, man sweat, and sulfurous estuary formed an oppressively balmy bouquet. "May I present my father, His M—um...I guess just Gonfrid now." It still felt odd to go from a lifetime of using the utmost honorific to none at all, even if he no longer deserved it. "Father, you may show deference to our guest, His Imperial Highness, Calosandros, Crown Prince of Urstille."

Father snarled. "You ungrateful brat! Where is my due respect?"

Conora pretended to ignore the outburst. "I wanted the two of you to meet before we leave. Calosandros and I—"

"I know." In a snap, he became a wolf, his hackles raised, teeth bared. "The Vistan Whore already told me about his demands."

Conora crossed her arms. "She's Queen Odelia to you. And it was an offer, not a demand—one I gladly agree to."

As she was speaking, Father had cocked his head, then began sniffing. A low growl grew in his throat.

Oh shit. She should've known better, but it was too late now.

He lunged at Calosandros through the bars, all claws and teeth, the clang reverberating loudly in the small space. "You bastard! You defiled her! I'll kill you!"

To his credit, Calosandros barely blinked as he casually took one step back with a disapproving sigh.

"Stop it," Conora scolded. "Calosandros didn't violate me. You're just embarrassing yourself."

Father turned his snarl toward her and recoiled. "You. A princess. *My* bloodline. How dare you debase yourself for this brute!"

Calosandros scoffed. "Rich words from a prisoner. And 'this brute' is the next emperor of Urstille."

Father snapped back into a man and glared. "So, does that mean women are all the same from your lofty position? Or is the satisfaction sweeter when you see a king's daughter on her knees?"

81

Conora approached him, half pleading, half warning, "You don't know what you're talking about." Not about the disposition of their relationship at least. As far as Calosandros had shown her, his proclivities were completely the opposite, drawing his pleasure from hers.

"It's bad enough to pretend you aren't covered in each other's scent, but don't lie to me when I can smell his seed on your breath." Though Father's voice was full of venom, his eyes held disappointment.

She froze, jittering her hand over her mouth. He'd finally deduced one thing correctly. Conora had picked the wrong morning to explore new sexual acts. Shaking her head, she took a step toward him. *Please stop!*

"You've had your fun with rebellion, but you're in over your head. Rid yourself of this invader before anyone else knows he's stolen your virtue." He gripped her shoulder painfully. "You can't leave. Your brother is a lost cause. You're the only one who can restore the throne to what it was. You must stay here. It is your duty to this family."

She had been afloat with confidence in his presence for ages, but the disappointment in his voice had cracked her hull at last. His focus was entirely on her, and he wasn't entirely wrong. She had no biting retort. She was drowning.

Calosandros loudly slammed his palms on the bars, startling Father into releasing Conora and stepping backward. "Hey, asshole, you aren't in a position to shame or control anyone—least of all her."

She backed away from Father's reach and put a hand over her pounding heart, trying not to gag as her faster breathing sucked in more fetid air.

"Conora is *my* daughter." He thumped his chest.

Calosandros rolled his eyes. "She's neither a child nor a possession, and she's more than capable of thinking for herself. Maybe you wouldn't be in here if you had listened to her more."

Father snapped into a grizzly bear and pounded on the bars. "She isn't yours!"

Calosandros shrugged. "You're probably right. But if and when she ever is, that is a declaration only she can make." He held out a hand to Conora. "We don't owe him or anyone else an explanation, but I will support whatever you want to do."

Escape. She had to get away from this moment, this sickening tightness in her chest. Still reeling, she wove her fingers between his, then spun on her heels and marched out. Nothing could stop her from getting fresh air.

Conora needed to tamp down her wild emotions, gather her racing thoughts. Calosandros's empathy notwithstanding, falling apart in front of two Urstillian soldiers would not commend Conora as their future empress. And if Gerid or Thaum repeated anything? She had to clean this up before it got out of hand.

Could she try to spin Father's accusations as pure madness? Too risky. Even if the guards were to believe her denial, that wouldn't stop them from talking. The ravings of their former king would be just as tantalizing gossip as their debauched princess. And unlike Conora, Father didn't have the secrecy protection that came with being their charge—assuming the guards still followed such a policy anymore.

At least she could trust that Father wouldn't spread word any further. Even if anyone visited him, impugning her "purity" would go against whatever delusions he had. Her carelessness had driven him to act out.

A solid tug on her hand yanked Conora backward and into Calosandros's arms. He brushed her hair off her face and softly tucked it behind her ear. "I'm sorry, dearest." His low tone of voice was soothing and tamed the wild rush of her thoughts. "But if you want to take me on a tour of the capital, could we take a more leisurely pace?"

Conora's confusion gave way as she realized they were standing in the middle of the—mercifully empty—bridge between the Cedar Palace and North Meria. So much for controlling herself. She snarled, the sound shriller than she'd intended. "I should've been better prepared. He hasn't caught me off guard like that since I was a little girl."

"Nobody can ever fully prepare for madness."

Conora shook her head and whispered, "I knew he could smell everything. This morning—it was a stupid mistake when I knew our plans."

"No. He was the one making stupid mistakes."

"He knew exactly what we did."

"Did he?" Calosandros raised an eyebrow. "He wrongly assumed you were on your knees this morning."

"I doubt the position was his main objection."

"True, but he was using it to further what he was most wrong about. Everything we have done is natural." He smiled gently and caressed her cheek. "Each encounter together makes you more beautiful to me, raises my regard for you. If he considers that debasing, then the fuckwit deserves his cell."

Conora stifled a giggle with her hand.

"Ah!" He lit up. "You don't mind my crudeness so much now, do you?"

"Sometimes..." she admitted, though speaking so lewdly with her guards nearby did not help the gnawing discomfort of the situation. "Sorry, but I need to check something." She held up a finger, then turned to one of them and raised her voice so he could hear. "Gerid, has His Majesty changed the private guards' secrecy policy?"

He cleared his throat. "No, Your Highness, but I must advise you to remember that it does not apply to the other palace guards. Thaum and I can keep our silence, but that will not stop others from asking questions, especially if they are inclined to listen to wild accusations."

"I'm aware, thank you." Conora nodded, trying not to let too much of her relief show.

Calosandros slid his arm around her waist. "Does this mean I don't have to crawl under carts anymore?"

Gerid gaped, and Thaum smacked his chest with the back of his hand. "I told you it was the carts. The men assigned to the Urstillians were talking about them. They're starting to get suspicious."

Panic rose in her chest again.

"What would you suggest?" Calosandros asked casually, either unaware or unconcerned that his previous flippant comment had undone Gerid's apparent willingness to accept Conora's version of events.

Gerid scowled. "It's one thing to keep our silence. It's another matter to ask us not to do our job to protect the princess." He puffed his chest out in self-righteous bluster, even as he repeated the lie.

Something in her snapped, and Conora laughed. "Oh, you're doing your job, but let's stop pretending it's about my safety."

Thaum was taken aback. "Your Highness?"

"What? You think my brother didn't tell me your assignment? It's futile. Instead of wasting all of our time on something that doesn't exist, why don't you protect something useful, like the alliance I'm securing with Urstille?" Conora didn't give them a chance to retort. Not ready to return to the palace—a little time and distance might cool her brother's head anyway—she turned away from the guards and curled her hand around Calosandros's arm. "I would be remiss in my diplomatic duties if I didn't give you a very detailed, very thorough tour of Meria."

The first place Conora took Calosandros was the finest jeweler in Meria, where he insisted she wait outside. Through the window, she watched him offer the proprietor a large sum of gold and a piece of paper—probably a ring he had sketched. It didn't matter what design he'd made; anything from his hand was going to be perfect for her wedding ring.

She showed him around the rest of the high-end merchants, the bustling wharf, a royal Meriverian vessel, and a renowned seafood restaurant on the waterfront, before the dark of night drove them back to the palace. Unfortunately, the fatigue from the morning's panic combined with the excellent wine collection at their last stop proved too much for Conora, and she found herself leaning heavily on Calosandros to return home.

There, he wordlessly undressed her, plying her body with soft kisses as he did so. When he guided her to the bed, Conora stifled sleepy giggles—nothing was particularly funny, yet everything was. He gave her a bemused smile, then rolled her over and cuddled her close, enveloping her body in his. Her thighs warmed in anticipation.

But nothing happened. No petting. No more kisses. Just the slow and even breathing that told her he'd fallen asleep. Her disappointment didn't last long before sleep claimed her too.

Thankfully, the corollary was Conora waking to overwhelming expressions of his desire: his beard and breath tickling her ear, a hand firmly holding her breast, another tucked between her thighs, and what felt like a whole tree of morning wood pressed against her back. Not so thankfully, a knock on the door prevented her from reciprocating the vigorous snuggling into more.

Conora tried not to glare too hard at Raina, who popped her head through the door before opening it completely to reveal Anabusos.

Calosandros bolted upright, excited. "They're here?"

Conora clutched the shifting blanket high on her chest, praying she hadn't accidentally flashed his friend.

Anabusos raised an eyebrow. "Cempusos pana?"

Calosandros gave a mildly annoyed huff. "Cempusos pana. Piros yos sid icloee?"

Anabusos smiled and nodded. "Mios." He tossed a folded green chiton on the bed. "Yis ictee oin tia icada icsinaba."

Calosandros put an arm around Conora and smiled at her expectantly.

"Does that mean your men are here?" she asked.

He laughed. "I should hope it's more than just the men. It's supposed to be an army." Then he grabbed the chiton and climbed out of bed to put it on.

Conora rolled her eyes. "You know I didn't mean that literally. Do Urstillians not assume the weapons and supplies come with the men?"

"Yes, but I expect their female comrades to be here too."

Conora gasped in delight. "You let women fight?"

"Why wouldn't we? Every hand is useful when there are lands to conquer."

So, women *did* help on the battlefield. Oh, she would make stuffy Grandilord Doneron eat his words. "Why didn't you bring some of them with you initially?"

Calosandros knelt to tie his sandals. "I did. Maybe you didn't notice because all the soldiers wear the same uniform."

"You'll have to point some out to me when we go out there."

He stood and looked between Anabusos and Conora, eventually settling his gaze on her chest. "No."

"*No?* You just said women are welcome at your camp!"

"That has nothing to do with it." He perched on the edge of the bed and caressed her cheek. "It's clear that you aren't comfortable yet with my Urstillian courtly manners. The army is as different from court life as our kingdoms are from each other. I don't want to subject you to that much culture shock at once, dearest. Not until you're better prepared."

She frowned. "What makes you think I couldn't handle it?"

"You looked flustered when I got out of bed naked, and you're holding onto that bedsheet like your life depends on it. I know those instincts will take some time to fade, but learning some of our customs before you meet more of my people would help too."

"You seem to have fared just fine with the cultural difference."

He smirked. "I've had a lot of practice in foreign kingdoms. But we can talk about this more later. I need to go." He gave her a quick kiss, then joined Anabusos and called back over his shoulder, "I'll be back soon, my little vixen."

12

FUCKED

Iclasar

Conora squinted at the spines on the dusty shelf. Most of the library was impeccably clean, but the books relating to Urstille looked like they hadn't been touched in ages. Did the librarians even remember this section existed? She picked one titled *A History of Urstille* and added it to the pile on her cart. The number of books was getting a bit ridiculous, but there was a good chance that most would have false or outdated information anyway. She would have to get Calosandros to sift through them and select the most accurate ones to learn from. That had likely been the last book she would find, so Conora had Thaum help her return to her suite with the haul.

When she opened the door, Cloudy and Spruce eagerly stood in their usual place in front of her, tails wagging, *Hello, hello, HELLO!*

Behind them, Calosandros jumped up from an armchair and greeted her with a smile. "There you are! Gerid refused to tell me anything." He glared at the offending guard, who glared right back.

"Her Highness has the right to go where she pleases without being stalked."

"For Giver's sake, it was a simple question of when she might be back. Even by guard standards, you're paranoid." Calosandros shook his head, then with a giddy grin, took Conora's hands. "I have presents for you."

Her cheeks warmed. "I'm afraid what I have for you is more of a chore."

"My little vixen is doing some scouting. What's your prey?" He peeked over her shoulder. "Impressive. I honestly wouldn't have expected you to find that many books on Urstille here."

She shrugged. "Not the freshest catch. The information is at least two hundred years old, and some of the books themselves almost look that ancient. I don't know how to determine which ones are worth reading, though. Studying the wrong things won't help me acclimate."

87

He grimaced. "No, it won't. Let's see what we have to work with." He approached the books, stroking his beard contemplatively.

Next to the armchair he'd been using when she walked in, Conora noticed a wooden chest on the floor that wasn't part of her decor. "Didn't you want to give me something before we get lost in this project?"

"Oh, we definitely need to finish this first. If I've learned anything about you yet, you're going to want to use what I have for you right away." He snaked his arms around her waist and kissed her cheek, then nuzzled her ear and whispered, "And then neither of us will get anything done."

She chuckled. "Well, now I really want to see it."

"Hmm..." He trailed a fingertip along her jaw to gently tip her chin up. "But anticipation is a potent aphrodisiac."

As she leaned into the kiss, memories of what they'd almost started that morning begged to be finished. Conora held onto his neck, pressing closer and kissing harder.

But he broke away, disentangling himself from her arms, with a besotted smirk. "Patience and focus, dearest."

He turned to a pile of books and picked up one from the top, his face screwed up in disgusted fascination. "Do you need me to look inside all of them? I feel confident in saying that *Urstille: A Brutal Land of Debauchery and Carnage* is not going to be a fair representation." Calosandros gingerly set the offensive book far away from the rest as if it were diseased.

"I'm so sorry." Conora put her hands up in apologetic surrender. "All I saw was Urstille on the cover. I should've read the subtitle."

He shrugged it off. "It's okay. You didn't write it, and I expect most of the books here to have similar opinions. Yours is not the first kingdom to develop a strong hatred for the empire." Then, snickering, he picked up another book and held it between them. "Are you sure you didn't write this one?"

It read, "*The Great Urstillian Penetration*," in stark black lettering.

"Only 'great'?" She laughed, then clicked her tongue and shook her head in mock disappointment. "I thought you took more pride in your work than that."

Calosandros momentarily fell wide-eyed and slack-jawed before bursting into a full belly laugh.

She took the book from him and riffled through it. "This is actually one of the newest texts I found. It's the most popular historical account we have about that period."

"What period?"

"The Great Urstillian Penetration. It's the name for the time before the Treaty of Meriveria was signed, when Vistan subjects were...disappearing."

He cocked his head in disbelief. "You don't actually call it that?"

"It's better than what the Vistans used to call it." She dug through the books for a moment, pulled out a somewhat frail old volume, and handed it to Calosandros.

"*The Abductions.* Lovely." He sighed. "It looks like I'm going to have to settle for the least hostile books I can find. Is there one on translation in here? I can give you better books than this if you can learn to read Urstillian."

They sifted through the pile until they found the two biggest and oldest-looking tomes. Calosandros opened to a random page in one book and read some of the text, which was a mixture of Urstillian and Meriverian. He scowled and did the same with second book, flipping through more pages.

"Iclas," he spat. She didn't need to understand Urstillian to recognize the crudeness of his tone as *fuck.*

"What's wrong?"

He sighed and slumped into the armchair. "I should've guessed. The Urstillian in here is *old*—old enough that even I can tell it's not right. If you learn Urstillian from one of these books, most people will understand you, but you'll be speaking a very stiff dialect that's only heard in old poetry." He passed the book to her. "Look, you can probably read how archaic the Meriverian is too."

"Let's see. 'Wherefore art thou fraternizing amidst mine enemies?'" Conora laughed. "Oh, that's terrible!"

"I have another idea." He grabbed the wooden chest by his chair and set it atop the cart. "I'll have to try not to let you distract me from looking through those history books for a while." Calosandros pushed the cart into the bedroom.

As soon as Conora joined him inside, she deftly locked the door behind her before Thaum and Gerid could follow them.

Rude! Cloudy barked from the other side.

She smiled at Calosandros. "I assumed you moved us in here for more privacy."

"Clever little vixen." He opened the chest and pulled out a book with deep red leather binding and fancy gold lettering.

"*Pusosio Sioria.* You called me *sioria* once. You said it means...'sexy'?"

89

"Yes, but in this case, it means 'sexual.' No Urstillian royal's education is complete without this book. All of the nobility and much of our populace read it before they come of age. This particular copy I'm giving you is actually mine."

She sat near him on the edge of the bed. "So, I'm borrowing it?"

"No, I don't mean it that way." He caressed her cheek. "Everything I own is yours now, including my personal treasures." He blushed as he handed her the book. "This is probably easier to just show you than to explain first."

Inside, the title page showed a large full-color illustration of a couple standing next to each other, completely naked. Something about it looked familiar. As Conora slowly turned more pages, each one filled with another full-page nude drawing, it dawned on her. "Calosandros...did you draw these yourself?"

His blush deepened as he nodded. "Many are passed down or bought new from a market, but to keep enough circulating, anyone with moderate artistic talent is encouraged to create their own copy as they come of age. It's also considered a good exercise for learning everything in the book."

She examined the book more. The first few pages focused on anatomy, not just labeling body parts but also showing close images of genitalia and other erogenous zones. Unlike the basic line sketches shown in the few anatomical texts Conora had found in Meriveria, these were carefully detailed, colored, and shaded to near realism.

Calosandros chuckled nervously. "If you can't learn anything else, at least you'll know which body parts people are talking about."

"It's certainly more useful than those translation books."

She flipped through more of *Pusosio Sioria*. The images began showing poses and short paragraphs of text, first with lone figures, then in pairs for most of the book, and a tiny section at the end with increasing numbers of partners and decreasing detail.

It was so much information to absorb, and her husband was intimately acquainted with *all of it*. How laughably ignorant was she in comparison? Even the pages on masturbation had new ideas for her. Was this his way of expressing disappointment in her sexual prowess?

Unable to look up, she took a deep breath. "Was there...um... Which page in particular do you need me to learn in here?"

"Conora." Calosandros laid a hand on her back. "I told you before, I would never demand anything from you. If it would make you more comfortable, we can get you a brand new one from the quartermaster. They always keep some on hand to sell to soldiers who lose theirs."

Pulling the book to herself, she shook her head. "The work is beautiful, *Cal*, and it means even more that it's yours. Thank you, truly."

"But you look upset."

She fidgeted her fingers together as she stared at the gold filigree of the book's cover. "It must be frustrating for you to have a partner who knows almost nothing."

"Not at all. Half the fun is exploring together, and you have yet to disappoint me. The *only* thing you lack is practice, something I will gladly give you as much as you like. Speaking of which..." He pulled a long black box out of the wooden chest and handed it to her. "This might help."

The book in her lap was nothing compared to the contents of the box. It was lined with red silken padding. One end had small jars of liquid nestled in it; most of the box was filled with the bulk of something cylindrical wrapped in cloth.

As she began to unwrap it, Calosandros blushed again. "I didn't think you had one already, and I didn't want to leave you without, in case you get lonely while I'm gone. In hindsight, it might be a little vain, but I thought you might prefer it a little more personal."

The unwrapped piece was wood, polished to a high sheen, in the shape of an erection. The artist had even traced faint veins along it.

Conora glanced at Calosandros's lap. How similar was it to the real thing? Similar enough to fool her body into arousal. She shifted her position. "Wait. You said 'personal.' This hasn't been used before, has it?"

He laughed. "Giver, no! I modeled for it this morning. I was going to leave it blank, but the carpenter was bored, and for a Speeder, he has a great eye for detail."

It was the last present Conora would've expected, an absolute scandal if anyone knew about it—and she wasn't sure she wanted to imagine what modeling would've entailed—but it was a sweet gesture in its own way. She set it and *Pusosio Sioria* on her bedside table, then threw her arms around Calosandros and kissed him vigorously.

He pushed her back just enough to sardonically say, "I thought you wanted me to help sort through the books."

"The books can wait. A practical lesson sounds better right now." She reached under his chiton. "*Cal*."

"Mmm...nuil yos cal yon siora..." He kissed her long and slow, breaking into a sly grin.

Taking her hand, he entwined their fingers together and held them aloft. "Yosee."

She repeated it back. "Yosee?" (Hand?)

"Mios." He nodded. "Yosee." Then he pointed at her mouth. "Toros."

"Toros?" (Mouth?)

"Mios. Toros." He brushed his fingertip along her lower lip. "Tumaos."

A soft kiss was *icthidoir*. The pleasant sensations built as he kissed her forehead (*cacos*), her nose (*ceree*), her cheek (*coindalos*), her jaw (*gradee*), her throat (*sendolos*), and her neck (*cianee*).

The last kiss made her giggle, and she said back, "Ci-nee?"

He chuckled and shook his head. "*Aah...* Ci-*a*-nee." He kissed her neck again. "Cianee."

"Cianee." She drew her fingers over her neck, inviting him to come back for more.

His eyes smoldered a deep green, like the beckoning of the forest at night as he repeated, "Cianee." Then he was nuzzling her neck, repeating it one last time before he began sucking and nibbling at the tender flesh.

She writhed with excitement and pulled at the top of her bodice, determined to have him name all of her favorite parts, whether she'd remember them or not.

After Conora finished putting her dress back on, she ran her hand over the chest Calosandros had brought. "May I look inside?"

"Of course. I told you, everything I own is yours."

Expecting to find extra chitons or the usual odds and ends to groom himself since he'd been sleeping in her room, Conora had no idea what to make of the chest's contents. Small dividers and leather straps held each item neatly in place, and *Pusosio Sioria* had left an obvious vacancy. A jar and bottles similar to the ones he'd given her were tucked in between small stacks of towels. Conora pulled out the large jar; it turned out to be filled with lotion. "No wonder your skin is so smooth," she said as she put it back.

Calosandros reddened. "I've been alone for a while... Speaking of which..." He took out a bottle. "I can throw this one out. It's probably no good by now. And you make enough of your own when we're together anyway." He punctuated the last statement with a kiss on her temple and a squeeze of her butt.

"What is it?"

He opened the top and showed the thick liquid inside. "Lubricant."

Conora felt too foolish to ask what the others were.

But Calosandros saved her the trouble, pointing to the other two bottles in the box. "Gentle soap for the loins and *sitrecayus.*"

Conora definitely wasn't going to ask. Whatever was in the last bottle was so foreign, it didn't even translate into Meriverian, and her mind was already trying to hold onto the last Urstillian words he'd taught her. Instead, she moved on to the handful of feathers clustered in the corner of the chest and plucked one out. "Okay. I know what this is, but why?"

He pressed himself behind her, wrapped an arm around her waist, and then took the feather. Nuzzling her ear, he whispered. "For fun." A pleasant chill went up her spine as he lightly brushed the tip of the feather up and down her arm and across her bosom.

She put her hand over his to stop the distracting sensation. "Is everything in here used for sex?"

He laughed and put the feather away. "What else would I keep in my sex box? Do Meriverians keep different things in theirs?"

"We don't have— What are these for?" She lifted the top piece from a stack of folded silk, only for it to continue unfolding into a narrow scarf. Assuming they were the same size, four more scarves remained folded underneath.

"Depends on the mood you're in." He took the scarf and draped it over her eyes. "Surprises can be sensual." Then he wrapped it over her wrist, trailed the ends across her palm, and closed her hand. "Or maybe one of us might enjoy a little surrender." He lifted the scarf, moving her arm gently but entirely under his control for a few moments. With a kiss on her cheek, he dropped the scarf. "But only if we both want it. Your pleasure arouses me more than any kind of play."

She reached up behind her and stroked his soft beard, snuggling into him.

A pounding on the door interrupted their blissful embrace.

Conora sighed and sulked across the room to answer it. Outside was Anabusos, along with two pouting dogs and an annoyed-looking Gerid, whose fist hovered over the doorway.

Anabusos bowed to her, then held up a bundle of papers and peeked inside. "Turoisos Loee?"

As Calosandros took the papers and began shuffling through them, Anabusos bowed again. Something about the way he looked at Calosandros and her struck Conora strangely, though she couldn't quite place it. She'd thought it might be distaste, but next to Gerid's obvious show of it now, Anabusos's emotions were clearly something entirely different but equally tense.

Unsure what to do with herself, Conora fidgeted with her hair, brushing it out of her face and over one shoulder.

With a smirk, Anabusos nodded toward Conora and clapped Calosandros on the shoulder. "Calisioree cian."

She didn't appreciate what felt like possible mockery and tried to keep the irritation out of her voice as she asked, "What did he say?"

Calosandros shrugged. "He was complimenting the love bite I gave you."

"The *what*?" Conora ran to the mirror.

Sure enough, a dark red circular mark had formed on her neck. Rubbing didn't remove it in the least. It was a bruise.

It was proof of Conora's secrets.

13

SISTERS-IN-LAW

Pintiotiaris

A t first sight, Calosandros was proud of his beautifully bold mark on Conora's delicate flesh, the physical evidence of the passion they'd shared. But her horrified gasp and wide eyes brought him back to the reality of their situation: it was *physical evidence* of the passion they'd shared. Anabusos had warned him about the danger of excess after a drought, and Calosandros had lost himself in desire anyway. He'd willfully embraced it.

He handed the reports back to Anabusos—none of them worth more of his attention than his distraught wife—and approached Conora cautiously.

Her breathing sped up. "I can't go to dinner. I need to talk to Kennard. But if he sees this? I mean, he already hates you, and now he has a reason." She bit her lower lip and covered his mark with her hand.

Calosandros rubbed her back. "Then we don't have to eat with him. We could dine in the city again?"

Her eyes glistened. "That won't make this go away."

"No, but it will buy us a little time."

She ran to her closet and retrieved a dark blue chiffon scarf, throwing it around her neck. "I might be able to get away with this if we go to the waterfront, right? Does the scarf cover it? Does it look suspicious?"

He gently pushed her hands down from her neck. "You're a princess. If you wear it with confidence, nobody will question it."

Conora swallowed hard and nodded, keeping her hands in his. "Of course. You've probably done this so many times before."

"Well...no, not really. Most people want to flaunt a love bite, not hide it." At her shame-filled pout, he quickly added, "But these are obviously unusual circumstances."

He slowly pulled her closer into an embrace and took deep calming breaths until she matched him. Though he could feel Anabusos's stare, he avoided meeting it. Such gentleness went against everything Calosandros had been taught as the future Emperor of Urstille, but it came so naturally when he was with Conora, this essence he'd buried so deep for so long. And he couldn't deny his fault in this; his honor demanded he make it right somehow.

"A shame that it's your brother who rules," Calosandros said. "If you had the power to make the alliance, none of this would matter."

Conora stilled. "But he's not the only one."

"What do you mean?"

She pulled back to look at him. "Odelia rules as queen."

"Yes, but the nominal power of a consort isn't helpful here unless the idea is to convince her to sway him." In a more equitable kingdom, the queen would be a formidable ally, but if they wouldn't let women raise arms, it was hard to imagine they allowed them any real voice in governing.

Conora frowned. "She's no mere consort. Her title is Queen Regnant of Meriveria. She was actually crowned as Queen of Vist before the coup. For a few days, Kennard was *her* consort."

Calosandros balked. "Are you saying she can make the alliance herself?" Why hadn't Conora mentioned this before?

She wrinkled her nose. "Technically, yes..."

Calosandros made sure to be prompt in calling on Queen Odelia. Conora had told him about the one reliable time to speak to her alone: the king's morning sparring session. Having attended enough himself, Calosandros didn't want to waste time—an injury or poor temper could end it early at any moment.

As expected, a retinue of four guards watched his every move in the queen's sitting room while he waited for her. Her maidservant had only been gone a few minutes when the door opened again, revealing a less-than-welcoming-looking Odelia.

He put on his best manners as he smiled and bowed. "Good morning, Your Majesty. Is this a convenient time to speak privately?"

She eyed him shrewdly as she waddled in. "Of course. I expect you're looking for a reply to Urstille's proposal?"

More confident since she hadn't rejected him outright, he nodded and continued, "As prudent as you are lovely. So, I trust that I don't need to guard my words with you?"

Odelia laughed. "Not at all. I'm hardier than I look."

At last, a sensible negotiator. Calosandros got straight to the point. "Then, I must confess, I don't understand the delay. For a kingdom so desperately in need of an alliance, you are slow to decide. As far as I know, the princess is willing to marry me, and your kingdom cannot possibly hope for a better offer than the one involving her." The tiniest fear rose up in him as he added, "Has she confided otherwise to you?" Despite her eagerness alone with him, he couldn't completely shake the king's accusations of undue influence.

"No. Conora has expressed nothing but eagerness." Odelia still eyed him cautiously.

"Are you certain? I know such an arrangement is outside your customs, but I assure you that I understand the gravity of my request. If she is unwilling or doubtful, I want to know before we exchange lifelong vows." He could always cancel the wedding ceremony if Conora would rather keep their marriage political and economic—however unlikely that seemed to him now.

Odelia shook her head. "Conora has no trouble speaking her mind—quite the opposite, in fact. If she harbored any dislike for you or your offer, it would've surfaced by now." She offered a tight now-fuck-off-please smile.

Calosandros pretended not to notice; he'd made too much progress to retreat now. "And as reasonable as you have been, I suspect that you are not opposed to it either."

Odelia sighed. "I can appreciate what you're doing, but I'm afraid it's not that easy."

Calosandros crossed his arms, trying to exude more confident power. "Are you not the reigning queen? With your signature, I could have my army marching to the border by morning."

She glared. "This is a decision King Kennard and I must make together."

Calosandros scoffed. "If you need your husband's permission to rule, then your kingdom is just as repressed as I thought it was."

She stood straighter, impressively composed for such a small person. "It isn't a matter of permission. It's a matter of trust and respect. I will not betray my husband by overruling him on something this important, and I trust him not to do the same."

"Hasn't he effectively done just that? As long as he refuses to make this deal, he holds all the power, and your choice is irrelevant."

Odelia's eyes widened, and she almost looked ready to shout, but then she rubbed her temples and sighed. "Tell Conora to come in."

"What?" That was the last thing he'd expected her to say.

"I know she's standing outside the door."

"Why are you so certain of that?" Maybe she would drop it if he continued bluffing.

Odelia rolled her eyes. "Because Giver knows I've done it enough times myself, and until now, you've spoken to me as if I were Kennard's consort, not a ruler in my own right. It doesn't take much to deduce who has corrected you."

Shit. Never mind. He motioned for the queen's maidservant to open the door to the hall.

When Conora walked in, she gave him an eager look that asked, *Did you do it?*

He shook his head as little as possible to say, *Not yet.*

Poor Conora could barely contain her distress. She turned to the queen. "I thought you were my friend."

"I am."

"Then, help me! You know how ridiculous my brother is being. You have the power to fix everything right now."

"How can you call on me to help you in the name of friendship if you can't be a friend to me?" Odelia asked.

Conora scowled at her. "How can you say that? I stood by your side when you were in my place!"

Curious as that statement was, Calosandros would have to ask her about it later. He didn't dare interrupt when she seemed to be holding her own.

The queen was turning red. "Because a true friend wouldn't risk that love I fought so hard for just so she can call herself an empress someday. Kennard is your brother, Conora." Odelia shook her head sadly. "And you call me your friend and your sister while you try to turn my insecurities, which I told you about *in confidence*, against him. But, by all means, tell me why I must help you."

"Need I remind you that, much like you before your elopement, I am running out of options to make sure this all happens. Our friendship didn't stop you from forcing my hand against my parents then."

"That was a matter of life and death."

"And this is a matter of the rest of my life."

What had they done to Conora? Whatever hold they had, Calosandros needed to free her.

Conora put her hands together. "Please, Odelia. There must be something you can do to sway him. Kennard has always been enamored with you, and judging from the way he looks at you, that's only gotten stronger over time. In that respect, nobody has more power than you do, not even close to it."

"Well, there is one thing I certainly have the power to help with right now." Odelia put a hand on her hip and beckoned Conora with a finger.

Calosandros didn't trust her, but before he could warn Conora, she walked right up to the queen. In one motion, Odelia snatched Conora's scarf to expose the love bite.

Conora gasped and clasped her neck. "Odelia!"

Odelia shook her head and scoffed. "It's the height of summer. Did you really think that was a sensible disguise?"

Conora blushed. "Well, I can't let Kennard see it!"

"No, you can't. Let me see it." Odelia gently pulled Conora's hand away and kissed her on the cheek.

To Calosandros's amazement, the mark faded away almost instantly.

Odelia cocked her head patronizingly at Calosandros. "Perhaps you should refrain from giving my sister-in-law love bites."

He sighed. "Nobody in Urstille would care about something so trivial."

She shrugged. "And when you take her back there, the two of you can do whatever you like, but doing that here will not help with your people's notoriety for taking advantage of our women."

Conora rolled her eyes. "It's so easy for you to judge me when my brother couldn't leave a love bite on you if he tried. You aren't even that pure, Odelia. I saw you enter his room in Iverish, and don't think nobody noticed all the time the two of you spent together during the tour."

Odelia snorted. "If you want the reputation I earned for that, you're more than welcome to it. And I'm not judging you; I'm trying to help you. If you must explore your passions, then for Giver's sake, come to me for a Healing before anyone else sees. You should get to leave home with your head held high, not hearing whispers against your virtue following you behind your back. If I had the chance to do everything over again, I would have been bolder with Kennard and more discreet around everyone else."

The queen's efforts not to condemn them hardly mattered when she admonished them anyway. It gallingly reminded Calosandros of his warnings to Anabusos. He groaned in frustration. "We shouldn't have to hide. She accepted my ribbon."

Conora put a hand on his shoulder. "I know, but like I told you, the publicity of it has put everything in question for now." She looked at Odelia. "Your signature would validate this."

Odelia sighed. "Betrayal is not the answer. I've had my fill of that for a lifetime. I will take your side in speaking to Kennard and urge him to listen to you, but you cannot ask me to sign without him."

"King or not, he can control neither whom I marry nor when." Conora lowered her voice. "And I don't need a treaty to do it."

Calosandros almost jumped at her near-admission. Conora clearly trusted Odelia more than she'd let on before.

Odelia put her hand over Conora's. "So, make him understand that. But before you do, Conora, you need to understand what that will mean for him. Because it's not truly about you." She looked around, then whispered, "You know better than anyone how much is at risk and how many loved ones and family he's already lost."

Conora slowly sank onto a sofa. "I know, but I can't... I'm not a replacement."

Odelia sat in the armchair next to her. "And it's not right or fair to ask you to be, but for all the influence I have with him, I can't force him to see reason through the fear. If you leave and the worst comes to pass..." She put a protective hand over her swollen belly.

"...he'd be completely alone." Conora clasped Odelia's hand in both of hers. "He won't let that happen. He's stronger than that, and he knows it."

Odelia laughed bitterly. "That's what I've been telling him for weeks. He thinks I'm in denial of my own mortality."

"Well, he will have to come to terms with it. I won't be chained by his paranoia."

So, the king was afraid of losing loved ones and counted his sister marrying as part of that? Calosandros sat next to Conora and put a hand on her back. "Maybe His Majesty needs to hear it from both of you together. Remind him how formidable the women around him are."

Then the hall door opened, and the king walked through, pausing halfway with a trapped expression. The queen smiled winsomely and reached out to him.

"I see the three of you are conspiring against me," Kennard half joked, still looking ready to run, before he finished crossing the room.

"Only a little." Odelia pulled him toward her. "These two are anxious to discuss terms."

"I suppose we must." As Kennard sat by her side, he asked hopefully, "Are there new terms on the table?"

"Not exactly," Conora said.

"As it is, my second offer already works greatly in your favor." Calosandros needed to infuse some logic back into the negotiations.

Kennard scoffed. "Making my only sister marry you? Enlighten me as to how that is in my favor."

Conora bristled. "He isn't *making* me do anything!"

Perhaps depending on their sibling bond wasn't Calosandros's best plan. He put a hand on her back to calm her. "Your Majesty, you underestimate what she stands to gain. Never mind that my inheritance would make her an empress one day. If you truly care about her well-being, marriage to me is the best protection she could have. I have no doubt you would miss her dearly, but is this kingdom the safest place for her? You have the Tehazians invading, and even with my help to stop them, the politics here seem...unstable at best."

Kennard took a deep breath and cleared his throat before responding. "It sounds like you're insulting our abilities as rulers."

Calosandros shook his head. "Regardless of your abilities, your coup was only a few months ago, and relations between Elgathan and Vistans aren't ideal either. Even in the short time I've been here, it's obvious that your marriage is an exception; your professed unity is far from a reality." It was a bit of a leap, but just as Iverish had been filled almost exclusively with Vistans, he'd seen suspiciously few of them while walking in the capital city with Conora—a divide that had to be engineered.

The king spat, "And you think you can justify this coercion because you're saving her from our pitiful kingdom?"

"Your own coercion to protect me is no better." Conora stood and jabbed her finger at her brother. "Nor is it any better than what Father did to you. You found your way around it, and I will too if you force me."

Kennard gaped. "You cannot be so desperate to marry him."

"I marry him, or I don't marry at all." Conora shrugged. "I'd rather not be alone."

The king groaned. "Conora, I know you're impulsive, but don't tell me you're foolish enough to believe in love at first sight. You're smarter than that."

"I'm not claiming any such thing, but I do believe this may be the only chance I have, and I'm trusting that love will come with time."

Calosandros had been insisting the same to himself, yet hearing her declare it left a sting in his chest.

The king snapped, "'Love will come with time'? You deserve better than that."

"Perhaps, but we both know that one like yours is as rare as Healing, and either way, the choice of my marriage is mine, not yours. I love you, Kennard, but you're an idiot if you let this alliance fail, especially if you do so because you're trying to hold out for something so unlikely. We cannot win the war without an ally, and I don't want to be here if and when Tehazy marches on Meria. I will gladly follow the prince to Urstille, but I'd rather do so knowing that it helps you as well."

The monarchs exchanged wide-eyed looks.

Good. Maybe a small dose of the truth would wake them up. Calosandros seized the chance to make himself magnanimous in comparison. "I am not so heartless as you seem to think. After speaking with Her Majesty, there is one last concession I am willing to make."

Clearly disbelieving, Kennard smugly waved for him to continue. "By all means."

"Much of your distress is over losing family, but you're about to add to that number soon. If we wait to marry until after the queen has given birth, I'm sure you'll be too occupied as a new father to feel the sting of your sister's absence so keenly."

Calosandros refrained from flinching as Conora clutched his leg. "No," she breathed.

"That's...actually a decent compromise," Kennard finally mused.

"It's a long time from now," Conora said, a note of desperation in her voice.

Why was she complaining? They were getting what they wanted! "There's no need to be dramatic. We can easily wait, what, a month at most?"

"Try five! They've only been married for four months."

Calosandros raised an eyebrow. He really needed to get her to read *Pusosio Sioria* completely. "You do know that wedding dates can have little to no bearing on—"

"For Giver's sake, yes. I'm not that naive, and the subject of their consummation has been discussed more at court than I ever wanted to hear about. But she looks far along because she's carrying triplets. It'll be winter by the time she gives birth."

What? How had he missed that piece of intelligence? His recent marriage had distracted him more than he realized—and the king had pounced on it. Calosandros scowled at Kennard. "You expect me to fight for that long before we marry? The Urstillian Empire needs an heir after me." It was literally the only thing he'd asked Conora for!

"You expect to leave my sister a widow? That doesn't sound like it would benefit her much. Besides, it's not as though you can bring her to the warfront with you, and even the mighty Urstillian army will take some time to crush the Tehazian forces."

"It's a reasonable concern," Odelia oh-so-helpfully added. "Most couples aren't as fertile as we are, and we don't have time to wait for you to secure an heir before Urstille joins our army. Conora will need to procure a dress and make other preparations for a wedding. Waiting until you return makes sense."

"Well, I am a man of my word, and I said I would make the concession," Calosandros said. "If it means we can formalize the agreement, I'm willing to wait." He had what he wanted anyway. What did it matter to wait on a ceremony that Conora might not even want?

"What happens if Conora changes her mind in the meantime?" Kennard asked.

"We can always return to the original offer," Calosandros bluffed. Only a fool would choose that.

"Please, Kennard." Conora squeezed her brother's arm with an adorable puppy-like pout, accentuated by her big brown eyes—it was a look that could wrap Calosandros around her finger if he didn't start being careful.

The king sighed in surrender. "We can have the documents drawn up by dinner."

14

A FOOLISH MISTAKE

Putrios Ginturosa

Conora should have participated in the wedding plans with Calosandros and Odelia—Kennard had fled the room at the first opportunity, of course—but knowing what she ought to do had never been enough to hold her focus. How could she trifle with pomp when other concerns were so loud? She nodded along with whatever was put before her; Conora couldn't care less who performed the ceremony, whose rituals to include, or whom to invite. She was already living as Calosandros's wife, so her purpose for the wedding, protecting her reputation in the eyes of her people and her family, was potentially moot.

But what recourse did she have? She couldn't raise any legitimate objection to the agreement without admitting what she'd done. If only Calosandros had pressed his interest in marrying quickly—he ostensibly had clear political interest in such an outcome and could have spared her honor without question.

Then again, he didn't truly need to press the matter, did he? Fool that she was, Conora had already given him everything he'd asked for. She couldn't regret the outcome for her people, but it had cost her dignity. Even if nobody else found out, she would know that he had played her with as much skill as he did the lyre. He had written the marriage contract, and all he had to do to fulfill his end was finish negotiations to the exact terms he'd asked for. Why would he care if they had a ceremony or not? Her legacy in her homeland meant nothing to him, and he had all the legality he needed for his empire.

And while this storm raged in her head and her heart, Conora had to put on a smile. For all everyone else knew, she'd gotten what she wanted, what she'd asked for, what she'd *begged* for. She smiled and thanked Odelia for her help as Calosandros put Conora's arm through his and rose to leave. She smiled as she walked out the door and down the stairs. She even smiled down the empty hallway to her rooms.

Then she ran.

She vaguely heard Calosandros call her name as she bolted, but she couldn't face him right now. She needed wilderness. She needed the calmness of trees, the simplicity of animals.

Spruce and Cloudy knew what to do. As soon as she entered the bedroom, they trotted toward the garden door with her. They ran outside together, cutting back inside just long enough to exit through the front of the palace, then made for the forest around Meria.

There, Conora could breathe. She could mourn her stupid mistake. She could curl up at the base of a giant red-cedar until the tears stopped flowing and everything in her felt as tiny as her hand against the dozen-foot-wide tree.

Cloudy nosed her other hand, plying her with sloppy dog kisses until she scratched behind his ears. *I here. I help.*

Conora touched her forehead to his. *Thank you.*

Several feet away, Spruce growled. He snarled and barked, *No! Get back! Go away!*

"Shhh... It's okay. It's just me." Calosandros sounded a little out of breath and confused. "Conora...?"

As she turned and saw him, her words caught in her throat.

When he tried to take a step toward her, Spruce lunged and bared his teeth. *No, no, no! Back! Bad man!*

Calosandros swallowed and put his hands up in surrender. "What's wrong with Spruce?"

Still too raw to speak, Conora recalled Spruce with a snap of her fingers and a flick of her wrist. As he reached her, she buried her fingers in the scruff of his neck and held him and Cloudy close. Why couldn't she be left in peace? What more could Calosandros want from her than he'd already taken?

He only took a few steps toward her before eyeing her warily. "No?" He slowly lowered himself to his knees and sat back on his heels.

For a long while, he watched her silently, and Conora could not look up farther than his knees, let alone meet his gaze.

"Is this a habit?" he finally asked.

Her voice small, she eked out, "I needed to be alone." She wiped her cheeks.

"I need to know if this will be a liability. I can appreciate the instinct to hide—Urstillians don't abide crying well—but fleeing the palace without warning is not an option there."

Of course. Her image would matter when it affected *his*.

Conora accidentally communicated her anger to Cloudy and Spruce, who growled at Calosandros.

"Intimidation is effective, though." He sighed. "Are you going to tell me what happened?"

"Why does it matter? You got what you wanted."

"We both did, didn't we? The king and queen signed the alliance."

"I should've known better." Conora sniffled. "You told me from the beginning that all you asked for was an heir. It doesn't matter to you if or when we have a wedding ceremony."

"I'm sorry I misjudged my offer. I shouldn't have made it without all the information, but you can't get upset about every decision I make in my position."

She scoffed at his absolute gall. "I think I have a right to be upset when that decision might ruin my honor!"

"What does your honor have to do with it?"

"Because if I turn out to be pregnant, it will be pretty obvious at our wedding in several months."

He cocked his head and chuckled. "So? Wives usually are at most weddings."

"Not here! It will be an absolute scandal if I'm pregnant before we're married."

"I don't understand. We *are* married."

"Then, what is the point of a wedding?"

He shrugged. "Sometimes spouses who have bonded want to display a pledge of devotion with a wedding ceremony. My own parents never had one. Neither have most at court. You asked about it so insistently, I thought..." He blinked and cleared his throat. "I thought it was what you wanted, but if you prefer, the marriage contract only fulfills our basic obligations."

"What?" Conora squeezed her eyes shut and rubbed her temples. "I know the words you're speaking are Meriverian, but it doesn't *feel* like it."

"I'm trying, Conora, truly, I am. But I can only tell you what I know. If you could meet me halfway, tell me what *you* expect, we might make sense of this." Still crouched, he crept closer to her. In fact, he somehow seemed much closer than when he'd first knelt.

"The distinction confuses me. A wedding marks the beginning of a marriage, which itself is a pledge of devotion. How are you separating them? If we aren't pledging devotion with the marriage contract..." It was nauseating to think about it, but she had to ask, "...what did we sign?"

"Marriage is a practical arrangement, just as I offered from the start, an agreement to create a household together. For royalty like us, that means you bear my heirs in exchange for the comfort, power, and protection that comes with my title. The pledge of devotion works much like you understand it, lifelong sexual and emotional fealty to each other. Without it, couples are only obliged not to produce children with nor spend excessive amounts of money on other partners."

Conora froze in shock. Had her husband just told her that he didn't need to be faithful?

He put a hand on her knee. "I was quick to agree to a wedding because, as I told you, I intend faithfulness either way. I'm sorry if I misled you about our traditions. I didn't realize yours were so different, and the way you spoke of foxes mating for life and the need for a wedding made me think you felt the same as I do."

She took a deep breath. How could she tell if he was being honest or just trying to seduce her all over again?

Abandoning his subtle sneak toward Conora, Calosandros boldly pulled himself up to sit beside her, then slowly asked, "Do you still want to make a pledge of devotion?"

With his body so close to hers, she couldn't lie. "More than anything."

He let out a relieved sigh and wrapped his arms around her, kissing her temple. "That's why you are my dearest."

In this moment, being his dearest was all Conora wanted. She leaned into him, resting her head on his shoulder.

Reaching into his chiton, he asked, "Would these make you more comfortable with the state of things?" When he opened his hand, two rings sparkled from his palm, matching gold bands set with a continuous channel of rubies. Though well-polished, the worn edges told her they were probably heirloom pieces, not something he'd commissioned in Meria. "Now that we don't have to hide as much, I was hoping we could wear them—unless there's another custom I missed?"

She picked up the smaller ring. "My family believes we're engaged, and we wear a ring for that."

"I thought that was the ribbon."

"The ribbon marked us as sweethearts. A ring marks the official betrothal." She slipped it onto the fourth finger on her right hand. "Like this."

He stifled a chuckle. "Dearest, that's where you wear a marriage band."

"No, it isn't. At the wedding, you'll move it to my other hand." She demonstrated, showing the ring off on the left hand.

"Wait. You go through all that trouble with private questions, the ribbon, and the formal engagement, but for the last part, you just move the jewelry?" He laughed. "We will do much better than that."

"What's your tradition?"

He took the ring off her and put it back on her right hand. "To start, this doesn't leave this finger. And these are just plain marriage bands. They've been at my disposal since I was a boy. Our devotion rings will be much nicer, made for us. Yours will go right here." He tapped her finger just above the marriage band.

"And yours?"

He offered the larger ring to her and held out his right hand, fingers splayed. When she put it on his finger, he smiled, then kissed her senseless.

15

DISTANCE

Prabliros

Calosandros had left Meria just two days after the agreement was signed. He led his troops to the northern border, where he quickly developed a routine around his wife's correspondence. The crows she'd trained to deliver their letters were adept at leaving them in the center of his cot every evening in return for the nuts and dried meat he left them. When he opened a letter, he liked to hold one of the sketches he'd done of Conora. Tonight's chosen image was from the morning he'd left Meria, her face serene in sleep, with wild curls cascading around her and a rumpled bedsheet barely covering her soft curves. He'd tried to hastily draw it before she awoke, but she'd caught him, and to his surprise, instead of stopping him, she'd flung back the sheet and offered to pose better. The thought still made him grin like a fool. Those sketches were not for letter time.

Calosandros spun the ruby wedding band on his right hand as he read Conora's latest letter.

> *My Handsome Lover,*
>   *I must thank you for the gift you left with me. It cannot perfectly fill the void you leave, but it helps. (I know you're laughing right now, but I couldn't think of something more appropriate!)*
>   *Spruce and Cloudy look for you at the door and ask when my mate will come back. You've been gone now for longer than you were in my bed, and yet they remember. They don't tell me if they are guarding against you or awaiting your return, and at this point, I'm afraid to ask.*
>   *I think the sentences you sent me to translate are improving my Urstillian. Please*

send more. I can't wait to practice more with you in the flesh. A cunning linguist like you is irreplaceable.

Your Little Vixen

"'*Your little vixen*'?" Anabusos asked over Calosandros's shoulder. "Is she calling you back to her den, foxy boy?"

Calosandros shoved him. "If you could read it, then she's improving, which means *my little vixen* will soon be able to outfox you in your native tongue."

Anabusos rolled his eyes. "It's one phrase."

"Like I said, soon she'll outfox you."

He whistled low. "Well, if I encounter her looking like that, you're probably right."

"You won't." Calosandros placed the sketch face down on his cot. "What are you doing in my tent right now anyway?"

Anabusos held up a stack of papers. "Reports."

Calosandros motioned for him to set them on a folding table.

Anabusos shook his head and laughed. "No need to be so jealous. You're the one she's agreed to bear children for."

"She means more than that."

"Great Giver, I *know*. Has marrying a Meriverian turned you into one? You used to take a damn joke."

"I just don't want you—or anyone else—to be in the habit of making that kind of joke when she returns with us to Urstille. It will be a big change for her, and she likely won't know enough context, language, or custom to know when it's a joke."

Anabusos sighed. "You cannot shield her from everyone. And, if we're being honest, we both know how earnest the inquiries to her bed will be. Don't tell me your pride has fallen so far that you can't stand a little competition. The court knows to play carefully with a consort."

"It's not a matter of my pride. It's a matter of vows. She is not a toy for the court."

One eyebrow raised, Anabusos leaned back on one hip and crossed his arms. "What vows?"

Calosandros clasped his hands together. He'd avoided the subject, but this was as good a time as any to ask. "Well...about that... I have a favor to ask of you. I need someone to perform the Urstillian rites for my w—"

"Fuuuck." Anabusos ran his hands down his face and groaned. "You really have lost it, my friend. I can believe that you'd marry her as part of negotiations, but a *wedding*?" He paced as he continued ranting, "That has no political or economic purpose. It's purely lovesick shit. And why rush into this? You barely know her. What if she can't give you an heir—unless you're doing this because you somehow conceived already—in which case, ignore everything I just said, and congratulations."

"Are you finished?" Calosandros asked.

"Fuck," Anabusos muttered, paused for a moment, then said, "Now I'm finished."

"We don't know whether she's pregnant, but it's what we both want. The connection we made in just a few days is incomparable. I've never been good at sharing my lovers, and the look on her face when I explained the common marriage arrangement—it would be her worst nightmare."

Anabusos stared at him. "You're serious. You've fallen madly in love with her."

Calosandros's cheeks flamed. "I wouldn't call it that."

"Shit. What are we going to do with you?" Anabusos shook his head with a pitying frown. "It's just like—" His eyes grew wide. "'Your little vixen' doesn't have anything to do with that fox story you told her, does it?"

Calosandros couldn't help but smile as he shrugged. "It suits the princess. It's a happy memory."

"And *I* remember the way you snapped when the fox was gone."

"What do you mean, I 'snapped'? It was sad that she ran off, but she had to. She was a wild animal."

"That. The way you rewrote what happened in your head, I don't think you could handle the truth of what happened when we were boys."

Calosandros didn't like the rising chill in his spine. "What are you talking about?"

Anabusos put a hand on his shoulder. "When that vixen disappeared, the emperor had a new fox-fur mantle made."

It had to be one of Anabusos's sick jokes. Calosandros slapped his hand away. "Just because you would rather get invited to our bed than our wedding doesn't mean you can take your envy out on our relationship. I trust you like a brother, and you repay me by lying to poison a story that means something to us?"

Anabusos glared, his eyes watering. "And I didn't think you were enough of an asshole to throw that in my face. I'm not stupid, Calosandros.

I gave up any genuine hope with you years ago when you made your orientation clear. I'm trying to save you from yourself before history repeats, because I can't bear to watch you fall apart *again* when the emperor sees how sentimental you've gotten *again*, and this inevitably falls to shit *again*."

Without any show of deference or another word, Anabusos stormed out of the tent, leaving Calosandros alone to sort out what truth there might be—if any—to the cruelty.

16

HEARTACHE

Cianos Sorosa

Thirty tally marks. It had to be too many, but Conora had only made one each morning since Calosandros left. And her sheets were still clean today. She couldn't keep putting off the obvious and inevitable.

Should she ask Odelia to confirm by checking her Vitality? Kennard was just as capable of the task, but asking him was out of the question. On the other hand, Conora had outright lied to Odelia when she'd stumbled across *Pusosio Sioria*, telling her she'd never tried anything in the book and only had it as a preparatory read. At least Odelia had never found Calosandros's other gift. Conora briefly contemplated using it to calm her nerves, but Raina would be arriving with breakfast soon.

After that would be a dress fitting with Hortensia. Conora's clean sheets meant there was probably no point, but how could she cancel? The only dresses Hortensia had made in months were for Odelia since the Queen Mother had no need to work anymore. It was generosity of spirit and enjoyment of being the finest seamstress in the kingdom that kept the sweet woman sewing at all. Conora was grateful to get one last dress from her and couldn't stand the thought of snubbing Hortensia.

And yet, despite the headache it was causing her, Conora longed to write to Calosandros and tell him he would have an heir. He was so patient and tender with her, it wasn't hard to imagine his brawny arms cradling a baby as he softly sang lullabies.

Feeling a slight twinge of a cramp on her right side, Conora decided to draw her bath herself instead of waiting for Raina. Though the bath was relaxing at first, the cramp came back with a vengeance, so Conora hurried to finish cleaning herself, thankful that she didn't need to wash her hair this time. As she patted herself with a towel, the moisture on her thighs didn't seem to want to dry.

When she looked down, there was no mistaking the large red stain on the towel.

She ran to the toilet and closed the door behind her, shaking as she sat, a silent sob slowly creeping up from her middle. Surely, Conora was losing her mind. This was a relief. She wouldn't have to confess her elopement or hide a growing belly.

And yet.

Her chest hurt; her heart physically ached. There would be no news of an heir to write to Calosandros, no person to remind her of him if he didn't return, no living proof of his touch on her skin.

"Your Highness?" Raina called outside the door. "Are you all right?"

Conora wiped her tears and nose with a clean section of the towel and tried to keep her voice level as she replied, "Yes, it's just a heavy flow."

"Did you want a warm compress?"

Conora sighed. "Yes, thank you."

As Raina's footsteps retreated, Conora chided herself for being so ridiculous: this was just her monthly cycle, Calosandros's time in her bed had been a brief affair, and crying would only bring her trouble. If only those thoughts would stop the aching hole in her chest.

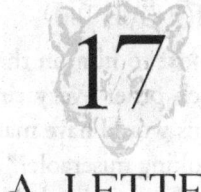

17
A LETTER
Oirayos

Each letter from Conora, Calosandros's anticipation grew. Without word of her cycle, it was becoming more likely that her predictions of pregnancy were accurate. It could cause problems with the Meriverian court, but in Urstille, they would be lauded as soon as he brought her home. Before Conora, Calosandros had always used at least two methods at a time—sometimes three—to avoid creating children, and now the potential was driving him to distraction. Just the night before, he'd been doodling while in a meeting and found himself drawing what she might look like while carrying his child. If he were with her, he could do something productive with these urges, but he had to press them down and do the job he'd been sent to do.

When Calosandros spied a crow flying into his tent after dinner, he nearly ran to retrieve the letter it left behind.

> *My Handsome Lover,*
> *   Our wedding will go forward as planned*
> *without any further impediments.*
> *   Your Little Vixen*

The air left Calosandros's lungs as if he'd been punched in the gut. Her earlier worry had made him believe this outcome would make her happy, but she'd never sent him a letter so short, and the brevity spoke of so much pain. She had always made a few quips, tried to translate some Urstillian.

"I'm so sorry, Conora," he whispered.

He looked up to see Anabusos staring at him with a look of confused concern, holding a stack of reports. "Is everything okay?"

Calosandros blinked and cleared his throat. "Thank you, Anabusos, but you were right. It's not right for me to depend on you on matters like this."

Anabusos sighed and sat next to him on the cot, resting a hand on his shoulder. "If we abandoned each other every time one of us acted like an asshole, I don't think either of us would have made it past twenty. What did your wife write that has you looking miserable?"

Calosandros explained all the meaning he'd gleaned from the letter. "I didn't have high expectations from our short time together, but I feel guilty that it distresses her."

"Then tell her that. It would do you both good to place less gravity on this relationship." Anabusos put a hand up. "And before you get upset, I don't intend to come between you—physically or emotionally. But you need to guard your hearts better before we return to Urstille. If you don't, this little vixen of yours won't survive the court much better than the four-legged one."

18

PAID

Icgrar

Shivering, Calosandros pulled his bearskin coat closed. The addition of a long shirt and thick leggings to his chiton and replacing his sandals with tall boots were not enough to keep the chill out. It would be colder in Urstille, where the snow was probably already blanketing everything by now, but something about this constant just-above-freezing drizzle seeped into his bones. He'd had no idea there were so many ways it could rain. It was rarely the recognizable shower he knew. It sprinkled, it drizzled, and it spat—different things, the Meriverians assured him. But the worst was when it misted—how the fuck did it rain *sideways*? His hair, his clothes, his tent, his supplies—everything had been damp for months. It was a wonder he hadn't started sprouting moss.

Anabusos had done an admirable job channeling their army's disgust with the weather into fighting fury. He'd promised that the sooner they thrashed the Tehazians, the sooner everyone could leave the Giver-forsaken rain behind and get back to their dry homes. And the army had run with that promise, driving back the enemy with a ferocity that Tehazy had never seen before. Some of the Tehazians even screamed about demon warriors as they fled the field.

Superior tactics, equipment, and training didn't hurt either. Neither the Tehazians nor the Meriverians wore spiked soles. Both lacked sufficient weapon variety to account for what should have been more tailored fighting styles. It was stupid to equip and train the Fire users the same as the Speeders, and the Meriverians wasted the range of heights between their Elgathan and Vistan men. Of course, only arming half their population was an oversight as well. Compared to the Urstillians, the local soldiers were basically untrained, experienced only in the hardships of recent battle.

Rather than spending precious time bringing Meriverians up to acceptable standards, Calosandros directed Urstille to press the similar weaknesses in Tehazy. The most fatal flaw to exploit was the very thing that had made Tehazy such a danger to Meriveria: their opportunism. Tehazians couldn't resist a perceived opening or vulnerability, and Urstille had no shortage of trap maneuvers.

In a matter of just four months, they'd driven them back so effectively that Calosandros and his army were now several miles north of the border into Tehazy. Only the stubbornness of their King Zamuk kept the fight going for so long.

But even stubborn kings have a breaking point, and Zamuk reached his. Over ten miles from the Meriverian Fort Gale, after a particularly fast rout, the Tehazian general Lord Jibiam flew the white flag.

Five days later, Calosandros was on a boat in the middle of Carum Sound to turn that truce into an armistice. The trip out there was more terrifying than he could ever let anyone know. A storm had rolled in, and Grandigeneral Wermer, Kennard's appointed leader of the Meriverian army, insisted it was mild. But Calosandros could swear it felt like the thrashing frigid waves would drown them all before they could board the ship owned by their neutral arbiter, Queen Barbenia of Uskev.

Calosandros followed Grandigeneral Wermer into the ship's cabin, grateful to finally be somewhere relatively dry. It seemed Calosandros and Wermer were just in time. Kennard was looking ready to brawl as he conversed with Lord Jibiam and King Zamuk.

Determined not to let this situation escalate and keep him from his wife any longer, Calosandros smiled and put a hand on Kennard's shoulder as if he were Anabusos. "Hail, Brother!" he said, motioning with his eyes toward the Tehazians to signal, *Play along.*

For once, the king responded favorably, going as far as patting Calosandros on the back.

"I apologize for the delay," Calosandros said. "The first boat sprang a leak, and by the time they replaced it, they were fighting a stronger wind to get out here."

"Our ride wasn't much smoother," Kennard admitted, "so you haven't missed much."

"How is my sweetheart?" Calosandros asked, thanking the Giver he hadn't accidentally slipped and called her his wife as he'd become used to with Anabusos.

"The princess is well, though I've never seen her spend so much time reading."

Calosandros laughed heartily. "I'd hoped so. Urstillian literature is quite engaging."

The king looked more confused than angry at the reference, so Conora must have maintained her façade of sexual innocence.

It was risky to inquire further, but Calosandros had to know where he stood with the king. "I trust nothing has changed, then?"

Kennard forced a smile and said, "Indeed, nothing has changed." The tinge of annoyance in his eyes confirmed that that included his attitude about the arrangement.

Despite the king's poor acting, it worked on the Tehazians, who looked at each other nervously. The continuance of this alliance would amplify their defeat.

But before either side could say more, a woman with midnight hair entered the cabin, holding the arm of a blond man. The room instantly fell silent and darkened as sailors drew shades over the windows. The woman removed the dark gray veil that covered the top half of her face—the hallmark of someone with Night Sight—revealing a hairline scar down the side of her nose.

She bobbed her head to Calosandros. "I am Queen Barbenia of Uskev, and this is my fiancé, Prince Elio of Boscada. Am I to presume you are Crown Prince Calosandros of Urstille?"

Prince Elio looked ready to speak when Calosandros nodded. "Yes, Your Majesty. It is an honor to meet you."

Under his breath, Elio muttered, "Never mind," then smiled and bowed to Calosandros.

Barbenia turned to Zamuk and introduced herself again. This time, Lord Jibiam repeated it, using the same method Calosandros did of eliciting a response before translating—the general was a fellow Speaker.

Lastly, Barbenia addressed Kennard, speaking with a heavy accent. "It is good to see you, Your Majesty. Dare I ask about your beloved? I confess I do not remember how much time she had left."

Between her concerned frown and what sounded to be a second or third tongue of Meriverian, the neutral arbiter seemed a little less than neutral. That could obviously work in their favor.

Kennard replied, "A month. She should be resting, but she's having trouble staying put."

Barbenia smiled. "Of course. We queens have things to do."

"You certainly do."

"I'll try to keep things simple so we don't waste what precious time she has," Barbenia said quietly.

Shit. She definitely wasn't neutral. If she didn't stop making it clear before the Tehazians noticed, negotiations would be screwed.

Barbenia addressed the room, still accented: "My main purpose here is as a witness to these negotiations. However, should you fail to come to reasonable terms, you have all authorized me to decide on a fair outcome. According to the documents I was sent, Meriveria seeks recompense for Tehazian raids on their lands, Urstille stands in support of the Meriverian cause, and Tehazy asks that the border between Urstille and Meriveria be reclosed. Have I interpreted your requests correctly?"

Calosandros and Kennard both answered yes, and after a few moments of translation between Jibiam and his king, Zamuk nodded.

"Are there any objections to Tehazy recompensing Meriveria?" Barbenia asked.

"Yes," Lord Jibiam said. "Casualties are part of war. If we must pay Meriveria, surely, Urstille should pay us for the territory they have recently taken."

"Urstille's conquests were part of an official alliance in pursuit of a formal war," Kennard countered with more maturity and kingly authority than Calosandros had thought him capable of before. "The raids we seek recompense for were unprovoked and forced us into declaring this war."

"As you say, they were preludes to war." Jibiam shrugged. "If raids concern you, maybe you shouldn't have such vulnerable towns."

It was the same obvious reasoning Calosandros had already surmised, but his brother-in-law had no appreciation for its simplicity. Fists clenched, Kennard took deep breaths. At least he was trying not to give in to his rage this time.

Barbenia put up a hand. "Though not conventional, Meriveria's demand is neither unreasonable nor unheard of. It may stay on the table for now. What of Tehazy's demand for a closed border?"

Not wanting to give Kennard a chance to say something stupid in anger and cut Conora off from her family, Calosandros jumped in. "It cannot be done. Meriveria and Urstille have obligations to each other that require open borders between our kingdoms as well as personal ties that would be severed." He said directly to Kennard, "It would be a waste to throw away the long-awaited peace between us for one with a kingdom that's already proven itself untrustworthy."

Kennard shook his head and sneered at Jibiam and Zamuk. "What kind of spiteful demand is this? Is peace so appalling to Tehazy that you must destroy the alliance we have cultivated with Urstille to stomach the existence of a new treaty?"

"Any Urstillian presence west of the mountains threatens all of Carum Sound," Jibiam said. "Just as we used the bridge to enter Meriveria, Urstille will use your alliance to take over all of our kingdoms. Your cowardly attempt to save your own hide has doomed us all."

Shit. He'd correctly assessed the emperor's goal. Of course, Calosandros had been doing his best to thwart that, but if everyone got the idea in their heads, it could destroy the rest of negotiations—and everything else he'd worked for. He crossed his arms and glowered at Jibiam, willing him to shut up.

Zamuk eyed the other royals, then asked Jibiam to repeat himself in Tehazian. The general recalled what they'd said, most of it verbatim.

Zamuk scowled. "You idiot. You don't open negotiations by calling the other party a coward! You have to work up to that kind of thing. And taunting the demon warriors? Have you completely lost your..."

"What are they talking about?" Kennard whispered to Calosandros.

"Lord Jibiam was just translating the conversation so far, but King Zamuk is rebuking him for calling you a coward and for inviting the wrath of Urstille."

"Good."

Zamuk continued, "...have to tread more carefully to block Urstille. We have to convince Queen Barbenia that we're the reasonable ones and let Urstille look dangerous. Then *she* will want to close the border."

Calosandros couldn't let that happen to Conora. He pursed his lips. "Hmmm."

"What now?" Kennard asked.

"He wants to stand by the request to close our borders."

Kennard huffed. "Forget that. I'd rather we continue to beat Tehazy back to their capital than accept peace on those terms."

"Agreed. Are you willing to pay for it?" As much as Calosandros himself would do it for free, the emperor would never.

"What are you asking for?"

How little could he ask for without crossing the emperor? "Spoils of war, the whole bounty of whatever comes out of Tehazy going forward."

Kennard immediately offered his hand to Calosandros, and both men quickly shook and nodded.

Zamuk's eyes widened, and he hissed to Jibiam, "Did you see that? Do something about it!"

Jibiam gave Barbenia a pleading look.

"Yes, Lord Jibiam?" she asked.

"Even now, Meriveria and Urstille are colluding against us!"

Kennard scoffed and sardonically said, "It's called an alliance—I understand that might be a foreign concept for Tehazy."

Barbenia and Elio covered their mouths and shared a glance.

"It's a danger to the rest of us," Jibiam said, "and Tehazy will not stand for it."

Once again serious, Kennard said, "Because it means you cannot take whatever you want from us without consequence."

"Enough," Barbenia said firmly. "You have both made your point. Prince Calosandros, Urstille had nothing in the initial request. Do you wish to change that after hearing the others?"

Oh, did he. Calosandros nodded. "Though Tehazy started this war, I don't believe they grasp that they are no longer in control of it. Meriveria is not your territory to exploit, and this meeting is meant to be a formality. You have only seen a piece of the Urstillian army. If Tehazy will agree to Meriveria's terms and cease all hostilities, Urstille will be a friendly neighbor to the kingdoms of Carum Sound. However, if you do not, or if you take up arms against Meriveria again..." As he'd seen the emperor do so many times, Calosandros took a step forward, deepening his voice and staring down the Tehazians. "Urstille will bring in enough forces to bring your entire kingdom to its knees. You will become nothing but another state in our Empire."

"Translation?" Zamuk asked Jibiam.

This was Calosandros's chance. If the emperor were here to see it, perhaps he would take more pride in Calosandros's Gift. Sure that he would now be speaking Tehazian, he repeated his threat, throwing behind it a weighty subtext: *I am the son of the emperor. I will be emperor. I will be obeyed.*

Zamuk blanched, muttering, "Yes, Your Imperial Highness."

Prince Elio, who had been quiet for so long, had clearly understood more than Kennard or Barbenia did. He pulled out a document and began writing furiously.

"What's happening?" Barbenia asked without an accent.

Elio sighed. "I *was* starting to draft in Tehazian what terms Urstille just set. Please, let me get it down before I forget or somebody else starts speaking another language again."

Another Speaker? Three of them in the same room. Calosandros nearly laughed. Maybe Conora was correct about it being more common on this side of the mountains.

It took Elio a long while to finish writing the treaty in four languages—Meriverian, Tehazian, Urstillian, and Uskevi—a tedious and thankless task Calosandros had done too many times himself. Kennard was restless, pacing a corner of the cabin as they waited. As a Speaker, Calosandros wanted to throttle Kennard on Elio's behalf, but as someone who also had a wife waiting back at the Cedar Palace, the impatience was contagious.

Both kings, their generals, and Calosandros had to sign all versions of the document, as did Barbenia and Elio as witnesses.

Kennard went straight to Calosandros as soon as they were both done. "Are you coming back with me?"

"Someone should stay until the Tehazians leave, and I'll need to speak to my people. Tell Princess Conora to expect me later tonight." As they left the cabin, Calosandros looked at the setting sun. Anabusos and the main army would be fighting the storm to set their camp and likely slowed by it too. Calosandros might not even get to sleep that night if it took too long to reach camp. "Make that the morning. It'll be inappropriately late by the time I'm done."

"Tomorrow then." Ken gave him a firm pat on the shoulder.

Camp was only a mile north of where it was supposed to be; the effects of the windstorm on land were a mild annoyance, nothing like the frothing waves Calosandros had seen on the water. Though he wanted to leave as soon as he'd settled plans, Anabusos convinced him to rest for a few hours and freshen himself up before heading to Meria. But between the cold wind and thoughts of Conora, Calosandros's rest was anything but restful, so he left before sunrise.

He contemplated sneaking into Conora's bed so he could surprise her when she woke up, but he wasn't awake enough for stealth and would probably get himself caught by the guards instead. And his sleep-deprived mind took an embarrassingly long time to realize that the idea was more likely to frighten her. Better not to try to be clever and just have a simple happy reunion.

When he reached the Cedar Palace, it was daylight—or as much daylight as it could be behind a layer of clouds—and the place was in a state of upheaval, more so than the usual morning rush of servants. He should've expected as much with the treaty to celebrate. After a few minutes of helplessly watching, he finally spotted a Speed messenger who wasn't rushing on to other duties.

"Please take a message to Princess Conora. Let her know I'm here and to meet me in her sitting room—if she's awake already, of course."

The messenger bowed, but when he ran off, instead of heading for the courtyard garden or one of the halls to Conora's room, he headed for a stairwell. Odd. In any case, Calosandros headed where he'd said he'd meet her. By the time he reached the sitting room, the messenger was standing outside.

He bowed again, his expression somber now. "She says she'll be here soon."

Calosandros let himself inside the sitting room, not even trying to stop the giddy grin that was taking over him as he greeted Cloudy and Spruce with lots of scritches. He bounced on his heels in the center of the room. How could he sit down now?

When the door slowly opened, there was his Conora in the flesh, her dark curls haloed in the soft morning light. "My little vixen!" He pulled her close, her body so soft against his, then caressed her cheek as he said, "I've come to take you home."

At the word "home," Conora sobbed.

Concerned, Calosandros took a step back. "That was not the welcome I expected. Did I say something wrong, or is this the custom here?"

As she wiped her cheeks, her warm brown eyes filled with more tears. "So many things have just happened, and it's all too much."

He had to help, fix whatever had gone awry. "Was my arrival one of those things?"

Biting her lip, she shook her head. And that's when he saw it in her eyes, a look he'd seen before, and it broke him. It was loss, grief, the look he'd seen on his soldiers after they'd watched friends fall. She wasn't supposed to experience it here.

Not knowing what else to do for her, he wrapped his arms around her and gently pressed her head to his shoulder.

She clung to him. "I'm sorry. I know Urstillians don't abide crying."

"Only in public. There is no shame in vulnerability with our true intimates."

"Like spouses?" she asked.

Calosandros was momentarily at a loss. Did she not already see them as intimates? "Sometimes...if they are so lucky. Such emotions are only shown to our closest friends and lovers. There must be a bond of trust."

She sobbed harder.

Words were only hurting her more. What could he do? He held her tighter, slowly stroking her back as she collapsed in his embrace and wept. She was crying herself into exhaustion. Should he carry her to bed?

Before he could decide, a Speeder in a guard uniform appeared in the doorway. It was a familiar face, possibly one of the king's personal bodyguards. The guard looked as tired as Conora, his eyes rimmed red. He leaned on the doorframe and wiped his brow, leaving a red smudge.

What the hell had happened in the palace?

"They need Her Highness," the guard said.

Conora was too lost in her breakdown to notice.

Calosandros pressed his cheek to Conora's until she pressed back, then whispered, "There's a message for you."

Conora sniffled. "What?"

He gently turned her around to face the guard, who said, "They're asking for you, Your Highness."

"Who?"

"Their Majesties."

Conora's knees buckled as she gasped, but Calosandros kept his hold on her. "They woke up?" she breathed.

The guard nodded. "They asked for you when we told them you named Elliana."

"Lies. She named herself." She laughed through the tears. "And I'm glad my brother survived because now I can kill him for abandoning her—that stupid self-sacrificing moose's ass."

Surprisingly, the guard laughed at her outburst and wiped his eyes. He cleared his throat. "I'll tell them you need to sleep first. But I thought you deserved to know sooner than later."

Conora nodded. "Thank you, Herman."

Then Herman was gone.

Calosandros checked that Conora was standing on her own, then closed and locked the door. Whatever insanity had taken over the palace, it needed to be kept away for a while. Standing farther away from her, he could finally see what a mess she was—still breathtakingly beautiful but objectively messy—her hair frizzed, her dress wrinkled and stained with what looked to be bodily fluids, and a sheen of sweat on her forehead.

He picked up one of her hands with both of his. "Dearest, what happened?"

She laughed bitterly. "Where do I even start?"

19

LIFE AND DEATH

Idos mio Icoilur

Calosandros tugged on her hand and slowly pulled her along to the bedroom. "Why don't we bathe you? And you can take your time to tell me from the beginning."

Conora giggled tiredly. "If you want to make love, you don't have to use any pretense to get my clothes off." She smiled slyly and started unbuttoning her dress with her free hand. Then her fingers dragged through one of the stains, so she examined it and gagged. "Oh, Giver, that's disgusting! You're right about the bath."

"Dare I ask?"

She shuddered. "Just help me draw the bath quickly. I'm not waiting for Raina."

He started the water while she grabbed flint and lit the heater. It wouldn't be as warm as asking a servant with Fire to heat the water directly, but it was convenient to have the option to do it themselves.

"What does 'make love' mean?" he asked, curiosity getting the better of his pride.

She chuckled. "What?"

"I mean, obviously, I understand the direct words, but I haven't heard them put together that way before. It's a little strange. Another euphemism?"

Conora eyed him suspiciously as she undressed. "Yes, and I think you've shown you know very well what it means."

Calosandros scrunched his face, confused, and undressed as well. "How? I can't make you love me. I don't want to make you do anything."

She stepped into the barely filled tub. "Not that kind of 'make.' It's about creation, not force." She crooked her finger at him, and when he stepped in, she continued, "It's what you and I create together, our connection, our passion."

127

He smiled as the idea took hold. "You're referring to the emotions of—I want *you* to say it." If he could contemplate emotions with her, she could say something crude.

She blushed adorably, as he'd hoped she would. "Fucking?" she squeaked.

He laughed. "Oh, I missed you." He kissed her soundly, the way he'd wanted to for months. The way she melted into him drove him wild. He never wanted to let her go again.

As they broke the kiss, she staggered, her eyes half-lidded. "I wish my body could keep up with my desire right now."

"We can make up for it later." He touched his forehead to hers. "I'm sorry. I distracted you. You were telling me why you're so tired and grimy."

"It started with my father." Her bottom lip quivered, and she dropped eye contact.

"He didn't escape, did he?" That would be truly terrifying.

Conora shook her head. "He was murdered...stabbed in his cell."

Not wanting to further her upset, Calosandros tried to hide his shock. "Do they know who did it?"

"No. That's where things turn stranger. When the guards found him, he was calling for Odelia, and the blade was one of her throwing knives."

Calosandros started. "The queen throws knives? I thought women here couldn't fight."

"Odelia isn't good at doing as she's told. Anyway, the idiot guard captain woke her from a nap to arrest her for it." Conora fumed. "She's the queen! He broke her door down, had her ripped from her bed... Even if she were a commoner, you don't handle a bedridden woman that way. I still can't believe he actually thought she was physically capable of carrying it out. She was too weak to harm him up close, and—you've been to his cell—there isn't enough room in the hallway for her to throw."

Calosandros let go of Conora to turn the water off and pick up the soap.

"Not to mention, why? If she'd truly wanted to kill my father, she had every right to take his head for his crimes against her. Why would she spare his life if she wanted to murder him? The incompetence, it just—" Conora wiped away fresh angry tears. "How can I feel safe here?"

Sinking into the water, Calosandros pulled Conora down onto his lap and cradled her close. "I will keep you safe. We can petition your brother to let you come home with me as soon as possible." He began to lather her wild curls and silky skin.

"We won't need to. You wanted to know what was on my dress?" She scoffed another bitter laugh. "As if the murder and arrest weren't enough, the ordeal put Odelia into labor." Conora sniffled. "She shouldn't have been alone, but Hortensia and I were working on my dress, and we didn't hear anything about it until Kennard came home and started looking for her."

Calosandros stroked her cheek. "You couldn't have known."

Conora shook her head. "I call her my sister, but she was alone in that cell for seven hours because I never thought to check on her when I thought she was stuck in her bed."

"But you did help her when you found out?" he asked as he dipped Conora backward to rinse her hair.

She nodded, her long hair dripping over both of them. "Hortensia and I held her upright until almost dawn. We felt her struggle and weaken. And Kennard spent so much of his Healing on their babies—they're so tiny—he tried to hide it, but we could all see there was nothing left in him when she collapsed. I don't know how she even delivered the last one."

"Was that why you were talking about self-sacrificing?"

"Healers who have no power left to give, they use their own lives. He just passed his newborn daughter to me and threw himself to Odelia without a second thought. He risked orphaning those girls to *maybe* revive her." Conora's whole body tensed.

"Ah." Calosandros massaged her shoulders with the soap until she relaxed. "So, Elliana is one of their babies?"

"She's the youngest—Azalia, then Valerzana, then Elliana. Oh, she's absolutely beautiful," Conora squealed, "and I think she'll be the smartest one."

He laughed. "How do you know that? Weren't they just born this morning?"

Conora straightened and turned to him, her whole face alit with excitement. "She told me her name. I didn't even know she could do that!"

Head cocked, he raised one eyebrow as he quickly scrubbed himself. "Are you sure it's not just the exhaustion? Babies don't have a language."

"Not a language per se, no. But they express their wants and needs much like animals do. It's very rudimentary. That's why it was so surprising to get a name. My youngest niece is going to have a powerful wit; you'll see."

He briefly slid underwater, then sat back up. "And the guard—what's his name? Herman?—he said the king and queen survived, that they woke up?"

"Yes, thank the Giver. You arrived after Kennard kissed Odelia, and nobody knew if they were alive or not yet. They were so still, we couldn't even tell if they were breathing." Conora shuddered again.

Calosandros splashed warm water on her and rubbed her arms. "But it's over now. They woke up, and you'll be safe with me." The sentiment probably wouldn't stop the image from haunting her, but he had to try. He grabbed towels for them. "After all that, I think the bed will be the best thing. The question is whether you need sleep or distraction more?"

She leaned on him as he wrapped them in towels. "Could you distract me to sleep?"

He kissed her forehead. "Of course, dearest."

Calosandros and Conora woke the same way they'd fallen asleep, wrapped in each other's arms, her head on his chest. He softly brushed his fingertips along her arm and kissed the top of her head, deeply inhaling the soft scent of gardenia and cedar in her hair. The aroma of elegance tempered with wilderness, it suited her perfectly. He would have to make sure she brought plenty of her usual soaps and perfumes when she packed for Urstille.

She kissed his chest and snuggled tighter, pressing her pelvis against his hip and stirring his already ravenous lust. When he clasped her ass, she grabbed his shoulder and pulled herself up face-to-face with him. Then her mouth was on his, his tongue deep inside, his hand full of her hair as he clutched her closer. Giver, he'd missed this passion between them.

When Calosandros couldn't bear it anymore, he pressed harder and rolled her over, pinning her under him. Though he worried it might have been too much, the wild sensual yearning in her eyes drove him on. He put his hand between her legs; Giver, she was almost wet already. He teased her with his fingers, kissing and nipping all over her delicious curves, up to her neck and back again, until she arched her back and moaned.

He needed Conora. Now.

He leaped off the bed and grabbed her legs. She spread wider, but that wasn't his aim. He yanked her across the sheets, sliding her on her back until her ass was on the edge. She gripped the bed, bracing, to offer her body to him.

So, he took her. Hard and fast he pounded, propelled by four months of pent-up craving that only she could satisfy. It was the obsession that had pervaded his dreams, an urge more primal than he'd ever known. The desperate need to join with her was as essential as water to life.

Nothing stifled her cries of pleasure, and each one pushed him further toward climax. He grunted and gripped her legs. His last push drew from her a guttural moan that racked her whole body, holding him fast inside and drawing every last drop from him.

Panting, he moved her legs aside to collapse next to her.

She slowly rolled over and curled against him, nuzzling his neck. "I think my practice with your present paid off."

"Yes, it did." Calosandros clasped her ass with an audible slap. "Fuck, I've never come so good."

Conora giggled. "Ah, delicate as always."

"I would say I'd leave that up to you, but that grip of yours is anything but delicate."

They both dissolved into heady, giddy laughter, basking in the glow of each other's presence.

He sighed and kissed her forehead. "You've left me famished. I wonder if Raina might have left lunch in your sitting room."

Calosandros hopped up and swaggered to the door, flexing a bit to show off in case Conora was still watching him. In the sitting room, he glanced at the table, disappointed to discover it empty.

"Well, well. You must be Prince Calosandros," a sultry but mature voice said.

Startled, he pivoted on his toes, hands up in defensive posture. "Who the fuck are you? How did you get in here?" He could've sworn he'd locked the door.

A gorgeous woman of regal bearing perched in one of Conora's chairs, her hands elegantly draped over her knees. She reminded him somewhat of Conora, though her features were starker: her hair a shade darker where grays did not peek through, her skin a paler bronze, her nose and cheeks sharper. Only her eyes broke the trend, being a more muted hazel instead of Conora's rich brown.

She pursed her lips. "We can work on your manners..." Looking down, she smirked and raised a key aloft. "...big boy. And I go where I please."

In spite of himself, Calosandros despaired at offending her. A flicker of a memory from his first night with Conora screamed in his mind, *She has Allure.* The way Spruce glared at the woman from across the room, his hackles raised, hinted at her true nature.

"And you must be Conora's mother?" Before Calosandros could stop himself, he added, "She never told me all her beauty comes from you."

Her mother smiled and held out her hand, palm-down. "Queen Melaine."

"That is *Lady* Melaine!" Conora came barreling through the door, a bedsheet wrapped haphazardly around her.

Calosandros bit back a smile at the silliness of it. How long until Conora stopped being so bashful about her body? It was such a beautiful one to hide.

Conora put a hand on her hip and cocked her head at Melaine. "She always seems to forget she was stripped of her regal title. If you're so concerned about manners, you should be curtsying to Prince Calosandros."

Melaine ignored her, examining Calosandros as if he were a portrait on display. She slowly smiled. "I heard he was handsome, but I must say, well done, Conora. At least one of my children can use her wits and follow instructions."

Conora stepped between Calosandros and Melaine. "Please, leave him alone. He's a good man."

"If you're referring to his prowess in bed, I know. I heard you."

Conora softly gasped and backed into Calosandros, who caught her arms to steady her.

Melaine waved a hand and rolled her eyes. "If you're worried about me revealing your arrangement to your brother, don't be. Winning his favor is a lost cause, and after yesterday, returning to the previous order of things is no longer possible."

Calosandros said, "My condolences for the loss of your husband, Lady Melaine. This must be a difficult time for you."

Melaine quirked an eyebrow. "I suppose?" She shrugged and continued with Conora, "It's in my best interest for this to continue unimpeded." She gestured at the pair of them. "A change of scenery suits me. Besides, how could I let my favorite child go off to a foreign land all alone?"

Conora wrapped her arms around herself to anxiously grasp Calosandros's hands. "What *exactly* do you know, Mother, and how did you find out? You only arrived this morning."

Calosandros was having trouble appreciating Conora's reaction to the delightful Melaine, but he nonetheless wanted to soothe his wife, so he slid his arms around her waist to snugly envelop her. "Relax, my little vixen," he whispered, "she's on our side."

"She's on her own side," Conora muttered.

Melaine laughed. "I never have trouble finding out what I want to know. Once she knew I wanted to help you, I found your servant quite accommodating. From what she told me, you played your hand with exquisite efficiency." She leaned forward with a conspiratorial smirk. "That contract? I wish I had thought of it." She shot Calosandros an inquisitive look. "And it *is* legally binding in Urstille, isn't it?"

He nodded. "As binding as any other marriage contract."

"Surely, Urstille allows retinues for its consorts?" Melaine suggested.

Conora fidgeted. "We haven't talked about it yet, but—"

"Of course," Calosandros said. "Conora will have courtiers and servants of her own, whomever she chooses."

Melaine grinned. "Then, it's settled. You will obviously want your widowed mother to accompany you, won't you, Conora?"

"Well, you *did* at least take my side in this matter." Conora sighed heavily. "Fine."

20
UNWANTED HELP
Icrelur Ca Icthed

The sun was already setting as the precious few winter daylight hours had been spent on their nap. Conora walked hand-in-hand with Calosandros, so much more at ease without Gerid and Thaum watching over them. Because the guard captain had been jailed, the palace guards were in an unfortunate state, continuing their usual routines but receiving no new orders—like being reassigned to the princess from their normal hall duty. She could engage them directly, but Conora preferred this situation, and neither guard had seemed happy to be placed in a pointless position anyway.

"What were the babies' names again?" Calosandros asked.

"Azalia, Valerzana, and Elliana."

"That second one, where have I heard it before?"

"Ah, Valerzana." Conora nodded. "She's named after her late uncle Valerzan—Odelia's brother."

Calosandros blanched. "Thank you. I definitely will not make the mistake of asking about him again. Azalia isn't named for anyone I shouldn't bring up, is she?"

"The flower maybe? I don't really know the origin of that one, but nothing as obvious as Valerzan." Conora opened the door to Kennard and Odelia's sitting room.

The doorway to their bedroom was empty; someone had finally cleared away the door the guards had broken down the day before. Just inside, Odelia's maid, Imery, paced and rocked a bundle. She smiled at Conora and Calosandros and walked over, lifting the infant to pass her to them. "You remember your Auntie Conora?"

"Yeeesss... Hiii..." Conora cradled Elliana close. "How is my little ray of sunshine?" She angled the baby to show Calosandros. "Isn't she precious?"

He smiled tenderly at her. "Yes, she is. See those eyes? I think she takes after Auntie Conora," he cooed.

"That's your Uncle *Cal*," Conora whispered. "Isn't he handsome?"

Elliana gurgled happily.

"See? She likes you."

He chuckled. "You made that up."

Conora shrugged. "Let's see what your sisters are doing, Elliana." She stepped into the bedroom.

Odelia sat up on fresh sheets in bed, her skin looking freshly-scrubbed as well. She was partly obscured by Kennard, who sat facing her on the edge while gently bouncing a baby in his arms.

Mama, one of the girls was crying.

"She's hungry. She wants Odelia," Conora said.

"We know. She has her. She's trying." Kennard glanced back at Conora, then eyed Calosandros. "No. Conora, he needs to leave."

Conora scoffed. "She needs help. Here. Elliana likes you." She handed the baby to Calosandros and walked up to Kennard. "Give me..." She peered over his arm at the little face that looked like Odelia if she were darker. "...Azalia."

He frowned. "What are you doing?"

"Freeing your hands so you can help your wife. Give me the baby, please."

He sighed and handed Azalia to Conora, then turned back to Odelia and stroked the head of the baby in her arms. "What's wrong, Zana? Why won't you drink?"

Odelia's lips quivered. "She's trying. I don't think she's getting anything."

Valerzana's cry became angrier, frustrated.

Kennard wrapped one arm around the pair. "I know. You're both trying. And you've done well feeding her sisters. There's no shame in calling the wet nurses back in. We need to feed her."

"Conora?" Calosandros called from the other room.

She carefully carried Azalia to him.

"How much of *Pusosio Sioria* have you tried to read?" he whispered.

"All of it. Wh— Oh!" Of course. There were pages dedicated to pregnant lovers and new mothers.

Calosandros held out the arm that wasn't cradling Elliana, and Conora gave him Azalia.

She hurried back into the bedroom. "I think I can help. You'll need the wet nurse for a short while to tide Valerzana over, but there's a technique that will make her unnecessary after that."

"How would you know?" Kennard asked.

"*Pusosio Sioria,*" Conora whispered to Odelia, giving her a look that said, *Remember?*

"Oh!" Odelia immediately gave Valerzana to Conora. "Have Imery take her to the wet nurse."

"What?" Kennard asked as Conora started walking out. "What was *that* about?"

"Don't ask, love," Odelia warned.

Conora quickly found Imery, who had taken Azalia from Calosandros and was changing her.

As soon as the baby was swaddled, Imery handed her back to Calosandros and took Valerzana. "I'll take her to the wet nurse."

Conora smiled at Calosandros. He looked so natural holding the princesses.

He smiled back at her and nodded his head toward the bedroom. "You should get back in there."

"Right!" Conora rushed back into the room, then cautiously approached the bed. Discussing this with her brother would be awkward enough, and knowing him, he would probably make it weirder somehow. But her friend would be easier, right? So Odelia would be the one to focus on.

Thankfully, Odelia was ready with rapt attention.

"You need to command your body to make more," Conora started.

Odelia's face fell, completely unamused. "That's the advice?"

"No, but that's your aim, right? Your body will make what you demand of it. The problem is that the babies aren't demanding much because they're so small, and they've been taking from the wet nurse."

Odelia huffed. "You just sent them back to her!"

Conora put her hands up. "I know. Just listen. You need stronger stimulation... You need to demand more..."

She vainly hoped that Odelia would pick up what she was alluding to so she wouldn't have to keep talking, but the new mother just frowned in confusion.

"There's a technique called..." Frog nuggets. Conora had never been able to translate it—if it translated at all, and the Urstillian was eluding her. All she could remember was that it was a cumbersome word.

"*Ictrarcanonee,*" Calosandros finished for her, his voice slightly muffled behind the wall.

"Thank you, *Cal*. Yes, it's ictra...ictrarca—what he said. You need someone stronger—" Conora couldn't look at Kennard as she talked about this but thumbed behind her in his general direction "—to do that for you."

Odelia mouthed, *Ohf*, her eyes alight with understanding.

Kennard sputtered. "I'm sorry. What?"

Hands up, Conora backed toward the doorway. "I'm definitely *not* explaining it again."

He put his hands on hips. "But you didn't explain anything."

"Oh for—" Calosandros stepped into the doorway. "Your wife needs you to suck on her breasts. Don't look so shocked. Giver knows you should be well practiced at it by now."

Kennard's jaw dropped. "*That's* the cretin you're marrying. Great Giver, you've lost your mind, Conora." He strode over to Calosandros. "Give me my daughters. Now, please."

Conora said, "Kennard, if it works..."

He finished taking the babies in his arms and turned to her. "It's not about what does or doesn't work. He can't just walk in here and say that. And I'm afraid to ask what else he's taught you if *that* sounds appropriate to you." He gently laid the babies on the bed next to Odelia. "Conora, it's still not too late to find another way."

Conora rolled her eyes. "It is. Calosandros has upheld his end of the bargain. The war is over. Your heirs are born. The contract is finished. It's consummated!"

Kennard put a hand on her back and steered her out of the bedroom, wrinkling his nose. "Poor phrasing choice. 'Consummated' has...other connotations, especially in this case."

Oh, she was well aware of what she meant.

He looked around the room. "Where are your guards? I gave orders that he wasn't to be left alone with you."

"I am a grown woman!"

"And I'm the king!"

"So what! I still have rights of my own. Whom I spend time with is not for you to decide."

"And the consequences for that—"

"Are for me to live with. Not you."

Kennard clenched his fists. "Again, where are your guards?"

She shrugged. "Calosandros would never hurt me."

"No, he just sullies your honor and your mind."

Conora laughed. "You're one to talk. You've done far more damage to Odelia's honor."

"How screwed up is that? Lia has done everything right and gets called a whore by the masses. Meanwhile, you actually sell yourself to the Urstillian—the very literal definition of whoring—and you're thanked for it."

Conora was quiet for a moment. The bit of truth in his barb stung, though not as much as hearing it from him. But she could not refute it; she couldn't bring herself to outright lie about her relationship again. And while Calosandros looked ready to speak up, she could not hide behind her husband either.

She squared her shoulders and forced herself to look her brother in the eyes. "Between the two of us, I'm not the one who plotted a coup. But by all means, call me whatever makes you feel better."

"You participated in that coup."

"You didn't give me a choice."

"As if the ultimatum he offered you was better?" Kennard pointed at Calosandros.

"It's more freedom and respect than anyone in this family has ever given me."

Kennard frowned. "You can't mean that."

Conora was done: done with this fight, done with her brother, done with this palace. She put her hands around Calosandros's arm. "We have everything we need to hold a ceremony tomorrow. Just leave me alone until the wedding, and say your goodbyes there. By Urstillian law, I'm already bound to Calosandros. Maybe you should pretend I am by Meriverian law as well."

21

WEDDING

Loidee

Conora slowly turned the small cedar wreath in her hands, watching its distorted reflection in her blue-green pearl bracelet. She'd filled the wreath with fresh red camellias and preserved white gardenias, and it smelled divine. To her mother's horror, she'd opted to leave her hair down, letting her curls mostly run wild, other than a few strands pulled back from her face to keep her blue-green pearl tiara secured. And even more scandalous, Calosandros had advised her to forgo a necklace—a better choice to keep her hair from tangling in anyway—though it did look rather sparse to wear nothing with such a low neckline.

She could appreciate that her cleavage looked amazing, but she felt a constant need to check that her bosom hadn't completely spilled out. Calosandros had mostly left her to her own Meriverian customs for her attire, with the exception that her chest be bared as much as possible within the constraints of public modesty. It wasn't a random or lurid request, but she didn't want to admit she hadn't been paying attention when he'd explained the reason and trusted it was an important Urstillian custom. The rest of her dress was a classic Elgathan-style wedding gown: tightly fitted from her waist up, the long flowing sleeves nearly off her shoulders, the spruce-colored ramie velvet was trimmed with embroidered gold, copper, and silver flowers.

It didn't make sense to be nervous—she'd already signed and consummated the marriage with Calosandros—but consciously planning to walk in front of the court as the center of attention made her fingers tremble. Were they ever going to announce her entrance or just make her stand in the hall forever?

Finally, a drumbeat sounded, and the doors began to open. Conora beamed as she walked out into the center of the throne room. Though she'd worried about all the eyes on her, it only took her a moment to forget them as she found the only pair she cared about, Calosandros's lush green ones. Despite the winter chill, he wore no shirt, and his chiton hung off one shoulder—much like the first time she saw him—but this time, the fabric matched her dress in blue-green velvet, and he had brown leather leggings and boots underneath. This was the first time she'd seen some of his imperial regalia as well, a furry bearskin cape and gold-and-ruby circlet. When he smiled back at her, it warmed her whole body.

As Conora joined him on the dais, he reached out and took her hands through the center of the wreath. This tradition she understood, the union of their hands inside an infinite evergreen circle—that their union be unending. The officiant would begin to address the crowd soon, most of it the boring speech about what they were doing that was the same at every wedding. Conora was more interested in the beautiful man before her.

So it caught her completely off-guard to hear her brother's voice beside her.

Conora looked at Kennard, who blushed and nodded to her as he continued his speech.

A lump caught in her throat. After months of horrid bickering and name-calling and his outright resistance to this wedding, he was here for her anyway, supporting her in the most active way possible.

"Do you, Crown Prince Calosandros of the Empire of Urstille, accept Princess Conora of Meriveria as your wife?"

Calosandros looked straight at Conora, his eyes intense as he swore, "I do."

"How do you pledge your devotion?"

He held up an ornate ring embedded with rubies and sapphires. "This ring is my pledge, the offer of my heart." Then, instead of putting it on her finger, he nodded to Anabusos, who stood beside him as Kennard stood by her.

"Iclusa oin tra?" Anabusos asked.

"Yis oid u padee iclusa, cianos ictradur yos," Calosandros said as he slipped the ornate ring on her right hand, just above her marriage band.

Kennard cocked an eyebrow—likely wondering if he should correct the placement—then shrugged and turned to her. "And do you, Princess Conora of Meriveria, accept Crown Prince Calosandros of the Empire of Urstille as your husband?"

She grinned at Calosandros and stifled a joyful chuckle. "I do."

"How do you pledge your devotion?"

Before Conora could panic that she had nothing, Calosandros slyly passed a large ring to her palm from inside the wreath and winked.

She exhaled and held up the match to her ring of devotion. "This ring is my pledge, the offer of my heart." Oh Giver, would she have to recite it in Urstillian now?

Calosandros rubbed her knuckles with his thumbs, letting her know, *You can do this. I'm here.*

"Iclusa oin tra?" Anabusos asked her.

Conora looked to Calosandros, who mouthed, barely whispering, "Yis oid..."

She followed his lead one word at a time, sure she sounded stilted and foolish to anyone who understood Urstillian, but when she finished, he squeezed her fingers and beamed at her proudly before letting go so she could place the ring on his hand.

This was normally the part where Kennard should have pronounced them married, but Calosandros looked back at Anabusos, who held aloft a bowl and spoke so rapidly in Urstillian that Conora couldn't even parse out words. Then he lowered it near to her chest, revealing dark reddish-purple liquid—blackberry ink?—and offered Calosandros a long-handled brush.

He blushed as he dipped for some ink, saying, "Tudos yos ee cianos oid."

When he put a steady hand on her waist and held the brush over her left breast, she held her breath, unsure what she should expect or do. He began to draw or write on her—it was hard to tell which since his head was in the way if she tried to look down—and she bit her lip to try to keep from laughing as the brush hairs tickled terribly on such a sensitive place. Giver, why were solemn events always the hardest places *not* to laugh?

Calosandros sighed, then chuckled. "Crebia icsura!" he whispered in what sounded like an attempt at a rebuking tone foiled by laughter.

Anabusos snickered and rattled something off in Urstillian that received hearty laughter from those who understood, including Calosandros, who pursed his lips and shook his head before laughing again.

Conora couldn't take it. "What did he say?" she whispered.

"He said I might need both breasts for all the letters in my name."

She covered her mouth with her hand, which did little to stop the laugh from shaking her chest.

Calosandros laugh-said, "Hold still. I have two letters left."

When he stepped back, she could see his name snaking across the top of her breast in a dark red scrawl so shaky and crooked, it looked like a child wrote it. The first letters he'd written had begun to turn a deep purple as they dried. She couldn't make eye contact with Calosandros without both of them laughing again.

He offered the brush to her. "Your turn now, dearest."

Thank the Giver her name only had six letters. She took a deep breath and tried to focus on writing her name on his muscular chest. It seemed to work until he started shaking on the second *o*. When she finished, her handwriting was jagged too. As she tried to step back, Calosandros held her by her waist.

Anabusos took the brush from her and declared, "Icoinur loee icpiayosagee!"

Urstillians recited it back, followed by whistles from several of them.

Calosandros, now red, held up his finger to Conora, then gestured to Kennard, who stifled his laughter with a throat clearing and announced, "Under my power as the King of Meriveria, I declare you wed. You may now seal your vow with a kiss."

Conora moved in slowly, but Calosandros vigorously pressed her flush against himself and dipped her. Then he gave her a deep, tongue-tangling kiss that would've weakened her knees if he'd left her standing. As the room filled with cheers in both languages, Calosandros righted Conora again, smiling and touching his forehead to hers while the dizzy giddiness washed over her.

Calosandros sighed happily. "Nuil yos cal, nuil yos *thiodoma*."

Conora didn't ask him to translate the last word for her; all of him was professing the same joyful sentiment: *My beautiful little vixen*, all *mine*.

Eventually, Kennard tapped on her shoulder, then ushered the pair to the side door to his office. There, Odelia sat just inside the open doorway with one of her babies in her arms. Her other two lay together in a large bassinet farther in.

Odelia smiled. "That was beautiful, Conora. You're a glowing bride."

Conora put one arm around her in a half hug. "Thank you. And you could see well enough from here?"

"Azalia and I had the best view of all," she cooed as she gently bounced Azalia. "We could see her sisters and the wedding. And when everybody else was watching Conora enter, we got to watch the groom's face." She laughed. "I'm so happy for you."

Kennard closed the door behind them, smiling but being uncharacteristically quiet.

Remembering what he'd done for her, Conora threw her arms around him and squeezed tight. "Thank you. I never thought... Thank you."

142

He squeezed back. "I was just being your brother. Even if I royally screw it up sometimes, know that I will always love you, Sis."

Odelia cleared her throat.

He blushed. "And Lia may have given me a much-needed dressing down."

Odelia smirked. "I'm glad to see the talk with Calosandros went well."

Calosandros shrugged. "We just need to speak man-to-man. I hope the small delay to the ceremony didn't worry you too much." He wove his fingers through Conora's.

"I thought it was just my nerves," Conora admitted. She'd never been a good judge of how long things took.

"We wish you didn't have to leave in the middle of the feast," Kennard said, "but I hear you already have everything packed and on route to Iverish?"

"It gets so cold there if we arrive late at night," Conora said.

Kennard nodded sadly. "That's sensible. Lia wanted us to give you something, so we should do that now so we don't miss you." He moved to the side of Conora.

Odelia stood and placed Azalia in the bassinet with her sisters, then came and stood on Conora's other side. Kennard and Odelia each put two fingers on Conora's wrists, and a breath later, they kissed her cheeks, sending a brief but powerful tingle from her head to her toes and making Conora giggle.

She'd never felt more refreshed or lively, like every inch of her had renewed.

Kennard's fingers lingered for a moment after Odelia let go. "Interesting. That's the nicest balance in Vitality... It's almost perfect."

"Really?" Odelia touched Conora's wrist again. "Huh. It is. We should tell Bertina about this."

"I don't think we have time for that," Calosandros said worriedly.

"Oh, you don't need to talk to her with us. I don't think it has to do with Conora," Odelia said. "It's a Healer matter. We'll confirm that with the rest of our present."

"The rest?" Conora asked.

Kennard sighed. "I was hoping she'd forget. Let's get it over with." He dragged himself over to Calosandros and grabbed his wrist as Odelia approached his other side.

"Wait. Me? What are we doing?" Calosandros looked to Conora with eyes that said, *Help!*

"It doesn't hurt, I promise," Conora said.

"Think of yourself like a cup of water," Kennard said. "We're making sure you're filled to the brim."

"That analogy doesn't make it any clearer," Calosandros said. "I don't know what the water is."

Kennard rolled his eyes. "It's your Vitality. Look, it's the best explanation I can think of right now. Would you like to be in the best health of your life or not?"

"I didn't know you could do that."

Conora laughed. "*Cal*, shush. Let the Healers work."

Calosandros cringed and closed his eyes—and thankfully, his mouth. When Kennard and Odelia kissed his cheeks, his eyes popped open, and he relaxed and stood taller.

"Oh, it's definitely us," Kennard said to Odelia, then patted Calosandros on the shoulder. "Congratulations, Brother."

22

CLOSER

Rianar

As the riverboat creaked, Conora snuggled closer to Calosandros and shivered against the icy wind.

He lifted the blanket that was resting over their knees. "You could be warmer on my lap."

"I know but..." She looked down at Spruce and Cloudy, who were sitting on her feet with their muzzles on her lap.

Cloudy whined, *Why is floor moving? Don't like moving floor.*

The dogs hadn't been on a riverboat before. It had neither the oneness with the water that a small canoe would have nor the stability of a ship, so the wide but wobbly ferry was confusing them.

Conora petted Cloudy's head. *Can I cuddle my mate? You can cuddle us.*

Cloudy sighed in the dramatic way only dogs can. *Fine.*

As Conora started to lift from her seat, Spruce's eyes widened. *Why move? No move! We fall!*

Conora scoffed. So much for her brave guardian. *Don't be such a puppy, Spruce.*

Calosandros frowned. "Is that a no?"

She pushed Spruce back. "They'll be fine if you let them sit on your feet."

"Then, get over here." He plucked her up by the waist, then started lifting the back of her poncho.

She gasped and stopped him. "What are you doing?"

"Just trust me." He pulled the back of her poncho up and over his shoulder and clasped her back against his chest, then wrapped his cape in front of her. "This puts another layer around us instead of between us." He nuzzled her ear. "We want more contact to share our body heat."

She wiggled slightly against his warmth. "Mmm. You're right. Much better."

Princess? Spruce whined.

All right, she huffed, and the dogs scurried onto Calosandros's feet.

"Oof. That's..." Calosandros's voice was a bit strained. He looked next to him at Anabusos, who was shivering. "Should I ask Anabusos if he wants a dog, or will they object?"

"Now that we've made some room, Cloudy could lie on his lap." His fluffy coat made for especially warm snuggles. Instead of waiting for the men to switch to Urstillian and talk, Conora told the dog to lie on their new friend.

"Yis? Phee?" Anabusos almost yelled as Cloudy came to him, then nervously said, "Lanos pana..." Then a loud "Oof!" as Cloudy crawled onto his lap, soon followed by "Oooooh..." as he started petting what was probably now his best friend for the duration of the trip.

Calosandros chuckled and said to Anabusos, "Yis icrion proee nointraian osis yos."

Without looking, Anabusos raised his middle finger at him, shielding it from the crew around them with his other hand.

Conora tensed, but Calosandros just laughed.

"You aren't going to tell him off for that?" she whispered.

"Why? I started it, and he knows better than to joke with me in front of the wrong people."

Perhaps it was traveling to Valerzan's burial place that brought it to her mind, but the banter was the kind of familiarity she and her brother had only ever had with Odelia and Valerzan—Kennard had once goaded Valerzan into throwing him in the lake at Oulley. The four of them had been close since childhood. How long must Calosandros and Anabusos have been friends?

"You two are close, aren't you?" she said. "Very old friends?"

"Yes, he's the brother I never had."

"You two remind me of someone. Do we have time for me to visit somewhere before we leave Iverish tomorrow?" It would be their last stop in Meriveria before they crossed the border at Acas Icsiol—or was it Acas Icsio?—she'd heard Urstillians using both names.

"Is it far away?" Calosandros asked.

"In the woods outside the city. I'd like to say a last goodbye to an old friend."

"Of course. Depending on which part of the woods, it might even be on our way." He softly grunted and shifted.

"Are you okay?"

"Yes. I think my foot just fell asleep," he whispered.

Conora sighed. *Spruce, go sit with Raina. She looks cold. And lonely.* He'd make better conversation for Raina than the cold silence of Mother, who wouldn't deign to speak to a servant if she didn't need something, and Raina could give him more attention than Conora had to spare at the moment.

Okay... He slunk down and crawled under the bench to get the row in front of them, where Raina and Mother were sitting.

"Mmm... Just us now?" Calosandros whispered huskily, reaching up to her bosom.

Conora laughed. "Almost." As he nuzzled her neck, she tilted her head, thinking back to the dramatic kiss he'd given her at the wedding. "What were they chanting at the end of the wedding?"

"Hmm?"

"Anabusos said something, and the other Urstillians repeated it."

"Oh, the wedding blessing."

"Which is..."

"They were wishing us an orgasmic marriage," he said casually.

Conora laughed. "What is it really?"

"May your marriage be orgasmic? I'm not sure what other way you need me to word it."

Conora laughed harder. "I'm so glad my family doesn't understand Urstillian!"

The inn was full of Urstillians as a portion of the army had traveled ahead of them and rented the entire place. Calosandros got the key and led Conora to their room alone as the dogs would remain with their boatmates for the evening. It was unfortunately the same room she'd slept in before Valerzan's funeral. The haunting must have shown on her face.

"What wrong, dearest? Did they give us the wrong room? I specifically asked for the best one."

"No, the room is lovely. It's just an unhappy memory. We can replace that." She kissed him hard, willing herself to think only of now.

Still kissing, she heard him lock the door, then a *clink* as he tossed the key onto a nearby table. He kissed her harder, moving his hands all over her, tugging at her clothes. He growled. "I have half a mind to forget tradition and just bend you over now."

As she puzzled over which tradition that would be, her poncho came up and off, and he buried his fingers in her cleavage, pulling on her neckline. She inhaled deeply, thinking she would spill out as he seemed to be trying for, but that wasn't as effective as she'd hoped.

He caressed her cheek and kissed her again. "I'll try to be careful. I don't want to hurt you."

"What? But you already took my—"

Riiiiip!

"What was that?" Conora looked down and gasped.

Her beautiful gown was torn open down the middle from her neckline to her waist, revealing her breast bodice and chemise. And Calosandros had a small knife in one hand and a far-too-satisfied smile on his face.

"My dress!" She screech-growled and shoved his chest—or tried to. "Why would you— *Whyyy!*"

He carefully set down the knife. "It's tradition."

"What stupid kind of tradition—" She futilely tried to put the pieces together. "You destroyed it..."

He shrugged, looking bemused. "There's no need to be upset. It's a wedding dress."

She gaped. "No need to be upset? That it's a wedding dress is *more* reason to be upset!"

"I don't understand. It's not as if you were going to wear it again, were you?"

"No, but this was a work of art. I thought I might show it to our children someday."

"Oh." He touched one of the raw edges. "If it means that much to you, there's no reason we can't keep it like this. You can still see most of the design."

"But why destroy something beautiful?"

Calosandros threw his hands up in exasperation. "I know, right? We discussed plans. I was surprised to see you'd chosen such a fine dress for this, but I assumed it was a royal show of wealth." He looked her over for a moment, and his face softened. "You really didn't know about ripping the dress at all, did you?"

She shook her head, blinking back tears. "If you told me, I didn't hear you."

He took her hand. "Why didn't you ask me to go over it again?"

"Because people get upset when I do that." She looked down at the hem of her sleeve, which now hung limply on her arm. "They get angry

148

that I'm not paying attention, so I pretend that I am and try to figure out whatever I missed from context later."

"Conora, that could be dangerous. If you miss the wrong information—"

"I know that, but do you know how terrifying it is to anger the wrong person?"

"Conora—"

"If you're going to tell me to just try harder and focus more, know that I have. Giver knows, the harder I try, the more I miss."

"Conora!"

"What!"

He grasped her face with both hands. "I'm not going to tell you that. I know your mind works differently. I married you as you are." He kissed her gently, then pulled her into a firm embrace. "It must feel like it's impossible for you to do right sometimes, but it doesn't have to be that way between us. Please don't feel you have to pretend with me. You can tell me when your mind wanders."

"You'll think it means I don't care. That's what people assume."

"Those people are wrong. I can think of at least five ways you showed how much you care just on the boat ride here. And the wandering twists your mind takes can bring you five steps ahead of those people." He leaned back and tipped her chin up until she was looking into his forest-green eyes, earnest and gentle. "It's what makes you my little vixen."

He kissed her slowly, tenderly, not burning with lust and passion, but caressing her with the gentle warmth of affection. Conora clung to the feeling. It was the closest he had come to loving her.

23

GOODBYES

Iario

Conora had just pulled on her chemise and was reaching for her bust bodice when Calosandros put his hands on her hips and kissed her neck. "You don't need that."

She laughed. "I do have to get dressed at some point if we're going to leave."

He reached past her and swiped the bust bodice, holding it up to dangle from his fingers. "This thing looks horribly uncomfortable. What is it for?"

She snatched it back. "I need it to hold up my bosom."

"But you didn't wear it when we met."

"I was supposed to, but I didn't want to wear my chemise in the summer heat, and I can't wear it without the chemise."

"So, you don't actually *need* it, then? You wear something nobody else can see just because you're 'supposed to'?"

Conora sighed and finished fastening the ties. She couldn't fully deny the silliness, but it was what she knew. "My winter gowns are more fitted. They'll look sloppy without it."

"My little vixen, your natural shape is anything but sloppy." Calosandros gave her another kiss and a pat on her bottom. "We'll have to get you some Urstillian clothes in the next couple of days so you don't freeze, and then you really won't need that thing anyway."

Conora turned over the thick red dress in her hands and looked at the stack of other dresses in her travel chest. It had apparently been a waste of time to pack her wardrobe. Since her title was hardly changing, she hadn't given much thought to changing what she wore. But she was supposed to be an Urstillian princess now, and that would mean looking the part, whatever that was. Her wedding gown, now discarded on the bed, had simply been the first article sacrificed to the change.

Outside the inn, Conora pointed across the frozen Lake Iver. "There's a dense grove on the eastern shore, just north of the old Vistan palace."

"The grove is right in our path," Calosandros said, "but I don't remember seeing a palace."

"It's very old, walled-off, and overgrown. If you were going through the burial woods, it would look like more forest in the distance."

Calosandros paled. "It's a burial grove? Shit. I didn't realize that when we walked through the first time. I'll tell Anabusos to reroute my people."

"You didn't damage the trees or stones, did you?"

"Not the party I took, but to be honest, I don't know what the rest of the army did. They likely bypassed it anyway in favor of a thinner section of forest to clear a path." He sounded confident, but the worry line in the middle of his brow showed he wasn't entirely convinced.

As they walked around the lake, Calosandros explained the situation to Anabusos. When they reached the eastern shore, Anabusos split off from them, followed by Cloudy, who hadn't left his side since the boat ride—that furry little traitor, he would do anything for a good ear or belly rub. Of course, Mother opted out of visiting a gravesite, and Raina and Spruce followed Anabusos with her.

So, it was just Conora and Calosandros hand-in-hand in the burial woods. In between giant trees, waist-high stones bore names, some of them with the Vistan crest engraved as well. Valerzan wasn't difficult to find as his stone was so new, it was the only one without moss. On the unengraved side, where his body lay underground, was something that brought tears to Conora's eyes.

A little seedling, bright green, barely peeked through the snow. The pine cone that had been burned open at his funeral had sprouted.

She dropped to her knees before it and dug a little well in the snow around the seedling, then kissed her fingers and touched the seedling. It probably looked ridiculous, and she knew Valerzan wasn't actually there anymore, but it felt right.

"I should've known you'd still be strong. You have a niece named after you now..." As she told Valerzan's tree about the weddings and births and the general upheaval of life since his death, Calosandros silently rested a hand on her back, softly rubbing when she talked about something too emotional. "...and I guess the Giver finally granted you justice, but you probably know that better than—"

She couldn't finish the last bit of news. It felt like a betrayal. It didn't matter what Father had deserved, it was still another loss, and it didn't undo this one.

Calosandros helped her stand and wrapped his arms around her, holding her head to his chest, still silent.

"I never talked to him again," Conora admitted. "When I took you to meet my father, that was the last time I saw him. I didn't even say goodbye when we left. It was just him yelling. My last moments with him were nothing but disgust and disappointment." She sniffled against the cold air. "And I was so eager to run that we're going to miss whatever burial he gets. But the worst part is that I don't actually miss him, and I feel like a terrible daughter for feeling that way."

Calosandros kissed her head. "You aren't terrible. If you were, you wouldn't question these feelings, and you wouldn't have said such beautiful things for your friend. Your relationship with your father was complicated. I understand too well, it probably never stops being that way."

She nodded and pulled back to look at Calosandros. "We should go. Thank you for indulging me in this."

"It's not an indulgence." He smiled and tucked a curl behind her ear. "I would feel the same way if it were Anabusos here, and I know you wouldn't begrudge me the same need to say goodbye."

He laced his fingers through hers and led her farther east, toward Urstille.

When they'd walked past several more trees, Conora's curiosity got the best of her. "Speaking of Anabusos, I was wondering something, but it felt rude to ask in front of him, even if he doesn't understand."

"What were you wondering?"

"There's something about him I don't quite understand, body language I can't decipher."

Calosandros laughed. "Well, with him, that could mean any number of things, but if you can be more specific, I'll answer as best as I can."

"It's the way he looks when you hold me. I thought maybe he dislikes or disapproves of me, but it's not the same as the look my guards gave you."

"Oh, that... I'm not sure even Anabusos can fully explain what he's feeling—partly happy for me, partly concerned for me, partly jealous."

Conora felt guilty for taking all of Calosandros's attention. "I don't mean to disrupt your friendship. If he's worried about it, we can make sure you have time for him too."

Calosandros laughed. "Wrong kind of jealousy. You don't need to worry about it, though. He's likely to flirt with anyone and everyone, but he knows where things stand and has made peace with it." He held up his right hand and wiggled his ring finger.

If the devotion rings defined things, then... "So, it's a sexual thing?" she whispered.

"Conora, if you have to whisper, I don't know if you're ready for this conversation."

She couldn't let this go. She'd seen enough in *Purosio Siora* to know that Urstillians were open to what most Meriverians would consider unconventional pairings. It wasn't a given whom Anabusos was jealous of. She'd given him little reason to be interested in her, and Calosandros had never explicitly told her anything more than a number regarding his previous partners. It left too many new questions.

"Fine," she said aloud. "So you're saying that Anabusos is jealous of—"

"Both of us."

Conora paused, brows knit in confusion. "Both of us? So, sometimes he's attracted to women and sometimes men?"

Calosandros laughed sardonically. "Oh, I wish it were that simple for him. I could've helped to match him up with somebody ages ago if it were."

"Then just explain it."

He sighed. "If you were Urstillian, I'd say that's already more than you have any business asking, but I know you're just trying to understand. As you learn more of the language, you must promise not to ask these kinds of questions to other people."

"I thought you were open about sexual matters."

"We are, but if you ask too many questions about what a particular someone does in bed, people will assume you're interested in participating with that person."

Conora nodded. "Understood. I will save all my questions for one handsome man."

He smiled.

"Now, about our complicated friend..."

"Okay, okay—*our* friend? He'd like that." Calosandros smirked. "For him, it's not just about attraction to a man or woman—he can play with anyone. But what he's most attracted to is men *and* women—together."

153

That was more unconventional than Conora had guessed. She tried to keep her face neutral. "Like the positions from the end of *Pusosio Siora*?" Those pages showed many examples of three people together.

"Yes." After a little while he added, "Conora, I can practically see the questions running across your face. Just ask."

"You told me your three previous lovers were all separate, so you haven't...?"

"No, and not for lack of opportunity. I've never had interest in a threesome. I honestly don't know how he does it. It sounds more exhausting than fun to me."

Conora sighed with relief that Calosandros wouldn't ask her to do such a thing.

He chuckled and slipped his arm around her waist. "Dearest, we had a wedding. I know we laughed a lot at the ceremony, but a pledge of devotion is one of the most significant vows a person can make. Not many people do that. It would be a stupid thing to do if I had the slightest interest in having anyone besides you in our bed."

Her cheeks warmed. It was surreal, accepting both the notion that Urstillians held such wildly different sexual standards and that Calosandros would rather be with her than participate in all of it. She still had another question. "If Anabusos sometimes has single partners, have you ever...?"

"No. All my exes are women. The most he's gotten from me is one *terrible* kiss."

Conora giggled, then immediately tried to stifle it. "I'm sorry. I shouldn't laugh, but the way you said it..." There had to be a story behind that reaction.

"It was years ago. We were both drunk off our asses. I said something about how much he meant to me—thinking of brotherhood and stupidly not considering other interpretations—and he took it as an invitation. Unfortunately for him, that was a moment that confirmed my own orientation. When he tried to lean in for a second one, I stopped him and admitted an aversion to men." Calosandros cleared his throat and grimaced. "And then I vomited on the poor man. I still feel awful about that part."

"But you're still friends after all that."

"He did stop talking to me for a week. Turned out it was the vomit that offended him more—he thought it was an intentional insult to his skill as a kisser. But we worked it out. We've been friends for too long to destroy it for something neither of us chose." He squinted ahead. "Looks like we're about to meet up with him. Any last questions?"

"Was he offended when you asked him to officiate for us? I would imagine he might not be fond of the ceremony."

"Oh, he hates it, which was why I was hesitant to ask him. But he's also fiercely protective. When he realized I wouldn't change my mind about our wedding, he actually *offered*. He was worried somebody else would ruin things."

Conora smiled. It definitely sounded like Valerzan's reaction when Kennard and Odelia were trying to run away together. "Then my last question is, what did you do to earn such a true friend?"

Calosandros laughed. "Giver if I know. Probably the same as I did to deserve such an exceptional wife." Her face warmed as he kissed her cheek. "Maybe you can answer a question for me?"

"What?"

"You don't seem as shocked as I would expect from your culture, more curious than anything. Is there a reason for that, or are you just hiding it well?"

She laughed. "For all your fear of culture shock, you keep forgetting I talk to animals. There is nothing further from court conversation than that. How do you think I know that bears are promiscuous?"

As they met up with the rest of their party, Conora turned back to take mischievous pleasure in her husband's open-mouthed stare, then bid a silent goodbye to the endless forest below them that was Meriveria.

24

FOREIGN

Upha

Calosandros led everyone over the border soon after sunset. Thankfully, the moonlight illuminated the snow enough to show the way, and Break Pass had lodging for them. At the patrol barracks, Calosandros brought the little family he'd accumulated to the reserved imperial apartment. Despite being in a bleak outpost, the imperial apartment was well-kept and filled with lush fur and fine leather furnishings. They'd barely settled in when he could hear the beginnings of revelry among the soldiers below.

Anabusos, who'd followed Calosandros up to the room, clapped him on the back and smiled. "Are you going to celebrate with us?"

"Not tonight. You'll have enough fun for all of us."

Anabusos shrugged and started for the door, then turned back. "Hey, the princess's maid is an Animal Speaker too, isn't she? Do you think she'd like to join us downstairs?"

"Are you asking because you think she'd enjoy the party, or are you looking for a new fuck buddy?"

He laughed. "If it makes you feel better, I'll take personal responsibility that she comes back unharmed."

Calosandros sighed. "I will ask for you, but she probably won't want to go." He turned to the maid. "Raina?"

"Yes, Your Imperial Highness?"

"Anabusos wants to know if you'd like to accompany him downstairs. The soldiers are celebrating our homecoming."

She frowned in confusion. "What does he need me to do down there?"

"He was simply hoping for..." How would the Meriverians put it? "...the pleasure of your company. It's an Urstillian party, so there will be lots of food, a lot of drinking and dancing..."

"And a lot of sex, I'm assuming?" Conora quipped.

Calosandros nodded. "He won't be lonely if you don't want to go, so

156

unless the princess requires anything of you tonight, the choice is truly yours."

Conora leaned on Raina's shoulder and whispered.

The maid's eyes widened, and she blushed. Then she waved for Conora to tell her more. Whatever she told her must have appealed, because Raina grinned and crossed the room to grab Anabusos's arm.

"Thanks!" With the smuggest grin ever, he scampered off with Raina.

Calosandros raised an eyebrow at Conora.

"What?"

"What did you tell her?"

She shrugged. "I just reminded her that we live in Urstille now, so the rules are different. And then I told her what he likes."

"Really?"

"I know. I'm as surprised as you are. Who could've guessed she was that free-spirited?"

As they both laughed, he pulled her close. "What about you? I told him we were staying up here, but I shouldn't decide for you."

"Oh, *Giver* no." Conora rolled her eyes. "All those crowds?" She shuddered. "I'd rather lick a slug."

"Oh really?" He chuckled. "If you're in the mood for licking, you can—"

"Not finish that sentence with her mother in the room, thank you." Melaine pursed her lips at them, hands on her hips.

He hadn't done anything wrong, but her look alone made him feel guilty for the unknown offense.

"Why don't you go downstairs, Mother?" Conora suggested. "Maybe someone will teach you what pleasure is."

Melaine gasped.

"Conora..." he halfheartedly scolded. Part of him appreciated the speed with which Conora had thrown the barb, but another part was horrified on behalf of his sweet mother-in-law.

"What?" Conora snapped. "She's the one who pulled me aside earlier to accuse me of faking pleasure with you."

Melaine placed a hand on her chest. "You make so much noise! Half the inn probably heard you moaning last night. There's no need for such dramatics."

"Critical as ever. This is what I was afraid of with you. I can't even orgasm without you intruding on my love life to tell me I'm doing it incorrectly!"

"No man can be that good in bed. If you keep carrying on like that, he's just going to demand it from you more, and you'll wear yourself out."

Calosandros frowned. The accusation contradicted his connection with Conora, but he couldn't think of Melaine as a liar. This was giving him a splitting headache. He closed his eyes and tried to shake the fog from his head.

"Mother, stop!"

Cloudy growled.

After a short scuffle, the door slammed.

Conora put her hands on the side of his face and turned him toward her. "*Cal*, listen to me, and breathe. Hold on to my hips—or my ass; I guess that works too." She chuckled sadly and rubbed her thumb on his cheek.

He peeked his eyes open one at a time, the pain slowly receding as he focused on Conora's beautiful face: her full lips pursing, her delicate brows knitting in concern, her garnet-like eyes searching his.

"There's my *Cal*." She smiled sweetly. "I should've warned you before we brought her along, but—Giver, she's really lost all subtlety—I've never seen her push someone so close to breaking so fast."

"What in the unbathed fuck was that?"

"Maybe she's scared after the way things went back home, but she was trying way too hard to push her Allure on you. It's normally more of a passive nudge toward liking her that naturally occurs around her, but she was doing it on purpose just now."

"But why did it hurt so badly? How does that attract people to her?"

"It's not supposed to, but she used too much, and she was foolish to do it while she insulted you. She's usually canny enough in her manipulation to actively Allure people *after* she's hurt them. Doing both was like trying to slap you and embrace you at the same time."

Calosandros rubbed his head and sat down. "I take it this isn't the first time she's done that?"

Conora bit her lip and fidgeted with her rings. "My father. She did it so many times, I've wondered if it was her driving him mad as much as his own overuse of Transformation."

"You didn't use the same method to calm him, did you?"

She laughed. "No, not exactly. I certainly wouldn't have asked him to touch me—he was usually in the form of something with claws. He'd turn a bit feral in that state, and I had to talk to him in the form he'd chosen until he calmed down and remembered how to speak like a person. I don't remember what he did before I had Animal Speech—probably roamed the halls and terrorized the servants."

Calosandros pulled Conora onto his lap. "I'm sorry you had to do something that reminded you of that."

"I'm not." She snuggled against his chest, resting her head on his shoulder. "I'm glad I was able to stop her before it got worse. But I don't want to talk about the past anymore." Walking her fingertips sensually across his collarbone, she tugged on the tie on his other shoulder. "We're supposed to be celebrating our future."

Calosandros wasn't sure how Conora kept her mother away, but he barely saw Melaine before they reached Siputreos, the first notable city at the foot of the mountains, around noon the next day. Had he been traveling with just the army, he could've pressed farther toward the capital, but he wanted new clothing for Conora right away, and it was a long way until the next city with remotely sufficient wares to partially outfit an imperial princess.

The city watch had seen their approach down the mountain, and a parade formed around them as soon as they set foot in the city. Although most of the city residents cheered the return of their imperial prince, he couldn't help but notice the questioning glances, whispers, and fingers pointed at the mysterious foreigner holding his hand and the two huge dogs trailing behind them off-leash. He made a point to wave to the crowd with his right hand, but of course, that seemed to encourage the questions.

Conora quickly wilted from bold and radiant to timid and overwhelmed, though she kept her smile up like the princess she'd been raised to be. She didn't have to understand the language to see the same thing he saw.

This would not do. He paused to give Conora a big showy kiss until people started properly cheering.

She gave him a real smile this time, her cheeks a lovely deep shade of red. "That only works for a little while. What are you going to do, kiss me all the way down the route?"

He laughed. "Would that be so bad?"

"It's just going to take us a long time that way."

"Worth it." He kissed her cheek.

Of course, words travel faster than feet, and the crowds were soon cheering them on their own. Eventually, groups of children gathered at the edges to get a closer look. She was still the foreign princess in the strange dress, but the fear of her had turned to wonder. One intrepid little girl with purple asters in her hand ran out to meet them and bowed.

Conora crouched down and smiled as she took a flower and patted the girl's hand. "T-thank...you," she managed to say in what he now recognized from her wedding vows and their brief lessons as a Meriverian accent—she was speaking Urstillian on her own.

Granted, it was only two words, but she'd spoken them without prompting! It was a start—and further proof of her diligence in her royal duties.

When they reached the imperial mansion at the end of the route, before they walked through the doors, Calosandros gave her another big kiss just for enjoyment's sake. Once inside, he called for a tailor—preferably a female one—then led Conora to their room. Unlike the barracks at Break Pass, Siputreos had rooms set aside for the imperial family and high nobility. They could set Melaine up in the second one and have complete privacy.

The tailor was prompt. Calosandros had just finished showing Conora the room and discussing lunch plans when she arrived with a cart full of cloth.

After staring at Conora for a while, she raised an eyebrow. "Was there something you wanted me to make, Your...?"

"Imperial Highness." Calosandros flashed his right hand. "She only speaks Meriverian unfortunately, so I'll have to translate. As I'm sure you can see, she needs something appropriate for an Urstillian princess."

The tailor picked up a bolt of green cloth from her cart. "What does Her Imperial Highness think of this?"

Calosandros got Conora's attention and let her speak so he could ask her to look at the tailor's offering.

She ran her hand over it and scrunched her nose. "Did you choose this one?" she cautiously asked him.

"No, the tailor did. Why?"

"It's the kind of fabric we would use for palace staff. It's sturdy and presents well, but it's...a bit stiff?"

He felt the fabric for himself and immediately noticed the same. Conora was sweetly trying so hard to be diplomatic about it, but it was definitely not fit for a princess. He shook his head at the tailor, who put the bolt back and presented a rich blue this time. Calosandros decided to try this one himself, and it was marginally softer than the first. What kind of game was this tailor playing at?

He immediately handed it back. "I said appropriate for a *princess*, not a palace servant. You will show her your *finest* fabric."

The woman paled and bowed. "I'm so sorry, Your Imperial Highness. I must have picked up the wrong ones by mistake." She returned with a smooth sky-blue ramie that received smiling approval from Conora. After several more fabric choices, the tailor showed her some options for fur trim.

Conora looked ready to vomit, her skin pallid, eyes watery. She shook her head. "Absolutely not."

Calosandros put an arm around her. "What's wrong, dearest?"

"What's wrong? I talk to animals. What do you *think* is wrong?" Her breathing was getting faster and more erratic. "Oh Great Giver, I think I'm going to be sick."

He waved to the tailor to take the fur away. "I don't understand. I've seen you eat meat and wear leather."

"Some things can't be helped. I have to eat, and even the animals eat each other. Hides can be used from the animal that already died for food. It's harsh but purposeful. But those?" Conora's bottom lip quivered. "I've had conversations with those in the wild. I recognize the fur. People aren't hunting mink and marten and...*fox*...so they can eat. Have you seen how scrawny they are? Those creatures were killed purely for those tiny scraps of fur."

Calosandros nodded. "I think I understand. It's like the difference between killing in battle and murdering someone in..." Considering the fate of her late father, it was best not to finish that.

"Thank you for understanding." She sniffled. "The tailor probably thinks I'm just a spoiled brat throwing a tantrum."

"I'll explain it to her." He got the tailor's attention and assent. "No fur or leather if it can be helped. If you must use it, it must come from common game, something like bison or deer—and nothing young."

The tailor frowned. "Just to be clear, you want me to use the *finest* cloths but the most *common* hides?"

"Exactly." After the stunt she'd pulled with the fabric, he didn't owe her any more of an explanation than to follow his instructions.

"Okay... I guess I'll just take her measurements then."

Calosandros translated to Conora, who began well enough, removing her outer layers, main dress, and three additional skirts that seemed to be reproducing as she took them off. Then she simply stood there in her chemise and bosom contraption.

"What?" she asked after several awkward seconds.

"You need to finish undressing."

She sighed and began unfastening. "I don't understand what you have against breast support. You seem to like it well enough when it gives you a better view of them." She dropped the piece on the floor and stood with her hands on her hips. "Happy now?"

"Giver, I've never seen you take so long to undress. The chemise too, please."

Her eyes widened. "Why?"

"So she can measure accurately." *Duh.*

She huffed. "I swear, if this is a ploy to embarrass me, I will find a way to make you sorry." Despite the threat, she pulled off the last piece of clothing.

He didn't dare tell her how cute she looked, glaring death at him while nude. She was clever enough to plan her threat and obstinate enough to carry it out.

Since they needed to give the tailor a few days to make Conora's clothes, Calosandros let her sleep in while he took care of some imperial tasks. He'd started compiling his summary report when Anabusos came by with his own summary. Calosandros whispered his thanks, not wanting to wake Conora.

Anabusos nodded, but instead of leaving, he approached Calosandros's sex box, which was still open from the night before. "It's still full? Or is this new?" he whispered, holding up the bottle of *sitrecayus*.

Calosandros silently raised his right ring finger at him with a look to say, *Really?*

"If you're not going to use it, I could take it off your hands."

Calosandros rolled his eyes, waving him on and mouthing, *Fine*. Then he closed the sex box and set it under the table.

A pair of servants entered, one with a breakfast tray, the other with outerwear and the first two completed outfits for Conora. Calosandros quietly directed them to put the items on the table and dismissed them.

He unfolded the first set of clothing: a sky-blue wrap dress with deerskin trim cord to fasten it, a slender but heavy long-sleeved flannel

162

underobe, and thick wool leggings. The second outfit replaced the wrap dress with a long chiton in deep crimson. As a member of the imperial family now, her mantle would've been bearskin like his, but the tailor had thankfully followed directions and substituted it with a dense brushed wool in a rich brown that matched her eyes. Satisfied with the quality, he neatly refolded the clothes into three stacks on the table so Conora wouldn't have to sift through a messy pile to figure out what was what.

Anabusos, who still hadn't left, picked up the hood of the mantle and rubbed it between his fingers. "That's a first."

"Well, I can't ask Conora to wear the traditional bearskin. At least the tailor tried to work within her parameters. Maybe it can pass from a distance."

Gasping, Anabusos dropped the hood. "But she's a princess."

"I know." Calosandros hadn't had a chance to teach her much tradition yet, and the middle of a fitting that already distressed her hadn't seemed like a good time to start a lesson that would upset her more—especially when he wasn't completely certain whether the bearskin was a rule or a habit so deeply entrenched that it feel like one. "Are you familiar with Siputreos? I need a bookseller."

"Yes. Do you want me to take you there?"

Calosandros nodded. "Just a minute." He'd probably be back before Conora woke up, but just in case, he'd leave her a note. Not wanting to dig out his translation card from his packed belongings, he'd have to keep the message short enough that she might understand the Urstillian.

My Little Vixen,
Food and clothes are for you. I'll return soon.
Your Handsome Lover

Anabusos was snickering as they left. "'*Your handsome lover*'—that will never get old."

Calosandros punched him in the arm. "That's *her* handsome lover to you."

After a productive visit to the bookseller, Calosandros returned to his room with books on history and tradition as well as a dictionary—there were no books involving Meriverian translation, but he'd expected that.

Raina bowed as she passed him in the hallway, where she was leading the dogs out for a walk. When he entered the bedroom, Conora was eating breakfast while wearing only a new underobe and each legging falling down past her knees.

She blushed. "Good morning."

He laughed as he put the books down. "Did you build up an appetite just putting that on?"

Her blush traveled all the way down her chest, visible through the open front, which currently had no overgarment to hold it closed. "I wanted to get dressed, but I got lost after this. I have no idea how any of this is meant to be draped or fastened." She set down her fork and held up the wrap dress—sideways. She put the waist over one shoulder.

He approached to help her. "These triangular pieces?" He lifted them away from where they straddled her neck and turned the whole garment right side up. "These are for your breasts."

"Oh, for Giver's sake." She tipped her head back and sighed. "In hindsight, that was obvious."

"Don't be hard on yourself. You've probably never seen something like this before." He set the dress over a chair, then slipped his hands inside her underobe, around her waist. "You know, I wouldn't mind if you wanted to wear just this."

"Maybe I will sometimes."

Clearing his throat in an attempt to clear his thoughts, he grabbed the front of her underobe and straightened it, pulling it taut and overlapping it around her abdomen, lingering his hands over her hips. "Hold that." Draping the top of the wrap dress over her chest, he found the seam and tucked it under her bosom, moving her hands. Then he pulled the skirt around her until it crossed itself completely once and temporarily tied it off.

Conora lifted the leather trim that trailed down to pool on the floor. "But why are these so long?"

"Because we're not done yet. We need to tie the top first, though." He led her to a mirror and turned her. "See these holes?" He pointed to the back of the dress, then took the trim from the top of her neckline, crossed it behind her back, threaded it through the holes, and tied it off securely. He chuckled. "This probably wasn't the best dress to leave on your own with for the first time."

"Do women really dress themselves alone in these?"

"You'd be surprised how many do, but we can add this to Raina's duties." He pulled the long strings around her, crisscrossing them down to her waist, then found the anchor loop and tied it securely into a long bow at her hip. "There."

Conora turned back to the mirror. "Oh!" she squeaked. "That's why I don't need a bust bodice?" She reached into her neckline and adjusted herself to better show off her cleavage—he liked to think that she'd done it for his benefit.

Smiling, he crouched down, then dragged his hands up her leg from her ankles, past her knees, under her skirt, and up her thigh. After he tied the garter, he repeated the process with the other leg, lingering to brush his fingertips against the still-bare skin and squeeze her ass.

She squealed. "*Cal!* I thought you were helping me put these clothes *on.*" She laughed and tugged upward on his shoulder until he stood. "I've never worn something with a hem above my knees before. I'll have to get used to seeing my legs."

Calosandros stared at her in the mirror, spellbound. She'd been devastatingly beautiful from the first moment he'd beheld her, but this set off all her best features to her advantage. She looked confident. She looked like she belonged at the imperial court. She looked Urstillian.

He put his hands on her hips and kissed her cheek. "What do you think? Besides the novelty, of course."

She bit her lip. "I'm afraid to say what I'm thinking."

"Because you don't like it?" He tried not to let the disappointment show in his voice. This was something he desperately wanted to see her in again, but her disliking the clothes would rob them of their appeal.

"If I admit I like it, will I have to give up the rest of my wardrobe?" There was grief behind the fear in her eyes.

He sighed. "No, dearest." He wrapped his arms around her waist and kissed her cheek again. "I never should've implied that. It's important that you can dress like an Urstillian, but I should remember that your love for your homeland brought us together." He pivoted around her so they could stand facing each other. "Is this your way of asking to change back into your Meriverian clothes already?"

She shook her head. "For now, it's enough to know they're there. I'm having fun trying this new Urstillian life."

Calosandros took a moment to appreciate his wife's Urstillian persona, then caressed her cheek and pulled her close for a kiss. Giver help him—he really was falling for her. He thought he'd simply pledged his body to her, but it was only a matter of time before his heart and soul belonged to her. Conora's pull on him only intensified with familiarity, and now she was in his homeland, in familiar dress. As he deepened the kiss, she even tasted familiar. It was the sweetness of berries cut with bitter herbs and sharpened with fermentation. And it was absurdly arousing. He'd trained himself to expect it for so long, his body responded on its own.

And it was *wrong*.

He pushed away from Conora, his chest heaving in pain at the unexpected betrayal. "What did you do?"

"What?" Her eyes were wide. "I don't know what—"

He backed away from her. "Don't lie to me! I know *sitrecayus* when I taste it. I only asked one thing from you. One. How could you?"

She clenched her fists, eyes full of tears. "If you're going to yell at me, make it about something I did! I don't even know what you're talking about!"

"You drank *sitrecayus*."

Conora furrowed her brow, looking around the table, then picked up a bottle. "Is it this?"

He snatched it out of her hand. A cup's worth had been poured from it, a whole dose. Calosandros took a deep breath. "If you've changed your mind, you should tell me, not try to sneak this past me."

She shook her head. "I still don't know what you're talking about. It was on the table with breakfast. It seemed a little early in the day, but I assumed you had a reason."

"You expect me to believe you drank a whole cup of *sitrecayus* by accident?"

"Well, no."

He couldn't breathe.

Conora grabbed a cup from the table. "I poured some to drink with my food." She held it out to him. "But I barely touched it. On the first sip, I spat it back out." She grimaced. "I'm sorry if it's your favorite wine, but it tasted rancid."

Though wary at first, as he took the cup, it was indeed full. "You spat it out?"

"Yes, but what *is* it? It's not a special gift for the emperor or something, is it?"

"You—you really don't know." Nearly crying with relief, he laughed. "Giver, I thought..." He shook his head and held up the bottle. "*Sitrecayus* is what a woman drinks before sex if she wants to prevent a child."

She gasped in horror, then immediately glared at him. "I would *never* do something like that to you. You say that I should've talked to you? I

166

would have. I didn't hesitate to tell you exactly what happened just now. You are the one who just yelled at me for something that I not only didn't do—I didn't even understand the accusation. You owe me an apology."

Calosandros blinked back tears. "Conora, I'm sorry. I..." He couldn't admit he belonged to her. "I'm sorry."

Conora sighed. "Why was it even here?"

"I was giving it to Anabusos, and he must have forgotten to take it with him."

She scoffed and shook her head, then reached for the bottle. "Then he had his chance. I'm giving it to Raina."

He nodded. "Good idea."

Part of him wanted to tell her what he was feeling. He'd lost his temper because he was caring too much. The sting of what he'd thought was betrayal had burned deeper in his softened heart. But even if he could admit it, what kind of asshole was he to have yelled at her because of it?

167

25

BEAR FEVER

Yolois Podia

After four days in Siputreos, Calosandros was ready to move on. Conora's wardrobe was far from sufficient for a princess, but he'd ordered her enough clothing to look presentable on the way to the capital city of Pasutrus. Each day, they'd enter a new city around sunset, greeted by a local parade, and spend the night in an imperial mansion at the center. The routine went uninterrupted until the sixth stop, Orosiad, which happened to be the halfway point.

Calosandros made his usual show of walking with Conora and drawing cheers. As they approached the imperial mansion, she began to grip his hand tighter and lean on him slightly, though she continued to smile and wave. Once inside, her smile dropped, and she began panting.

"Are you okay, dearest?" He held his arm out for her to embrace him if she was feeling overwhelmed.

"I'm so tired. I just—" Her eyes rolled back as she collapsed into his arms.

"Conora?"

No response. Shit.

He shifted her weight so he could carry her and made straight for one of the reserved rooms. Thanking the Giver he could hear her breathing, he laid her on the bed. Cloudy and Spruce were pacing around them, distressed at the mysterious state of their princess.

"Conora?" He ripped his gloves off and put a hand to her cheek. "Dearest?"

She was hot, much more so than she should have been after walking in the snow. Her forehead was no better. He hurriedly began undressing her down to her underobe, which was when she finally stirred, groaning. When she tried to sit up, he removed her last clothing, then gently shushed her and pressed her back down. She fell back asleep as he tucked the sheet over her. The dogs snuggled down on the other side of the bed, their muzzles resting on her.

Calosandros looked around the room. Where was that damn maid when they needed her?

He headed out to find Raina and nearly ran into Anabusos, who happened to be dragging said maid down the hallway with her arm over his shoulder as she stumbled in a drunken-looking stupor.

"I looked for her as soon as I saw your wife swoon," Anabusos whispered quickly. "Raina had made a comment about feeling tired before we entered the city. She's feverish."

"Fuck." Two of the Meriverians with them were sick at the same time? That didn't bode well. He needed to find the third. If she was sick too, they were all in deep shit. "Has anybody seen Lady Melaine?"

Anabusos shook his head.

Calosandros took Raina and tasked Anabusos with finding Conora's mother. Although Calosandros normally preferred for the maid to lodge separately, he laid her in a servant's cot in a corner of the room he'd chosen for Conora. Until they knew more, he had to keep them quarantined together. He left Raina in her chemise before tucking her in, out of respect for her Meriverian sensibilities—even if he doubted how seriously she held them.

As Calosandros checked on Conora again—still burning—Anabusos returned with a belligerent but somewhat tired-looking Melaine.

"She's warm. That makes all three." Anabusos shut and locked the door. "I told anyone who asked that they're suffering from exhaustion. All of our people appear to be fine for now. I alerted a trusted man to fetch a medicine kit and stand by for orders at the door." He took off his gloves. "Who do you want me to start with?"

"Conora," Calosandros said without hesitation.

Anabusos nodded. "Track me." He hovered his hand over Conora's forehead.

"Of course." Calosandros would make sure Anabusos used enough Ice to cool her fever without giving her hypothermia or frostbite. As Calosandros sat on the edge of the bed and softly wrapped his hand around the side of her neck, the glands under her jaw felt swollen beneath his fingers. He nodded to Anabusos, who laid his hand down on her. As the heat slowly leached away, Conora groaned and shifted uncomfortably, then began shivering. But it wasn't until she felt cool under Calosandros's hand that he called to stop.

Anabusos backed away and wiped his sweaty brow with his sleeve. "Shit. That was a lot." He stripped down to his shirt and chiton. "Raina next?"

Calosandros followed him to repeat the process for Raina. By the time they finished, Anabusos was visibly sweating circles through his shirt.

He held up a hand and took a deep breath, venting his chiton with his other hand. "I need a break. Lady Melaine seems well enough to wait."

She huffed and crossed her arms. She'd been sitting in a chair, watching them warily. "Why don't you call for a real physician?"

Calosandros sighed. "We cannot call for anyone else without trapping them in here with us. Any competent physician would be calling for an Ice user anyway. And we're both as experienced with triage and field medicine as any other Urstillian soldier, Anabusos more so."

Conora shivered and curled up on her side. "*Cal?*" she groaned.

Calosandros grabbed the thick blanket and cover and wrapped them over her, pausing with his arms around her. "I know how miserable that is, but it had to be done."

"Everything hurts," she cried, her voice small and broken.

"I'm sorry, my little vixen."

Melaine seethed. "You cannot let her suffer like this. Who cares if the physician is forced to stay in here?"

He shook his head. "That wouldn't help. You must understand, a foreign contagion is not allowed to run unchecked in the empire. In a situation like this, an imperial physician will prioritize Urstillian safety over the comfort or health of any of you—over your *lives.*"

She glared. "You cannot be serious."

"Until we know what this illness is, the safest thing we can do for you is to keep you contained and keep this quiet."

A knock at the door signaled Anabusos to check. He unlocked the door and opened it just enough to retrieve a box and a stack of buckets before relocking it. Setting the box on a table, he set a bucket on the floor near Raina, then handed one each to Calosandros and Melaine.

She frowned. "What is this for?"

Anabusos's trusted man had been just in time; Conora began twitching and convulsing. Calosandros propped her up and placed his bucket in front of her as she gagged and retched. Then she forcefully vomited into it.

Melaine shrank back and held her bucket close. "Never mind."

By the end of the night, Raina and Melaine were in the same condition as Conora, taking turns alternating between blacking out and vomiting. Anabusos had to cool them every half hour. Melaine occupied one of the two cots that Anabusos's man had brought after the medicine kit.

Since Calosandros wasn't the one wearing himself out with his Gift, he set to work on creating a tincture for the women. Still unsure what they were fighting, he had to use the symptoms he knew and hope one of the ingredients he used brought them some relief: nettle leaves for the aching; yarrow leaves for fever; mahonia berries and alder bark for vomiting; cherry bark and salal leaves for general contagion.

They were most lucid just after Anabusos lowered their fevers, so that's when Calosandros gave them the spoonfuls of tincture, chased with sips of water. All the women understandably gagged on the dense mixture, but thankfully, they didn't immediately vomit it back up. Most of the food went to the men and dogs as the women could only manage an appetite for small amounts of broth.

Anabusos's man was diligent about bringing them food and linens. He'd knock on the door, then back away from the fresh supplies on the floor. Anabusos would swap them for soiled towels, sheets, clothing, and dishes. Somewhere, secret stockpiles of the used items would grow until they could name the disease and decide whether to burn it all or wash them to safely return them to normal use.

Time dragged on through the night and the next day and the next night and the day after that. With nobody else to take care of their charges, Calosandros and Anabusos took turns stealing catnaps between fever spikes, alternating use of the cot. When he sat vigil, Calosandros would hold Conora's hand—if and when she had moments of wakefulness, the connection seemed to soothe her.

There were so many sicknesses it could be, and if there was anything distinctive about this one, they weren't seeing it. That was, until the third day.

Conora finally stopped vomiting—or had nothing left to bring up—it was hard to tell which yet. She woke during one of Calosandros's vigils and squeezed his hand. More alert than usual, she sat up weakly and leaned against the headboard. Her forehead still felt hot, but it didn't burn like it had before, and yet her cheeks were flushed redder than ever.

"How are you feeling?" he asked her.

"Tired...a bit foggy? The pain is better." She grimaced. "I feel disgusting, though, like I want to claw my own skin off just to be rid of the grime."

He chuckled. "That's understandable. We'll run you a bath."

He turned on the faucet and waited until half the tub was filled before striking the flint to heat it. Hopefully, it would keep it from being shockingly cold without setting her fever off again. Then he helped her in and took over scrubbing her down. As he worked, she scratched at her chest, her arms, her neck, getting more agitated and scratching more frequently as the bath went on. She twisted to scratch her back and immediately moved back to her chest, her fingertips ready to dig into her own skin.

Calosandros grabbed her wrist to stop her. "What are you doing?"

"It itches so badly!"

He grabbed her other hand, which was already moving to scratch. "But you're hurting yourself, little vixen."

Her eyes welled up. "Please make it stop."

If he added sagebrush, the yarrow and alder he'd used in the tincture could soothe rashes. But if he let go of her hands, he didn't trust her not to impulsively scratch again. He called to Anabusos.

"Did something happen?"

"We have a new symptom. She's scratching at herself like a little girl with bear fever. Can you start a salve of sagebrush, yarrow, and alder while I protect her from herself?"

She leaned back and tried to scrape her back against the tub.

He cleared his throat at her and gave her a look that said, *What did I just say? Stop that!*

She sighed in defeat and rested her head on his arm, which stretched out her back, and Calosandros gasped. Long welts ran across her skin in rows, like miniature bear claw marks. It was a distinctive symptom, but it didn't make sense to see it on a grown woman. Urstillian bear fever was strictly a childhood illness; people got it once as a pre-Gift child or not at all. At least the rapid spread made sense as it tended to rip through whole villages at a time.

Calosandros shook his head. This was too intense for bear fever. Although the symptoms they'd displayed so far technically matched, for children with bear fever, they were never this extreme: a mild fever, some nausea, a need to stop running outside and rest for a few days.

"Anabusos, do you see this?"

He set down the mixture he was making, staring at her back. "Fuck. You weren't kidding about the bear fever. But..."

"It doesn't make sense to see three adults with bear fever?"

Anabusos nodded, brows furrowed. "Do you have one of those history books you bought for Conora in here?"

Calosandros thought back to the day they'd arrived... "Yes! She was carrying one because she was still studying when we left that morning. It should be near the bed where I took her clothes off."

Anabusos quickly found the book and riffled through it. "Aha. Let's see..." He read for a bit, then snapped it shut. "Fuck!"

"Well, that's not good," Conora said.

"You followed that conversation?" Calosandros asked.

"No, but I've listened to you two enough to know what 'fuck' means."

At least he'd taught her the important things... "Anabusos?"

"Well, the good news is that they're not a danger to anyone in Urstille."

"The bad news?"

"The first time this thing showed up about one hundred and fifty years ago, adults were getting it too. It just spreads so well that it's almost impossible not to encounter it before adulthood now. It was in the history book because it killed a large number of the infected adults back then."

No. He hadn't met the woman of his dreams just for her to die of something as trivial as bear fever. What perverse sense was there in that? Besides, they'd learned to treat it in the last century and a half.

"You look scared, *Cal*. What did he say?"

"Conora, how old were you when you had bear fever?" He knew the answer but casually asked the question, praying she would answer it as normally as anyone else in Urstille would.

"I've never even heard of it."

"Maybe it was called Urstillian fever or Urstillian bear fever?"

She shook her head. "Is that what this is?"

He nodded. "Anabusos and I were nine years old when we caught it, and that was considered late. You're supposed to be immune to it one way or another by the time you reach adulthood."

"That's good, then, right? If children can usually handle it, it must not be that serious."

Unable to voice it or lie to her face, he grabbed a towel. "Anabusos is almost finished with that salve. Let's get you dried off so we can apply it." He drained the tub and helped her stand.

Anabusos handed him the bowl of salve, not bothering to make a joke about helping to apply it. Though Calosandros obviously would have objected, the lack of the offer was unnerving.

It took a while to apply since the salve had to go everywhere, but that gave Anabusos time to change Conora's sheets and lay a fresh towel in the middle of the bed so she didn't soak it completely while she was covered head to toe in the herbal concoction. Calosandros helped Conora back to the bed while Anabusos moved on to checking Raina and Melaine.

"Raina's cooling a bit. We might as well mix up some salve for her next." Then Anabusos checked Melaine. "Fuck."

Knowing Conora understood, Calosandros exchanged looks of concern with her.

"Melaine's fever is worse than ever," Anabusos said.

Calosandros grabbed a pair of mittens from Conora's clothes and handed them to her. "To keep you from scratching by accident." Then he kissed her forehead and went to Melaine.

Anabusos was physically ready, his hand over Melaine's forehead, but his eyes held warning. Calosandros placed his hand on her neck and nodded. Anabusos had understated the fever. It was almost painful to touch her skin. And she wasn't cooling.

Anabusos shook his head slowly, then whispered, "She's past the threshold. I can't safely pull enough power to fight the fever without freezing her skin."

They both looked down at Melaine, who was shivering violently. What else could they do?

"What if you freeze the bath?" Calosandros asked.

"It might work, or the shock of that might kill her instead." Anabusos started drawing the bath, freezing chunks as it filled.

He'd barely covered the bottom of the tub when Melaine twitched. Calosandros wanted to get her into the tub, but he couldn't pick her up while she was spasming. Then, in the midst of the horrifying sight, a piece of the horror just...dissolved. This wasn't a poor sweet widow who was traveling with her beloved daughter. She was a calculating manipulator who had coerced Conora into bringing her along after a lifetime of control. And if her Allure wasn't working now, under these circumstances, it meant something terrible.

174

"Anabusos, stop." Calosandros backed away from Melaine and moved on to someone who wasn't beyond help.

Conora was drifting but fighting to stay awake, her eyelids heavy. "What's going on? The dogs are scared."

He tucked a stray curl behind her ear and rubbed his thumb on her cheek. "Just look at me. I promise to tell you everything later, but I want your focus here right now. Snuggle with Spruce and Cloudy, look at me, and rest."

Conora did not need to see her mother's death throes, have them seared into her mind, especially when it could mean the difference between her fighting this illness or succumbing to that same death. It didn't matter if she hated him for it later. She would survive. He would do whatever was necessary to ensure it.

He could not let go of her, not ever.

Anabusos approached them and quietly said, "She's gone."

Calosandros nodded. "Your trusted man is safe to enter and help you remove her."

"Where to?"

Conora should get a chance to bury her mother, but knowing the course of bear fever, she still had days ahead of her to fight this. "You'll have to keep her out in the snow for a while."

"And what do I say if anyone asks what happened to her?"

A horrid pit settled in the bottom of Calosandros's stomach. They couldn't afford questions. Or, rather, Meriveria couldn't afford them. If it became known that the Meriverians were susceptible to bear fever, the emperor would see it as an opportunity, and the kingdoms of Carum Sound would be devastated. All that he and Conora had done to protect her homeland would be for nothing.

Anabusos tried another question. "Since people can safely enter, how many servants should I bring back to help with the princess and Raina?"

"Nobody else in Urstille can know about the bear fever in this room," Calosandros said.

"But we need help."

"I know that. But more lives will be lost if this is not kept secret." It was the one line he could not cross to save his dearest little vixen. She would rightly never forgive him if he doomed her home.

"We can't keep this secret forever. People know the princess fainted, that she's been kept in this room. Soon they'll know her mother is dead."

Anabusos was right. Calosandros had to do something with the information they'd learned before it came out naturally. Even if they somehow managed to keep this room a secret, it was only a matter of time before another Meriverian crossed the border and contracted bear fever.

"Prepare Lady Melaine to return home immediately. We also need a discreet Flight messenger," Calosandros said. "I have to send a letter to Meria as fast as possible."

Conora had fallen asleep as they talked. Though not exactly peaceful, it was the least fitful sleep she'd had in days. Calosandros kissed her forehead and left her under the dogs' dutiful watch as he found paper and pen.

What would he write to Kennard and Odelia? He had to warn them in a way that they would understand without arousing suspicion if the emperor wanted to intercept the message. After Calosandros's actions so far, warning Meriveria would be seen as a betrayal of Urstille. It didn't matter that the kingdom posed no threat to them. Helping the kingdom was a threat to the emperor's ambitions. Calosandros would have to use as many allusions and euphemisms as he could think of.

As Calosandros pondered the letter, Raina stirred. "Where did Anabusos go? And Lady Melaine?"

"A friend is helping him take Lady Melaine to more suitable lodging."

"I thought we all had to stay together while we're sick."

"Lady Melaine is no longer sick." Maybe he was more capable of this lingual sleight of hand than he thought. He picked up a bowl of salve that Anabusos had prepared and handed it to Raina. "If you aren't itchy now, you will be soon. This will help."

She thanked him as he sat back down at the table to write.

Your Majesties,
Queen Odelia and King Kennard of Meriveria,
    Conora and I must thank you profusely for the
wedding gift. Our greatest wish is that you would share
it with all of your subjects as soon as possible. Iverish
would be a lovely city to start with. As the first
Meriverians I met, the residents there gave me such a
warm welcome.
    Unfortunately, I must inform you that Lady Melaine
is no longer with us. It seems she needed to reunite with
her husband. I am certain that this letter will reach you

before her, and I wish for you to be prepared for her
arrival. The children will react much better than grown
men and women to this development, but I believe that,
among all monarchs, you both are uniquely qualified to
handle this.

I am sending you a gift with this letter as your
Urstillian history texts seem to be lacking. You will likely
find the period fifty years after the Great Urstillian
Penetration to be particularly illuminating. Conora finds
knowledge to be an itch that must be scratched.

Your Brother,
His Imperial Highness,
Crown Prince Calosandros of Urstille

For the next two days, Conora's fevers ceased to be dangerously high;
herbal teas were enough to manage them without further intervention from
Anabusos's Ice. Calosandros would not leave her side, ever. When he needed
to sleep, he gently nudged his way onto the middle of the bed, relieved that
the dogs regarded him with enough respect to allow him in—as long as they
could rest atop him to reach Conora. Considering that he'd given her all the
blankets on the bed, it wasn't a terrible trade-off to sleep under the fluffy
creatures, even if they each were half his weight.

But Raina still could not keep food down, and eventually, not even
water. Calosandros had to concede to allowing Anabusos's trusted man to
be brought into the room to give Anabusos rest from watching Raina. She
was slowly wasting away, her lips dry and cracked, and none of them knew
what more they could do for her. The poor woman was fighting like hell to
hold on, surviving on sheer will. With just a little food and water, they were
certain she could claw her way back to health, but the retching never
stopped.

Calosandros had to distract Conora from the state of the other
Meriverian. He knew she could see and hear what was happening with
Raina, but when Conora was awake, her attention was best used for
practical needs: bathing, applying salve, eating, and drinking. She didn't
speak much, not even a mention of her mother's absence, which didn't help
his worry for her.

So he spoke enough for both of them. Knowing he was speaking Urstillian from his conversations with Anabusos, he narrated everything he did for her. He recited poetry, nursery rhymes, folktales, fairy tales, war stories, whatever came to mind. And when Raina was retching, he'd sing to Conora. They were mostly simple lullabies, but they'd coaxed a few weary smiles out of her. Calosandros didn't care if he talked and sang himself hoarse, as long as it kept her with him, not drifting into despair or grief.

He was not going to lose his little vixen.

26

ALONE

Grabia

Conora had lost whole days. It all ran together, strange memories of fever, pain, and a maddening rash. But she also remembered Calosandros, Anabusos, Spruce, and Cloudy, ever-present, watching over her. Talk of bear fever. Salves and mittens. Swearing and crying. Mother disappeared. Raina gagging and retching.

Calosandros talked and sang, his voice a lifeline whenever she got confused. Not that she understood much of what he said. But she understood *nuil yos*. It was the name always on his lips as he cared for her, *nuil yos*. She just wanted to hear him call her *nuil yos*.

He sang louder once, his face near to hers in as close to an embrace as he could get without touching much of her searing-rash-covered body. It was a melancholy song, not the softly lilting tunes he'd been singing. And when he was done, the room became so quiet.

Nobody told her, but Conora knew. She was alone. She was the only Meriverian left.

But Calosandros kept talking, kept singing. He would not let her stay alone completely. It sparked a desire she wasn't used to: she wanted more than anything to simply be held. And at some point, that desire became stronger than the pain of her skin. When he carefully lay beside her, she curled into him until he slowly wrapped his arms around her. She didn't know if it was the salve or time or purely desire, but the sting was not as bad as she anticipated, and she lingered, enduring it for the warm comfort of his embrace.

He kissed her forehead, her nose. "Nuil yos...yis sid icidoin."

"Yis sid icidoin, Cal," she said. (I am here.)

He let out a gasping sigh and laughed softly. "Mios, nuil yos, oin sid icida." (Yes, you are here.)

Then he kissed her tenderly, reminding her why she was here.

Though Conora had made it through the worst of bear fever and was on the mend, it took two more days after the kiss before Calosandros would entertain the idea of leaving. He insisted the rash be completely faded and that Conora be past the need for medicinal tea. He said there was nowhere they needed to be quickly enough to risk a relapse.

And Conora had one requirement before they left. She asked to see the graves.

Calosandros looked so guilty. "*Nuil yos*, I'm so sorry."

"I know why you shielded me, that you were sparing me the worst details when I was at my weakest. It took time for my mind to catch up to what happened, but I still knew that Mother and Raina didn't make it. I just want to say goodbye."

"Anabusos can show you where Raina is, but your mother..." He took a deep breath. "She's on her way back to Meria, if not there by now. I had to write to your family a week ago."

Conora's eyes widened. "You sent the letter a week ago?"

"Dearest, you were sick for ten days. I had to warn them as quickly as possible." He caressed her cheek. "We weren't even sure that you would..." He blinked and cleared his throat. "But you're here, *nuil yos*, and we can say goodbye to Raina."

She nodded, and he sent for Anabusos, who led them out of town to the graveyard. A dark red mound of freshly disturbed dirt was stark against the white snow, like the ground had been cut open and bled.

A man was laying a purple aster on the grave, and when he saw them, he bowed and began to leave. Something about him seemed familiar, but Conora couldn't place it. His eyes watered as he shook hands with Anabusos. The pair exchanged whispers and sad nods, then moved on from one another within moments. The man's voice was more familiar than his face, connected to fleeting memories from the fever. Even Calosandros put a hand on the man's shoulder and squeezed as he passed—a gesture that seemed to say *sorry* as much as *thank you*. Conora did not ask about the man; the parts of Raina's life that she'd chosen not to share could remain private in her death.

Conora crouched by the graveside. Unlike with Valerzan, she didn't have a lifetime of memories together with Raina. But she'd been loyal and gone beyond her duties as a maid to help Conora.

She kissed her fingertips, then picked up a handful of dirt and let it slowly fall from her hand. "There was more to you than we'll ever know, and I think you and I were on our way to being dear friends. You deserved to explore more of Urstille. Rest well and find peace, Raina." Then Conora finished with a quiet howl for her fellow Animal Speaker: *Goodbye.*

She stood and dusted her hands, and Calosandros put his arm around her. "That was beautiful."

Anabusos stood there, staring past them at the grave. Though Conora couldn't exactly remember all he'd done, she knew he'd been at their sides for days and used his Ice to fight their fevers. And she knew he'd probably shared a bed with Raina at least once. Burying her could not have been easy.

Conora didn't know much Urstillian she could say to Anabusos, and it would probably come out broken, but it felt more meaningful than asking Calosandros to translate. She approached Anabusos and cautiously opened her arms for a hug—the gesture terrified her when it wasn't with those closest to her.

As he embraced her, she said, "Yis oid icredoin yis sid icidoin." (Thank you I am here.)

He squeezed her and sniffled. "Pana. Yis siad icpiloin oin sid icida sa." Then he patted her back and let go, turning to hide his face as he walked away.

She asked Calosandros what he said.

"Good. He's glad you are here too."

When it was time to depart in the morning, Conora steeled herself for the long journey to the next city. As daunting as the exertion was, she couldn't wait to leave Orosiad. Most of the army had already gone on without them a week ago when they realized the soldiers were in no danger of spreading a foreign contagion. With Calosandros's arm around her, Conora walked outside the imperial mansion to find a basket sled lined with pillows and woolen blankets.

Calosandros rushed over to fluff one of the pillows, waving her closer. "Come, sit!"

She gasped and smiled as she approached. "I assumed we'd keep walking."

"Not you." He held her hand to help her settle into the seat. "What kind of husband would I be if I made *nuil yos* walk after what you've endured? Anabusos and I redistributed the supplies to free a sled for you." He began wrapping the blankets around her, tucking them tightly underneath and behind her.

"What about you?" she asked.

He smiled. "I'm going to push you."

"*Cal*, you've already done so much for me..."

He crouched and caressed her cheek. "I'm perfectly capable. It's not as if I have these muscles just to look handsome for you." He winked. "And most importantly, there is a duty that comes with the privilege of calling you dearest." Calosandros kissed her.

As he stood back up, Spruce began jumping excitedly around the sled, leaning down onto his front paws and wagging his tail. *Pull? We pull sled? PULL!!!* He jumped on Cloudy and tugged at his ear. *Pull! Pull!*

Cloudy was too busy wagging his own tail and stamping his front paws to fuss with Spruce. *Please, please, please, please, please..."*

Conora laughed. "You have two volunteers to help you if we can find their harnesses."

"And I thought they were just guard dogs," Calosandros said. "I'll check our gear." Soon he had Spruce and Cloudy attached side-by-side to the front of the sled. Behind Conora, Calosandros took hold of the cart. "Can you tell them not to go too fast? I don't want to leave Anabusos and what's left of our company behind."

Spruce, Cloudy, not fast. Stay with the pack. Go!

After two days of riding in the sled, Conora felt guilty about making Calosandros push her, so when they cuddled in bed that night, she offered to walk to give him a break the next day.

He sighed. "Are you *sure*? It's not a hardship. I really could push you all the way to Pasutrus."

"Why are you so determined not to have me walk with everyone else?"

He shrugged. "I like the sled. That little stretch today when we let the dogs run like they wanted? That was fun."

There had to be more to it. She tested him: "I could teach you commands to run the sled with gear."

"Clever *nuil yos*." He sighed again and kissed her forehead. "When I think about you marching with us, all I can think about is you collapsing. I know it's weak to admit it, but you scared the shit out of me."

"You said people only get bear fever once. It won't happen again."

Pulling her closer, he held her tightly. "I know that. I know." He pressed a firm kiss to the top of her head. "I just liked not having to think about it for a little while." Taking deep controlled breaths, he almost sounded as if he'd fallen asleep when he finally asked, "What about you? Do you really want to walk in the snow? If this is about showing how strong you are, you've already done that by surviving."

Conora laughed. "No, it's not exactly my favorite activity. I'm feeling better and stronger, but I can't do anything but sleep and ride in the sled. I'm getting restless." She pushed up from his chest to look at him. "I need to *do* something."

Reaching for his soft beard, she kissed him tentatively, waiting for him to tell her she needed rest. He'd been like this since the bear fever, affectionate but lacking any sensual desire. Conora was tired of being fragile, too delicate to kiss passionately, too breakable to make love. She needed to feel alive, feel desire rage through her veins and consume her.

When he broke away, she wanted to scream. But she held her breath in, rolling over and curling into herself, trying not to cry. She couldn't rightly be angry with him when he had been putting his all into caring for her.

He shifted in bed behind her and brushed the backs of his fingers over her cheek. "*Nuil yos?*"

Not wanting to confront what was bothering her, she focused on the other conundrum that had been slowly pestering her. She rolled onto her back to look at him. "How are you doing that?"

"Doing what?"

"Calling me *nuil yos*."

He frowned, puzzled. "That's what I've always called you."

"But you're saying it in Urstillian, even when you're speaking Meriverian."

He blinked and laughed. "What? Since when?"

"I don't remember you doing it before I got sick, but since I've gotten better, I don't think I've heard you say it in Meriverian at all."

"Ah...I did so much talking through all that, and most of it was probably in Urstillian." His cheeks turned red. "And I may have favored my pet name for you a little too much. Now it feels like a valid name."

So, he did see her differently. It haunted him.

He brushed a curl off her forehead. "I'm sorry if you miss hearing it in your native tongue. I don't know how to undo it."

She shook her head. "It's fine. It sounds prettier in Urstillian anyway."

"Well, you certainly don't look fine with it. What's upsetting you?"

Conora closed her eyes so she could focus on keeping her words calm. "It's another change to accept. I understand why you see me differently—I can't fault you for that. But it still hurts."

"What do you mean 'differently'?"

Inhaling deeply, she willed her bottom lip to stop quivering. "We've been together such a short time, and through most of it, you've seen me weak and disgusting and covered in a rash..." She laughed bitterly.

"*Nuil yos...*" Calosandros caressed her cheek. "Look at me, dearest."

Though she opened her eyes, she still couldn't meet his gaze, staring at his lips instead. "Of course, that would erode your attraction to me."

Holding her chin in place, he moved himself into her eyeline, his brow deeply furrowed. "Bullshit. That is complete and utter bullshit, a whole bison's worth." He stared intensely into her eyes, making her heart pound against her chest. "I never knew the true madness of desire until I met you."

"Then, why do you push me away?"

"Because I need you to ask. I don't want to hurt you, and I desire you too badly to trust my own judgment in this."

Conora raised an eyebrow. His judgment? She hadn't known it to be suspect before.

"The day you collapsed, you showed me just how far you will push yourself to look strong, and the selfless courage you displayed when you accepted my proposal is admirable and endearing. But it means that, as you recover and grieve, if I come to you with my desire, you might put on a brave face and accept it, even if you aren't feeling strong enough. Instead of putting that pressure on you, I am waiting for you to tell me what you want when you are ready."

She reached up to stroke his beard and kissed him vigorously. "I want to make love," she breathed.

He kissed her back with matched passion, then pulled back a few inches. "Just to be sure, that's your euphemism for—"

Conora put a finger on his lips. She chose the clearest words he would understand, annunciating carefully. "Cal, yid iclasa." (Fuck me.)

He grinned. "Mios, nuil yos sioria *coir*." (Yes, my *very* sexy little vixen.)

27

COMING HOME

Coiyos A Iciban

Conora did not object to the sled again. Her night with Calosandros had been as tiring as it was satisfying—and completely worth it. When he harnessed the dogs and offered without commentary to help her into the seat, she gratefully limited her response to a simple *yis oid icredoin* (thank you) and a quick kiss, which became a routine of somewhat normalcy for the last few days of their trip.

When they finally sighted Pasutrus ahead of them, Calosandros told Conora to look out for a bear statue. "There's one posted half a mile out from the capital at each cardinal and ordinal point. When we reach it, you may need to cover your ears."

She passed the message along to Cloudy and Spruce: *Humans get loud. Do not be scared. Keep pulling.*

Sure enough, when they passed a snarling life-sized black granite grizzly bear, Calosandros let out a whoop. He called to Anabusos, who clapped three times, then shouted, "Na lulos!" (Another success!) After the next three claps, more men clapped and shouted in time with him, quickly growing in volume until the whole company was chanting together.

Thankful for the warning, Conora had pushed a blanket up to hold around her ears, hopefully making it appear as a response to the cold, rather than overwhelmed as Calosandros joined in the booming noise just above her head, projecting himself at full volume. For such a simple chant, it seemed to go on forever. The city gates began opening at their approach, timed to clear their entry without pausing their march, and the company mercifully ended the chant with a brief whooping cheer. Inside, crowds had lined up for a parade, just like in previous cities, though now with a much larger population spilling over the sides of the streets and leaning out of windows.

"Icra," Calosandros told Conora as soon as they cleared the gates.
Cloudy and Spruce, stop.

He smiled as he helped her up out of the sled. Then he pulled her close, his arm tightly wrapped around her waist. "Sima su coiyos, nuil yos."

She had a guess as to the meaning from the context, but she hadn't heard the words before, so she asked, "Translation?"

He laughed, his green eyes alight with joy. "Welcome home."

Then he kissed her, genuinely at first, but it turned into the showy, exaggerated kind that had always brought loud cheers and whistles from the onlookers. While it did garner some response, it wasn't anywhere near as enthusiastic as the other cities, even before accounting for size. When he broke the kiss, Calosandros looked visibly shaken for a moment. But he forced a big smile before taking her hand and waving to the crowd. Conora played her part as well, smiling and waving in spite of the worry his worry inspired in her.

The palace at the center of the capital looked like nothing she'd ever seen before. Though bigger than the Cedar Palace, the *entire* building was made of stone; a structure like that would have sunk half into the ground in Meriveria. Most of the imposing structure had been formed from limestone into a sprawling oval and steeply roofed with slate. Several jutting towers seemed from a distance to be covered with climbing greenery on the south side, but a closer view revealed decorative inlays of serpentine and black marble that spiraled and twisted upwards. The top of each tower had what looked to be an open section supported by pillars.

Because the palace faced south, instead of heading due east, the group had to wind their way southeast to reach the gate separating the city from the imperial grounds. Pairs of black granite statues of snarling bears flanked both the gate and palace entrance itself. Behind the oddly lightweight entry doors, temporary-looking wooden panels enclosed a long portico that ended in a much more substantial-looking set of double doors.

Conora took deep breaths as they passed the bear statues. Fake as they were, their aggressive pose was unsettling, a warning against trespassers—and hauntingly familiar as something her late Father had done all too often. The Urstillians might as well have hung giant signs saying, "Go away!"—or, more likely, "Fuck off!" Even the interior oozed aggression: axes, shields, leather, and antlers were the primary decor.

Calosandros, on the other hand, acted with complete nonchalance from the moment he unharnessed the dogs just in front of the palace, strolling casually inside. Whatever had unnerved him before seemed to no longer concern him.

Grinning, he slipped an arm around her waist and brushed his lips against her ear. "Would you like to tour the palace first or see my—*our* room?"

Conora was torn between desire for solitude and curiosity about her new home. "How about a partial tour? You can just show me whatever is on the way to our room."

With the excitement of a dancer, he pivoted the pair of them to take in the room. "This is obviously the entryway." He paused cheek-to-cheek with her and breathlessly continued, "You see those grated doors against the wall? In the summer, we use those and leave the wooden doors open. And we take down the wood panels we passed on the way in. It's a pity I couldn't introduce this to you when it's all open and airy—and brighter." He pointed straight overhead, where a mostly empty tower rose above them to what looked like a flat wooden ceiling. "We open those shutters too."

The entryway split to the right or left, and Calosandros led her right, nearly bouncing with each step. "The emperor has the northernmost rooms. We live to the east of him, literally at his right hand. My mother lives to the west."

Conora wasn't entirely new to the concept of the empress having separate quarters—unlike Odelia and Kennard, her parents had chosen a similar arrangement—but then she remembered that Calosandros said his parents had never made a pledge of devotion. The Urstillians likely used the separate spaces for more than some time to be alone.

"Ooh!" They'd barely walked down the hallway when he gave her a quick giddy squeeze and pointed out a smaller corridor to the left. "That leads to the throne room. There's another way into it from the other side of the entryway."

All the way down the larger, curved hallway, doors lined their left side, while windows lined the right, even as they rounded east and north. Cloudy and Spruce sniffed out their new surroundings. "All the rooms are on the same side?" Conora noted.

"They all face the courtyard garden, like your room at the Cedar Palace. This one hallway circles the whole perimeter. I've never had a knack for engineering, so you'll have to ask someone else how it works, but this whole place is designed for the interior rooms to stay warm in the winter. And, in the summer, everything opens to be pleasantly cool and breezy."

Halfway between doors, there were alcoves hung with curtains and lined with padded fabric. Conora pointed to one as they passed. "Are these part of that engineering, or do you know what they're for?"

"The fuck-closets?" He laughed. "I think those are self-explanatory."

Of course. Why had she expected something in Urstille to be anything but sexual or violent? "Is that really what they're called, or are you teasing me?"

Calosandros smirked. "Do you need a demonstration?"

"I think a bed sounds more comfortable."

He laughed. "It definitely is. These are for unexpected passionate encounters." He playfully patted her ass.

"That's all they're for? Nobody uses them for midday naps or private conversations or something?"

"No. In fact—" he lowered his voice to one of concern "—there is only one reason to invite someone to a fuck-closet, so you should never follow *anyone* else into one—not even family. Don't let someone try to trick you by saying they want to gossip in there."

Conora nodded. "I assume these devious courtiers won't be asking in Meriverian. What is it in Urstillian? I assume something with *iclas*."

"Mios, griliclasee."

She tried the word out a few times until she began to feel confident she'd recognize it.

Eventually, the limestone floor ahead of them became more ornate, inlaid with a giant bear in black marble. Conora pointed to the door centered behind the design. "I'm guessing that belongs to the emperor." She pointed to a door several yards closer to them. "So, this must be ours?"

"Nicely done, *nuil yos*." He kissed her cheek and slipped a heavy key into her hand. "I'll let you have the honor."

Conora turned the key in the thick cherrywood door, opening it to a large room that seemed to function as both bedroom and sitting room. A desk and bookcases sat on one side of the door, and on the other, a dressing table, mirrors, and tub. A small door behind the tub presumably led to a toilet. Across from a bed with red curtains, a sofa and chairs faced a giant hearth—which someone had lit. A large table with chairs was at the back of the somewhat wedge-shaped room, where pillars had been filled in with wooden panels to create a temporary wall. She would have to make sure the dogs could find a way through one of the panels to the garden on the other side.

But a second glance around the room began to turn her stomach. The red-curtained bed was covered in wolf hides, and above it, a mounted bear head snarled at the room. Over the hearth were three antlered buck heads. A bearskin rug lay in the middle of the floor.

189

Conora froze. She might learn to live with the wolf and bear furs for the warmth they provided, but she could *not* sleep in a room with severed heads. And yet it felt like overstepping to demand changes from the moment she entered. What if he was proud of how it looked?

She backed up into Calosandros, who put steady hands on her shoulders and asked, "What do you think?"

She swallowed. "W-who chose the decor in this room?"

"I'm not sure. It's looked like this for as long as I can— Shit. I see it now." He led her to the desk chair that faced the bookshelves instead of the rest of the room. "We're changing this as soon as possible." He pulled a thick cord that hung next to the door, then returned to put his arms around her.

She leaned against him. "Thank you."

"I really should have thought this through more. I'd forgotten how those stupid trophies used to give me nightmares."

"You grew up in this room? But you aren't even hesitating to change it for me?"

He shrugged. "I never liked those things anyway. I just hadn't thought about what I'd replace them with until now." He kissed the top of her head, then walked over to the bed. "Let's start with this ugly thing." He pulled off his boots and climbed up to lift the bear head off the wall, grunting as he grappled with the unwieldy trophy and dropped it on the bed. Then he folded the fur bedcover over it until it formed a rough bundle, which he deposited on top of the bearskin rug.

The dogs rushed over to inspect it, then turned their snouts up in disgust and backed away. *Wolves bad.*

She hushed them. *It's okay. The wolfskins are leaving.*

Dusting off his hands and smiling at Conora, Calosandros hopped onto the bed, then patted the space next to himself.

She removed her boots, then sat next to him and leaned on his shoulder. "You might change your mind about that cover if we freeze tonight."

"Our room is well heated. Wool will be enough. Besides, isn't that what we let the dogs in the room for?"

Conora laughed and playfully shoved him.

"So, other than the hunting trophies, what do you think of it?" Calosandros asked.

"It's cozier than I expected." She looked at a bookcase and gasped. "A lyre! You played so beautifully that first night we spent together." Hopping off the bed, she rushed over to the instrument and picked it up.

Somebody knocked on the door. Calosandros opened it and ushered in a manservant, who bowed before entering, carrying a tray of food, which he set on the large table at the far end of the room. He and Calosandros exchanged Urstillian so rapidly, Conora couldn't catch a single word. But the man picked up one end of the bearskin rug and dragged the pile of trophies just outside the door as Calosandros began pouring wine.

"It looks better already." Conora said.

"I thought the same thing when you walked in." Calosandros handed her a cup of the fragrant raspberry wine.

Her cheeks warmed. "Should we close the door?"

"Nnn-mmm." He had been taking a sip and shook his head as he swallowed. "It's just for a little while, and the servants know to mind their own business anyway. He'll be back with a ladder and a cart for the rest. I said to take every single trophy and pelt out of this room and the unused one next to us."

"Why the room next to us?"

He caressed her cheek. "Because that's where our children will live one day, Giver willing." Unhurried, he gave her a soft, sensuous kiss. The way he lingered made her sigh blissfully.

With a sly grin, she lifted the lyre between them. "Watching you play this might make that happen faster."

"Is that so?" He laughed and took the instrument from her, testing out the strings. After a quick tuning, he strummed it and smiled. "Let's see. What is the most seductive song I know...?"

"The one you played before was effective enough to get you in my bed, *Cal*."

With a nod, he began a reprisal of the first tune he'd sung for her. Conora sat back on the bed and drank in his beautiful voice and the sweet wine and the way his fingers danced over the strings. And this time, there were only the two of them, no family members to interfere or interrupt her enjoyment.

As if she'd thought it aloud, a tall, brown-winged woman burst through the open door, gushing, "Calosandros! Yis ictee sul yis icar a icso oid!" (I thought that I heard your ——!)

Conora wasn't sure what *icso* meant. Perhaps "playing"?

Calosandros stopped playing and beamed, throwing his arms around her. "Madee!"

Conora slipped off the bed to stand behind him. Though she hadn't heard the last term before, his reaction and the passing resemblance between them made it clear: mother.

"Yis oid icthiol." (I missed you.) The empress grabbed his face and kissed his cheek with a loud *smack*. Then she turned and, upon seeing Conora, staggered back with a dramatic gasp and swatted her son's chest with the back of her hand. "Calosandros! So u grenguree *papes* icidaree?" (Who is this —— ——?) From her breathless delivery, whatever she had called Conora at least sounded like a compliment.

Calosandros smiled and blushed. "Madee, u Conora Duboinee pan Meripheree icidaree, gras Cabalee pan *Urstil*."

The empress gasped again, then clasped her hands and grinned. "Onee oid?" (Your wife?)

He was positively red as he nodded.

Then the empress squealed and flew at Conora with her arms open, trapping her in a tight bear hug until Calosandros cleared his throat and rescued her.

"A quick introduction, please?" Conora whispered to him.

"Of course, dearest. This is my mother, Empress Nemonee."

Though it was a bit frightening to be tackled by her mother-in-law for their first introduction, Conora was grateful that no threats were made and everyone was fully clothed.

28

MOTHER

Madee

Calosandros's mother always held a great appreciation for beauty. It had been her encouragement to pursue his talents in art and music that had driven him to continue them in spite of the emperor's distaste for sentimentality. So, of course, it took her a matter of seconds to notice the radiant treasure sitting on his bed.

Mother's face showed the same awe he'd felt when he first beheld Conora. "Who is this *gorgeous* creature?"

Calosandros could hardly contain his excitement, so he summarized the formal introduction a bit. "Mother, this is Conora, Royal Princess of Meriveria, now Princess Consort of *Urstille*."

"Your wife?" Mother made her deduction ecstatically—thank the Giver—though perhaps a little too ecstatically.

Flying in for an exuberant hug was clearly too much for Conora, who stiffened, her eyes wide with panic and pleading for release. As he laid the lyre on the bed, Cloudy and Spruce came running, to either investigate this new person or rescue Conora—probably both. Silly as it was, he didn't want to laugh as his poor wife was smothered. He coughed to cover it and pulled his mother away from her as he silently shooed the dogs back with a wave of his hand.

Spruce slunk back with his tail between his legs, while Cloudy let out an offended sigh and sauntered off.

Conora whispered, "A quick introduction, please?"

"Of course, dearest. This is my mother, Empress Nemonee."

Conora gave Mother a nervous smile and an awkward bow, then carefully said in a thick Meriverian accent, "I...am...glad to meet you, Nemonee Empress..." Her eyes widened as she realized her mistake. "Empress Nemonee!"

Imperfect as it was, the effort and recovery were impressive. Calosandros proudly put his arm around Conora, whispering, "My clever little vixen." He kissed her cheek, making her blush adorably as she nestled closer to him.

"Glad to meet you too...*Conora*." Mother pronounced her name as carefully as Conora had spoken Urstillian. Then she turned back to Calosandros. "How long?"

He spoke slowly and held up six fingers, hoping to help Conora follow the conversation somewhat. "Let's see. I've been gone for almost six months now?"

Mother nodded.

"So...we've been married about five and a half months?" He bent one finger halfway down and looked to Conora for confirmation.

She stared at his fingers for a moment, face scrunched in thought. Understanding seemed to dawn as she lit up and nodded with an accented *yes.*

Mother raised an eyebrow and laughed. "What did you do, marry when you met?"

Was the room suddenly feeling very warm? He looked away and shrugged. "It was part of negotiations."

Mother sobered, deeply concerned. "Tell me you didn't alter the terms. Your father—"

"Also told me I needed a wife, didn't he?"

Mother crossed her arms. "*Calosandros.* Those were separate discussions, and— Why are there dogs in your room?"

He followed her gaze to Cloudy and Spruce, who froze mid-crouch, trying to pretend they'd been lying down the whole time. The sneaks had been slowly crawling toward Conora on their bellies. Conora sighed and shook her head at them, then gave a split-second growl and a *huff-huff.* Their ears drooped as they gave her puppy eyes and a whiny hum.

Conora looked up at Calosandros with a similar expression. "Can we introduce them, *Cal?*"

He nodded, letting her speak dog while he spoke human. "Mother, these are Conora's companions. They will be living here now. The white one is Cloudy. The dark one is Spruce."

Conora sent Cloudy, then Spruce, to trot over and sit politely at Mother's feet.

Looking at the dogs and pointing, Mother attempted their names. "*Clodee* and *Sperus?*"

Conora smiled and said with an accent, "*Yes. Good!*" She told

Calosandros, "Could you also let her know they're friendly? You know how they love being petted, *Cal*."

Calosandros passed along the message, demonstrating with a vigorous scratch in the softest part of Spruce's fur, behind his ear.

Mother warily bent down and stroked the top of Cloudy's head. "An Animal Speaker? I can't say I ever expected you to find a consort more fluent in dog than Urstillian," she mused.

Calosandros sighed, annoyed that his normally friendly mother might be so judgmental. "She's clever, and her Urstillian will improve with time. It already has since we crossed the border. You should hear how you sound attempting Meriverian."

Mother put a hand on his shoulder. "I meant it as a compliment, Calosandros. You've always been special, and it should've been obvious that you could never settle for someone who wasn't equally unique."

He bit back a laugh. After being in a meeting where half the room were Speakers, he certainly didn't seem so special anymore, but there was no use arguing with her maternal bias.

She continued, "Besides, it all makes sense now. Beauty like that and a novel Gift? I would've brought her home too if I were you." She took a step back and looked Conora over again, smiling. "Oh, yes, my ladies could do with some novelty."

As Conora instinctively shied away from her gaze, Calosandros pulled her closer to him, taking her right hand with his. "Before you get anyone's hopes up, you should know that Conora and I have made a pledge of devotion." He punctuated the declaration by lifting their right hands so she could see the rings.

Mother grabbed his right hand and gasped, eyes wide. "I'm going to be a grandmother?" She beamed pure joy as she reached for Conora's abdomen.

As Conora flinched, Calosandros grimaced and put his arm out to block his mother from pouncing on his wife again. "Not quite yet."

"'Not quite yet'? What is *that* supposed to—" Mother's eyes filled with pity. "Unless..."

He quickly shook his head. "No. Everything is fine. A royal wedding was part of the negotiations, nothing to do with conception."

"*Calosandros*..." She shook her head at him, disappointed. "You know better than that."

"Mother, she's Meriverian. It's the only form of marriage they know."

She lowered her voice. "You've been married this long without impregnating her, and you've already pledged devotion? It's possible she might be barren. How will you produce an heir, then?"

"It's too soon to be so pessimistic. Due to Meriverian customs, I couldn't bring her with me to the warfront. We've only truly had a chance to try in the past few weeks. And *somebody* has interrupted the foreplay for our most recent attempt to create an heir." He gave her a pointed stare.

She put her hands on her hips. "Well, why didn't you say something? Besides, your door is wide open." She turned to indicate the door and must have finally noticed the manservant climbing down the ladder behind her, carrying the last mounted buck head. Whipping back to Calosandros, she looked aghast. "What is going on here?"

Calosandros shrugged. "I told him to remove all the hunting trophies and hides."

"Those are your father's. You can't just throw them out."

"Well, they can't stay in here now that I'm married to an Animal Speaker. If they're so important, you're welcome to put them in your room."

Mother scoffed, her wings twitching irritably as she grumbled, "I *am* his trophy. I don't need to be surrounded by more of them."

Conora wrapped her arms around Calosandros's waist and looked up at him, those warm brown eyes sparkling in the light of the fireplace. "Translation? Or should I just wait for her to leave first?" she asked softly, brimming with curiosity and a touch of worry, but offering patience.

He brushed the backs of his fingers against her cheek. "She thinks you're wonderful. There are just a lot of changes for her, like there are for you."

Conora narrowed her eyes. "That was all?"

He chuckled. "And she's worried about me, but that's always true." Giver, he wanted to kiss her so badly, audience or not, he leaned in...

Mother sighed loudly. "Oh, my sweet boy, you really do take after me too much." She scoffed and shook her head sadly. "I'll take the damn trophies. But you and I are going to talk more about this situation later. Alone." She gave orders to the servant, then walked out, flying as soon as she cleared the doorway.

Calosandros put a finger to Conora's lips, then broke from her embrace. After following the manservant who was carrying the ladder out the door, he quickly closed and locked the door behind him. Calosandros leaned against it for a moment and sighed.

Then he caught Conora's eyes and smiled. "No more interruptions."

29

EMPEROR

Uboios

Conora squeezed Calosandros's hand and took a deep breath. No matter how many times she smoothed out her skirt and patted her hair, she couldn't shake the feeling that something about her appearance looked completely wrong. After what felt like ages of discussion about whether it was more appropriate to wear something old or new, they had agreed she would choose one of her familiar Meriverian dresses for her introduction to the emperor. Commissioned before her brother's coup, the deep cobalt-blue gown was full of Elgathan symbols: swirling silver waves along the hem splashed up into a dissipating spatter of stars over her skirt, and matching waves around her neckline dipped down to meet a little fox head just below her bosom. It was one of Hortensia's ingenious designs with hidden fastenings, which had vexed poor Calosandros as he helped her dress—though he changed his mind when he saw the effect of the seamless illusion. A silver tiara and necklace, both studded with pearls and sapphires, matched the dress. And to complete the Meriverian look, he'd called a maidservant to arrange Conora's hair using drawings he'd made of Raina's work. The only Urstillian addition was the fluffy brown wool mantle, which complemented the blue dress perfectly and kept her from freezing in attire better suited for a temperate forestland.

It had seemed like such a good idea when they discussed it. This was everything Conora was used to, the way she'd always dressed for court at home. It should have been comforting. But it also reminded her of whom and what she had lost.

She tried to hide her fidgeting free hand behind her skirt. "What if we chose wrong? Maybe I should have worn something new."

Calosandros looked up and down the corridor to the throne room, then pulled Conora into a gentle, loose embrace. "Relax, *nuil yos*. I'll be with you the whole time." He tipped her chin up to meet his gaze. "And you couldn't look more perfect."

His lips on hers temporarily banished the unease.

Rubbing his thumb on her cheek, he smiled. "Truly, this color is stunning. It reminds me of that first, absolutely breathtaking, moment I saw you. Your dress was almost this same hue, just a little darker."

Though the compliment initially warmed her face, something was off about it. But before Conora could respond, the murmur of a crowd swelled over them as a door opened.

Calosandros put his right hand at the small of her back and guided her left arm to drape behind him, her hand resting on his right shoulder—despite practicing the awkward position earlier that morning, it still felt strangely intimate compared to resting her hand on his arm as she'd been raised to expect from a formal pose. He led her to a grand set of double doors, which seemed to instantly open to their approach, and handed a slip of paper to the herald.

The servant bowed, then waved for them to follow him behind a row of pillars, in front of which, a large crowd stood with their backs to them. A wall of wooden panels covered the other side of their path. When they reached a wide aisle through the crowd, the herald announced in a booming voice, "Turoisos To Ubalosa, Calosandros Duboinos Guroiyionosa pan Urstil, noee..." Then he took a big breath before adding, "Turoisee Pun, Conora Duboinee pan Meripheree, gras Turoisee Pun Ubalosa, Cabalee Guroiyionosa pan Urstil."

Great Giver, that was a long title! No wonder Calosandros had to write it down. Their formal introductions had felt so much quicker in Meriverian, not that she would have complained about lingering at that first meeting—one she remembered vividly, with his half-undone red chiton and her own attire carefully chosen to entice...

Wait. She'd specifically chosen her most plunging neckline, a soft camas-blue gown—a pastel bluish purple that looked nothing like the rich Elgathan blue she was currently wearing. What nonsense had Calosandros been on about?

As she grappled with the sudden confusion, Calosandros pressed her forward, and Conora nearly stumbled. Thank the Giver for a long full skirt to hide her clumsy steps.

Or perhaps not. Partway down the aisle of the vast pillared throne room, the Urstillians were whispering, and though Conora didn't understand most of it, she could swear she heard the words *uphaian* (foreigner) and *nandoros* (tent). The way Calosandros tensed at the sound only confirmed it.

Conora inhaled deeply. She couldn't do this if she kept thinking about the other people in the room, and running away or breaking down would only add to her and Calosandros's humiliation. She had to find something, anything else to focus on. The novelty of the architecture would have to do. She counted a dozen limestone pillars holding up the high arches of the ceiling, four flanking each side of the aisle and two additional pairs where the room widened. And over the dais...

Another mounted bear head?

No, it was a collection of five—*five* decapitated creatures adorned the wall behind the throne, all of them with grotesquely aggressive expressions. The throne itself was upholstered with a full bearskin and adorned with antlers.

Conora could feel a tremble beginning in her stomach, one that would spread through her body if she could not tamp it down or channel it soon. She slid her free hand just behind her hip and clenched a fistful of fabric, using the fullness of her skirt to hide the nervous gesture.

Next to the throne, Empress Nemonee sat in a much simpler fur-covered chair. She at least had a warm and encouraging smile for Conora. Nemonee leaned toward the emperor and whispered something, still smiling.

Conora finally dared to look at the man himself. At first glance, he looked much like an older Calosandros, with similar clothing, hair, and beard, though the angles of his face were harder, longer. His mouth cut a harsh line of disapproval, and his beady eyes sent a shiver down her spine. In addition to the expected imperial regalia, he had thick golden spectacles hanging from his neck and his golden crown was studded with rubies and spiked with five-inch grizzly bear claws. But the detail that made her blood run cold was the extra mantle that he wore over his bearskin one.

It was made of an entire fox, its face and legs still attached. The front paws had little white toes.

Desperate for a lifeline, Conora looked at Calosandros, who was staring at the same mantle, his face ashen. When he looked back at her, he forced a smile, but it didn't fool her in the least. How was she supposed to remain calm when even he could not?

When the herald announced, "Cercanos To Ubalosa, Cuintos Uboios pan Urstil, noee Cercanee Pun Ubalosa, Nemonee Goree pan Urstil," Calosandros bowed, pressing Conora forward with him. Having been raised to curtsy in her Meriverian attire, Conora felt like she was exposing herself with the forward motion of the bow, but what other choice did she have?

Emperor Quintos eyed her coolly and drawled, "Conora *Cabalee...?*" (*Princess Consort* Conora?)

She swallowed and nodded, then repeated the statement she'd learned for this moment: "Yis siad icpiloin su loisos pan Calosandros Duboinos icloid." (I am glad to meet Prince Calosandros's father.)

Calosandros inhaled sharply and muttered, "Iclas." (Fuck.)

The emperor raised an eyebrow. "Yis rio icplioin sul oid icpila." (I am sure that you are.) Then he laughed, the sound echoed by Nemonee and all of their courtiers.

Calosandros leaned closer to Conora and frantically whispered, "Lois-*i*-os, nuil yos... Loisios, ca loisos." (Father. Father, not ——.)

As soon as she asked, "What did I say?" she remembered, to her complete mortification, how she'd learned the word *loisos*.

"You just announced to the court that you're glad to meet my cock."

There wasn't a big enough forest in the world for her to hide in. Conora put a hand to her chest and shook her head. She couldn't breathe.

With a firm grasp, Calosandros shifted his hand to the side of her waist and put his lips to her ear. "Do not move, *nuil yos*. Show them you are still a princess."

She took a shaky breath and nodded. "Yes, *Cal*."

The emperor raised his hand, instantly silencing the room. "Calosandros, yis padayos mio guroltis oid yis icpoimoia?" (What news and —— do you bring me?)

He tentatively let go of Conora and, seemingly satisfied that she wasn't going to bolt, walked to the edge of the dais. "Na lulos, Loisios." (Another success, Father.) He bowed again, presenting a leather portfolio to the emperor. "Thia dungaos noee Odilia Thiadee mio Cenurd Thiados. Mer—" (A contract with Queen Odelia and King Kennard.)

"Thiadee mio thiados?" (Queen and king?) The emperor asked. "Dulta?" (Both?)

Calosandros nodded. "Mios, car as icsindan." (Yes, they —— together.)

It was likely that *icsinda* meant "rule" and the emperor was confused by Odelia having a ruling title instead of a married one. As Conora had discovered, her own title of princess, unchanged for an introduction in Meriverian, changed completely in Urstillian from *duboinee* (royal princess) to *cabalee* (princess consort).

Calosandros continued. "Meripheree guroltis icebomoimu ia pingus traosio." (Meriveria —— —— for five years.)

The emperor held up his glasses and opened the portfolio, his frown deepening as he read. "Oid toee ichnar." (You changed it.)

Calosandros swallowed, then held his arms out and flashed a winsome smile. "Yis toee ictumos." (I improved it.)

The emperor spat, "Noee u yid icha?" (By —— me?)

Calosandros swaggered back two steps and gestured to Conora with both hands. "Noee ictida ia pan guroltee ianois pan Meripheree." (By —— *the* greatest —— of Meriveria.)

Conora buried another hand in her skirt, clenching her fists as though she might physically anchor herself. She didn't know what was worse: the emperor's growing displeasure from the moment she'd stepped in the room, or the glaring reminder from her own husband that she had come here as a war prize.

Calosandros launched into smooth but rapid Urstillian that she had no hope to follow, gesturing with his hands and pausing dramatically every so often. The emperor sat stone-still as he listened, giving no indication of his opinion in the least. Nemonee put her hand on the emperor's arm a few times, clearly siding with Calosandros in whatever he was explaining. The speech was likely not that long, but without a way of understanding it, it felt interminable to Conora.

Eventually, Calosandros finished with a deep nod, a flourish of his hand, and a charming smile.

The emperor stood, leaning heavily on an ornate gilded cane, his eyes locked on Calosandros. "Crenos," he said, beckoning with his free hand.

"Mios, Loisios." (Yes, Father.) Hands behind his back, Calosandros casually stepped closer.

Emperor Quintos took a deep breath. Then he struck Calosandros across the face, hard. The audible *slap* reverberated through the throne room, and the force spun him almost doubled over facing Conora.

"Oid *gis* yid icrengadaba coimiar," the emperor seethed, not shouting but full of venom. "Iciana...?"

Eyes watering, Calosandros blinked and put his hand to his cheek, taking measured breaths as he righted himself. Just before he turned back to the emperor, he momentarily caught Conora's gaze and put his hand up palm-out as if to say, *Wait.*

Conora was rooted in place, her trembling now unfettered, blinking back tears of her own. For all the terrible things her parents had done, neither had ever laid a hand on her like that.

Calosandros nodded. "Mios, Loisios."

The emperor waved his hand. "Loee icnoindiosar icpilampre, crendios oin yolicthiar."

Though Conora understood his disgusted tone, the words were lost in her need to breathe, to keep herself still.

Calosandros bowed as he repeated, "Mios, Loisios." Then he turned on his heel and walked over to Conora.

Seeing that they were clearly dismissed, she curtsied to the emperor. The logical part of her mind knew it was not the right motion, but she could not will her body to correct it. As she lifted from the curtsy, whispers rippled around the room, and Calosandros put his hand on her back. She let him silently lead her out of the throne room and around the perimeter of the palace.

When they reached their room, Calosandros quietly closed the door, his face an impassive mask.

Conora wrapped her arms around herself, finally letting the tears stream down. "I'm so sorry."

Calosandros frowned and shook his head. "What?"

"I'm sorry. I screwed up everything. I didn't know that it would lead to... I'm so sorry."

He cradled her face in his hands, wiping her cheeks with his thumbs. "No, *nuil yos*, you have nothing to apologize for. I earned that slap myself." Then he pulled her into an embrace, the comfort of his strong arms slowly calming her trembling.

She sniffed. "I was an embarrassment to you and to my homeland."

"No. You fucked up a single word. It was an easy mistake." He tipped her chin up until she looked into his eyes, as green and reassuring as the forest. "I was proud to call you my wife in there. I still am."

"I know you and the emperor were discussing me. I didn't have to understand all the words to know I'm a disappointing war trophy."

His eyes widened, searching hers and full of so much conflict, she had to look away. He swallowed loudly and squeezed her tightly with a sigh. "Oh, clever *nuil yos*. I...I should have been honest with you sooner." He whispered, "I need you to sit in the middle of our bed and wait for me."

Then he suddenly let go of her. Confused, Conora still did as he'd asked, removing her boots and climbing into the center of the bed to curl up with her arms around her knees. He checked the hallway, locked the door, and double-checked it.

Meanwhile, her mind reeled with what he might have been dishonest about. Was he promised to someone else? Had the emperor wanted her for some other purpose? She shuddered at the thought.

Calosandros retrieved two bones from a cabinet and tossed them to the dogs, who panted *TREAT!* as they leaped to loudly gnaw on them.

Then he began pulling drapery around the room, most of which she hadn't even noticed before: sets of curtains over the doors to the hall and the toilet, a thick velvet blanket dumped into the tub—suggesting his main concern was a Hearer, though it still seemed a bit excessive—more curtains strung between pillars at the back of the room, and finally, the red curtains that surrounded the bed. With a soft *thunk-thunk*, his boots hit the floor, and he crawled through the curtains to join her. He sat next to Conora, his arms around her, and touched his forehead to her temple. The proximity in this strange context sent her heart pounding, but she willed herself not to flinch or push him away.

He spoke soft and low. "Thank you for waiting, dearest. You may be the only one who understands Meriverian, but I still cannot risk anyone overhearing. I got off lightly with a slap—the only lasting wound is my pride. If I were not his heir, the emperor might have called for my head."

Conora dared a look at Calosandros, his eyes truly fearful. "What could you have done that's so bad?"

"The empire is vast, but it's never enough, and I can be a skilled negotiator when I try. I can convince a kingdom to promise more than they could ever hope to deliver, indebt themselves, essentially hand the land to Urstille. When the emperor saw a foothold in Carum Sound, that's what I was sent to Meriveria to do. But I...I subverted the deal to favor them in the contract."

"Why?"

"As I said, the empire is *vast*. As it is now, some of the more remote areas are neglected. Despite the emperor's ambition, we could never effectively rule anywhere past the Western Mountains. We'd strip the land of all its worth and leave it essentially lawless. I couldn't bring myself to do that to your kingdom."

"But that first offer you gave us—wasn't that the emperor's demand?" she asked.

"Not exactly. I know better than to work so blatantly. I asked for a grossly excessive amount on purpose to guide you toward my second offer, one I believed your kingdom was capable of fulfilling on its own."

"And asking for my hand..." The reason was obvious and painful, but she had to hear it from him.

"Yes, I saw it as the way to make that possible."

Conora closed her eyes and sank onto her back, trying to remind herself that she'd accepted the offer for the same reason.

"But that wasn't the only reason I asked." Calosandros caressed her cheek. "*Nuil yos*, when I told you about the connection I felt, every word I said to you was true."

Eyes still closed, she shook her head. "I want to believe you, but you can't even keep your details straight. You don't remember what I wore when we met."

"Of course I do. That soft purple dress that showed off your cleavage? Before I was finally alone with you, I'd spent the whole day imagining pulling those straps down." He traced a finger along her collarbone as if to reenact the moment.

She squinted her eyes open. "Then why did you say this dress reminded you of it just before we walked in the throne room today?"

He chuckled. "I said it reminded me of the first time I *saw* you, not the first time we met."

She popped up onto her elbows. "What?"

"When I arrived at the palace, I saw you attending to an injured dog, and I watched you work while the servants were arranging our rooms. I'd never seen anyone more beautiful."

"Why didn't you say something? I would've welcomed you."

"I wanted to make a good first impression." He blushed. "I'd just hiked down a mountain. If you swooned, I didn't want it to be from smelling me."

She gasped. "That's when you planned it all, isn't it? That's why you had a piece of your chiton to give me, why you had your offers ready. Giver, you were even looking for me in the throne room that morning, weren't you?"

He nodded.

"Why did you keep this from me? I would have understood."

"I couldn't afford to tell *anyone*. If the emperor ever found out I actively worked against his interests..." Calosandros shuddered.

"But he did. You were punished anyway, weren't you?"

"For incompetence, not willful defiance. I argued—truthfully—that Meriveria's greatest treasure is worth far more than what I bargained away. I tried to convince him that an alliance through marriage would be more advantageous, allow us access to Carum Sound without having to directly oversee Meriveria. But—forgive me, *nuil yos*—I put all of my emphasis on you, on your value as my consort."

Conora puzzled. "So it *was* about his dissatisfaction with me, then."

Calosandros tenderly slid his hand around her waist. "No, my redirect worked. His displeasure was about your effect on me. He called me a lovesick idiot. And he'll find proof. Anabusos already believes that I'm wrapped around your finger, and the emperor is likely questioning him about it as we speak."

"If it worked, why do you look perturbed? You made the same face when we greeted the emperor." She put her hand over his, stopping it. "What are you still not telling me?"

He sighed and rubbed his hand down his face. "I know you noticed his trophies, especially the one he was wearing."

The fox. It felt like a personal slight, a symbolic threat to her as a Meriverian.

"Anabusos was right. I don't know how I never saw it before, but..." Calosandros shook his head and whispered even quieter, "I recognized her white paws."

Her? He had to mean the vixen he'd befriended as a child. The betrayal he must feel to realize his own father had hunted her—Conora's heart broke for Calosandros. She put a tentative hand on his chest, offering comfort but not assuming he'd accept it. "Oh, *Cal*...I know how badly that must hurt."

"How...?" Brow furrowed, he put his hand over hers. "*Nuil yos*, you have every right to resent me right now."

Shaking her head, Conora reached up and stroked his soft beard. "How could I resent you for saving my home?"

"Because I forced your decision."

"No." She put a finger to his lips. "I'm not some innocent victim to your whims. I knew what you were doing, even if I didn't know the reason, and I chose to play along. I chose to wear my most revealing gown to meet you. I chose to invite you to my bed. Even the request for aid that we sent to Urstille was my idea."

He frowned again, his eyes searching her face in bemusement. "Really?"

She nodded. "A Seer once told me that there was no lover for me in all of Carum Sound. So, when a handsome prince from Urstille asked for my hand, it was as if you'd been sent by the Giver, and I didn't hesitate."

Calosandros chuckled. "A lifetime of celibacy, with your passion? That would be a tragic waste."

"Yes, it would be." Ready to show him, Conora grabbed his shoulders and pulled him down closer to her.

He put his hand out to stop himself a few inches above her. "I still feel like a coward for using you to save my own ass."

"Well, it's a fine ass to save." She reached up under the back of his chiton and squeezed to emphasize her point, indulging in the pressure of his body's response to her touch. "And after all you've done, I'm glad I could return the favor. I would have volunteered if you'd asked me."

He shook his head, blushing. "*Nuil yos*, why?"

Now was finally her chance to try a phrase she'd taught herself. "Because...*yis oid icthian*."

His eyes grew wide, and this close, she could not escape the intensity there, so much of it conflicting: joy, lust, confusion, wonder—and fear?

"Did I say it right?"

He gulped. "You—you love me?"

She laughed. "Yes, I love you. Of course I do. Is it really so surprising?"

"You say it so easily."

She shrugged. "I admit it did take an effort to look that one up, but I think the pronunciations are coming easier now."

"No, I mean you so easily admit it." He furrowed his brow, his eyes somehow searching her more intensely.

"Why shouldn't I? We're lovers, Calosandros." When he continued staring at her, she rolled her eyes. "I forgot, expressing your feelings is more taboo than cursing in Urstille."

"You're talking about more than feelings. Those words..." He brushed his fingertips down the side of her throat, and she stretched her neck to savor the sensual shivers. He shook his head. "How can you be so trusting? I never asked for all of you."

Conora groaned. "What are you talking about? We had a wedding. We pledged our devotion to each other for life. I swear, if there's some other Urstillian marriage loophole that you haven't told me about—"

"No, nothing like that. As promised, you and I share our bodies, our pleasure, only with each other. But your mind, your soul should never belong to anyone. I-it makes you vulnerable." His voice and eyes betrayed his own vulnerability, that beautiful side of him that he'd cruelly been taught to hide away.

207

Conora's heart longed to hear him reciprocate her words, but if he could show patience with her struggles, she would do the same for him. She would trust that he would say it someday when he was ready. For now, she had his tender touches, his steadfast loyalty, and the glimmer of affection in his eyes.

She held his face with both hands. "Then, don't say it. You don't need to. But I won't take back my words. You're going to have to get used to being loved." Before he could object again, she kissed him hard, refusing to break until his passion matched hers.

Calosandros softly growled and kissed her neck. "You're stubborn, dogged, *nuil yos.*" Another kiss. "And, fuck, that's sexy..."

With another growl, he nuzzled her neck. The kissing and sucking combined with his wandering hands to overwhelm her senses until her ticklish giggle gave way to a lustful moan.

He sighed, then laughed. "I'm guessing you'll try to kill me if I rip another dress off you." His fingers were already inching up between her thighs.

Smirking, she opened her legs more. "Getting impatient?"

He returned her smirk and nodded. "And we still haven't tried what I would rather have done that night."

"Oh?"

His cheeks bloomed as he confessed, "I'm dying to test the old adage about Animal Speakers."

"Which is?" Her curiosity burned almost as strong as her ardor.

"That you have an affinity for being on all fours."

She remembered looking at those pages in *Pusosio Sioria.* Now her cheeks were the ones burning. "You're saying that because I talk to animals, I'd want to mate like one?"

His eyes went wide. "Giver's hands...when you put it that way..." He sighed and buried his face in the crook of her neck. "I shouldn't have said it. I'm being a prejudicial asshole. You don't have to—"

"Oh, yes, I do!" She couldn't hold back a laugh. "We have to try it now."

He popped his head back up and tilted it like a confused puppy.

"What if it's true? I'd be lying if I said the idea to try that position has never crossed my mind. I just couldn't think of how to ask without, well..." She shrugged.

They looked at each other and giggled until he kissed her, softly at first, then swiftly returning to the wild passion of where they'd left off. His fingertips teased her inner thighs, relentlessly igniting her flesh with flickers of delight but keeping the flame just out of reach. She whimpered her desire into his lips, pleading for more. But he pulled away instead, keeping one hand on her hip. With the same firm yet benevolent control he would use to lead when dancing, he flipped her face down and, before she could get her bearings, grasped both hips and hinged her up onto her hands and knees.

Too overwhelmed by the urgency and momentum of the present, Conora abandoned memories of illustrations from *Pusosio Sioria*. She would let her instincts guide her—they demanded control anyway. Dropping onto her elbows, she arched her back and tilted her pelvis toward her mate while he moved her skirt aside. She gasped as he fluidly mounted her and plunged deeper than she'd ever felt before. He gripped her ass, his fingers digging into her flesh with sensuous strength. Though his long, deliberate thrusts had her panting and bracing her arms down against the bed, when he sped up, the greater force not only increased the intensity inside her but also swung his balls to brush against her clit in a way that had her clawing at the sheets in ecstasy. She bit her lip and buried her face to grunt out the fervent cry that tore at her throat.

"No." Calosandros stretched himself over her and grabbed her shoulders, pulling her head up from the bed. "Please...don't hide from me."

Every sense and sensation and emotion writhed together, swirling and boiling until, overwhelmed and enraptured, she could not separate or contain them. Her grunt grew into a growl, then burst into a scream and euphoric tears as the release consumed her.

Yet he had not stopped as she feared he would. His hands once more grasped the thickest parts of her hips as he continued pounding, and her scream died into a delirious sob.

This finally did slow him down. "Are you hurt?"

She shook her head and clenched onto him inside, begging, "Don't stop!"

He gasped and wrapped her in a crushing embrace as he filled her, his shuddering becoming her own until they sighed as one. Then he gently released her and rolled onto his side as she collapsed in the other direction.

Reaching for Calosandros's hand, Conora let out little sighs to slow the fit of laughter and crying.

"I hope I didn't..." He furrowed his brow, his eyes almost scared. "How do you feel?"

"Mmm..." She closed her eyes and smiled, basking in the most exquisite bliss she'd ever known. "Perfect. Ridiculously perfect..." Another giggle escaped her lips.

"That good?" He laughed with her and wiped the tears from her face. "*Nuil yos*, did we just bring you to a new level of orgasm?"

All she could do was nod.

He put his arm around her, kissing her cheek. "I guess that answers our question about Animal Speakers in bed."

30

TROPHIES

Impresosio

Calosandros held his wife close, proudly marveling over her. This foxy princess who was uneasy with most of the world—she *loved* him. When he'd told Conora he wanted to be an exception to that unease, he never fathomed just how much of one he could be. He did not understand how she trusted him so profoundly, but wild carnal pleasure was the least he could give her in return.

When her breathing steadied, she rolled over and snuggled into him. "I'm sorry I scared you. I just—it felt so good—I lost control."

He chuckled. "What did I tell you about apologizing for orgasms?"

As she tucked her head against him and giggled back, he kissed the top of her head, taking a deep breath of gardenia and cedar.

"And losing control is the aim. Do you know what some people would give to experience *piationos*? When I realized *that* was what affected you...I've never felt more manly pride or arousal."

Conora tilted her head back to peer at him. "You liked it?"

"Of course." Calosandros brushed stray curls back from her face and cupped her chin so he could gaze into the depth of those warm brown eyes. "Seeing your pleasure will always bring mine, and piationos is supposed to be the most intense kind."

Her heavy-lidded eyes lit up at the admission. She chuckled and shook her head as if enjoying her own private joke. Then her lips curved into a saucy little smile before she pressed them to his. She nuzzled the tip of her nose against his, then met his gaze again, her dark eyes glittering softly. "*Pia-tio-nos?*" she slowly sounded out. "Why doesn't that translate? We have the word 'orgasm.'"

"True, but do you have a separate word for the violent intensity of feeling when you came this time?"

Her brow wrinkled in thought for a while before she shook her head, then smiled coyly at him. "Have you ever experienced *piationos* before?"

He caressed her smooth bronze cheek until she closed her eyes and nestled under his touch. "Not without you, *nuil yos*." It required enough passion and vulnerability with a lover to feel it. Even if he'd experienced or inspired either of those before Conora, the Urstillian taboo on crying in public had dampened it as a natural response. That was what made the legendary *piationos* so coveted; it was a hard-won victory. "Yet another reason you are my dearest."

A little bell jingled on the wall near the bed.

Conora started. "What was that?"

Calosandros sighed. "Someone is at the door. I'll see what they want."

She closed her eyes again as he kissed her forehead and smoothed her skirt back over her legs. Then he sat up and crawled out through the bed-curtains, making sure to close them behind himself for the sake of his bashful wife. On the way to the door, he swiped a towel from the dressing table and wiped himself off before adjusting his chiton back down.

The bell rang again.

He scoffed as he withdrew the curtain. "So impatient," he muttered.

When he unlocked and opened the door, his mother stood on the other side, arms folded. "You and I still need to talk." She didn't wait for him to respond before pushing past him into the room. "Where is your wife?"

He sighed and shrugged, then closed the door. "She's on the bed."

"So, that's where she's been hiding." Mother kept walking toward the bed. "Nobody has seen either of you for the past two hours."

Calosandros chased after her. "Please don't—"

But Mother was already pulling open the curtains to reveal Conora, who still lay curled on her side and didn't stir. The drowsiness of the glow had apparently finished her off already, leaving a blissful little smile playing at the corners of her lips. The tranquility of her face belied her wildly tousled hair and rumpled dress.

Mother raised an eyebrow, then put her hands on her hips and shook her head.

"What?" he whispered.

She grabbed him by the arm and yanked him several paces away. "I told you we need to talk about this," she hissed. "If you take seriously your marital duty to protect her, you will listen to me."

"Then, talk."

"Not here. You've put that poor girl through enough. She doesn't need to watch us talking about her."

212

Calosandros bristled and shook his arm free. He didn't know what exactly Mother was accusing him of, but it clearly disappointed her. "Fine. I need to let Conora know that I'm leaving so she doesn't wake up alone and confused." He went to the bed and gingerly sat next to Conora, curling his arm around to gently shake her and kiss her temple. "*Nuil yos*," he whispered low.

"Mmm...?" She stirred and squinted one eye open, then pouted. "I fell asleep..."

He chuckled. "Only for a moment. You know I wouldn't let you forget to piss. If you want, you can continue napping while I'm gone. I just wanted to tell you that I'm going to my mother's room for a while, but I'll come back soon. Would you feel safer with the door locked or unlocked?"

"Locked," Conora said without hesitation. As she rolled onto her side and sat up on the edge of the bed, Calosandros impulsively put his arm around her waist, mostly for the enjoyment of touching her. But when her feet touched the ground, she immediately leaned into him, her eyes wide. "Please don't let go. I think I have sea legs."

"Sea legs?" Though he hadn't heard of such a thing before, the meaning became clear with a just a couple wobbly steps. "Oh, you mean fawn's legs?" With a surge of pride in his performance, he reached for her knees with his free hand and swept her off her feet.

She let out a squeak of surprise and clasped her hands behind his neck as he carried her across the room. When he set her down by the door to the toilet, she gave him a quick kiss. "Thank you, *Cal, I love you.*"

The words made his heart flutter, but he still could not repeat them, not aloud. Instead, his weakness seeped through his tone as he called her stubborn *nuil yos*, which earned him a smirk and a giggle as she slipped inside and closed the door.

He quietly followed Mother out to the hall, taking care to lock the bedroom door behind him. Neither of them spoke until they were alone in her room, where she began pacing, with one hand clutching her stomach. "Please, tell me that I misheard you referring to her as your little vixen."

"It suits her."

Mother scoffed. "It does, too well." She slumped onto a plush stool, her wings drooping. "My son, you're going to destroy that girl."

Bullshit. He would *never* hurt her; he had put all his efforts into protecting her. "What do you mean, 'destroy' her?"

"You're in so deep, you have pet names for each other—handsome and little vixen?" Mother raised an eyebrow. "And the adoration when you look at her, anyone can see it—including your father."

Calosandros rolled his eyes. "I know. We all heard him call me a lovesick idiot."

Mother shook her head. "It's much more than that. At least in the throne room, you were trying to hide it. Even then, he saw her as a threat to your loyalty. But, when you let your guard down with her, there is no question that you are hers completely."

"I mean, I wouldn't say I'm—"

"Do not try to deny it, Calosandros. Not with me. I gave birth to you. I've known you since before you took your first breath. I know the look of love on you when I see it. And did you think I didn't hear her say, 'I love you'? Whether you admit your feelings or not, you accept hers—you accept responsibly for protecting that vulnerability. Now, sit down."

He huffed but did not argue again and plunked himself down in an armchair. "What are you suggesting I do about it?"

"To start, get better at acting. Until you can convince your father that she is not a threat, you cannot let him see the full depth of your feelings for her."

Calosandros groaned in frustration. "You know she isn't a threat. Help me convince him."

"I tried. What he sees from the two of you is more convincing than anything I could tell him. His first worry is weakness in you as the next emperor. Show him that you are the one making decisions—even if you have to lie."

"So? I did all of the leading and talking in the throne room."

"Yes, but he also noticed that you let her substitute the bearskin cape and wear clothing from her kingdom—not to mention how your affection for the princess spoiled the plans for Meriveria."

Calosandros took a deep breath. He'd made so many miscalculations, and now his little vixen was trapped. "And what did Conora and I do wrong when we were alone in our room? Can we not even have that?"

Mother reached over and grasped his hand. "Of course you can. That had nothing to do with your father's suspicion. I taught you to be considerate of your lovers. Leaving her tired and disheveled in the middle of the day is just rude. Save that for the evening." She wagged her finger at him, then paused, pensive. "But I will grant you that conceiving as quickly as you can is essential. I know from experience that bearing an imperial heir is the way to secure her place here."

Calosandros was woefully aware of the circumstances of his conception. Emperor Quintos wanted no emotional attachments to rule him, so he'd chosen his empress from his many lovers at random, letting fate and fertility decide.

Calosandros shrugged. "Her situation is hardly the same as yours was. Conora isn't biding her time as I fuck half the palace, wondering if she'll be the one fertile enough to win a crown. She already has a marriage contract and a pledge of devotion with me."

Mother crossed her arms and raised one eyebrow. "Don't be naive. If the emperor wants to get rid of your wife, do you really think he can be stopped by some piece of paper that you signed outside the bounds of Urstille? A blood tie is the one thing he has no power to undo—" she leaned forward and dropped her voice to almost mouth her words "—especially since his injury."

It was an open secret that, two months before Calosandros's birth, the emperor had sustained a deep gash to his groin while in battle. Though Mother swore function had returned to all his parts, his cane and Calosandros's lack of siblings suggested the recovery was less than complete.

"I know," Calosandros said, "and it's possible Conora is already pregnant, but unless you have some miraculous method for immediate detection, we need more time to find out."

"How much longer?"

Calosandros thought back to the last place he wanted to remember, Orosiad. It had been two weeks since he'd discovered what was either unlucky timing or the additional toll the bear fever had taken on Conora's body. He blinked and swallowed back the dismal memories. His little vixen was alive and well now. "If she isn't pregnant, we should know in two weeks."

Mother nodded. "So, likely three or four more weeks until you see other signs to confirm that she is." She stood and began pacing again, her wingtips softly fluttering as they were apt to do when she was thinking hard. "She needs to show she's adapting...but she needs to avoid the emperor as much as possible as well..." Mother stopped and turned to Calosandros. "What do you have planned for her right now?"

He grimaced. "Honestly, not much. She's spending much of her time studying."

"You would keep that girl locked up?" Mother rolled her eyes. "She's coming with me. I will introduce her to my ladies."

He scowled. "Like hell you will. You think I'd leave my wife alone around those she-wolves?"

She cocked her head. "Do you not trust your wife?"

"Of course I do. It's your she-wolves I don't trust."

Mother shrugged. "Yes, it would be stupid to trust my ladies, but I would hope you have a little more faith in me to watch out for her." She gave him a chiding stare.

He shook his head. "She's not ready yet. At least give her a fighting chance to speak back to them."

She crossed her arms and leaned back on one hip. "Well, the whole court has heard what you've taught her. She needs to practice with other people."

Calosandros crossed his own arms and stared back mutely. Conora did not deserve to struggle with her words in front of the she-wolves. They would delight in nothing more than eating her alive. He would not back down on this.

"Fine. If you cannot let your little vixen out of her cage, then I will send someone else into it. Boinee has Memory, and she's read everything we have on Meriveria. It's a bit outdated, and I don't know if she could speak any of it, but she should understand your wife well enough to keep the conversation going when she struggles with Urstillian."

He inhaled sharply. "Boinee? Are you sure—"

"What's wrong with Boinee? Her Gift is useful, and she's very sweet. She would be more patient than anyone else I can think of."

"Oh, I *know* how friendly she is. But do you really have to send one of my few exes to compare notes with my wife?"

Mother laughed. "It's not as if you can avoid that forever. Besides, the very natures that drew you to both women should make them kindred spirits. I truly can't think of anyone better suited to befriend your wife and keep her occupied enough to quiet the emperor's suspicions."

Calosandros sighed. Though he was loath to admit it, Mother was right. Boinee was the most amiable of not only his exes but probably all the ladies at court. And he would do anything to protect Conora, even if it meant wounding his own pride. At least the ex in question wasn't Agilee—that bitch would sooner set his wife on fire than help her.

31

EXES

Tidoias

As she peeked over Calosandros's shoulder, Conora gasped in delight. The large canvas he was working on in the middle of the room, which had started with seemingly haphazard splashes of paint, was beginning to evoke nostalgia as he formed dark island silhouettes along the horizon.

She mused at the familiar landscape. "It's a sunset on the water. You're painting my homeland?"

He blushed. "Of course. I couldn't capture it well enough with pencils that evening you took me to the beach. I'm hoping my memory won't fail me on the details now that I have proper supplies. But I thought you were reading..." When he turned from the painting to look at Conora, his face fell into a worried frown. He set down his brush. "Oh, *nuil yos*, I didn't mean to upset you. If it makes you homesick, I can stop."

"Don't you dare stop." She smiled, even as her eyes welled up. "I love it, *Cal*. It's just what we need above our mantel."

He smiled back. "You can choose every piece of art on our walls. I want our home to be a happy place for you." Then he tenderly tipped her chin up and briefly kissed her, smirking as he pulled away. "If you keep looking at me like that, you're going to end up with paint under your clothes."

She laughed. "You mean on my clothes?"

"No, I mean *under*." He wiggled his eyebrows and pantomimed groping her bottom.

Conora backed away, giggling. "Fine. I'll get back to my reading."

When she turned from him, she suddenly noticed a woman standing in the doorway with an awkward, almost panicked expression. The woman's silk-smooth black hair was as flawless as her golden bronze skin—unlike Conora's wild mane, which was currently escaping its braid.

The woman asked, "U pamoiyos cia ipcilaree?" (Is this the wrong time?)

217

Calosandros waved his hands. "Lud, lud. Yis icporul." (No, no. I forgot.)

That's right. He'd said yesterday that one of Empress Nemonee's ladies would be visiting to help Conora dip her toes in the water at court. It was the whole reason they'd left the bedroom door open.

He beckoned Conora back to his side with his finger and spoke slowly—not condescendingly so but with careful annunciation as he must have deduced his language change. "Conora, u Boinee Ucuee icidaree. Pus oid Urstilios icnoidamu." (This is Lady Boinee. She will teach you Urstillian.)

Calosandros grinned as he put an arm around Conora. "Boinee Ucuee, u *onee yos* icidaree, Turoisee Pun Ubalosa, Conora Cabalee Guroiyionosa pan Urstil." (Lady Boinee, this is *my wife*, Her Imperial Highness, Crown Princess Consort Conora of Urstille.)

The formal introduction still felt long, even without the Meriverian part. Her title of consort made the emphatic *my wife* redundant—though it was a welcome addition. Conora kept her response simpler than her throne-room mishap. "Yis siad icpiloin su oid icloid, Boinee Ucuee." (I am glad to meet you, Lady Boinee.)

Boinee smiled warmly as she bowed. "Yis siad icpiloin su oid icloid iba, Conora Cabalee." (I am glad to meet you also, Princess Consort Conora.)

Conora gestured to the chairs at the desk. "Ar icalba?" (We sit?)

"Ar yis icalba...?" Boinee's face scrunched up in confusion for a moment. "Ohhh...*ichalba*. Ar ichalba?" She tentatively walked toward one of the seats.

Conora nodded. "Ar icalaba."

Boinee shook her head, then pointed at her throat and coughed out a *k*-like sound. "I-*ch*-alba. Ichalba."

Frowning, Conora sat in the opposite chair. "I don't understand the difference."

Without looking away from his painting, Calosandros chimed in, "You asked, 'Shall we save?' which is why Boinee asked you what to save. Now she's teaching you to say 'we sit.'"

"But they sound the same!"

"So do animal sounds, but you somehow differentiate those."

Conora huffed and rolled her eyes, then gave Boinee an apologetic smile.

Shrugging, Boinee picked up a pencil from the desk and wrote down a *C* and a *CH*. She alternated pointing at them while making a *k* sound or the cough-like sound several times. Then she gave a your-turn gesture to Conora.

The *C* was easy enough, but the *CH* came out as a horrible rasping bark, like a dog choking on too much food.

Boinee winced, and Cloudy and Spruce perked up with concern, while Calosandros snorted back a laugh. She rolled her eyes and nodded back toward him, whispering conspiratorially, "Ictheda oin toee icpamu?" (You want him to go?)

Conora laughed and shook her head. "Lud."

Boinee wrote out a note, then turned the paper right side up for Conora.

> I have Memory. I found an old translation book and read it all, so I can understand the written form of your language. However, I don't know what the words sound like. You can write things down if you need to ask me a question you don't know how to say in Urstillian. You do not need him here to translate if he will be a distraction.

Conora asked, "Phee?" (Why?)

"Phee yis?" (Why what?)

"Oin...?" (You...) Conora tried then wrote, *Do you dislike him?*

Boinee blinked in surprise. No. I'm just annoyed that he didn't finish something. Typical Calosandros. She chuckled and smiled knowingly.

Conora looked up at Calosandros, who was now engrossed in his art, then at Boinee, trying to parse her meaning. *I don't understand.*

Boinee cocked her head, then shook it. "Guran." (Nothing.) She eyed Conora pensively before writing again.

> I heard him try to convince the emperor that you were a valuable war trophy. Your situation is regrettable. Has anybody asked what you think of your husband? Your truth is safe with me. I will burn this paper when we are done.

Conora read it over twice. Indeed, nobody in Urstille had ever asked her, though she'd assumed that the language barrier was most of the reason.

Her face heated, and she shrugged, whispering, "Yis toee icthian." (I love him.)

I know you are his. He bought you. But how do you feel about it?

Frustrated, Conora sighed. *I told you. I love him. Did I mispronounce my Urstillian again?*

Boinee's eyes widened as she smiled. "Oin toee icthia? Sundodoma?" (You love him? Truly?)

Conora nodded, her face flushing even warmer. "Mios."

Boinee wrote, *I did not mean offense. Icthia has two meanings, and I mistook the one you intended.*

Conora poised her pencil and held up two fingers with her other hand. "Grar?" With a nod from Boinee, she wrote, *I love him,* and, *I am his.*

"Mios," Boinee said. *Honestly, at first, I was very confused by the two being separate concepts in Meriverian.*

Was Calosandros still confused by it as well? If so, Conora might never hear the words from him. After all, wasn't that what he'd been trying to tell her? The future emperor could never surrender himself with such a declaration. Perhaps he'd already given her all that he could. But would she ever be satisfied with that?

Boinee reached toward Conora's hand, stopping short of touching her. "Loee tee icpila?" (Are you okay?)

Conora nodded. *We should probably work on my Urstillian.*

Crumpling the paper, Boinee started a fresh piece and began showing Conora letters as she demonstrated different sounds. Conora practiced them over and over. Then they reviewed the pronouns she'd learned while studying on her own—most of which she thankfully had right—before working on new vocabulary. Eventually, both she and Boinee grew so parched from talking that they were stumbling over words.

Conora offered to let Boinee dine there with her and Calosandros if she had no other plans, but Boinee graciously declined.

I must thank you for being so kind to me, Princess. I was so worried that you would hate me.

What? Conora cocked her head. *Why would I hate you?*

Boinee eyed her nervously before writing, *Because of the history between Calosandros and me.*

Conora sucked in a breath. She knew she wasn't Calosandros's first. But she hadn't imagined actually facing one of his former lovers. He'd insisted that Conora was incomparable, nothing like the women he knew in

Urstille, so she never would've expected someone so pretty and nice, someone she wanted to be a friend.

She pointed at the bed, eyebrows raised, to ask the question she could neither voice nor write.

Boinee gasped. "Tia oid ca icloiya?" (He didn't tell you?) She hissed in his general direction, "Iclasian." (Fucker.)

Conora scoffed and admitted, "Mios, pabia." (Yes, sometimes.)

They caught each other's mirrored scowls and burst into commiserative laughter.

Calosandros strode over to them, looking nervously intrigued. "Loee grar loiyosio icthiampre sud?" (You two are friends already?)

Conora bid Boinee goodbye, then turned to Calosandros and forced a saccharine smile. "Oh, she was just telling all the details of your exploits in that bed right there!"

All the color drained from his face. "Oh, Giver, no..."

"No, not really. But she did call you *iclasian*, and it's rather fitting. Why didn't *you* tell me about your past together?"

He grabbed her hand with both of his. "Because it's the past. With you, all I want is our future, *nuil yos*."

She shook her head. "It doesn't work that way. This is your childhood home. You cannot keep the past hidden from me when you've brought me to where it still lives."

He hung his head and sighed. "I'm sorry, Conora. I know it's too late for me to say anything this time, but what if I promise that when we encounter one of my exes again, I will tell you right away?"

"Why can't you just tell me now?"

"Because, until you've met more ladies of the court, they'll just be names to you."

Conora pulled her hand back and crossed her arms. "Then, at least I'll have that. If I know their names, there's a chance I won't be blindsided again when one of them knows more than I do."

He ran his hand down his face. "Please understand that I'm not...proud...of all my choices. There's one that I deeply regret."

"*Cal*, just tell me."

"Fine. Boinee was the first. Then there was Siasee—last I heard, she married a lord who prefers to stay on his estate, so you might never meet her. And the last was Agilee." He grimaced and shuddered. "That poor excuse for a lady is probably still at court. Stay away from her."

221

Conora wrapped her arms around his waist and leaned into him. "Thank you for telling me. And please don't get upset with Boinee. She thought you'd already told me."

"So, you *are* friends already." Calosandros kissed the top of her head. "I'm happy for you, *nuil yos*. She's always been amiable."

"So, why isn't she your princess?"

He laughed. "What? Her?" Then he tipped her chin up to meet his gaze and softened his expression. "We were incompatible for many reasons. To start, there is a long way between amiable and setting my passion ablaze. And, unlike you, she was not born into the pressures of being a princess and does not want them. She would be happier with someone a bit more unbound and adventurous. Beneath all that amiability, she could never truly hide her boredom with me. But compare that to *nuil yos*?"

As he softly stroked Conora's cheek, she closed her eyes and relished his affection.

"Mmm... You know what those adorable reactions of yours do to me." Then he showed her with a dizzyingly lusty kiss.

For the next week, it seemed that whatever time Conora didn't spend learning Urstillian with Boinee, she spent being seduced by Calosandros. He did not hang around for most lessons, having imperial business to attend to that he could no longer put off. But, no matter how long the emperor kept him working, her husband somehow always had energy left for their bed every morning *and* night. After a couple of days, she began to expect the pattern, and with Boinee gone before Calosandros returned in the evening, Conora would remove everything but her underobe in anticipation—something he showed immense appreciation for. Cloudy and Spruce had learned the pattern as well and developed a keen interest in frolicking outside in the garden soon after Boinee's departure each day.

The Urstillian lessons themselves became more focused and efficient, depending on writing in Meriverian less each day. However, they never turned completely academic as Boinee would seize every opportunity to use the vocabulary she was teaching to share bits of court history and gossip or ask Conora about herself. Though initially worried that all their diverting conversations would hamper their lessons, after several days, Conora realized just how helpful of a friend Boinee truly was. The information

222

about court was making her less nervous about the prospect of meeting the other ladies, and the need for that had propelled her to soak up much more than learning the language for its own sake.

From their conversations, Conora learned that Boinee's account of her past with Calosandros matched his, including her boredom with him. Apparently, she fancied Anabusos, but he had never approached her. When asked why she didn't ask him herself, Boinee claimed that he probably wasn't interested in her since he had plenty of partners to choose from already, enough to always keep his bed warm. But Conora doubted Anabusos would turn Boinee away, considering that he had propositioned her maid.

So, the next time he visited Calosandros for a lunch break, Conora decided to put some of what she'd learned into practice and simply asked him if he'd ever considered pursuing Lady Boinee.

Calosandros and Boinee both stared at her in shock, and for the first time ever, Anabusos *blushed*.

So much for Urstillian openness. Conora took a sip of wine and sat back to see what else they'd do.

Anabusos stammered something about Calosandros, who put his hands up and shook his head. "Yid? Lud. Yis onee icsisoin. Oin icthio ria icoee oin ictheda." (Me? No. I have a wife. You can do whatever you want.)

After an awkward silence, Anabusos shrugged, then casually said, "Thioros yos ca ictumu canus. Ar icparun so icsimaree." (My door won't close tonight. We'll see who enters.)

Boinee's blushing smile seemed to answer that.

Though a week was hardly sufficient to make Conora fluent, after the lunch with Anabusos, Boinee decided she'd learned enough for a brief introduction to the ladies' court. So, two days later, Boinee brought Nemonee to take Conora under her wing—literally and figuratively, according to Calosandros. He was even more reluctant than usual to see her go, walking with them through the hallways, then lingering with his goodbye kiss outside the *celudos ucuisa* (ladies' haven) until Nemonee cleared her throat at him.

It would be disrespectful for Calosandros to enter the room unless he wished to be referred to as 'lady'—even the emperor himself was said to remain outside. They had their own *celudos ucusioya* (lords' haven) next door, which Conora did not belong in. It seemed strange to have such divided spaces when the empire distinguished little between the sexes in terms of fashion or occupation. Calosandros had explained that they were purely social places for the nobility and imperial family to relax or play beyond their private rooms and that the larger *celudos iarosa* (central haven) welcomed any gender.

Conora took Nemonee's offered arm, which really did partly shelter her under one of her mother-in-law's large wings. It was hard not to be nervous. Despite the assurances that Nemonee would watch over her, it was hard not to remember how she had sat by as the emperor struck Calosandros. But, without the emperor, the empress would have more power in the *celudos ucuisa*, right?

The room was about twice the size of Calosandros and Conora's bedroom, lavishly draped in copious amounts of velvet, satin, and chiffon in various shades and hues of red, purple, and orange. In one corner was a massive pile of cushions, where several ladies reclined in much closer proximity than Conora could comfortably share with a friend. One corner had more structured sofas and chairs around a hearth. Another had several small tables and chairs. And the last had chairs and musical instruments. The center of the room was left wide open. Almost unnoticed amid the drapery, three of the four walls had what Conora hoped were changing rooms for ladies to try new fashions together—but they were probably just more fuck-closets. Why would they have so many in here, where only women could— Giver, this room had to be for more than just female trysts, right? Calosandros would've warned her if it weren't.

The hum of conversation stopped as ladies saw their empress and dropped whatever they were doing to bow.

"Ucuis," (Ladies) Nemonee said when the room was silent, "Yis icthion poid cebalitiaree yos icnamoee, *Conora* Cabalee." (I can finally present my daughter-in-law, Princess Consort Conora.) She stumbled a little on Conora's name, sounding it out carefully as if it was still too foreign on her tongue. Yet she smiled proudly, treating it as a privilege to make the introduction.

Ladies around the room began sizing Conora up, all with different intents in their eyes. Most were naturally curious, while others looked mildly annoyed with her. A few looked deeply critical, and yet others were almost predatory in their ogling. But one lady looked at her with pure seething hatred in her icy-blue eyes. She had to be Agilee, the ex Calosandros had warned her about—who else would have reason to loathe Conora on mere sight?

Nemonee waited for them all to bow to Conora before pointing at her own marriage band and then up, signaling Conora to show off her ring of devotion. She obliged, lifting her right hand palm-in and wiggling her finger as Nemonee launched into rapid Urstillian that had clearly disappointed many ladies. Most of them were likely upset that Calosandros was now forbidden, though there was ample enough evidence in the room that at least a few had been hoping for a chance with Conora. Thank the Giver that her ring of devotion now spared her from having to awkwardly explain how she preferred to keep her distance from people—that had been awful enough back in Meriveria, let alone somewhere as loose with personal boundaries as Urstille.

With her announcements finished, Nemonee bid the ladies to return to their leisure.

As conversations returned, Conora leaned closer to Nemonee and subtly gestured toward the hateful lady. "Pus Agilee Ucuee icidree?" (Is she Lady Agilee?)

Nemonee raised an eyebrow. "Nabad, oin yon *icpila*." (Damn, you *are* clever.)

As all the other ladies dispersed, Agilee began whispering to passersby. Despite the ugly look of disgust on her face, she clearly took great pride in her beauty. Her dark ribbon-like curls were unnaturally perfect in a way that could only be achieved by a long sitting with an iron, and her lips were stained a deep shade of red that complemented her light bronze complexion. From her haughty bearing, Agilee looked to hold herself above the other ladies, so it was no wonder that she would have pursued Calosandros as the future emperor. The real question was, what had he seen in Agilee?

Focus!

Conora could not waste all her time on one bitter woman. But what was she supposed to do now? Nemonee's announcement had sent the ladies scattering, and nobody dared to be the first to approach their new princess. Was it Conora's role to choose for them? She had no idea whom she should talk to first.

But Nemonee didn't let her flounder for long. She promptly led her to a hearthside sofa, where Boinee had begun chatting with another lady. Soon an individual introduction was made, quickly followed by another and another as ladies slowly meandered their way to her. It was more names than Conora could ever hope to remember in one day, but she trusted she would figure it out over time as they all had.

Some of the ladies had simple questions for her. Did she miss Meriveria? Yes. When had she married Calosandros? In the summer. How old was she? Eighteen—no, nineteen. Conora couldn't tell anyone that she'd missed her own birthday because she'd been delirious with bear fever. It was even more embarrassing that she had been so wrapped up in everything new in Urstille that she hadn't even realized it until now. She played it off to the Urstillian ladies as poor counting in her new language—oops, was it *riansios* or *tiarsios*?

At that point, Agilee had moved closer and become more audacious. Instead of whispers and snickers, her comments were almost audible. When Conora messed up her age, Agilee dropped the subtlety and clearly spat out, "Semiaos cechee."

Conora didn't need the translation to understand someone calling her a stupid bitch. She shrugged and smiled as she shot back a phrase she'd heard many times between Calosandros and Anabusos: "Oid gir." (Same to you.)

There was a loud collective gasp.

Then Nemonee laughed, patting Conora on the back, and ladies around the room began laughing as well. Agilee turned red, her face somehow screwed up in more hatred than before. They treated it as a moment of great wit or boldness, but Conora had reacted on pure impulse, merely guessing at the meaning of the insult. She was completely out of her depth.

Nemonee stood and offered her arm to Conora again. "Us yos, sul gul noiros crel icpilaree su ia od iclois." (My child, that is the perfect moment to leave them with.)

Overwhelmed, Conora gladly followed her out of the *celudos ucuisa* and back to Calosandros and her bedroom.

Nemonee smiled and patted her arm as they walked down the hallway. "Tiosee pana." (Good girl.)

To Conora's joy, Calosandros was in the room, eating an early lunch, when they walked in. She abandoned her pretense of royal grace and ran to him. As if anticipating her need, he immediately stood and met her with a tight embrace. The pressure of his hold centered her, and she listened to his heartbeat until her own began to fall in sync with it.

Nemonee spoke quickly, likely explaining what had happened, and Calosandros thanked her. Then the door closed.

He rubbed Conora's back. "*Nuil yos?*"

"Yes?"

"Are you ready to talk? Mother said your introduction was eventful."

She nodded.

He sat back in his chair and pulled her onto his lap. "Start from the beginning."

She mentally retraced her steps, and the first thing out of her mouth was, "I assume they have fuck-closets in the *celudos ucusioya* too?"

Calosandros laughed. "Yes. Obviously, I've never used them, but that is a correct assumption. If the ladies are anything like the lords, I would suggest only visiting the havens during the daytime."

"It was a bit overwhelming with all those ladies, but your mother led me well. I think my Urstillian was okay until someone asked me how old I am." She explained the mix-up and her missed birthday.

He frowned. "Oh, *nuil yos*, that's terrible. It was clever thinking to not tell anyone about the fever, but I feel like a shitty husband for not knowing. I should've asked you ages ago when it was. I need to give you something extra special as a belated gift."

Conora shook her head. "You gave me my life. I can't think of a better birthday gift than making sure I get to have another one." She kissed him.

"I'm still going to give you a gift." He bopped the tip of her nose with his finger. "So, what happened after you 'mixed up' the numbers?"

She sighed. "I learned a new phrase. One of the ladies called me *semiaos cechee.*"

"*Yis!*" (What!) Calosandros hissed, his eyes full of rage. "*So?*" (Who?)

Even the dogs understood his anger and slowly approached them, growling low.

Calm, Conora signaled, then put a hand on his chest. "It's okay, *Cal*. I've been called a stupid bitch before. I know I'm not stupid, and 'bitch' is such a ridiculous insult. Some people aren't even worthy to be compared to dogs."

"That's not what that means. You deduced 'stupid' correctly, but she did not call you a bitch. And who dared to call you such a thing?"

"I think you know who."

"*Agilee...*"

Conora shrugged. "Well, at least your mother and the ladies seemed to like my response."

227

"What did you do?"

"I copied you and Anabusos. I smiled and said, '*Oid gir*,' without skipping a beat."

Calosandros chuckled and shook his head, grinning. "Perfect. I'm sure she was not expecting that."

"No, she was not. But what does *semiaos* mean? You didn't actually say."

All his mirth left again. "You embarrassed her, but I will make Agilee pay. Nobody is allowed to call my wife a cunt, especially someone who deserves the label herself." He deposited Conora onto her feet and stood, his fists clenched.

Remembering how Urstillian punishment tended toward violence, Conora cringed. "What are you planning to do?"

"You'll see."

He was already moving toward the door.

32

BURN

Icduchio

A terrifying realization froze Conora in place: she truly had no idea what her husband was capable of. She wanted—needed—to believe in the gentler side of his nature, but she could not afford to be so naive when he acted in her honor. With a deep inhale, Conora chased after Calosandros, with Cloudy and Spruce at her heels.

He had headed in the direction of the *celudosio*, where most of the nobles' rooms were as well. Conora had almost caught up with him when he stopped at a door and pounded on it. Passing lords and ladies paused to gasp and whisper—the palace bell system made even normal knocking rude, let alone his blatantly loud thumping on the door.

Agilee answered, simpering at Calosandros. "Oh, duboinos yos, yis oin icthiol...!" (Oh, my prince, I missed you...!) She batted her eyelashes and threw herself at him as if for an embrace.

He deftly dodged backward and blocked her with his arm. "*Ca* yid icamprana!" (Do *not* touch me!)

Now the passersby stopped moving entirely, everyone within earshot deeply intrigued by whatever drama had the prince raising his voice.

Agilee pouted and whispered something in a breathy tone that was too soft to overhear but overly obvious in her attempt at seduction.

Calosandros backed up farther, rolling his eyes, and scoffed. "Lagusee oid iclasa." (Fuck yourself.)

Then she whined something—Giver, she was difficult to understand when she wasn't being directly spiteful.

He held up a finger. "Yis sid icpiloin ia gu pasee. Icmior oin onee yos semiaos cechee?" (I'm here for one reason. Did you call my wife a stupid cunt?)

She put a hand on her chest. "Yiiis...yid?" (Whaaat...me?)

"Ca iciala!" (Don't lie!)

More people had gathered to watch, and between his mention of *wife* and raising his voice again, they were beginning to eye Conora and back

229

away from her dogs as if she were orchestrating all this. In reality, she felt entirely powerless; she could neither escape their prying stares nor find her voice to call Calosandros back, her body refusing to comply with any kind of logic. Adept with her panic, Cloudy and Spruce tucked themselves close by her feet, and she buried her hands in their scruffs.

Still pouting, Agilee sighed and muttered with a dismissive wave of her hand, then said, "Coee tiosil so cechee icpilaree, pus ca pios pos icpiree pubiad." (That little girl is so stupid, she doesn't even know her age.)

Calosandros glared, then suddenly smirked. With loud and deliberate annunciation, he slowly taunted, "Pus oid icadolur ician nara thia cendiodos sul tus nara tichindaos pos icoindar ia graramod traosio, mio pus oid icnuicar crebia." (She understood your insult in a language that nobody in her homeland has spoken for two hundred years, and she still outfoxed you.)

Agilee's contrived pout finally broke as her face screwed up.

But, just as she opened her mouth, Calosandros let a little more growling anger into his voice as he continued, "Mio oin pin crendiosa icpil su onee *yos* icadol, cabalee guroiyionosa *yos*, pan *goree* coiyia." (And you were idiotic enough to insult *my* wife, *my* crown princess consort, the future *empress consort*.)

He laughed sardonically. Then his voice deepened to a menacing tone that sounded hauntingly like the emperor's as he sneered, "So, yid icloiya, so thia semiaos cechee *sir* icpilaree?" (So, tell me, who is the *real* stupid cunt?)

Conora actually felt a sliver of pity for Agilee when she saw the tears fill her eyes. The lady's lips quivered as she took a few steps toward Calosandros, who looked at her as if she were made of dung. She dropped to her knees and hastily whined unintelligibly, clutching at him—the closest part of him unfortunately being his skirt.

He grabbed her wrists. "Iclois. Yis oid ictraliyionosoin chas u puree boid oin icura." (Go. I —— you from this palace until you ——.)

There was a collective gasp; being the only one to not know what was happening made Conora almost as uneasy as the confrontation itself.

Agilee's eyes bulged as she shook her head. "Lud. Lud! Oin ca icthio coee icoee!" (No. No! You can't do that!)

"Yis icthion, mios yis icpiloin." (I can, and I am.) He flung her hands away from himself with just enough force for her to flail under the momentum as he backed away again and spat, "Yis icthedoin su *gis* oid icpar coimiar." (I *never* want to see you again.)

230

Conora let out a tense sigh. It was banishment—a harsh punishment for Agilee's crime, though not the worst that could befall her. But his proclamation somehow felt even crueler. Conora had to avert her gaze from the tears that finally fell down Agilee's cheeks.

Calosandros glanced at Conora and suddenly looked worried. He turned on his heel to head back and, without breaking his stride, reached over Spruce to wrap his arm around Conora's waist, pulling her along. He gently kissed her temple and whispered, "Icgrara, nuil yos." (Breathe.)

The instant change in his temperament made her head spin. It was difficult to reconcile the sweet tenderness her husband showed her in private with the coldness that he had just displayed—like emperor, like son, apparently.

Everything was too much. She could feel the eyes of the palace on her, hear Agilee shrieking curses behind them. All Conora wanted was to run to the forest, but she didn't even know which direction the nearest woods were from here—if she could even leave.

As they walked back into their bedroom, Calosandros curled his arm tighter around her and closed the door. "Icrendiola, ca icundo, namayos." His voice was soft, and they were words she should know, but they slipped through her mind like water through her fingers.

Cloudy and Spruce had become accustomed to not interfering with Calosandros lately, but perhaps they were getting better at deciphering when Conora was truly distressed and not simply playing her confusing human games.

Spruce whined, *You okay? Your mate yell. Scary.*

I'm okay. He fights for me, protects me. Conora had to stop herself from adding *for now.* It would only confuse the dogs, and she didn't trust the intrusive thought herself.

Cloudy barked, *He is strong. He keeps you safe.* Then he happily trotted off with Spruce.

Conora wanted to call them back, but as she leaned toward them, Calosandros pulled her closer and softly pleaded, "Icrendiola, ca icundo, nuil yos."

She turned around in his arms and put her hands on his chest. She needed to say something to make him speak Meriverian, but she needed to slow down her mind enough to get out human words. "What?"

"I said, 'Please, don't run, *nuil yos.*' You had that look in your eyes that you get right before you panic." He tucked a curl behind her ear and stroked her cheek with his thumb. "I hope I didn't hold you too tightly. I

231

wasn't sure if you were going to run away or pass out. Either looked distressingly imminent."

"I-I've never seen that side of you. Even when you yelled at me about the *sitrecayus*, I could see you were hurting more than anything, not... Did you mean what you said to Agilee, or were you just trying to wound her?"

"Both," he admitted. "Why does that trouble you? She was terrible to you. I can tell you from experience that she wouldn't hesitate to destroy you if given the opportunity."

Conora took a deep breath and squeezed her eyes shut. "I know, but I can't help thinking about what I might do someday to be on the receiving end of that temper."

Calosandros sighed, "Oh, *nuil yos*, no." He kissed her forehead. "Never. You are my dearest, the one my rage only exists to defend."

"And Agilee and you were lovers once, but now you despise her."

"Lovers?" He scoffed. "We were fuck-buddies—at best. Look at me." He gently tipped her chin up until she was gazing into his ardent green eyes. "You two aren't remotely comparable. You are a wonder, *nuil yos*. You stir me with more passion than I ever believed could exist."

"And with Agilee and you?"

"It was meaningless, just sex." He shrugged.

"Oh." Conora looked away, feeling hopelessly naive. Why did it keep surprising her that he didn't care as deeply as she did? Why did she always let herself hope for more?

"What's wrong?"

"I nearly lost my honor in my homeland over something that's meaningless to you."

"*Nothing* between you and me is meaningless."

"But you just said—"

"I meant that what I did with Agilee was meaningless."

Annoyed, Conora furrowed her brow. "That doesn't make sense. Am I supposed to believe that what you shared with Boinee and what's-her-name were meaningless too?"

Calosandros stifled a snicker. "Her name was Siasee. And I did have real relationships with each of those two, but they were not as intimate as what I have with you—neither emotionally nor physically."

She shook her head and sighed. "Just because you're my first for everything doesn't mean you have to make up some reason I'm special."

"I don't have to make anything up. The significance of that first night we spent together... You're the only one I've ever *wanted* to impregnate."

Conora hadn't thought it possible for his answer to be worse than her confusion, but there it was, another knife in her heart. She took a step back. "Right. Of course. I have a duty. Because we have a marriage contract."

His eyes widened as he grasped her shoulders. "No—I mean, technically, yes. You're the only one I could have complete intimacy—I'm explaining this all wrong." He took a deep breath and pulled her close again. "You and I have never really talked about contraception. I was mistaken to think our desire for a child makes it unnecessary. How can I expect you to understand the difference when I've never told you what my sex life used to be like?"

"You mean how the women used *sitrecayus*?"

He nodded. "Every time, without fail. But that was just one method, and I always used at least two, sometimes three."

"Three? What were the other two?" She wasn't sure if she could think of that many off the top of her head.

"A sheath when I had them, but whether I had them or not, I always pulled out."

"Always? Did you not believe the *sitrecayus* would work?"

"I like to be cautious."

She chuckled. "I noticed."

Calosandros blushed. "But do you understand how different that makes things with you? How beautiful it was to complete our intimacy that first night, knowing it was just the beginning of our passionate exploration?" He nuzzled his nose against hers, his breath soft against her lips. "We are bound together, *nuil yos*. You could never be anything less than my dearest."

Then he kissed her tenderly as she relaxed into the protective strength of his embrace.

The next day, Conora spent much of her lessons with Boinee going over the events in the *celudos ucuisa* and Agilee's banishment. Naturally, word had spread throughout the palace, and it was bound to be a favorite topic with courtiers for a while. Boinee explained that banishment from the palace did not destroy Agilee's title nor affect her family or their estate; however, she would not be allowed within the walls of the palace until she made amends. Much like the emperor slapping Calosandros, the banishment punished via humiliation more than anything else. With enough groveling or ridiculous sums of money, Agilee would find her way back—albeit with the shame attached to her name at court.

Learning to pronounce *ictraliyionosur* (banishment) was the hardest lesson of the day. By the time Conora felt reasonably comfortable with that mouthful, it was almost past a reasonable hour for lunch. Boinee suggested heading to *celudos ucuisa* to catch new gossip while they ate. Despite the lingering exhaustion from Conora's interactions there the day before—and the unseemliness of appearing to all the ladies with her hair lazily tossed into a lackluster braid—her curiosity won out.

When they walked into the *celudos*, which was bustling with excitement, a wave of gasps spread across the room. It only took a moment to realize why. Standing by the hearth was Agilee, a smug smile on her face.

Conora quickly scanned the room until she found Nemonee. Then she hurried over to her mother-in-law and whispered, "Tra?" (How?) "Calosandros—"

Nemonee sneered at Agilee as she whispered, "Pus gul uboios icantresoin." (She petitioned the emperor.)

Conora huffed and began to turn back.

But Nemonee put a hand on her shoulder and urged, "Ca icphiboia, pad tia Calosandros icnoilamu poiran." (Don't complain, or he will punish Calosandros further.)

Conora forced herself to look Nemonee in the eyes but saw no malice there, just a mother's worry. "Yos icloiya?" (Tell me?)

Nemonee nodded and led her and Boinee to one of the small tables in the corner of the room. "Loee icsinampre su icama?" (You both need to eat?)

Boinee responded before Conora could think of the words. "Mios, ar oid icredu." (Yes, thank you.)

Nemonee picked up a small bell from the table, then gave orders to the maidservant who approached before leaning in to whisper rapidly. Thankfully, Boinee was transcribing as Conora strained to understand Nemonee.

Between listening and reading, Conora gathered that Agilee had gone straight to the emperor immediately after Calosandros and Conora left. In her petition, she'd used Conora's presence during the confrontation to claim that Conora had forced Calosandros to turn on Agilee. Since her version of events suited the emperor, he only required a minor service to grant her request.

Conora shook her head. "Yis *ca* toee icgrio." (I did *not* ask him.)

Nemonee grasped Conora's hand with both of hers and leaned to her ear to whisper even lower, "Yis icpin. Tia ca icthio lagusee to icra dudod tia oid icthiaree." (I know. He could not stop himself because he loves you.)

Conora shook her head again. "Tia ca iclointreree—" (He does not say—)

Nemonee wagged her finger at Conora, then pointed at herself. "Yis crenos yos *icpin*." (I *know* my son.) She sighed. "Cadu oin icgrio pad tia yolicthiar icilaree ca uboee icpilaree. Gul uboios noil icpilaree." (Whether you asked or he is lovesick is irrelevant. The emperor is upset.)

Before Conora could ask for clarification, the maidservant came back with platters of food and drink.

Conora leaned back out of the way to swap notes with Boinee while the servant filled the table. *Should we ask what the minor service was?*

Boinee wrinkled her nose. *Why would you want to know?*

What if he asked her for an errand that—

Boinee snickered and put a hand over Conora's pencil, then wrote back, *Definitely NOT an errand.*

"Oh." The disgust suddenly made perfect sense. Agilee servicing the emperor was something Conora had less than no desire to pry into.

Boinee laughed harder. "Coindalos oid..." (Your face...)

Conora laughed back. "Oid gir." (Same to you.)

They set down their notebooks to start eating lunch, but a horrid smell was making it much less appetizing.

Though she worried it might be rude, Conora had to ask, "Ichpan gradosio icdol...?" (Should the food smell...?)

"La namoiyosio icduchior?" (Like burnt hair?) Boinee gagged and shook her head. "Lud." (No.)

She suddenly gasped, eyes wide, then grabbed a napkin and lunged at Conora, hitting her shoulders and back. Conora curled up under the assault, which was over as quickly as it had started, though Boinee did not move her hand from behind Conora.

As Conora slowly peeked out from under her own arms, there was a flurry of activity around her. Nemonee and Boinee put their free hands under Conora's arms to direct her to stand, then led her out the door. Even as they walked down the hallway and into Conora's bedroom, Boinee did not remove her hands until Conora was seated with her head down on her dressing table.

Boinee was muttering in Urstillian as she searched through drawers, placing items next to Conora. She felt a hand gently stroke her back as a woman softly murmured—it had to be Nemonee, as Boinee was still rummaging through Conora's things. Cloudy and Spruce crawled under the dressing table and rested their muzzles on her lap.

Her braid lay strangely down her back, but Conora was not ready to assess the damage. How had this even happened? She hadn't been near the hearth or a candle. *Someone* had done this to her. If only she could rest, catch her breath—but she couldn't stop shaking. Was this a petty act of cruelty, or had the assailant attempted greater harm and failed?

Hot tears pricked her eyes, purely the product of emotion and sensation—since she couldn't feel any pain or rawness on her flesh, she assumed her body was largely unscathed. The same could not be said for her hair. The real question was, how badly was it ruined?

Someone removed her woolen mantle and laid towels over her. There were small splashes of water nearby and quiet metallic sounds—and then a firm tug on her hair as a piece of paper slid under her hand. Conora lifted her face just enough to read it.

I will try to only cut what is necessary, but much is melted. Is it okay to start cutting your hair?

Conora almost nodded to get it over with, but she needed to regain control of herself, not drift away with the tide, no matter how strong it was. Cutting pieces of hair might salvage it with some creative styling to hide the patchiness, but leaving it free as she normally liked would look and feel strange. She held out her hand for a pencil and wrote, *How high up does the damage go?*

Boinee pulled and examined the hair, then pressed on Conora's spine, scant inches below the bottom of her neck, to indicate where.

Conora took a deep breath to steel herself. *Cut it all to there.*

Are you sure?

Conora nodded. She had lost her parents, her home, her friends, her family, her language, her wardrobe, her customs. If she couldn't hold onto anything else, what did her hair matter at this point? She was not going to cling to some meager strands and try to pretend nothing had changed. She would make this change *hers*.

There was another firm tug on Conora's hair. With a ripping, scraping sound, wet curls sprang up, first to cling to her neck, then falling against her arms. When the last of it released, the braid was pulled away, leaving Conora feeling strangely light.

She forced herself to lift her head, then slowly squinted her eyes open to see the result. For a moment, it was shocking not to recognize herself in the mirror. Although the hair had been cut much lower, it coiled up to hover just above her shoulders. A foot and a half of melted braid lay on the table before her; it had all the appeal of a carcass. But the hair left behind on her head was fresh and shiny and bounced when she moved.

She...liked it? Well, mostly. It still didn't look quite right with the front hanging a bit longer than the back and random pieces longer than their neighbors.

Conora held her hand out for the razor, which Calosandros normally used to keep the edges of his beard neat, and which Boinee was still holding.

Boinee exchanged a worried look with Nemonee and eyed Conora warily.

Conora sighed in frustration. It felt like all the words she knew in Urstillian had chosen this moment to abandon her, so she used what came naturally to her: she mimicked scissors with her fingers, evening out her hair.

"Ohhh..." Boinee let out a huge sigh of relief and nodded, though she still didn't hand over the razor. Instead, she readjusted the towels around Conora's shoulders and did the cutting herself.

Spruce nosed around in the growing pile of hair. *Ooh, a snack?*

Conora yipped, *No! Not snack. Get out of there. Hair is not for eating.*

Snack? Where? Cloudy asked.

Conora rolled her eyes. *No! No snack! Leave hair alone!*

Rude, the dogs huffed, then sauntered off.

Sculpting the style meant a lot more hair coming off, but the end result was worth it. The smoother horizontal line where Conora's hair ended sharply highlighted her neck, exposing one of her favorite spots for Calosandros to kiss. And the extra cutting changed the shape completely. It had started as an ungainly triangle from the top of her head to where her waves widened at the bottom, but now her wild curls separated to frame her face with lively coils. As she studied her reflection, Conora turned her head back and forth, enjoying the freeing lightness. It was satisfying, how the perky style moved with her, softly swinging around and back into place. The longer she stared at the image, the more she felt like herself, *truly her* in a way she hadn't seen before.

Nemonee put her hands on Conora's shoulders and smiled sweetly, slowly asking, "Yis ictia oin?" (What do you think?)

Conora smiled back and nodded. "Pana, cal coir." (Good, very beautiful.)

Boinee was pursing her lips in thought, flipping her own hair back behind her shoulders, when she began dipping her fingers in a bowl water, then wetting a section of her hair. Though the next step was clear, it was still a bit shocking to see her grab the razor and hack off over a foot of hair without hesitation. Nemonee gasped, but Boinee just shrugged with a sardonic smile. "Yis? Ucuee icelteree gul pastos grayar icor!" (What? A lady must wear the latest style!)

33

THE BEST REVENGE

Gul Dumpredos Pid

Ordinarily, Calosandros would do translation work in the privacy of his own room, but until he could prove Conora's trustworthiness to the emperor, he was forbidden from conducting any sensitive imperial business in her presence. And the emperor considered anything that wasn't presented in the throne room to be sensitive information. Unfortunately, Calosandros's attempted banishment of Agilee had set his progress back, and the emperor was more distrustful of Conora than ever. It made Calosandros sick to think how badly he was failing his wife. In return for her giving up everything, he'd promised to protect her under his power as the imperial prince—power that was apparently worthless in his hands.

So, Calosandros was translating reports from the outermost territories under the watchful eye of the emperor when Anabusos rushed into the office, hastily bowed, and said, "There's been an incident in the ladies' haven, involving both the princess and the empress."

Shit. Not again. Could Conora visit the haven in peace just once? Calosandros tried not to show any hint of his anxious fear as he asked, "What happened?"

Anabusos waited until the emperor gave an annoyed nod to give his account. "In the lords' haven, we all smelled something acrid, and when we went out to find the source, the ladies were emptying theirs, which smelled much stronger. I asked some of the ladies what the odor was, and they said it was burnt hair. Lady Agilee had been seen walking past the table where the empress, the princess, and Lady Boinee were eating and paused behind the princess. Then the smell started, and Lady Boinee threw herself onto the princess."

Fuck. Agilee's Gift was Fire. It worked like Ice in reverse, heating things with a touch of her hand.

Calosandros leaped out of his chair. "Was Conora harmed?"

"Nobody knows. The empress and Lady Boinee escorted her out before anyone could see anything or ask any questions."

"I have to see her."

"Calm yourself, Son." The emperor sighed. "Or have you already forgotten what I said? You dote on her too easily."

Calosandros shook his head. "Have you forgotten that she may be carrying my child—the heir you insisted I need for our line? This is not a mere matter of honor or emotions. If you expect me to fulfill my duty to the empire, I need to ensure that she is safe and cared for." He started toward the door.

"I did not dismiss you," the emperor scolded.

Calosandros stopped, jaw clenched, and took a deep breath. "Neither did you allow me to banish Lady Agilee, which seems to be what made this incident possible." He glared, daring the emperor to argue against Calosandros's logic about the situation.

"I expect a report on the condition of the empress and the princess," he finally conceded. "You are dismissed."

Calosandros and Anabusos bowed and hastened out the door. When they passed the havens in the hallway, both men covered their noses as the caustic sulfuric odor still lingered. But terrible as it was, at least it only seemed to smell like hair; if Conora's skin had burned at all, it hadn't been deep enough to add to the stench. Giver, if she was hurt, he would repay Agilee for every wound in kind.

The door to Calosandros's bedroom was locked, so he had to fetch his key out of his pocket. By the time he'd finished turning it in the lock, Mother stood on the other side of the door, her wings outspread, blocking his entrance.

"What are you doing?" Calosandros asked. "I need to see her."

Mother held up a finger and whispered, "Don't worry. She is not injured."

"Then, why are you stopping me?" he snapped.

"Because you look ready to pummel someone, and that is the last reaction she needs right now."

Calosandros crossed his arms and gave her an annoyed, please-explain glare.

"As I'm sure you've smelled, there was some burnt hair, so your wife has a lovely new haircut. However, no matter how beautiful you insist it looks, she will never believe you if you continue in here with this anger. It will be all too easy for her to think you are as angry over the loss of beauty as you are over Agilee's treachery. You are free to show her whatever feelings are true, but I advise you to think before you react this time."

240

He sighed, trying his best to calm himself. "Is that all?"

"I think this may be a battle Conora needs to fight her own way. Her resilience will torture Agilee in ways that you cannot." Mother punctuated the advice with a pat on Calosandros's cheek. Then she glanced over her shoulder. "Ready?"

"Yes," Boinee's voice said.

Mother tucked her wings in, revealing Conora and Boinee standing in the center of the room, both with their hair cropped above their shoulders. Mother patted both men on their backs. "I'll leave you to it, then."

The door clicked shut.

Conora's hair had been so glorious, thick and long and lustrous, a part of her elegant beauty. But this shorter style was bold, untamed, playful, and sexy, an outward expression of his little vixen's spirit. As if he needed any more reason to like the new look, the way it teasingly skimmed above her collarbone made him want to leave a love bite there.

Awed, he approached and gingerly pulled on one of the curls to watch it spring back, the freshly cut ends soft on his fingertips. "When she said you cut your hair, I never imagined this much."

She blushed under his gaze and said without her accent, "I thought it would be better to start over than to try to save the length. It should grow back eventually."

He tucked one side behind her ear and smiled. "Only if you miss it." Then he brushed his finger over that tempting dimple between her neck and collarbone. "I think I'm going to enjoy this wild and sexy look." Pulling her to him, he finished with a tender kiss.

Hearing a giggle, he turned to see Anabusos with one arm slung over Boinee's shoulders, combing through her silky hair with his other hand. "I didn't think your hair burned too," Anabusos said.

"It didn't. I was just feeling *adventurous* today."

"Really?" Anabusos grinned. "In that case, why don't we leave the lovesick pair while you tell me who and what you have in mind?"

As they made their way out, Calosandros followed behind to lock the door.

"You really like it?" Conora asked.

He grinned and nodded, then swept Conora into his arms once more and kissed her eagerly, digging his fingers into her soft hair. He trailed kisses across her jaw and down her neck, driven wild as she tilted her head away to offer the spot he was going for. He let his lips graze her skin as he whispered, "If I leave a mark, it will show more now."

"Good," she sighed huskily, then gasped as he nibbled her flesh.

He would take his time. After all, the emperor had told him to report on her condition, and Calosandros needed to check every inch of her.

242

34

SQUIRREL

Sonee

Conora took one last look in the hallway mirror in front of the *celudos ciarosa* to appreciate the love bite Calosandros had given her. It was much more vivid than the accidental one had been, and the blue, purple, and pink florals of her new dress brought out the color. Calosandros had commissioned the clothing weeks ago; he'd had the tailor in Siputreos send Conora's measurements ahead to the palace. What had taken so long was not the construction since Urstillian garments tended to be simple in that regard. Instead of using pre-dyed bolts of fabric, this dress had been sewn first, then painted in fine detail, and finally embroidered with tiny quartz beads around the neckline and mid-thigh hem. Conora's return to the *celudos ucuisa* to confront Agilee was the perfect time to show it off.

Calosandros wrapped his arms around her from behind and kissed her cheek. "You're going to destroy her with how gorgeous and desirable you are."

Her cheeks warmed as she giggled. "*Cal...*"

"Nuil yos sioria..."

She turned in his arms and whispered, "I love you too," on his lips before she kissed him.

He cupped her cheeks. "Please, just promise me you'll keep a wary eye out for trouble. If something goes wrong, I'd rather you be safe than brave. Remember, I'll be right next door."

"Of course, Your Imperial Cautiousness," Conora teased. "I'm surprised you aren't planning to stand out here and wait."

Calosandros blushed. "To be honest, I probably would if it weren't rude and creepy to linger alone outside the other haven."

She chuckled. "I promise I will do my best to stay out of trouble."

With one last kiss, they each went to the doors of their respective *celudosio*. Conora inhaled and held herself as tall as she could as she walked inside. She was a royal princess by birth, an imperial princess by marriage, and she would not be intimidated by a mere lady, no matter her Gift.

As planned, Nemonee awaited her inside and gushed about how happy she was to see Conora and how fabulous she looked—truthfully, Conora couldn't quite follow her excited rapid Urstillian and trusted what Nemonee had told her before. The empress showed her true power over the room as her excitement spread, and ladies began to *ooh* and *ahh* over Conora. A few were bold enough to try to touch her hair and dress, which had her instinctively backing away, but Nemonee pushed her way through, shooing ladies away and shielding Conora's back with a wing.

Boinee arrived soon after, smiling and patting her hair as the compliments were now directed at her. She approached Conora and loudly thanked her for the inspiration. Then she laughed and gestured to the love bite. "Yis icparoin sul gul duboinos gulee oid coil icoibosaree sa!" (I see that the prince enjoys your new fashion too!)

The room bubbled with enthusiasm as ladies gasped and whispered and chattered. Several were already sneaking out the door—perhaps they wanted to adopt the new trend as soon as possible?

But, of course, one lady in particular was not joining in the craze: Agilee. She was seething, staring daggers at Conora, and at the mention of Calosandros's appreciation, Agilee began to shake with rage. She muttered something to herself and stormed out of the room.

Over the next few days, ladies began showing up to the *celudos ucuisa* and around court with the latest hairstyle, abandoning their combs and pins for cropped curls or sleek bobs. Agilee had made herself scarce, though it remained to be seen whether it was because she was weathering the storm of embarrassment or plotting vengeance.

However, as glad as Conora was to gain acceptance with the ladies of the court, the *celudos ucuisa* was beginning to feel like anything but a haven. She was so tired. The overwhelming colors and chatter inside, ladies who did not share her concept of personal space, the pressure to pretend all of this was acceptable and enjoyable to her—it was all exhausting enough. But the added need to translate everything she said and heard made it harder. Not to mention the fear that Agilee might either return or convince someone else to harass Conora on her behalf.

One day, she could not take it anymore; everything and everyone was getting under her skin. It had started with Calosandros unintentionally making an obnoxious amount of noise as he left their room early that morning. Then Spruce had bothered her about some smell. She wasn't aware of any new scents, but once the idea was in her head, every odor in the palace seemed stronger—the dogs' breakfast was especially foul. And, of course, Boinee had chosen that day for an intense lesson on compound words. Then, when Conora sought a reprieve at the *celudos ucuisa*, one of the ladies was playing an out-of-tune lyre, and Nemonee practically smothered her with her welcoming hug.

Not wanting to offend her mother-in-law, Conora found a relatively empty corner of the room to pull herself together in instead of running. But as Nemonee soon flitted off to a new interest, and Conora lost the need to stay put. So, she simply got up and walked out. She didn't have a plan, other than wanting to be alone. It wasn't as if she could get lost; the entire palace was a circle, so if she walked down the hallway in either direction long enough, she'd eventually recognize where she was.

It was pleasant to look out the large windows in the hallway, though seeing the trees outside reminded her how long it had been since she'd walked through a forest. She stopped at one of the windows with more trees outside and leaned against the sill to look for animals in the branches. Most would have fled south or be hibernating for the winter, but there were always a few creatures who remained through the snow.

Sure enough, a pine squirrel stirred and scurried across the trunk of the nearest tree, its rusty gray fur camouflaged against the bark. Conora quickly examined the window casing and unlatched it. Careful not to startle the jumpy little rodent, she slowly opened the window and chirruped out a greeting.

Who goes there? the squirrel predictably barked back. *I'll fight you to the death!*

Conora laughed and rolled her eyes. *I don't want your hoard, little one. I just want to talk.* Giver, it felt good to use her Gift with something wild again.

Show yourself, coward!

Over here, in the building. I'm a human.

The squirrel stopped his wild roving and stared at her, his little body showing each rapid breath. *Human? Nonsense! Humans can't talk!*

I can.

What do you want?

Conora shrugged. *Nothing. I just wanted to say hello.*

Then, why are you bothering me?

Conora reached into the pocket where she kept bits of dried meat for the dogs and pulled out a tiny piece. *Would you like me to give you some food? I have bison meat.*

Give it!

Knowing he couldn't trust her enough to take it from her hand, Conora tossed the morsel at the base of the tree. *How big is your territory?*

He retrieved the meat and scurried back up. *All the trees around and inside the human circle are mine.*

The human circle must mean the palace with its garden in the center. *We humans are messy. You must find a lot of food.*

Yes, and lots of shiny things. You bring me more food and shinies?

Maybe. It might be easier to find me inside the human circle. It would be more convenient to access the garden from her bedroom than search for a window to open in a random section of the hallway.

What do you want for it?

I don't know. Friendship? Maybe a favor to hoard for the future?

The squirrel stared at her again, then scurried farther up the tree and back down. *Okay. You bring food to my tree?*

Yes.

Go to the biggest tree inside the circle, then go two north—

Wait. Conora grabbed the notebook and pencil she used with Boinee, then wrote down the directions as the squirrel continued. They were ridiculously convoluted, and she suspected that it could be narrowed down to just a couple points, but without knowing where he'd end up, she had to get it all down.

She was sitting in the windowsill, writing as quickly as she could, when someone painfully gripped her arm and yanked her to the ground.

The emperor's scowling face was inches from hers as he snarled a question at her in furious Urstillian that was too harsh and rapid to decipher. When she flinched away, he grabbed her jaw and forced her to look at him, yelling at her again.

"I d-don't understand." Before the words had fully escaped, Conora knew it was a mistake to say anything in Meriverian.

Still holding her by her arm, he yanked her up from the ground, wrenching her shoulder, and shook her. "Yis-icpee-su-oin-crelos-icthia, semiaos!"

The only word she'd caught so far was the worst insult she knew in Urstillian, which didn't help her understanding at all. Her mind struggled to string words together correctly in either language. She tried, "L-lud, c-ca ician." (N-no, n-not understand.)

He growled wordlessly at her, then began to pull her across the hallway.

Conora, seeing that the nearest thing on the other side was fuck-closet, struggled against his pull and screamed as loud as she could, though it twisted into an eerily similar animal sound. Pitched as a cougar scream, her nightmarish shriek came out louder than her human voice should have. This bought her a moment as he loosened his grip and winced at the sound, but it wasn't enough time. He quickly grabbed her arm again and twisted it.

Tears sprang to her eyes, and she yelped as the pain shot through her arm. She begged, "Icrel! Icra! Ca ician..." (Help! Stop! Not understand...)

The emperor shook her again. With a nauseating snap, fresh pain flooded up her arm.

35

FRACTURE

Pangioros

Calosandros was translating more correspondence from the outermost territories when the emperor stood up to stretch his legs. The lingering effects of the injury that had given him a bit of a limp also made it uncomfortable to sit in one place for too long, so for as long as Calosandros had been alive, the emperor had been known to take frequent walks along the portion of the hallway nearest to his office. In fact, it was so expected that Calosandros had barely noticed the departure.

A few minutes later and halfway through one letter, a bloodcurdling scream pierced the air and startled his pen across the page in a jagged line. It was a terrifying sound to hear outside, where it revealed the presence of a cougar, but the wild animal sound had come from inside the palace. An animal inside the palace?

Conora!

He dashed to the door in time to hear a pitiful canine yelp come from down the hallway, and his breath caught. Not his little vixen.

Calosandros sprinted toward the sound, hearing her beg in a thick accent, "Help! Stop! Not understand..." Giver, the distress in her voice physically pained him, and after all the pride she'd taken in her progress with Urstillian, to hear her speak it so brokenly...

But then the source of his horror came into view with the gruesome crack of bones. The emperor stood over Conora, shaking her, twisting and pulling her arm behind her at a grotesque angle as she sobbed, and he bellowed at her, "Stop playing stupid! Answer me!"

Her tear-streaked face was full of pain and confusion as she let out a defeated whimpering sob.

Calosandros had nearly reached them now, and rage like he'd never known utterly burned within him. "Let her go!" He growled out an angry roar as he charged at the emperor. A kick to the side of the knee buckled the leg, and Calosandros used the rest of his momentum to slam his shoulder and elbow into the chest, knocking the emperor to the floor.

248

Then Calosandros turned to Conora and put his hands on her waist. "*Nuil yos?*"

Trembling, she held onto him tightly with her good arm and buried her face in his chiton as she continued sobbing. Instead of her Meriverian accent, it was her crying that slurred her speech as she gasped out, "He's so angry. What did I do? I don't understand."

As Calosandros gently embraced her, he stroked her back. "Shh...*nuil yos*... It's okay. I'm here." However, since a small part of him recognized what he'd just done, he also slowly pivoted to keep the emperor in his view and walked backward to create distance.

The emperor pulled himself up to his knees and leaned heavily on his cane to stand up. All the while, he stared at Calosandros with a strange and intense look in his eyes. The fear and anger were obvious, but there was more that was too unfamiliar to place. "What have you done, Son?" he spat.

"What have *you* done?" Calosandros snarled right back. "Screaming at a terrified woman and breaking her arm? How dare you!"

"Your 'little vixen,' did you call her? How fitting. While she distracted you with feminine wiles and sentimentality, she's been a spy. I finally caught her in the act." The emperor brandished a small notebook. "She was writing her secrets in this. Translate it. What has she been recording?" He tossed it toward Calosandros so that it slid across the floor to his feet.

Though he let go of Conora so he could bend down and pick it up, she held onto his chiton. The notebook was familiar; it had been one of his until he gave it to Conora. She mainly used it to swap notes with Boinee, and a cursory glance at the pages showed just that: random pieces of idle conversation between friends. Though a few bits of court gossip mixed in here and there, they would be trivial outside the walls of the palace. Sometimes she left notes for herself, reminders to do personal errands like commissioning new dog beds for Spruce and Cloudy.

Calosandros shook his head.

"What does it say?"

"Nothing! They're just mundane tasks and her personal thoughts."

The emperor scowled. "I saw her! Check the last page she wrote in."

Calosandros sighed and flipped to the last written page.

Squirrel hoard – biggest tree, north two, west three, over the bendy branch, south five...

It went on that way for a while until it abruptly cut off in the middle of the last word, leaving a long scribble down and across the page—presumably when the emperor had "caught her spying."

"Well?"

"Congratulations." Calosandros flung the notebook at him in disgust. "You've intercepted the location of a squirrel hoard. I hope the seeds and trinkets in there are worth harming my wife over." He put his arm around Conora's waist and began leading her backward toward their room.

The emperor stared at the notebook in disbelief. "It has to be a code for something else."

"Or she was simply an Animal Speaker talking to a squirrel." Calosandros finally turned his back to him and walked away.

When they'd gone far enough that Calosandros felt comfortably out of sight, he quickened the pace until they were nearly running. He needed to get both of them into the relative safety of their locked bedroom. To the first servant he saw in the hall, he gave orders to retrieve Anabusos and a physician with a splint as quickly as possible.

Of course, Calosandros hadn't been the only one to hear the commotion in the hallway, and curious onlookers were beginning to block the path. He loudly ordered people to make way, prepared to shove back anyone who approached, lest they jostle Conora's arm.

Well, anyone except Anabusos, who was considerate enough to rush toward Calosandros's other side. "I just overheard you call for me and a— Oh fuck. That arm is definitely broken."

"Is there any chance you can Ice it while we're moving?"

Anabusos pulled off a glove. "I don't want to risk the arm until it's stable, but I can help with the shoulder. The way she's holding it looks like a sprain or dislocation."

Walking behind them, Anabusos pulled back Conora's mantle and grabbed the top of her shoulder above the joint. Her knuckles went white as she gripped Calosandros's chiton tighter, and she let out a small whimper—likely more from the initial shock than added pain as she did not try to remove Anabusos's hand or otherwise complain. When they reached the bedroom, Calosandros led Conora to the bed, fending off the worried and inquisitive dogs. She huffed something, and the dogs backed away to sit by the foot of the bed. He quickly but carefully helped her remove her mantle, then began to untie her dress.

Her red-rimmed eyes went wide as she asked without her accent, "What are you doing?"

"I promise to be careful, but your sleeve is in the way. We need to expose your arm."

She nodded at first, then gasped. "But my sleeve is part of my underobe."

Calosandros unwound her waist ties. "I know. That's why I brought you over to the bed. You can keep warm under the covers."

"That's not what I meant." She tried to subtly point toward Anabusos with her good hand.

Calosandros frowned in confusion as he pulled the overdress away and she held her underobe closed. "What? You might have been too delirious to remember, but he already saw everything back in Orosiad."

"Oh." Conora's bottom lip quivered as she numbly dropped her hand and slid the underobe off her good shoulder.

Calosandros slowly peeled back the other shoulder and waited a moment for Anabusos to put his hand back and cool the joint again. Then he gingerly shimmied the sleeve down her arm, trying not to jar it or snag fabric on the bump where the break was. He helped her onto the bed and covered her to her chin, leaving her right shoulder and arm out. And, finally, Anabusos was able to Ice her broken forearm.

Crawling onto the other side of the bed, Calosandros offered Conora his hand. She wove her fingers though his and clutched their hands to her chest. The dogs took this as a cue to join them, lying with their muzzles on her legs.

"The physician should be here any minute with a splint," he assured her.

Fresh tears trailed from her eyes into her hair. "I still don't know what happened. What did I do wrong?"

"Nothing to deserve this, *nuil yos*. What do you remember before he hurt you?"

"I saw a squirrel outside and opened a window to talk to it."

"An old friend?" It wasn't impossible that an animal would have followed her here.

She started to shake her head but immediately gasped and winced as the motion transferred into her arm. "No." Her voice strained into a whine as she added, "I'd never seen him before."

"Shh... It's okay, dearest. You don't have to convince me of anything." Calosandros caressed her cheek. He didn't want to interrogate her, but keeping her talking would serve the dual purpose of clarifying the situation and distracting her from the pain—provided he didn't get her so worked up that she moved her arm. "So, what did you want to talk to the squirrel about?"

Conora sighed. "Anything. He was the first wild animal I've encountered in weeks."

The guilt. Calosandros knew too well how the need built up when he could not use Speech, and he'd pressured her so much to stay busy that he'd sequestered her from nature. How sadly ironic that he'd done so to keep her out of trouble with the emperor.

"The squirrel didn't trust me," Conora continued, "which is typical—they're feisty little things. I promised to leave him bits of food and maybe a few shinies if he told me where to leave them. But his directions were too convoluted, so I tried to write them down. And that's when..." She tensed, and her breathing picked up. "I was so scared and confused..."

"I know. It's okay. You don't have to talk about that part right now. The only thing we need to know is if he hurt you anywhere else so that we can have the physician look at it when they get here." Where was the damn physician anyway?

"Just my arm and shoulder. You stopped him before he could do anything else." A haunted look passed over her eyes, and she swallowed. "D-do you know what he wanted from me?"

"The paranoid old fool thought you were a spy, that he'd caught you sending a message or recording information."

Her brows knit with worry. "W-what was he— What is the punishment for that?"

"That depends on how much damage a spy has done and how cooperative they are. But even if I hadn't intercepted you in the hallway, I would've been given a chance to argue on your behalf before any official punishment was carried out."

She closed her eyes. "Please, I need to know. The way the emperor demands services to grant requests—does he do that with the accused too?"

Calosandros felt sick. "Not that I'm aware of... Conora, what made you ask that? Did he hurt anything other than your arm and shoulder? Because I swear on the Giver, I will rip that crown from him and—"

"No. He didn't. When he was pulling me across the hallway, the first thing I noticed was a fuck-closet, but I didn't really know what was happening or what he was yelling at me. It was just the first explanation my mind could come up with in my confusion, and I want to have been mistaken."

Calosandros sighed with relief. "Yes, *nuil yos*, I believe you were mistaken, if only because I don't think he would've been yelling so much himself if he were doing something he wouldn't want other people to witness." It wouldn't erase the violent attack from her mind, but at least he could ease her fears about that.

The door burst open, and a physician *finally* came rushing in, carrying a bag full of supplies for a splint in one hand and the kit of herbs and tools in the other. She set them both on the desk and approached Conora. "How did the injury happen?"

Conora's face scrunched in concentration as she said with her thick accent, "I...arm my—no, my arm..." She let out a frustrated growl.

"It's okay," Calosandros told her, then turned to the physician, choosing his phrasing carefully to avoid a direct accusation. "The emperor found Conora in the hallway. She was lifted and shaken by her arm, and it was twisted behind her back until it snapped."

The physician wearily sighed and nodded. This wasn't the first time she'd heard an explanation like that about the emperor, not even the first time she'd heard it from Calosandros, who'd suffered his share of "spontaneous" injuries as a child.

She gestured for Anabusos to take a rest from using his Ice. "Can you start mixing ingredients for a poultice? Mint, red-cedar, yarrow, and salal." Then she quietly examined Conora's arm and shoulder. "We need to set the break first. Then we can splint the whole arm and sling it tightly for the sprained shoulder."

"Is there something you can give her for the pain first?" Calosandros asked.

The physician raised an eyebrow. "You didn't do that already? But you and Captain Anabusos both know basic pain relief."

"We were taught military application, which doesn't include any contraceptive side effects since they're considered an added benefit. And my wife is two days late. I know that's too soon to be sure, but I didn't want to take any chances." He tucked a stray curl behind Conora's ear. She needed the protection of carrying his heir now more than ever.

The physician grimaced. "I'm afraid the poultice is the best I can do. There is nothing that she can take internally. All the best medicines for pain that I have will encourage her body to begin its cycle. The safe herbs for this stage aren't much use for pain. We can try adding a little kinnikinnick to the poultice, though."

"Wait. Slow down," Conora said to Calosandros, her accent clear and natural again. "I didn't understand all of the Urstillian, but did you say that I'm two days late?"

He nodded sheepishly. "I thought it would be prudent to keep track myself since you find it more difficult than I do."

She scowled, not at him but lost in thought. Then her eyes widened, and she muttered, "Smell? Of course. Giver, I'm so stupid..."

She yipped at Spruce, who instantly perked up and began sniffing her, focusing intently on her crotch.

Conora explained to Calosandros, "They both learned the scent from Odelia, but Spruce has always had the better nose. I should've listened when he was pestering me about a smell this morning."

Spruce flattened his ears back and softly whined, giving Conora a doggy pout as he snuggled his head onto her belly.

She gasped and gripped Calosandros's hand. Her rich brown eyes were wide as they met his. Though the tears flowed again, Conora was smiling this time.

The awe and sudden joy nearly took his breath away. "He can smell our child inside you?"

She laughed. "I don't think it's the child he's smelling per se, but yes."

"Dearest *nuil yos*..." He leaned in for a passionate yet salty kiss. Then he rubbed Spruce behind his ears. "Such a good, good boy!"

When he looked back to the physician, she had Conora's forearm straightened and was beginning to attach the splint. "Thank you for keeping her still and relaxed. Whatever that was, it was a useful distraction."

Calosandros grinned. "Apparently, it's not too soon for a dog to detect a child."

Anabusos's jaw dropped into a gaping smile. "You're going to be a father? Congratulations!" He took a step toward Calosandros, then looked down at the poultice in his bare hands and shrugged. "I'll have to owe you a drink later."

Anabusos continued holding the poultice until it began to frost, then spread the cold herbal paste over a bare patch of skin where the break had been, as well as the shoulder joint. Behind him, the physician tightly wound bandages around the splint and over the poultice, all the way up the arm and over the shoulder. Then Calosandros helped Conora sit up so the physician could fashion a sling, which was further strapped down with more bandages wrapped around her chest and shoulders to completely immobilize her arm.

As Calosandros eased Conora back down, her eyelids were heavy. He gently kissed her forehead. "You can rest now, *nuil yos*." Between the injuries and the pregnancy, she would certainly need it.

He closed the curtains for the bed while Anabusos and the physician cleaned up her supplies. Calosandros thanked them both and walked them to the door. And, after he'd locked it shut behind them, he let out a trembling sigh of relief. His dearest was safe now, and they would welcome a child together.

Yet an aching dread would not let go of him. Calosandros would have to answer for what he'd done, and he'd made it all too clear to the emperor that Conora was his biggest weakness.

36

SURRENDER

Ichendo

Mother visited just a few hours after the incident, having shown up along with the servant bringing dinner while Conora was still resting. As Calosandros checked the hallway for the emperor or guards, Mother pressed her way in. "The court is in quite a stir. Nobody seems to know what has happened, other than hearing terrible screams and seeing you escort your injured wife in here. The physician who treated her has said nothing, even to me."

He held up a finger to tell her to wait while the servant set the platter of food on the table and left. Then he quickly locked the door. "So, nobody else knows who was involved?"

Looking worried, Mother shook her head.

Calosandros dragged himself toward the hearth and slumped down onto the sofa facing it. "What has the emperor said?"

"Nothing. He seems to be the only one with no interest in the subject."

Calosandros let out a breath. "Oh, thank the Giver." If nobody knew, the emperor might not feel the need to make a spectacle of punishing Calosandros and Conora. And the emperor revealing the information himself was unlikely as it would mean admitting both that he'd made a mistake and that his son had physically taken him down.

Mother stood behind Calosandros, combing her fingers through the top of his hair as if he were a little boy again. "My sweet boy, it's not good for you to worry like this. Whatever happened, you know you can tell me."

He stared into the blazing fireplace. "To be honest, it doesn't make sense to me. Conora has done everything asked of her to adapt to our way of life and proven herself more than worthy as a princess consort."

"True. I've been impressed with her in the ladies' haven."

"And yet one moment alone and the use of her Gift were all it took for the dick who created me to invent a crime to condemn and brutally punish her for on the spot."

Mother froze. "And your part in this?"

"My marital duty to protect her—less than what I desired but nothing more than was necessary."

"I see..." Mother knelt next to him and put her hand on his. "I know it doesn't mean much now, but perhaps you were right to keep her close to you before. If her cycle hasn't started, at least there's still hope for an heir to protect her soon."

"About that..." Calosandros softly smiled at the reminder of his joy. "We discovered today that, according to one of Conora's dogs, she smells pregnant."

Gasping, Mother hopped up and rushed over to the table.

"What are you doing?"

"What are *you* doing? Wake that girl up before the food gets cold. We need to make sure she eats!"

While Mother assembled a plate, Calosandros woke Conora with a kiss to her cheek. Then he helped her don a fresh underobe and one of his chitons over the splinted arm affixed to her chest. Though he hated seeing her in pain, he did like her wearing his oversized garment—something he should get used to anyway since, by the time her arm fully mended, the extra ease would be needed again, but by her belly instead. Of course, he'd have new dresses made for her to wear in public, but for just the two of them, there was a comforting intimacy in sharing his belongings with her.

Of course, Conora didn't seem to care what she was wearing. As soon as his chiton was pulled down over her, she took a deep breath, and her eyes lit up. "Is that dinner?" Without waiting for a response, she headed for the table and started eating from her plate with her hand before her ass even reached her seat.

Mother laughed and raised an eyebrow. "Hungry?"

Conora blushed and swallowed before answering back in her thick accent, "I missed lunch."

"Have you been sick at all yet?" Mother asked.

"No." Conora shook her head, then turned to Calosandros. "You told her already?"

He shrugged. "I was excited."

Mother put a hand on Conora's back. "This is good news. If you have evidence of an heir, perhaps I could speak to the emperor."

Conora shuddered.

Calosandros stepped between them. "Mother, I know you mean well, but can we let her eat in peace for now?"

"She needs this protection."

"I know." Conora gestured to her bandages with an irritated huff. "I am late, I am tired, and Spruce smelled me." She ticked off three fingers, then gave half a shrug with her mobile shoulder.

Mother pursed her lips in thought. "How reliable is the dog?"

"Very," Conora said.

"Please, be careful how you talk to him about her Animal Speech," Calosandros said. "He accused her of spying for speaking to a squirrel."

Mother patted his cheek. "Trust me. I know how to tell your father about an impending heir. Timing is key."

For the next several days, Calosandros refused to leave Conora, who refused to leave the room. Besides her understandable fear, she needed rest, and since she was right-handed, she required help for even simple tasks like eating, dressing, or writing a note. He actually enjoyed helping her dull her pain with pleasure—not with wild intensity, but with an abundance of tender caressing. The first time he touched her sensually, she apologized that she couldn't reciprocate until he shushed her with kisses and reminded her what *Pusosio Siora* taught about medicinal masturbation. He was offering her the best pain relief she could safely use, and all he wanted in return was to know that it worked.

Of course, Calosandros's reasons for staying in weren't *entirely* centered on Conora. He was not yet ready to face the emperor again, and the lack of missives from him calling for Calosandros's presence meant the feeling was likely mutual. He still kept the door locked, just in case. Thankfully, few people tried to visit anyway. Boinee and Anabusos showed up together each day, but Conora's inability to legibly write left-handed to her friend inevitably led to tears of frustration and an early end to visits.

The physician came by each morning and evening to change her compresses with fresh poultice and bandages. Though Calosandros initially worried this would hinder the stability of her broken arm, the physician always left strategic pieces intact to keep the splint in place. After about five days, Conora no longer needed the extra bandaging to completely immobilize her shoulder and could support it enough simply by resting her arm in the sling. This allowed her to wrap the arm to just above her elbow, instead of tucking her arm inside her clothes, which also meant she could wear her own clothes.

258

To celebrate the minor return to normalcy, Conora insisted on going for a walk in the garden—or rather, she wanted to find some woods to get lost in but settled for the garden when Calosandros pointed out how much of the hallway they would have to traverse to exit the palace. Thankfully, the emperor was not fond of the garden in the winter, so it promised to be the safest place on the palace grounds, aside from their bedroom. The air outside was pleasantly bracing and crisp, though Calosandros used the chill as an excuse to hold Conora close. For a while, it was relaxing to simply walk together and watch the dogs bounce around and chase each other through the snow.

Then Spruce stopped in his tracks and barked a warning.

Conora whispered, "He said a man is in the garden."

"The emperor?"

"He wouldn't know. He's never met or smelled the emperor before."

Calosandros looked around, but he could not see where the person was, which made him nervous. "I think it's time to go back in."

Conora quickly nodded and called the dogs back to her.

Though the man who had entered the garden did not appear to them before they returned to their bedroom, Calosandros still felt uneasy about the intrusion right up until he locked the door behind them.

Two days after their stroll in the garden, a week after the attack, Calosandros finally received the thing he dreaded most: a summons to meet privately with the emperor. It was addressed to him alone.

Calosandros held his head high as he walked next door to the emperor's bedroom, his righteous anger outweighing his fear at the moment. The meeting truly was alone; not even a manservant or guard stood within the trophy-laden walls. As Calosandros bowed, the emperor ordered him to sit by the fire. Since this wasn't an invitation Calosandros could remember having been offered before, he sat uneasily in one of the armchairs.

The emperor leaned back with his ankle crossed over his knee. Steepling his fingers, he coldly sized up Calosandros for an uncomfortably long time. Finally, he said, "You have been dutiful, carrying my orders without fail for years. So, explain to me how my right hand, my heir and protégé, the only one born of *my blood* has become such an astounding disappointment in the last seven months."

The same way the emperor had been such an astounding disappointment as a father?

He answered his own question, "It all comes back to that Meriverian you let grab onto your balls."

Calosandros shook his head slowly. "That isn't—"

"I will tell you when you can speak," the emperor snapped, then coolly returned to his dry rebuke. "Now, I admit to one mistake on my part. Given your history, I trusted that you wouldn't fuck it up, and I overlooked the contract you sent to me. Of course, you had intended it to look correct at first glance, wording the deal so close to what I originally asked, keeping all the items in order and changing the amounts by specific numbers. And you tucked the marriage clause in with everything else to make it easier to miss, didn't you?"

There was no use denying the written evidence. Calosandros reluctantly gave a single nod.

"So, when I received word from Siputreos that you had returned with a woman you were calling your wife, you can imagine my surprise. It had to be a mistake. After all, why would my trusted right hand not tell me such a thing? Still trusting you, I told everyone that the rumors were false."

Calosandros looked away. His tactic had only been to delay the emperor long enough to prevent him from reversing negotiations, assuming that he'd eventually notice after the army was too involved to back out. It had never occurred to Calosandros that his father might trust him so deeply as to avoid noticing indefinitely.

"And then the army arrived without you, which was strange. And every soldier swore that not only were you indeed married, but you had sequestered yourself in Orosiad with her. A little rumor reached me about your so-called wife's swooning. Later, there was another about a coffin being sent back west. Through all of this, I heard nothing from you—not even when the Meriverians reclosed the border."

So, he hadn't heard about the bear fever. At least that had gone according to plan.

"That was when I reread your contract. Your betrayal was unfathomable. I gave orders that you not be lauded until you made amends, and I foolishly hoped that might be the end of it. But you returned lovesick, rearranging things and making special requests for her whims. And her power over you only seems to grow with time, spreading through the court like a disease. You tried to banish poor Lady Agilee just because your wife dislikes her, and now most of the ladies in the palace have chopped off their hair, thanks to the princess's mere influence."

Calosandros frowned in confusion. "You're upset with her for being likable?"

The emperor scoffed. "You've been thinking with the wrong head all along. That's why you can't see it, but she is playing you. I thought it was about spying, but recent information tells me something much worse. Were you aware that we received an ambassador and guards from Meriveria three days ago?"

Calosandros shook his head. Nobody had told him anything about it.

"Apparently, that coffin contained their former queen, which was news to me. They were concerned about their princess because they haven't heard from her since she left their kingdom, and it's said that on her last night there, shouting was heard coming from her room. And, even worse, you left behind a ripped dress."

Calosandros groaned. "It was just her wedding dress. They don't follow the same traditions, but I explained it to...Conora..." Who hadn't been listening to him at the time and therefore couldn't have told her family. "Shit."

The emperor continued, "The Meriverians were giving you the benefit of doubt until they arrived in the palace. They were told that the princess would not receive visitors and, when they asked to speak to the maidservant she'd brought, were told that there was no such person."

Fuck. Calosandros hadn't considered an ambassador asking after Raina. Most of the Meriverian court had never seemed to notice her existence.

"This already concerned them, but the ambassador saw the princess in the palace garden, looking tired, her arm in a sling, her hair cut off, and you acting quite possessive. When he tried to approach, you spirited her away, and she looked scared." The emperor shook his head. "Given that you bargained for her as your war trophy, seeing her in such a state with you has the Meriverians distressed. They are asking for us to send the princess back to her homeland and are willing to pay handsomely to free her from her terrible husband."

"No." Calosandros shook with anger and disbelief. "We can't. You must tell the Meriverians that it's a misunderstanding."

The emperor shrugged. "Why would I tell them that? They're offering to not only free us of her disturbing hold over you but undo the damage you caused to negotiations."

"Because you know it's bullshit, for a start! *You* were the one who broke her arm. I protected her!"

"Do you really think that will satisfy the Meriverians? Whether it's you or me, they can see she is in danger here. And frankly, her attempts to wrest power make sense in the context of escaping a husband who forced her into marrying him."

"That's not true. She chose to marry me." Calosandros held up his hand and pointed to his ring of devotion. "She even pledged her devotion. I welcome the ambassador to ask her himself."

"Even if she made the choice, circumstances have changed. Dissolving this marriage would be better for everyone."

"Only better for you, and even that..." Calosandros rose out of his chair. "How can you do this after you told me I need an heir? If you send her away now—"

"We can find you a more appropriate wife, and if the princess happens to deliver a child anytime within the next nine months, we can retrieve it when it's old enough to wean," the emperor said as casually as if he were discussing the weather. "It would save us the trouble of hiring wet nurses to care for an infant. And, unlike you, your child wouldn't be softened by its mother's influence."

The absolute cruelty left Calosandros speechless. How could he not only forsake Conora but rip their child from her? He turned in disgust and began to walk away.

The emperor called after him, "Before you try to abscond with her, know that I have extra guards watching until we surrender her to the Meriverians in the morning. And other guards will be sent to fetch her within the hour, once a guest room is ready for her to use tonight."

37

MY DEAREST LITTLE VIXEN

Nuil Yos Namayos

Since Conora had done most of her earliest learning of Urstillian via books, her understanding of the written language far surpassed the spoken word. While she struggled to keep up with live conversations if nobody slowed down for her, reading was fairly easy to grasp. There was freedom there too; she could re-read what she needed to and move at her own pace without worrying about how everyone else perceived her. And though much of her seclusion with Calosandros had been spent in his arms, reading filled her time as well, especially history books.

Conora had been comparing the Urstillian historical account to Meriveria's. She'd brought to Urstille the best texts available in her native tongue, *The Great Urstillian Penetration* and *The Abductions*, despite Calosandros's poor opinions of them. He had been much more interested in his art than her reading anyway until she began thinking aloud to make up for being unable to write her ideas. Then, next to his easel, he began to keep the journal she'd been using for history notes, interrupting his painting to diligently jot down whatever she said while reading.

When the emperor summoned Calosandros, Conora needed something to prevent her from ruminating over the meeting, and history seemed as good a subject as any for that. Reclining on the sofa by the fire, she went over her notes. She was so close to piecing things together, weaving the disparate accounts into a truer image of the past. Both lands agreed on the timeline and major events. The disagreements were in the details and motivations, each ascribing the most noble and defensive intentions for themselves and the most selfish and insidious intentions for the other side. As contradictory and incompatible as they were, elements of either felt believable in the context of the Meriveria and Urstille she now knew.

Conora was lost deep in her notes, searching for answers to this enigma, when the thud of heavy steps between her and the hearth jolted her out of her thoughts. She nearly scolded Calosandros for startling her. But as she looked up at him, his eyes were wet, the reddened lids making their greenness hauntingly vibrant.

Conora gasped. "*Cal?*"

His lower lip trembled. "Yis oid icthian," he choked out, then sank down and wrapped his arms around her, burying his face on her shoulder to weep for a moment before meeting her gaze again. "Yis oid icthian, nuil yos namayos. Yis ca oid icthion icpias." (I love you, my dearest little vixen. I cannot lose you.)

Conora's heart raced. She had wanted to hear those words from him so badly, and yet they hurt him. He'd been showing her love for a long time, and that would have been enough for her if she'd known just how much pain such vulnerability would cause him.

Conora tried to blink back tears of her own as she wiped his with her thumb, one cheek at a time. "I love you too." Then she proved it with a kiss.

The staggering desire behind his lips, an undying thirst for her, almost distracted her from the frightening implications of his second statement—almost.

She caught her breath and wiped more tears from Calosandros's beautiful face. "But what could make you think you would lose me? I am yours, *Cal.* I made a vow to be yours for life."

"The emperor...he told me..." Calosandros spoke slowly, as if he had to rend each word from his soul, piece by piece. "He's going to dissolve our marriage...and send you back to Meriveria...tomorrow."

Conora shook her head. A hundred angry and terrified thoughts screamed through her mind, but she just whispered, "No."

"A Meriverian ambassador and guards arrived three days ago, and when they leave tomorrow morning..."

"No. I won't go. Why would they do this?"

"To save you."

"What!"

Calosandros sighed. "The Meriverians have been kept away from us, except for the ambassador, who saw us in the garden and was distressed by the state he saw you in. Combined with the mysterious circumstances around your illness, Raina's disappearance, and your mother's death, it paints a convincing picture of me as an abusive husband."

"I'll tell them the truth."

He shook his head. "It won't matter because the truth is that I fucked up, Conora. I should've protected you, and I failed. Either way, your family is willing to pay for your safe return. And in spite of my selfish desire for you, I can't deny that removing you from the emperor's grasp would protect you."

Conora fumed and sat up straight. "By sending me back to the palace where my father was murdered? Where the queen was arrested by her own guards? I would absolutely deny that 'protection.' At least we know the danger here. One day, it will die with the emperor. I chose this life to protect my homeland. To undo that—every risk you and I took, every choice we made—it would all be for nothing."

He ran his hand down his face, looking utterly defeated. "I know."

"And what about our baby, Calosandros? Surely, the emperor must see the importance of keeping your heir here?"

"He does, but *only* the child. Not you. Dearest *nuil yos*, we cannot let the emperor know about our child, or he will take them from you." Calosandros stroked her cheek. "As much this is killing me, I couldn't bear to make you say goodbye again, not to a child you've borne and cared for."

"You're talking like it's already decided." A hollow aching filled her chest. "You won't fight for us?"

"I would if I knew how to do it without making things worse. But do you realize what it will look like if I try to stop them from taking you away? I'll end up confirming their accusations."

"Then, *I* will fight. If they want me, they'll have to take me back in chains."

He frowned. "The emperor would not hesitate to deliver you drugged and bound if you refused to go. Please, don't make that be my last sight of you."

"It won't, because I swear to the Giver that I am not leaving you." She hugged him tightly with her good arm, pressing her head against his chest where she could feel his heartbeat. "We have all night to come up with a way out of this."

"Oh, *nuil yos*," he sighed. "*You* have all night until the Meriverians come for you, but you and I only have about half an hour left together."

It was too little time. A sob worked its way up her throat, and Calosandros held her as they cried together.

"I don't care what the emperor declares, I will always be your wife. Even if it's years from now, when you take his throne, we *will* return to you."

He squeezed her tighter. "It wouldn't be fair to expect that of you when I can't promise the same. Without a known heir, the emperor will make me marry again."

"Fair or not, it's my destiny. Remember, there is no lover for me in all of Carum Sound."

"I love you, *nuil yos*," he told her again. "I always will, no matter what happens. I need our child to know that too."

She nodded, her face rubbing against his chiton. "They will. I'll tell them about the handsome Urstillian prince with gentle hands and tender words, who tamed my wild heart by setting me free."

A fresh wave of tears came over her. How could she go back to her life before him? His love had forever changed her; she could no longer be the dutiful Princess Conora, politely standing in her brother's shadow and hoping to be of use. Calosandros loved her for more than the role she played—though he may have feared love itself, he had never been ashamed of loving Conora exactly as she was. How could anywhere without him be home now?

Calosandros kissed the top of her head. "I hope they can believe you. Everyone else will teach our child that their father is a monster."

It was history repeating itself, Meriverians and Urstillians seeing the worst in each other. At least the past had taken dozens of couples and many years to fall apart. Conora and Calosandros alone had managed to see everything destroyed in a matter of months. Maybe if they understood the past, they could do something different now. She stared down at her notes, which had fallen on the floor at some point while she and him were talking. They were open to an early page, still in Conora's handwriting.

Nobody disputes that the Vistan women went to Urstille. Vist said they were kidnapped or seduced. Urstille said they followed the men. Who was right?

What if they both were? With so many people, it was likely their situations weren't all the same. Some probably were unfortunate cases of abduction, while others were genuine love matches. With both happening, it would also be conceivable that individual stories would be conflated, either by mistake or by design. If some of the Urstillians of the past were like the emperor, it wouldn't be hard to imagine the women saying whatever pleased their captors to survive, making the Urstillian history look a bit cleaner than reality.

But the reverse situations were much more relevant right now. Some couples had to be like Conora and Calosandros, willingly chosen but maligned. Meriveria wasn't perfect, and Vist hadn't been either. How many women escaped their lives by fleeing east and letting their families and neighbors believe whatever suited them? Even in Conora's case, her living family members cared deeply for her, but it still seemed easier for them to believe the worst of Calosandros than to imagine her willingly leaving them.

"How did they stay?" Conora asked herself.

"How did who stay where?" Calosandros asked.

"The women the Vistans thought the Urstillians had abducted two hundred years ago—why were none of them brought back? They must have done something to stay in Urstille."

"I don't know, but before we get our hopes up, you have to know that many laws have changed since then. Even if you can find out the answer tonight, I don't know if it will still work."

"I have to try."

The bell rang. Conora had never hated a sound so much.

Calosandros let go of her so he could stand and dry his tears, then walked toward the door with the solemnity of a funeral. Halfway there, he spun on his heels, eyes wide. "Boinee! She's read lots of law, enough that even if you come across something she hasn't read, she'll at least know where to find it."

Conora ran to him and gave him one last kiss, lingering long enough that the bell rang again. "Thank you. If the ambassador will not listen to me, Boinee and I will find something, I promise."

Then she held his hand as he finally answered the door, reluctantly acknowledging the guards who asked for her, and she called for Spruce and Cloudy to follow her. She tried not to let the tears flow again when she had to let go, but even as she walked away, she couldn't bring herself to put her arm down.

Calosandros pressed a book into her outstretched hand. "Yis oid icthian, nuil yos namayos. Yis nara oid icgudoin." (I love you, my dearest little vixen. I believe in you.)

Conora nodded back. "Yis oid icthian sa, Cal."

She swallowed down her feelings as she turned to go with the guards.

There was no more time for crying. She had a journal of notes and two more books tucked in her sling.

And she had a plan.

38

PRINCESS CONSORT CONORA

Conora Cabalee

Calosandros stood in the doorway, helplessly watching as his only love was hauled away until she disappeared around the curve of the hallway. Everything in him wanted to fight this, but doing so physically would damn their marriage, and attempting to speak to the Meriverians himself would poison anything Conora said or did with more accusations of manipulation. He had to trust that she could find the solution herself; it was the only way he could live with this powerlessness. With a shaky hand, he closed the door and stood in the wretchedly empty silence of forced solitude.

Soon he found himself on the sofa, which was still warm where his wife had been sitting, with a bottle of raspberry brandy in his hand. Not bothering with a cup, he took a swig and grimaced. It burned like hell, but that would help to numb everything faster. Calosandros stared into the fireplace, watching the flames dance, only breaking the trance for the occasional drink until his eyelids began to grow heavy.

He hated the emperor. Father or not, this treachery was unforgivable. It spat upon Calosandros's lifetime of loyal duty to the empire. Maybe he had shown that fucker too much mercy when he struck him down in the hallway. Maybe he should've continued to fight him, delivered the pain he was due.

Then the bottle of brandy was pulled from Calosandros's hand.

"What are we drinking?" Anabusos asked before tasting it. He sputtered and coughed out a laugh. "Fuck. You went straight for the good stuff, didn't you?"

Calosandros tilted his head, brows knit in confusion. "Why are you here?"

Anabusos plunked down next to him and casually draped his arms over the back of the sofa. "Since your wife has my favorite fuck buddy occupied with a long project, I thought I might as well make sure you don't do something stupid."

"You have a favorite? That's new."

"Oh, you caught that? Good to know you're not *completely* shit-faced yet."

Calosandros groaned. "I wish I were."

"I'm sure you do, but this drink is giving you bad ideas."

"It dulls the pain of uselessness."

Anabusos gripped his shoulder. "You know that you cannot challenge the emperor to a duel."

Calosandros shook his head. "So what if he sired me! It's not as if that soulless bastard gives a shit about me!"

Anabusos sighed. "A week ago, I wouldn't have stopped you. But with the ambassador involved, it can only end badly for you."

Of course, he was right. With a frustrated growl, Calosandros rubbed his face. "How did you know I was thinking that?"

Anabusos pointed. "The pair of axes lying on the floor might have given you away."

Calosandros blinked and stared at the weapons he didn't remember gathering. "Oh...shit." He'd drunk more than he'd realized.

Chuckling, Anabusos hefted Calosandros's arm over his shoulder and helped him stand up. "Let's go. You need to sleep this off."

As they were stumbling toward the bed, panic set in, and Calosandros hunkered down, trying to back up. "No, I can't..."

Anabusos scoffed. "You've got to be kidding me."

"I can't face our bed without her." The admission brought back the tears Calosandros had thought were over.

Pivoting to face him, Anabusos wrapped Calosandros in a bear hug. "You won't lose her. Conora and Boinee are clever. If there's a way, they'll find it. And even if they somehow fail, I wouldn't put it past your little vixen to slip away from her people and find her way back to you."

Calosandros took a step back and shook his head, which made the room spin. "She won't sleep tonight. How can I?"

Anabusos grabbed his arm and righted him. "The brandy has other plans. Why don't we compromise and put you back on the sofa?"

Calosandros slowly nodded, almost nodding off where he stood, and Anabusos led him back to the sofa. Soon a blanket and pillow appeared around him, and before Calosandros could protest again, the warm fire melded into a dark foggy abyss.

A shock of cold water to Calosandros's face rudely woke him up to glaring daylight. He gasped and sat up, his skull pounding.

"Much better. Drink this," Mother's voice said as a miniature cup was forced into his face.

He quickly swallowed the hangover tincture, a familiar herbal-berry mixture of yarrow, salal, and mahonia.

"Change your clothes quickly," she continued. "We need to get to the throne room now. I just convinced your father to allow your wife a final audience, and you are not going to make her face him alone."

Conora needed him? Calosandros threw off his blanket and rushed to his wardrobe, grabbing the first clothes he found. Within a few minutes, he had changed and met Mother at his bedroom door.

"Does this mean Conora found something?" he asked as they started down the hallway.

"I believe so, but she didn't tell me. Boinee said the poor girl was up most of the night until she passed out with her head on a stack of books. When I went to say goodbye, the Meriverian ambassador had just arrived to fetch her, and Boinee was insisting that the princess was too unwell to travel. She looked the part too—visibly exhausted and frequently gagging."

A flicker of hope lit inside. "Did that work?"

"For now. They agreed to a short delay while they rearrange their transportation to be more comfortable for her. The request bought a few hours at most."

"Enough time for an audience?"

Mother nodded. "Exactly. She asked me the moment the ambassador left. But I fear your father must be confident in his decision, because he was nonchalant about the request for an audience."

Calosandros had to know: "Was she acting for the ambassador, or is she truly unwell?"

With a sardonic laugh, Mother rolled her eyes. "She hasn't slept, and her body is mending a broken bone and a sprain and growing a child—not to mention being at the most notoriously nauseating stage of it. So, frankly, I'd be surprised if she *didn't* feel like shit right now."

Right. Stupid question. "What does she need me to do?"

"Be there."

"And?"

"That's all." Mother paused to look Calosandros in the eyes. "You should've seen the look on her face when she said you had finally confessed your love. She would do anything for you. She just needs to know that you are there for her."

When they entered the throne room, he examined the crowd. As a hasty gathering of any courtiers who were awake to answer the summons, the court assembly was much smaller than it had been when he'd presented Conora, though there were enough there to form a substantial witness to whatever she had planned for today.

Mother put a hand on his back and whispered, "Take your place at the emperor's right hand. Remember that this is not the moment to let your discontent show, not until your wife is safely in your arms."

Again, she was right. His hatred and anger at the emperor would only be liabilities to keeping Conora home if anyone mistook their source or target. So, as he took his seat to the right of and slightly back from the emperor on the dais, Calosandros averted his gaze and forced his face into a neutral expression.

Before long, a herald announced, "Her Highness, Royal Princess Conora of Meriveria."

It took all of Calosandros's self-control to not yell out a correction. There was no Urstillian title, no acknowledgment of her marriage to him. At least he could take solace in seeing that, as Conora approached, she looked equally irritated with the omission as she shot a glare toward the herald.

Unfortunately, Mother's assessment of her physical condition had been understated. The slight sway of her form, clammy pallor over her skin, and dark circles under her eyes belied the determined and regal set of her chin. Seeing her this way reminded him too much of the last time he'd almost lost her, when she'd put on a stoic front just before swooning.

As she bowed, Conora kept her eyes on the emperor—a sign of defiance that few would dare, minor though it was.

"What business do you have with our empire?" the emperor asked as if she were a visitor.

Conora took a deep breath and spoke slowly and deliberately, her Meriverian accent thick. "I must protest the deal with Meriveria. You cannot fulfill it."

"It is not your place to tell me what I can or cannot do."

"Prince Calosandros and I pledged our devotion. If we separate, your only heir will be alone forever."

The emperor scoffed. "Stupid girl, your own ambassador believes that the pledge was made under duress. Therefore, I do not recognize it."

Dread rose up. Surely, after spending all night on it, she hadn't settled on the same useless tactic Calosandros had already tried?

Conora was quiet for a moment, her brow crinkled in concentration, then firmly replied, "No duress. I chose. I would pledge my devotion again."

He waved her off. "Is that all you have to say?"

She shook her head, then bit her lip and blinked slowly, breathing deeply as she pulled a slip of paper out of her sling. Her chest heaved as she proclaimed, "I, Royal Princess Conora of Meriveria, hereby renounce my homeland and its titles. From this day forward, I will be neither a royal princess nor a subject of the kingdom of Meriveria."

Calosandros gasped. No wonder she had made the futile attempt first. Conora took too much pride in her heritage to abandon it carelessly.

She continued reading, "Therefore, you have no Meriverian princess to trade back to Meriveria."

The emperor scoffed again. "A clever technicality."

Conora raised an eyebrow. "I am not finished." She slowly approached the dais, veering slightly off-center, and knelt.

Giver, no. The next step was obvious, but how could she swear fealty to someone who had so recently terrorized and battered her?

"I, Princess Consort Conora, hereby pledge the rest of my life in loyal allegiance to the empire of Urstille and its *future* emperor, Crown Prince Calosandros."

He stared at her, wide-eyed. It was a bold yet understandable alteration, but he never would have thought of it. She did not raise her head, keeping to that part of the ritual at least, waiting for acceptance of her pledge.

The emperor hissed, "You can't—"

But Calosandros was already bending down to Conora, taking her left wrist to raise her up from the floor since her hand still clutched the thick paper. "As a subject of the empire, you honor Urstille and me, Your Imperial Highness."

Her beautiful brown eyes shone as she smiled wearily at him, leaning comfortably into his arms, where she was meant to be.

The emperor gave an annoyed sigh. "If you are done with the theatrics, it is time to order my newest subject to leave."

Calosandros froze. No. Her pledge couldn't have been for nothing.

Conora scowled at the emperor. "I am not done." Then she whispered to Calosandros without her accent, "I love you. Please forgive me."

Before he could ask her what she meant, she turned to face the assembly. "I read your history and laws. Now I understand why the border was sealed." Conora shook out her small slip of paper with one hand, unfolding it into a full sheet.

This looked more like a full night's worth of preparation. Calosandros couldn't help a little smile of pride in his foxy trickster as she began to read aloud again.

"Two hundred years ago, the Vistan women who came to Urstille could not return, regardless of whether they left willingly or were kidnapped, because of two Urstillian laws, one of which is still valid."

From this close, it was clear that the tiny handwriting was Boinee's, which made sense since Conora lacked both the mastery of Urstillian and the use of her writing hand to compose a speech, though Calosandros had no doubt that Conora understood the gist of what she was saying.

"The abandoned law was a short-lived tradition of granting the title of *ucusodoil* to those who had returned from the Western Mountains with treasures. It conferred no real power or land as it was lower than a pettilord and could even be assigned by other nobility. Odder still, it could only be inherited through one generation of descendants."

"We know our own history," the emperor said. "Is there a point to talking about that obsolete class?"

"Yes," Conora said, then returned to the paper. "Because the true purpose of ucusodoilio was to allow any Urstillian with a foreign spouse to make use of one of your inheritance laws."

A pit settled in Calosandros's stomach. There was only one reason for Conora to bring up inheritance laws. She'd already surrendered her heritage and lain her dignity at his feet. Their child was all she had left, and she would lose them too if this failed. She was risking everything but her own mortality.

He put a hand on her shoulder and whispered, "Dearest, no. You don't have to do this."

Conora softly kissed his fingers and whispered back, "I do."

Then she took a steadying breath and continued reading, "You should be familiar with it. The heir to an Urstillian title is never to be removed from their lands before the age of five, when they may leave for one week at a time. When they are Gifted at twelve, they may leave for a month at time until they come of age at sixteen, when they may finally choose their own home. The only exception is to protect a child from peril. By this law, a foreign woman is unable to return to her homeland if she is pregnant by an Urstillian man with a title—even if he has to buy it, which was what the ucusodoilio did."

The emperor glared at her, likely deducing the natural conclusion to her speech.

But she continued, "Therefore, as I bear Prince Calosandros's lawful heir, I cannot legally set foot beyond the borders of Urstille. To force me to do so would violate your own law."

Then she moved Calosandros's hand from her shoulder to her lower abdomen, stepping back to press herself close as he gently folded his arms around her. His admiration for her could not be contained, and by now, even if someone mistook his affection for possessiveness, she had made her choice clearly enough for everyone to see.

With a clenched jaw and one eye twitching angrily, the emperor slowly rose from his throne. "It takes either ovaries of steel or profound idiocy to challenge my application of the law."

Calosandros immediately stepped in front of Conora. "I think she's proven it's not the latter." Fuck the appearance of obedience. He would not let the emperor threaten her. Calosandros stepped toward him and ground out, "Try it. I went easy on you last time. I will not make that mistake again."

"You are weak for her," the emperor spat.

Calosandros clenched his fists and puffed out his chest as he stared the emperor down and boomed, "Do I look weak to you?"

The emperor blinked and took a step back, glancing alternately at Calosandros and Conora with the same strange look in his eyes as the last time Calosandros had fought him. Then, with a slight smirk, he muttered, "So, that's where my side of you has been hiding."

Calosandros finally understood what the strange emotion in his father's eyes was: respect. In his outburst, Calosandros had inadvertently used a posture and turn of phrase he'd learned from him, shown the emperor a reflection of himself in his son.

But Calosandros couldn't care less about earning that respect now. Keeping the emperor in his peripheral vision, he turned his head to address the assembly. "Princess Consort Conora has clearly demonstrated both the law and her desire. She will *not* be leaving Urstille."

The emperor swiped at Calosandros, barely snagging the front of his chiton, which the emperor balled into his fist. "I warned you never to defy me again..."

Enough. Calosandros would not shrink back this time. He met the emperor's glare with his own. "Or what! You'll strike me again? Or will you break my arm like you did my wife's? Do it! Show everyone how easily threatened you are, taking a swing at every little shadow like a child afraid of the dark."

A long silence passed as neither man broke their hateful glower.

"I will not put up with your shit anymore," Calosandros whispered. "You will leave my wife alone and stop superseding my decisions. Otherwise, I will have no choice but to challenge you to a duel. And we both know that's a fight you will lose—even if you win."

The emperor's eyes widened in fearful realization, but he did not move. Despite the truth, he could not afford to back down or look weak in front of his court.

Calosandros took a measure of pity on his father, knowing he would have to lead the same court one day. "You still have a chance to save appearances. You've just been told that you'll be a grandfather soon."

Nodding soberly, the emperor let go of Calosandros's chiton and smoothed it, then turned to the assembly with a loud but uncomfortably hollow laugh. "It seems the fervor of good news briefly provoked this old warrior to fight again! But in light of this impending heir, the prince has correctly anticipated my judgment of the law. We shall honor all of the princess consort's oaths: her previous pledge of devotion to the prince, her recent pledge of fealty to the empire, *and* her renunciation of the kingdom of Meriveria. In addition, until she has weaned her first child, neither her body nor her words shall cross our borders."

Cruel and unnecessary as it was to silence Conora, if that was the worst the emperor could do anymore...

Calosandros turned to Conora, who looked thoroughly worn but determined as she furrowed her brow, probably trying to interpret what had just been said. He gently wrapped his arm around her, pulled her close, and tipped her chin up to face him. He spoke slowly to be sure she could follow every word. "You will stay with me, *nuil yos*, and you will be safe now."

With a teary-eyed smile, she let out a relieved chuckle. Then she hooked her good arm behind his neck and kissed him fiercely.

39

YIS OID ICTHIAN

With her splinted arm resting on the edge of the bath, Conora laid her head back onto Calosandros's shoulder. As he held her, she let the warm water begin to relax away the anxiety that had built up since her arrival in the palace. She was at peace, home, loved.

This close, Calosandros smelled of alcohol, which was understandable under the circumstances and would disappear soon. He hummed a contented sigh. "You're safe now. No more living in fear, and no one will separate us again."

"At least for the next couple of years. Hopefully, I can come up with a more permanent solution in that much time."

"Oh, I took care of that already. I made certain that the emperor will never hurt you again." There was a fierce edge to his serious tone.

"How? What did you say to him? You were speaking too fast and quiet to understand."

"What I should've done from the start—I stood my ground. If he were to threaten you again, I would rightfully challenge him to a duel."

She froze, her heart thudding. "*Cal*, what if you do have to fight? I don't want you to risk your life."

Calosandros ran a soothing hand along her side and nuzzled her ear. "That won't happen. He's subjected me to a lifetime of intimidation, but the truth is that I'm the one person he cannot afford to fight, because there is no good outcome for him. If he doesn't lose his life, he loses his only heir. And he knows it. Trust me: the emperor will not threaten you again. I just wish I'd realized that sooner."

Conora nodded. "Don't blame yourself. I understand the hesitation. I never truly stood up to my father until my brother was deep into his coup. What seems obvious now can be impossible to see when you're under their control. And you saw for yourself how easy that can be to forget when the intimidation comes back."

"True, but what you did today…" He gave her an affectionate squeeze and kissed her temple. "I'm in awe of you, dearest. You showed everyone who you are, and you did what I couldn't. I'm just sorry for what it cost you."

"I'm not," she softly admitted.

"*Nuil yos…*" He turned her head to meet his gaze and frowned. "I would never want you cut off from your family."

Conora sighed. "I knew the risk when I presented that law. It's the same risk I'd already accepted when I married you. The restrictions are just more solid."

"Keeping you from communicating at all with them is beyond the law."

"I know, but I'm familiar with how vindictive powerful men can be when they're thwarted. That's why Boinee helped me write a letter, which I left with Grandilord Ambassador Patricius in case the emperor imposed further confinement on me."

It had taken a couple drafts to get it right. But the letter was too important to ignore. Conora dictated in her limited Urstillian vocabulary, supplemented by the occasional word scrawled on scraps with her left hand, and Boinee wrote the resulting message in Meriverian. Then Conora checked that the translation was correct. Given the obstacles, Conora had to keep her message woefully brief: a simple goodbye and assurance that she knew what she was doing.

Calosandros gasped. "You realize you've given the ambassador contraband?"

Conora held up a finger. "Technically not. It was written and out of my possession first thing this morning, long before the emperor's proclamation."

Calosandros laughed. "You are completely untamable, *nuil yos*." He kissed her neck. "Speaking of which, I understand why you had to swear fealty, but I must reject part of it. I will not hold you in obedience or bend your will to me. I already trust in your love, and that's more than enough."

She turned around to face him, resting her arm over his shoulder. "I know, which is why I did it. Because you're the only one I would ever trust to not control me. You actually hear me. With you, I have peace and safety because you accept all of me." Her cheeks warmed as she smiled. "I've never felt freer than I do in your arms."

Smiling back, he cupped her face with both hands. "Neither have I."

EPILOGUE

Conora put a hand to her slightly rounded belly as a pleasant summer breeze cooled her bare legs and stirred springy curls around her cheeks. It felt like a lifetime ago that she'd last been to Acas Icsiol (Break Pass), which she now knew not to call Acas Icsio (Shit Pass)—not that anyone would criticize her if she did. The imperial prince's fierce defense of his consort had become legendary throughout the empire.

The gate had been widened, and locals had been paid handsomely to remove some of the buildings from the road so that trade could flow. Near the gate, Spruce and Cloudy blocked a little boy from passing through. His mop of brown curls bounced as he ran back and forth in a futile attempt to get by.

Calosandros sauntered up to them and singsonged, "Tibalos..." Then he snatched up the little boy, who squealed with laughter. "As sneaky as your mother." Calosandros smiled as he carried him back to Conora. "*Nuil yos*, I'm afraid our cub has gone feral again!"

As Calosandros set him down, Tibalos giggled and wrapped his little arms around Conora's leg. "*Madee!*"

She ruffled his hair. "We can cross the border when you're older, baby."

At least now Conora was allowed to make contact outside Urstille again.

Calosandros crouched down and put a hand on Tibalos's back. "But that's okay because, today, you get to meet some very special people. *Madee*'s family is going to be so happy to meet you..."

GIFTS

Allure – naturally more likeable, possibly seductive; can lead to paranoia from overuse

Animal Speech – can speak to animals; socialize better with them than people; trouble with impulse control

Far-Sight – telescopic vision; terrible near vision

Fire – can expel heat from body

Flight – can fly; large wings can be unwieldy on the ground

Healing – can heal others; compromised self-healing and immune system

Hearing – extremely sensitive ears

Ice – can absorb heat into body

Invisibility – cannot be seen by others

Listening – always reads everyone's thoughts

Memory – can never forget anything

Near-Sight – microscopic vision; terrible far vision

Night-Sight – enhances light for constant nocturnal vision; daylight painful

Seeing – receives visions of the future; no control over visions

Speech – can speak any language; cannot identify languages

Speed – can move at incredible speed; eats four times as much

Stone-Skin – skin is armored; also lacks emotional sensitivity

Strength – has the strength of four men; eats as much as two men

Transformation – can turn into a known mammal; can go insane from overuse

Water-Breathing – can breathe underwater; cannot leave water for more than a day

REGARDING "THE WILDNESS"

As you may have suspected, if you are familiar with the traits of autism and ADHD, Conora presents with both of them. She is not meant to be a perfect representation, because nobody can be—every individual experiences those conditions differently. But, rather, she is *a* depiction of an AuDHD (autism + ADHD) person, based much on my own neurodivergence.

While fantasy often uses magic to represent a condition or trait, in Conora's case, most of how she experiences the world is innate. Animal Speech is simply a by-product, given because it suits who she grew to be. To put it another way, "the wildness" doesn't come from Animal Speech; she received Animal Speech because of "the wildness" inside her.

Conora doesn't need her AuDHD or "wildness" to be cured or fixed; it's part of who she is. What she needs is the same as everyone else: love and acceptance. As someone like her, I hope that is the lasting message of my story.

ABOUT THE AUTHOR

Brandi Spencer's love stories of Carum Sound are heavily influenced by the beautiful Pacific Northwest, where she lives with her husband and two sons. The scenic views of Puget Sound and the Cascades provide plenty of inspiration for her superpowered fantasy romances. A Western Washington University alumna and former cosmetologist turned work-at-home mom and homeschool teacher, she writes in between family life and work for A4A Publishing. She loves crafting, baking, and video games and spends far too much time researching for her stories.

Follow her online:

www.BrandiSpencer.com
Twitter: @Meriverian
Facebook: @Meriveran
Instagram: @Meriverian

AUTHORS 4 AUTHORS
PUBLISHING

A publishing company for authors, run by authors, blending the best of traditional and independent publishing

We specialize in speculative fiction: science fiction, fantasy, paranormal, and romance. Get lost in another world!

Check out our collection at https://books2read.com/rl/a4a or visit Authors4AuthorsPublishing.com/books

For updates, scan the QR code or visit our website to join our semi-monthly newsletter!

Want more fantasy romance? We recommend:

FYR
by Lisa Borne Graves

At seventeen, Toury arrives in Fyr, where magic is power, a prince's love is deadly, and female autonomy is a dream. Alex, the Prince of Fyr, has to face his father's ailing health, the expectation to marry soon, and the hidden necromancers trying to take over the realm by exploiting his dark curse. At least there's hope in a cheeky savior, but Earth girls aren't so easy. Can they trust each other enough to save Fyr? Or will everything they hold dear turn to ash?

books2read.com/fyr